Pelican Point

Pelican Point

DONNA KAUFFMAN

KENSINGTON PUBLISHING CORP.
www.kensingtonbooks.com

KENSINGTON BOOKS are published by

Kensington Publishing Corp.
119 West 40th Street
New York, NY 10018

All Kensington titles, imprints, and distributed lines are available at special quantity discounts for bulk purchases for sales promotions, premiums, fund-raising, educational, or institutional use.

Special book excerpts or customized printings can also be created to fit specific needs. For details, write or phone the office of the Kensington special sales manager: Kensington Publishing Corp., 119 West 40th Street, New York, NY 10018, attn: Special Sales Department; phone 1-800-221-2647.

KENSINGTON and the K logo are Reg. U.S. Pat. & TM Off.

ISBN-13: 978-0-7582-9277-3
ISBN-10: 0-7582-9277-5

First Kensington Trade Paperback Printing: November 2013

10 9 8 7 6 5 4 3 2

Printed in the United States of America

First Electronic Edition: November 2013

ISBN-13: 978-0-7582-9278-0
ISBN-10: 0-7582-9278-3

This one is for Sue & Don Edwards.
Thank you for introducing me to Maine.
I think we're going to be very happy together.

Chapter 1

Logan McCrae loved everything about his hometown of Blueberry Cove, Maine. From the rocky, isolated shores that fronted his generations-old family home out on Pelican Point, to the quaint but comforting heart of the small town nestled around Half Moon Harbor and dotted with businesses that had been run by the same families for generations. Gentle rolling hills shifted to thick forests as they moved inland, providing the townsfolk with a variety of living choices, from tidy little houses that marched along the handful of streets branching off the main road around the central harbor, to the farm properties that took over as town turned to field, and the more isolated cabins as field turned to forest. Blueberry Cove was a place where neighbor helped neighbor and no one remained a stranger for long.

He enjoyed the steady pace of small-town living, even the predictability of it. There was something to be said for handling the day-to-day issues that arose, while knowing they weren't likely to be anything earth-shattering. He'd had enough of earth-shattering, thanks.

Not that being the police chief didn't come with moments of danger, worry, and, on rare occasions, tragedy, but that's why he'd taken the job. A fair share of that tragedy had been visited on him personally. So, he had a vested interest in keeping things going as smoothly as possible, for himself as much as for his fellow townsfolk. It was a bonus that being there when folks needed him had turned out to be so deeply gratifying. It was remarkably fulfilling, living a life surrounded by people who mattered to him; old friends, new acquaintances, family.

Well, most of the people, anyway. The downside to small-town living was that you couldn't escape the thorns that came along with every rose. But he handled that, too. He just didn't enjoy it as much.

That meant making yet another stop by Eula March's antique shop. Apparently another "helpful" citizen had decided to make shutting down the store a personal mission. Funny how those do-gooders were never actually from Blueberry Cove. Or they'd know better.

He climbed out of his town-issued SUV cruiser and walked under the canopy of the sparsely leafed oak, pausing a brief moment to admire the lingering colors of fall dotting the ancient branches before pulling open the heavy teak door by its *Alice in Wonderland*-themed brass handle.

Everything about Mossy Cup Antiques was whimsical, from the flamingo mallet–shaped door handle, to the beautifully restored range of antiques that began with an array of practical items like tables and chairs, and ran all the way to the decidedly impractical but far more interesting bits of unique statuary and home decor—what Logan's grandmother had called dust-catchers. He imagined there were few, if any, Blueberry Cove residents who didn't own and proudly display in their homes at least one piece from the shop. Many, including some in his own home, had gone on to become treasured family heirlooms, their Mossy Cup origin only the beginning of their story.

But nothing was more whimsical or fantastical than the giant oak tree that grew up right through the middle of the generations-old building . . . much to the chagrin of the occasional activist-minded soul who discovered the store and became convinced the tree was a fire hazard and a home for any number of potential infestations.

The townsfolk all knew it had been there in some form or other for as long as there'd been recorded history in the coastal fishing village. And since it was one of his own Mc-Crae forebears who'd help settle the little harbor town in Pelican Bay back in the early 1700s, that had actually been a substantial length of time.

As yet—though the shop built around it had seen a variety of changes over the years, with parts added and restored, and upgrades for things like central heating and plumbing and the like—the tree still stood, with nary a single incident in all those years. It had, however, spawned hundreds of well-told tales of lives changed and fortunes turned. Logan thought that part might have had more to do with the long line of eccentric March women who'd run the place since its first days. Most passers-through found the shop's history and unique construction to be charming rather than alarming, but there was no accounting for how some folks chose to expend their energy.

"Morning, Eula," he called out, doffing his uniform hat and wiping his feet on the beehive-shaped brush mat inside the door. "What's the complaint this time?"

"Same as it always is," came a scratchy, irritable voice from the back room. Eula March was tall and thin, rawboned and robust. She sported wire-gray hair of indeterminate length—it was always pinned up in a net-covered bun—and a manner that managed to be gruff and informatively helpful at the same time. When she wanted it to be, anyway.

After the first complaint under his watch as police chief some years back, Logan had tried to ask, as kindly as possible, if perhaps there was some other, underlying issue between Eula and the suddenly righteous-minded patron.

She'd flatly and quite directly informed him that it was her shop and she'd treat those who crossed its threshold in the manner she felt they deserved. If they wanted to be disagreeable about it and run around filing complaints and such, that was their time to waste. She wasn't about to mollycoddle those who needed anything but mollycoddling.

Logan had made a fast note never to do that again. He was pretty sure he still had a permanent scar or two from the blisters on his ears.

Eula came out from the back. Her face and hands were wrinkled and age-spotted, her skin appearing perennially tanned, though he'd have called it weathered. Her tall frame was slightly stooped but balanced by squared shoulders and a stiff posture that made a man remember to watch his manners. Her age, however, remained indeterminate. She looked exactly the same to Logan as she had in all the years he'd known her, which would be all thirty-four of them.

Her standard uniform of a floral print smock-like dress was in shades of lavender, buttoned to the throat, the hem ending just above spindly calves, the entire outfit neatly pressed and made by her own hand. It was all but covered by one of her handmade, whimsically stitched shop aprons. It was a scene from *Winnie the Pooh*—the original, not the Disney version—that had Pooh, Piglet, and Christopher Robin frolicking across the front of her apron pockets.

Apron notwithstanding, Logan would have said he'd never met a less whimsical woman in his life. If you looked up "stern New Englander" in the dictionary, her photo could have easily run next to it. But he knew, as did everyone else in the Cove, about the other side of Eula March, and the real reason folks felt such a strong bond to her and her shop. Eula harbored a unique array of skills that went far beyond her unparalleled ability to master any antique restoration, bringing back to life pieces others would have sooner turned to kindling. As had, apparently, the March women before her, hence the longevity and renown of the shop. On its own that was enough to make her something of a local legend.

When you factored in that . . . thing, that mystery in her clear gray eyes, if one chose to look past the disapproving set to her mouth and really notice, there was a certain sparkle, a kind of . . . knowing . . . as if she could see straight through any and all artifice and look right into your very soul. Most of the townsfolk were fairly certain she could indeed do just that.

"Nothing more than a nuisance," she said in her clipped tone, looking faintly annoyed as always. She wiped her hands on a shop towel tucked into her apron pocket, indicating she'd been in the workshop at the back of the shop where she did her restoration work. Or some of it, anyway.

The backroom area was tiny, whereas some of the pieces on display were of a size that would have been impossible to have been restored in such a narrow space. Yet, she lived in rooms over the rear workshop and accessed them by a winding set of interior stairs. As far as anyone knew, she didn't lease, own, or rent any other space. Hence the whispered questions about the true origins of some of her beautiful pieces, and how folks couldn't recall seeing them delivered to the back door, in any condition.

Logan dismissed that chatter as the kind of fanciful gossip that went hand in hand with a shop as old and storied as hers, the same way old buildings always seemed to have a ghost or two, whose stories were continually embellished as the years went on.

He met her halfway through the shop beside an English walnut keyhole desk that acted as countertop for the shop's beautifully restored and fully functional antique sales register.

"I told you not to worry about it," she informed him. "It will amount to nothing, just as the others have. Don't waste

Tom's time making him come over and run tests on the damn tree, again. It's not good for the tree and surely your fire chief has better things to do with his time. If it was going to infest the town with parasites or burn us all to death in our beds, surely it would have done so by now."

"You're absolutely right. But we still have a process—"

"The process is a waste of time. And mine is too valuable to be spent filling out ridiculous paperwork every time some tree-hugging nitwit gets his we're-all-going-to-die-if-we-don't-respect-the-environment knickers in a twist. It's not like I'm keeping the tree captive. And here's a news-flash for you. We're all dying. From the moment we come out squealing, we're counting down the days to the end. Mother Earth, on the other hand, will outlive us all, each and every one. I see no purpose in making what days we're blessed to spend with her any more of a challenge than they already are by lecturing folks on how she should be treated."

Logan barely blinked at the diatribe. Nor did he even consider any discussion that had the words *global* or *warming* in it. They were both just going through the motions, each knowing their part in the routine by heart, having played the scene too many times to count.

"Well, Eula, I can see your side in this, and I know these complaints are an occasional thorn in your side." *Mine, too,* he wanted to add. *If you wouldn't antagonize some of your customers, no matter how well deserving, maybe they wouldn't become so hell-bent on sticking it back to you.* But he said, calmly and deliberately, "If you'd complete the paperwork filing your own formal complaint, I'll process it and have a chat with—what did you say his name was?"

"Elmer Alvin Swinson. Can you believe that? Even his mama knew he was going to be an annoying whiner."

Logan hid a chuckle behind a sudden, short cough. "Be that as it may, I still need to question Elmer—er, Mr.

Swinson—and get this over and done. Just make your nuisance complaint official and I can get started."

Eula grumbled the entire time she filled out the forms, her shaky, spidery scrawl at odds with the intricate restoration work Logan knew she performed with those very same hands. She pushed the finished papers at him in a dismissive gesture. "Now, I've got work to do. Good day, Chief."

"Good day to you as well, Miss Eula." He turned to go, thinking not for the first time that both of their lives would be made a lot easier if she'd hire some sweet-natured local teen to run the register out front while she stayed in the back doing the work she clearly loved most. But since he rather liked his ears still attached to his head, he kept that suggestion to himself.

"Logan Matthew McCrae."

He stopped and turned back to Eula, eyebrows arched in curiosity at her use of his full given name. She used to call him Logan, or the more old-fashioned Master McCrae, right up until the day he'd become a sworn member of the local police department. Then he'd been Officer McCrae, and eventually, Chief. Never his given name. He'd taken it as a sign of respect. He had no idea what, if anything, this sudden reversion meant. He wasn't sure he wanted to find out. "Ma'am?"

She pointed a bony finger at him. "Change is coming."

He smiled at that. "To Blueberry Cove? Well, unless you're referring to the weather, nothing much changes here. It's—"

"To you," she said, more specifically. "Be open to it."

He frowned then, and fought the urge to rub away the little tingle that ran across the back of his neck. "I like to think I'm open-minded."

"Change hasn't generally been a harbinger of good for you." Her stern expression relaxed slightly. "It's the reason you love it here, as I believe you were about to say. The reason you stayed on, even after your sisters grew up and moved away. They wanted change, needed it. Not so with you. You made your life here—where nothing changes. Nothing to worry about. Nothing to fear."

Her comment about his past had caught him off guard. Who knew what she might have seen flash through his eyes? He didn't bother trying to bluff. Everyone in town knew all the details, so there was no point. "Eula, I appreciate the concern. I do. But I'm fine. It was all a very long time ago. I'm not hiding. I'm here because I want to be here. I belong here."

"Not all changes are bad, Logan."

"I never thought they were."

Her lips curved in what, on anyone else, might have been a hint of a smile. Whatever it was on her, it made him feel distinctly uncomfortable, and, well . . . exposed in some way. Vulnerable.

"Just because it's difficult, or challenging, doesn't mean it isn't a good thing. Sometimes the best changes need to be both."

"Agreed."

"Good. Keep that in mind. Good day now." With that, she turned and headed back to her workroom.

Late in the afternoon, Logan was more than ready to head home. After spending an hour and a half dealing with Ted Weathersby's pompous posturing and general obnoxiousness at the latest council meeting, he'd ended up having to mediate a scene between Becky and Walt Danneker in the middle of the Cove's one and only intersection that had involved single-handedly keeping Becky in her vehicle while convincing Walt that if Becky's temperature was where the doctor said it needed to be and Walt not only wanted children, but wanted to keep Becky from doing something that would permanently prevent him from ever being able to have them, maybe he should reconsider his afternoon meeting and go home with his wife.

Privately, Logan wished him luck in the performance department because Becky was, well, let's just say, not at her most enticing at that moment.

He had been hoping to use the remaining daylight hours to tackle the stacked stone wall he was uncovering, but Fergus had asked him to stop by the Rusty Puffin. From his overly cheerful tone Logan knew something was up. The lunch crowd had departed and the evening crowd had yet to start making their way in. His great-uncle Fergus, who owned the place—and was actually his grandfather's cousin some number of times removed—was nowhere to be seen.

A *clang* came from the kitchen, followed by a strident string of rather blue language that would have made the local fishermen proud.

"Fergus," he called out. "What's the trouble?"

There were a few more clangs, a lot more swearing, followed by a short bellow and what sounded like a wrench being thrown against—well, he didn't really want to know—then Fergus pushed through the swinging door, wiping grease-covered hands on the bottom edge of his apron. He was a short, broad-shouldered man with a thick neck and a stout frame, like an old-school pugilist. At seventy-three, he still had a full head of dark hair, though there were threads of gray and white in it. His thick thatch of beard had turned faster and was mostly steel gray and white, as were the matching bushy eyebrows. His eyes were a bright sky blue with the sparkle of a much younger man, and he was quick to flash a wide grin.

"Confounded contraption. We'd be better off with a bloody pellet stove and a stack of peat than that piece of—"

"Why don't you let me have a look at it?" Logan set his uniform hat on the bar and unzipped his jacket.

Fergus waved him off. After scrubbing his hands clean at

the small sink, he set two short glasses on the bar instead, smacking the bottoms on the varnished teak surface. "We'd be better off warming ourselves with a sip than swearing at that auld heap. I'll put a call in to young Broderick. Boy's a wonder with a wrench, or so I hear."

"Broderick. You mean Brodie Monaghan?"

"One and the same. Have you spent any time with the lad since his arrival? He's about your age."

Logan smiled. "I'm a bit too old for afterschool pals and playdates, Uncle Gus."

"Well, it's never too late to make a new friend," Fergus went on. "He's a good lad. Sharp mind, good with his hands, not afraid of hard work." He smiled. "Quite the charmer, too. Good with the ladies, if you know what I mean."

"So I've heard." In a town the size of Blueberry, it would have been impossible not to. Brodie Monaghan had come over from Ireland just the previous spring, intent on restoring his family's centuries-old shipbuilding business. Monaghan's Shipyard had been one of the founding businesses in Half Moon Harbor centuries before, but over the course of the previous three decades, it had slowly become a rundown relic, a mere ghost of its former glory. "Wouldn't mind hearing a story or two of home," Fergus went on, "or just a bit of the brogue." He grinned. "After all, 'tis no fun swearin' alone."

Logan eyed the glasses Fergus had set on the bar, and was tempted, but tugged the zipper back up on his jacket instead. "If you've got the problem in hand, I'm going to try and get out to the Point before another call comes in. I've got a stone wall needing some attention."

"I didn't call you here about the furnace." Fergus set a bottle on the bar anyway and motioned to the stool. "Park yer bum there, laddie. We need to talk."

Logan paused, his hat halfway to his head. "About?"

"You know how there's all this plottin' and plannin' going on, for the town tricentennial."

"Which is almost two years from now. But yes, I'm very well aware." It was another looming headache as he tried to quell the tensions already brewing as folks began taking sides on how the town should best celebrate such a monumental occasion.

"Well, then you've been hearing talk about the lighthouse."

Surprised, Logan leaned back. "The lighthouse? You mean our lighthouse?"

"You know of any others in Blueberry?"

Pelican Point was not only the sole lighthouse in the Cove, it was the only one on all of Pelican Bay. The only one left, anyway. The tower was a big part of Blueberry Cove's history and Maine's rich seafaring history. A book had been published by one of its keepers—Logan's great-great-great grandfather, in fact—with an account of his life on the job as its first keeper during some of the more turbulent years of the bay's history. It was still available in several shops dotting Harbor Street.

The lighthouse had been decommissioned in the early 1930s and listed for public auction by the early '70s. A member of the McCrae family had manned the Pelican Point light during all of its years in service, all the way back to 1821 when it had first been built, and the family had continued to maintain a residence there even after decommission, so they'd made a deal and bought it outright before the auction. The family had been struggling to keep the place from crumbling down around them ever since, but at least the burden was on them, and not the community.

"Folks have been talking about wanting to get the lighthouse up to snuff in time for the town celebration. Blue-

berry's tricentennial coincides with the lighthouse's bicentennial, give or take a handful of years. Close enough anyway."

"Up to snuff?" Logan laughed. "Gus, it would take an
army and a state lottery win just to get it up to code, much
less functional or safe enough for the public. And what
'folks?' I haven't heard any talk."

"You would, if you spent any time in here. This is where
all the real chatter happens. You spent enough time tending
bar here through your college years to know that."

"Gus, I have—"

"A job. I'm well aware. What you don't have, boy-o, is
a life. One that includes things like socializing. When was
the last time you shot a game of pool, threw a dart or two,
or, God forbid, bought a woman a drink? Wouldn't kill ye."

"I have two jobs," Logan said. "One, seeing to the people of Blueberry Cove, and the other to trying to keep two
hundred years of McCrae history from crumbling into the
sea. Both are full-time."

"I know, and we're all proud of ye, working so hard like
you do. But you could do with a bit more socializing. Can't
hide out there all the time." He eyed Logan. "Would help
curb that irritability of yours."

Logan smiled. "I'm only cranky when *some people* bug me
about living my life as they think I should rather than leaving me to live the life I already have and am liking just fine,
thankyouverymuch."

He rose from the stool and leaned over the counter to
give his uncle a one-armed hug and hearty buss on the
head. McCraes were, by nature, huggers and kissers and he
realized it had been far too long since he'd done either.
With anyone.

He picked up his hat. "I'll be in, okay? Scout's honor.
Now, I need to be getting on the road if I want to—"

"Have a seat there, laddie. We've a bit more to discuss." Logan lowered his hat once again.

"We haven't finished discussing the lighthouse." Fergus grabbed a towel and was making quite a business of wiping down the perfectly clean bar.

Ah, so now we're at the real reason I've been summoned to the bar. Eyeing Fergus's too innocent expression, a knot of tension started to ball up in Logan's gut. He put his hand on the towel. "What did you do, Uncle Gus?"

"Now, now, I did this with your best interest—with all of our best interests—in mind."

The knot jerked a little tighter. "What did you do?"

"I . . . hired on some help."

"You hired on help where? Here?"

"No, laddie. For Pelican Point. I hired someone who specializes in lighthouse restoration. Now we'll find out exactly what needs to be done. Alex MacFarland is—"

"A waste of your good money. Gus, I can tell you for free that the list of what needs to be done is longer than any of our bank accounts is deep—even if we combined them."

"You've got the trust."

"Yes, there is the trust, but that's not enough by itself. Get your money back, Gus, and invest in a new furnace."

"If the lighthouse is as bad as you say, then let MacFarland's report prove it. You can use that as your final word with the council and the townsfolk, and the matter will be put to rest."

"I'm confused. I thought you were trying to get the thing repaired."

"I said it would be a wondrous thing, but I'm nothing if not a realist."

"So, this is helping me out . . . how, exactly?"

"They'll listen to an expert with generations of experience in such things whereas they might not so quickly with you. Or, more to the point, Weathersby and the council won't. Teddy will make it his personal mission to make life hard on you."

Logan eyed the older man, not believing for one second that Gus had spent a dime of his hard-earned money to hire someone to prevent a headache that hadn't even happened yet.

"Just keep an open mind, okay, laddie?"

Change is coming. Be open to it.

Logan did rub the back of his neck this time, but he knew better than to argue. Not with Eula, or with Fergus. He drained the ale and tucked his hat under his arm as he rose to leave. He was halfway to the door when he thought to ask, "When is this MacFarland due to arrive?"

Fergus suddenly got busy again, ducking his chin as he wiped perfectly clean glasses with a fresh towel. "Should be waiting on you out at the Point as we speak."

"*What?* He's—at the house? Please tell me you didn't give him a damn key to the place."

"Didn't have to. Since when do you lock up, anyway?"

"And you told him that?" Logan opened his mouth to say something else, then snapped it shut. He pushed through the door of the pub, climbed in his truck, and decided he could get some satisfaction out of this lost cause of a day by heading home . . . and firing Alex MacFarland before he even started. What Fergus had done could just as easily be undone. Logan could have the guy on his way and still have a bit of daylight left to do a bit more surveying on the stone wall.

"What the . . . ?" Logan braked as he rounded the final bend on the coast road before crossing the causeway over to the Point.

An old truck with an even more beat-up trailer on the back had broken down on the short ramp leading to the bridge, blocking it completely. In fact, the back end of the trailer was jutting out onto the main road.

So much for getting to the damn wall. Hell, he'd be lucky if he managed dinner before eight—which reminded him that in his frustration with Fergus, he'd forgotten to stop by the grocery and pick up a few things. Preferably edible things, as he was presently all out of those.

Swearing under his breath, as much at himself as at the latest thorn in his day, he rolled closer and angled his truck behind the trailer before flipping on his lights. It would be dusk soon and he didn't need anyone zipping around the bend and slamming into the damn thing.

Then he saw the sign painted on the side of the truck, chipped and peeling, but clearly legible. MACFARLAND & SONS.

"Seriously, Gus? This is our expert?" The old pickup truck and dented trailer looked more like they'd been abandoned by a gypsy caravan, than the work vehicle of a trustworthy restoration expert.

Yes, he loved Blueberry Cove, but, oh, there were days. As he climbed out of his truck, he thought *there are days.*

Chapter 2

Alex MacFarland should never have taken the damn job. What had she been thinking, attempting something like this on her own? Except . . . she was on her own. And that wasn't going to change. So, it was either figure out how to keep MacFarland & Sons afloat for yet another generation—specifically hers—or . . . what? Give up? Lie down and die? Both of those had been pretty tantalizing options fifteen months ago.

Losing her father, so abruptly, so . . . horribly, how was she supposed to get over that? Much less figure out business stuff? She couldn't give less of a damn about business, about restoration, about any of it. All those things she'd loved for as long as she could remember, all the satisfaction, the dreams, the challenges, the hard work, every last bit of it, all of which had defined her . . . had died right alongside her father.

She wasn't entirely sure she wanted to find a way to resurrect it.

But, plain and simple . . . she needed to eat. And though her skill set was broad by some definitions, it was ultimately good for only one thing—building things. More specifically, restoring things someone else had built. Even more specifically, things that happened to be lighthouses. Not just everyone had one of those in their backyard, so she could hardly be choosy.

It had been a long, painful, frustrating, and very exhausting year. The lawsuit and the estate—if you could call it that—had finally been settled. What could be sold off had been sold off to resolve the debts her father had owed, none of which she'd known about, and the rest had gone to the lawyers. Thank God there'd been some life insurance money to cover the medical costs from the day of the accident, and, later, her father's burial. She'd been grateful to have had that much, but nothing was left.

Less than five days after packing up and moving out, she sat in her grandfather's banged-up sideboard truck a thousand miles away on a wind-whipped coastal road on the edge of Maine. Their oldest and only remaining trailer was hooked on the back. Between the two, she was carrying pretty much everything she owned. Well, everything worth hauling anyway. Except for four generations' worth of accumulated tools and her laptop, she'd sold off everything else of value, including their newer and sturdier work trucks.

No one had wanted Grandpa Mac's old truck or trailer, which had been parked at the house back in Thunder Bay after he'd passed four years ago. She'd hung on to them, then used every trick she had to get the damn truck running again. But running it was, and had been—with a few additional nudges and a steady string of swearwords along the way—all the way from her home on the shores of Lake Huron. The home that someone else lived in now.

She'd made it all the way to this ramp, leading down to the beautiful old stone causeway that ran across a corner of Pelican Bay and out to a rocky point jutting into the sound, atop which sat Pelican Point lighthouse. The entire vista was picture postcard perfect—from the boats dotting the water, the shops and homes lining the harbor across the sound, to the weathered keeper's house perched on the promontory, fronted by the lighthouse itself, a proud, majestic old sentinel, keeping watch over it all.

It was hers to rediscover, to heal, to make whole.

After everything she'd been through, all that she'd had to arbitrate, settle, overcome, and simply live through and survive . . . and with the answer to her most pressing needs sitting right there in front of her . . . the very last thing that should have undone her was a blown tire. She even had a spare, buried . . . somewhere in the back.

There was no reason, none at all, to be sitting there, blubbering like an idiot. *Or,* her little voice piped in, *like a woman who'd lost one too many things and just didn't have it in her to lose so much as a single tire more.*

She was working her way through the onslaught of tears, knowing that at some point she'd surely get her act together, climb out, and do what she always did, what she'd been taught to do since before she could walk, and what she'd been doing ever since . . . she'd fix it.

A big, white, sports utility truck pulled in behind her, with official-looking blue lights flashing on the roof. It looked like someone else was going to beat her to it. Or try, anyway. They'd soon discover it wasn't the busted tire that needed assistance . . . it was the broken-down mess of a driver sitting behind the wheel.

Alex instinctively scrubbed at her face only to realize she'd crumpled up the paper with the names, contact information, and directions on it into her fist. She smoothed it out, thinking she should have stopped in town and talked to Fergus McCrae directly before finding her way out to the Point. That had been the plan, actually, but she'd arrived early, a full day early in fact. Sleep hadn't been her friend for quite some time, so she'd driven on. She hadn't felt like talking to anyone as she'd pulled into Blueberry Cove any more than she had on the long drive.

She had called the number, however, and spoken to Mr. McCrae. She'd asked if it would be okay to head straight

out to Pelican Point to take a cursory look around, then
come back into town and meet up with him later, around
dinnertime, when they could discuss business. It was the
smart thing to do, but in complete honesty, she didn't care
what kind of shape the place was in, or what shape the Mc-
Craes were in for that matter. The job came with a guaranteed roof over her head for the duration, and, at the very
least, would put grocery money in her pocket. She was going to take it.

She'd really only headed out to the Point first as a means
of putting off the inevitable—having to open herself up to
a new set of people. She wasn't sure what anyone knew
about her, or the job she'd been hired to do, but with small
towns, she'd discovered everyone knew everything. So she
had to brace herself for that inevitability. And she didn't
have much left with which to brace.

There was also that other part. The part she hadn't admitted, even to herself. At least, not until the moment her
tire had gone out on the ramp, giving her some extended
viewing time of the lighthouse and no way to avoid thinking about it. The part where she was hoping, praying,
maybe even begging her soul a little, that just seeing the
lighthouse would open something back up inside her. Or
prove, once and for all, that it was truly dead forever.

To be more brutally honest . . . she wasn't sure which
one she'd been hoping would happen.

So, she'd skipped stopping in at the Rusty Puffin. *What
the hell kind of name is that anyway?* Weren't puffins cute,
cuddly little penguin-looking birds? If it had to be a rusty
bird, why not the Rusty Pelican? The brown, ungainly
creatures were the state bird, after all—so a sign in one of
the endless small towns she'd driven through had told her,
anyway. Except she was pretty sure it was the state bird of
Louisiana. What had that sign said? It was all a blur now.

Now that she had made the stupid decision to bypass both meeting up with Fergus McCrae and grabbing a much-needed bite to eat, she had a grumbling stomach to quell along with the red eyes, swollen nose, tear-and-mascara-streaked tragic clown face that looked back at her from the rearview mirror as she tried to do some basic repair before her good Samaritan made an appearance.

A light rap on the driver's side window of her truck got a choked squeal of surprise—stealthy Samaritan he was—causing her to spin toward the window a little too quickly. Her forehead connected with the glass.

Oh, yes, this was *so* how she wanted her first meeting in Blueberry Cove—her home for possibly the next year or so—to go.

Her Samaritan was tall, so much so she couldn't see his face, just his torso, and hips, and . . . thighs. All of which looked quite sturdy and muscular and . . . um, well-packaged. Wow, she really shouldn't have skipped lunch. Or breakfast for that matter. When had she eaten last, anyway?

A hand appeared, making a rolling sign with the forefinger.

He'd yet to speak. Weren't officers supposed to announce themselves when they approached? Of course, he hadn't pulled her over, exactly. Wouldn't it be her luck to be stopped by some rural coastal psycho who dressed up like a cop, then preyed on women along a distant, lonely stretch of road nobody traveled? Maybe she should have looked up local news reports.

The tap came again on the window, and she blinked away her bizarre, rambling thoughts and blinked again at the little twinkly lights flickering in her peripheral vision. She really should have eaten. She grappled with the window handle . . . only to have it fall off in her hand. A fresh wave of tears stupidly threatened all over again. She held up the handle in shaky fingers for him to see, lifting a shoulder in a half shrug, but not daring to look up at his face. Mostly because she didn't want him to see hers.

If she'd been hoping for some kind of sign about what her next step in life should be, she was pretty sure she'd been given several of them already. All bad.

"Can you unlock the door so I can open it from the outside?"

Wow. Deep voice. Very baritone. The kind that vibrated along the skin. And sexy. Just like his torso. And his thighs. Not to mention his . . . um, package. None of which she had any business thinking about.

"Sure." It came out as a croak. She cleared her throat, or tried to, but the ball of emotions still wedged there made it impossible. She just nodded, helpless to stop the tears leaking out and tracking down her cheeks. Beyond caring, she fumbled with the little lock nub on the door, trying to pull it up. Grandpa Mac's truck pre-dated automatic locks.

The policeman stepped back and positioned himself at an angle, hand at his side, where she saw his gun was holstered. *Just in case I'm the crazy psycho and he's the one being stalked.* The thought caused a little splutter of choked laughter, which led to another, then another, except it wasn't funny. Her heart was pounding and it felt like her lungs were constricting. She knew all the signs. Well, she'd learned them the hard way, fifteen months ago. *Panic attack.*

And for what? Because a cop was trying to help her change her damn tire? *Jesus, Alex, get a freaking grip.* She knew it wasn't easy or as simple as that. It had been a while since one had triggered, and she'd thought they were mercifully, finally behind her. *Yeah, well, think again.*

Her door was carefully and slowly being opened from the outside, which was when she realized she'd kind of slumped against it, and didn't have time to adjust her weight. And that was how she ended up falling into the arms of Mr. Tall, Tight, and Baritone.

My humiliation is officially complete, she thought, somewhat woozily. She was having a hard time focusing. Must be the tears blurring her vision.

"Hey, it's okay. I've got you. I've got you," he said, voice steady, calm.

And seriously sexy as all hell. Honestly, he should have gone into radio. Or made a career out of singing those Barry White kind of sex songs.

"Can you stand?"

She would have nodded yes, but he turned her in his arms just then and their gazes collided for the first time. Her knees went distinctly wobbly. Because if his voice was all sexy sex songs, his eyes were . . . well, they were just plain sex. On a platter. With a big heaping side of *oh my*.

They were the color of hot, melted caramel, with alternating flecks of gold and burnished bronze radiating out from the dark center. Like . . . shattered topaz. And if that wasn't a generous enough gift from the gods, they were framed by thick, dark, ridiculously lush lashes. He was saved from being too pretty by the small scar that ran in a thin silver line from his hairline, across his temple, and cut a jagged line through the corner of one eyebrow. It looked old, pale, but it wasn't a clean slice and hadn't healed neatly.

His cheekbones were a shade too sharp, as was the angle of his jaw, and the strong slope of his very patrician nose. But then her gaze continued, and all of that, every bit of it, was balanced by his mouth—which had clearly been a gift from the same god who'd designed those eyes. Full, sensual, even with the corners pulled too tight, as they were. She must have hit her head harder on the window than she thought, because she felt distinctly woozy again, and a little giddy. That had to be bad, right?

So was wanting to lift her head, just a little, so she could nip that bottom lip, see if it felt as warm, as soft, as inviting as those eyes. Add in that sex voice and wow, she'd be putty in his arms. Actually, she kind of already was.

How convenient.

Her gaze drifted to his eyes, then back to his mouth.

He cleared his throat. His sexy, sexy throat. She wanted to bite that, too.

"Ma'am?"

"Alex," she breathed, not even trying to stand on her own two feet. "It's . . . Alex." She felt his hold on her tighten momentarily.

"Alex. Of course you are."

There was another pause and she thought perhaps a little sigh, though it didn't sound anything like the kind of sighs he was eliciting from her.

"Alex, have you been drinking?"

Mmm. She liked it when he said her name.

"Have you taken any medication?"

She shook her head, which made her vision swim a little and the twinkly lights come back, so she closed her eyes. And just focused on that voice. That calm, steady as rock, sexy voice. "Sex god voice," she murmured.

And then there was the feel of his arms. So strong, so supportive. She could trust those arms. She could stay in those arms. The world was making a lot more sense as long as he held her. She felt safe. Cocooned. And at the same time, she felt alive, all of her dead parts coming burningly, achingly alive. And she wanted to trust that, too. To just . . . let go. Let herself feel without fear of finding pain and all-consuming grief.

She could let him be the strong one, the steady one. Not like it had been for the past year—when it was all on her. So much on her. But here . . . now . . . she could let go. Because he wouldn't.

Don't let go, she thought. She couldn't be set adrift again. She wouldn't survive it. She'd drown for sure. Feeling suddenly panicky, she grabbed him. *I want to stay right here.*

"Don't let me go." She dug fingers into his jacket, clinging, clinging . . . but feeling so distant, so far away, like she was falling. She gripped harder. "Don't let me go!"

"It's okay, I've got you. I've got you."

So steady. So strong. Then she felt . . . airborne. Weightless.

"Alex? Come on now. Alex!"

He sounded even sexier when he got all urgent like that.

"Stay with me. Open your eyes. Come on, stay with me. What are you on? What did you take? Alex!"

She smiled and let her cheek rest on his chest. Nice hard, warm chest. Silly, sexy sex god voice. Telling her to stay. She wasn't going anywhere. She liked it when he said her name. All demanding and commanding. She liked it a lot.

The next thing she remembered was the sound of something metal snapping. And then the warmth, the solid chest, the strong arms were gone. She was floating. No, she was on something soft. Flat. *Where am I?* She blinked her eyes open, then squeezed them back shut again. She must have been having the most excellent dream, but the suddenness of being jerked out of it had sent the vision floating, drifting just out of reach. Not fair. She wanted it back again. It had been warm . . . safe. Not confusing, like whatever was happening on the other side of her closed eyelids. *Or like her life for that matter.*

"Miss MacFarland?" said a young voice. A woman's voice.

She closed her eyes more tightly. Really unfair. She hadn't slept well, or at all really, in . . . she couldn't remember exactly. Months. A lifetime. No matter how exhausted she was, whenever she closed her eyes, she relived that horrible, horrible day. The day her life—the one she used to have—had ended.

Warm. Steady. Safe. That's what she remembered feeling. She hadn't felt any of those things in so . . . so long. And . . . that voice. The visions in her mind had been so . . . good. And more than warm. They'd been downright hot. She couldn't remember where the sexy voice had come from, but she wanted it back.

"Alex?"

That's the one. She smiled, and relaxed, willing the dream to completely return.

"Alex." More commanding this time.

She sighed. She remembered liking that, too.

"Open your eyes."

Okay, she thought. *But only for you.* She risked cracking her eyes open, just a tiny bit. *Oh . . . right.* He was real. The voice was real. Her Good Samaritan.

And it all came crashing back . . . right along with the accompanying mortification. She closed her eyes again.

"Alex, I'm Logan McCrae. I'm police chief here. Fergus McCrae, who hired you, is my great-uncle. Sort of. I own Pelican Point. You were headed out that way?"

She groaned. So, she'd been wrong about another thing. *Now* her humiliation was complete.

"Miss MacFarland? Can you hear me?" The woman's voice again.

Alex had noticed her during her brief eyes-open stint, standing beside Sexy Sex-god Voice. The woman was dressed in what looked like some kind of EMT gear. Alex knew exactly what that gear looked like.

She squeezed her eyes more tightly. No longer hoping for the happy dream place, because there wasn't one, but trying not to think about the last time she'd seen EMTs.

"Miss MacFarland? We need you to keep your eyes open. Come on. That's it." The young woman with pretty brown hair pulled up in a tight ponytail smiled at her. "Hello."

Oh, she's way too chipper. Wanting nothing more than to sink right back into oblivion, Alex had to work at maintaining eye contact. "Hey," Alex said, though it was more gravelly croak than actual language. "What . . . happened?"

As soon as she asked, she wished she hadn't. She had enough of the tidbits floating around in her head—she could figure out how it had likely gone down. She really didn't need chipper EMT girl rehashing the whole thing in front of Sex-god Voice, otherwise known as her new boss. She forced herself not to look at him. Seriously, hadn't she paid enough karmic dues over the past year? Wasn't it her turn for a little good? Or at least something not entirely awful?

"Miss MacFarland—"

"Alex," she repeated. "I'm—fine." Clearly untrue, but maybe if she said it and often, she could will it to be true. That trick had gotten her through the past fifteen months, anyway, hadn't it?

"You're dehydrated and I'm pretty sure your blood sugar just bottomed out," the EMT was saying. "Are you on any prescribed medications? Have you taken anything else? Cold, flu medicines? Allergies?"

"No, none of those things. No illegal things, either," she added, remembering her Samaritan's queries from before. She worked to clear the grit from her throat, and the remaining wisps of fog from her brain. "You—I think you got it right pretty much the first time." She struggled not to look at Mr. McCrae. A vision of her reflection in her truck mirror with the tear-streaked tragic clown face passed through her mind, which admittedly made not looking his way a bit easier. If he was police chief, he'd probably seen it all. But she was pretty sure he hadn't hired it.

Well . . . shit. The one thing she'd had going for her, and she'd managed to screw it up before it even started. "I just . . . need to eat something. Get some sleep." *Good luck with that.* She struggled to prop herself up on her elbows, which was when she realized she was strapped to a stretcher. Her head thunked back on the pillow, making her groan.

She gave the EMT a questioning look, but it was Chief McCrae who moved into view. "Did I do something wrong?" she asked him.

He waited half a beat too long, then said, "No, we were just keeping you from falling if you startled when you woke up."

They were still outside, she realized, feeling the chilly breeze on her cheeks and nose. She shifted her head, noticed the ambulance, and beyond its open rear door she spotted her truck. Good. Because she wasn't going anywhere in anything with a siren on top. "I'm fine—or I will be. Really." There was no money for a medical bill, so as long as she was breathing, she was fine enough. "You can let me up." She looked back to the EMT. "Thank you. Sorry for the trouble." She prayed there was no bill for that. She hadn't called for them, after all. "I'll take better care. Promise."

Alex glanced at Chief McCrae, then decided the EMT—Bonnie, she noted on her name tag—was the better bet. She tried a smile, then thought, recalling her mascara-streaked face, that it might look a little . . . manic. She went for earnest instead. "I was just in a hurry to get here. Start work. For the McCraes." She spared a tiny glance at the Chief. *God, why can't I stop thinking about the Sex-god Voice?* His expression was unreadable.

Just then his phone buzzed. He pulled it out, clearly not thrilled with whatever name was flashing on the screen. "What's up, Gus?" There was a pause, then a glance at her, his expression still unreadable. Okay, maybe it was a little readable. None of it good. "Yes, we've met," he said, then turned and stepped a few feet away, but not before she heard him say, "No, I don't think that's going to happen. We'll discuss it later."

"Well, Miss MacFarland—Alex," Bonnie corrected, still smiling, as she reclaimed Alex's attention.

Alex hadn't missed the placating note to it. *Wonderful.*

"You really aren't fit to drive," Bonnie told her. "It would be best if you'd come on in for a few more tests, make sure it's nothing other than fatigue, improper diet."

More like exhaustion and no diet, Alex thought, then realized Bonnie thought the same thing, but was being gentle with her when she saw the EMT and Sex-god—er, Chief McRae share a look as he stepped back over to the stretcher. *Be nice to the crazy lady who drove into town, fell apart over a blown tire, then passed out on the chief of police.*

Since she assumed Gus was Fergus, and Chief McCrae's "I don't think so" was pretty much going to translate to "sorry, you're fired," her only other option was to get the hell out of Dodge and figure out what her next step was going to be—which meant convincing them she could drive. Who wanted to start a job heading into a Maine winter, anyway? Maybe she'd find something down south.

She couldn't exactly ask them to take her to the nearest motel. No budget for that. She'd been counting on the promised lodging in the keeper's cottage that would be part of her fee. She tried to sit up again, then sighed. "Could you unstrap me?"

Bonnie looked at Chief McCrae, then smiled at Alex. "All right. But don't get up, okay?" She undid the straps. "I'll assist you."

Alex smiled back, all convivial, the picture of health. She might have managed that if it wasn't for the crazy, streaky clown face, quite likely paired with a nose and eyes both red from crying. Still, she went for it. What choice did she have?

"That's okay. I'm good." She shifted her legs off the stretcher and sat up all at once, intent on demonstrating just how good she was. Will didn't trump desire. However, she swung up, the world swung the other way, and she went careening off the other side . . . right back into Sex-god Voice's arms. Like she'd not only planned it, but executed it with such perfect placement and precision that the Russian judge would have given her a ten for sticking the landing.

Chief McCrae didn't look all that impressed. Possibly because she was seeing two of him. She blinked her eyes a few times, but that made it worse, so she gave up, shut them, and kept them that way.

Bonnie stepped up. "Chief—"

"It's okay. I'll take care of it."

"But—" Bonnie started.

"No, really, I'm—" Alex said at the same time.

"I'll take care of it," Logan repeated.

Bonnie stepped back. Alex might have sighed a little.

But the Sex-god Voice mixed with the Man of Steel attitude was really more than she could handle in her diminished state. Had she been healthy and hydrated, surely she'd have stood up to him. *As opposed to now, when you can't seem to stop thinking about being under him.*

He turned toward his SUV.

"Where are you taking me?" She should be alarmed. Or care what his answer was. All she could think about was how good it felt to be snuggled back up against his broad chest again. She really needed a snack.

"Out to the Point. You were headed there, right?"

"Yes, but—"

"It's dark. Or close enough. And cold."

"My truck—"

"Still has a flat. I'll get it taken care of. You need rest. We'll talk tomorrow."

"No need for that. You can fire me right here."

"Who said I was going to fire you?"

"You did. I mean, isn't that what you just told Fergus?"

"Do you want me to fire you?"

Why is he being deliberately obtuse? "What I want is to not needlessly draw things out only to be fired later. I'm not a fan of drawing things out. Rip the Band-Aid straight off. That's my motto."

"That hurts more, you know. It's a myth that it doesn't."

She looked at him. "First, it's a metaphor, and secondly, yes, it hurts like hell. But it goes away a lot faster."

He stared at her for the longest time. "Does it really?"

As horrifying as they were unavoidable, the tears sprang right back.

"Exactly. You're coming with me. We'll sort the rest out later."

Chapter 3

Mercifully, for both their sakes, she remained silent as he drove out to the Point. He'd glanced at her a few times, but told himself it was to make sure she didn't do anything stupid. Like fling herself from the moving vehicle into the sound.

He didn't think she was intent on doing herself any harm, but, to be honest, he didn't know what she was. Okay, that wasn't entirely true. He knew she was wounded. Maybe not in some obvious way. But in a way that was still unmistakable. If you knew the signs.

He knew all of them.

What he didn't know was how damaged she'd been by whatever had happened to her. Though, given the present circumstances, he was putting together a pretty good idea. Still, he didn't think she was a jumper. More like a runner. He wondered what she was running from. And how long she'd been at it. A good while, given the shape she was in.

They pulled up in front of the house, saving him from having to think about it any longer. He didn't want to be thinking about it at all. She wasn't his problem. He shut off the engine. "Stay put until I come around the other side," he said, pocketing the keys. "The ground is rocky and uneven and the lights aren't on yet." Remembering her distinct lack of respect for instructions, he added, "If you so much as move, I'll call Bonnie and tell her to come out here and pick you—"

A death rattle wheezed out from the passenger side of his truck. He instantly popped his door open so the overhead dome light came on, not wanting to admit that his heart had done a pretty hard stutter at the sound. He and Bonnie had agreed that they didn't think the new arrival was on anything, but it wouldn't be the first time he'd been wrong.

He snapped off his seat belt and was already reaching for her, intending to check her pulse, when her head lolled to the side, toward him . . . and she let out a nose-sucking, throat-gurgling, chest-rattling snore that would have put a three-hundred-pound man to shame.

He couldn't help it. He grinned. Okay, he might have chuckled. "Alex?" he said quietly.

Nothing—if you didn't count another nose-sucking snort. *Probably stuffed up from all the crying,* he thought, trying to be charitable. But mostly to offset the continued chuckling. He reached over anyway and, careful not to disturb her any more than necessary, touched the pulse on her neck. *Steady, solid. Good.*

Before he could take his fingers away, she shifted and trapped his hand between her cheek and the back of the seat. Her skin was soft, delicate. And surprisingly warm. If he could find a way to look past the red swollen nose, the splotchy cheeks streaked with mascara, and the significantly whacked-out hat hair that had emerged when Bonnie had taken her knit cap off to check for injuries earlier . . . she looked fragile. Vulnerable. In ways that had nothing to do with the superficial wreckage of a single day's events.

The glow of the overhead light wasn't great for making any real diagnosis, but he didn't need to see her. He'd gotten a very good look earlier when she'd first passed out. Faint purplish shadows were under her eyes, the fine skin look-

ing drawn, stretched almost too thin. Cheekbones and a jaw-
line that were probably a bit more pronounced than they
might normally have been. Not gaunt, but heading in that
direction. Long-term illness would have been most people's
guess.

He'd held her, looked into those eyes before they went
permanently spacey. Beautiful, haunting eyes the color of
the deep blue sea. A very turbulent, deep blue sea. Actually,
not *haunting*. Haunted.

Yeah, she was suffering all right, but she wasn't sick.
Though she was doing a pretty damn good job of getting
herself that way.

He belatedly realized he was slowly stroking her cheek
with the side of his thumb and went still, then shook his head
at himself. *Because, what? You're suddenly sixteen and so dorky
you're afraid to touch a girl?* With a dry smile aimed at himself,
he carefully slid his hand free, trying real hard to ignore how
long it had been since he'd stroked a woman's face.

He climbed out his side of the truck and closed the door,
then hunkered his shoulders against the constant breeze and
circled around to the passenger side. He carefully opened
the door and leaned across to unhook her seat belt, then
scooped her up before she could slither to the floor of his
truck in a boneless, snort-snoring heap.

Smiling again as she let a particularly staccato one rip, he
shifted her in his arms so she tipped against his chest, her
cheek against his jacket, then toed the truck door shut.

The air had a pretty good snap to it and she shivered as
he made his way over the rocky drive to the smoother
brick path that led to the side porch. He tucked her closer
and tried to angle himself to shield her as much as possible . . . and found himself noticing that for all her hair
might have looked like it hadn't seen a shower recently, it
actually smelled . . . nice. Sweet, a little fruity.

He chuckled. "Like its owner."

"Hmm?" She made another little groggy sound and he firmed up his hold on her.

"I've got you," he said quietly, calmly. "Go back to sleep. You're fine." *Far from,* he thought, but didn't want a repeat of her trying to throw herself off the stretcher to prove her independence.

That thought made him loosen his hold slightly. *Is that it? Is she running from a threat?* He stepped up on the porch and shifted her weight so he could turn the knob, and boot open the side door to the mudroom and kitchen. No, he decided, discarding that possibility as instantly as it had occurred to him. *That isn't it.*

He was mostly certain because he recognized the difference between a haunted look and a hunted one. He grinned as he made his way down the hall, past the bathroom, to the first-floor guest bedroom. He was 100 percent certain, however, because at one point in her exhaustion-induced delirium she'd called him Sex-god Voice . . . and had seemed pretty pleased about it. A woman on the run from a threat, particularly the male kind, wouldn't likely say anything like that, especially to a stranger, no matter what kind of shape she was in.

Sex-god Voice.

He probably shouldn't get such a kick out of it. Women had commented on his deep voice any number of times, but that particular description was a first. He hoped Bonnie hadn't picked up on it. It was one thing for him to be privately amused as all hell, but the idea of anyone else in town getting hold of that moniker made him shudder to even contemplate.

He leaned over the bed and started to lower her to the mattress, but the instant her body angled away from his, she grabbed the front of his jacket and tugged hard. "Don't let go!" she cried, the words muffled against his jacket.

He paused and looked down. Her eyes were still closed. She was still asleep. But her expression was contorted, strained. He paused for a moment and her hands relaxed a bit, so he tried to put her on the bed again.

"Don't go! Just hold on! *Hold on!*" She wasn't clutching him any longer, but she was shuddering, and her voice was shaking, thick with emotion. "Come on, hold on. You can. Just . . . *don't let go.*" The last came out on a choked sob, and then she gripped his jacket again, pressing her face against it, shaking. Tears squeezed out.

A dream. More like a nightmare.

"Dad! No! *Daddy!*" That last part had come out on a heart-wrenching wail. She clung to Logan, crying, keening.

Shaken up, he didn't quite know what to do. Force her awake? Or let her cry it out? He had the burgeoning feeling that the episode on the ramp earlier was likely because she'd spent too much time forcing herself to stay awake, and not enough time just letting it all out. Whatever *it* was.

He turned and slowly lowered his weight and hers into the oversized stuffed chair angled in the corner next to the bed, shoving the matching ottoman out of the way with his heel as he settled her against him, and simply held on.

There were no more words, no more pleas. Just wrenching, frame-shaking sobs. He questioned himself several times on whether it was the right thing to do, but saying her name, stroking her hair back from her damp cheeks, didn't elicit even a ripple of awareness in her. He couldn't bring himself to do anything harsher or more abrupt to shake her out of it. So he did what she'd asked.

He didn't let go.

He wasn't sure when the tears stopped. At some point, he'd drifted off. He felt her stir against him . . . and lifted his cheek from where it was resting on top of her head.

The room was in deep shadows, with only a glimmer of light coming from the mudroom back down the hall, and a sliver of moonlight peeking in through the curtains. Just enough so that when she opened her eyes and looked up at him, they were deep, luminous pools.

"It's you." Her words were raw and gritty.

He didn't know the best way to handle it, and he was still a bit foggy, so he simply said, "Yeah. It's me."

"You didn't let go."

The combination of wonder and affirmation might have made the corners of his mouth kick up a little, but it was some other emotion entirely that pinched at his heart. "No," he said quietly. "I didn't."

"I thought you were a dream."

He didn't want her to think about her dreams. "You're awake now. It's all okay."

"Your voice," she said, hers gravelly. She was still only half awake, groggy.

Sex-god Voice. His body surprised him by stirring, remembering how she'd smiled when she'd first called him that.

She wasn't smiling. She was warm, and soft, pliant in his arms, all tucked up against his chest . . . with big, bottomless eyes looking straight into his. When that gaze dropped to his mouth, his body went from stirring to leaping. Then he wasn't smiling, either.

"Alex—"

She made a soft little moan at the sound of her name, and then completely and utterly shocked him by lifting her head up and nipping his bottom lip.

He made a little grunt of surprise, while his body made a far more enthusiastic shout of hello.

"I knew it would be," she murmured, then slid her hand over his cheek and into his hair, pulled his head further down, and kissed him.

And damn if he didn't let her.

For the first split second, he told himself it was because he was simply too stunned to do anything else. But then she moaned a little, suckled and nipped at his bottom lip again, and he was suddenly kissing her back. *Instinct,* he told himself. Because she was warm and soft, and her firm little butt was pressed against his now raging hard-on. And because she was a hell of a kisser. Slow, but greedy, unhurried yet demanding. He felt like he'd just been tossed into the endless sea of her deep blue eyes without a lifejacket. He was drowning, and he just didn't care.

He let her pull him under for a third time before he finally shook awake some part of what functioning brain cells he had left and broke it off. Her lips, warm and damp, her bottom lip all soft and full, clung to his until the last second before he broke contact entirely. He wasn't sure who groaned softly, and didn't want to know.

She sighed, and he was all caught up in the wonder that was the sweet, satisfied smile on her face as she settled right back against his chest again, as trusting as a kitten.

"That was even better," she murmured drowsily.

And then she was out—leaving him sitting there, half dazed, pulse thundering, hard-on throbbing, wondering how the hammering of his heartbeat wasn't jarring her awake. *He* was sure as hell awake. More awake than he'd been in . . . well, too long.

He squeezed his eyes shut, trying not to think about all the things that were wrong with what he'd just let happen, and figure out what the hell he was going to do about it. But closing his eyes just enticed him to want to sink right back into the moment. *Jesus.* The friction of her sweet backside pressed against him was making him a little crazy. So the first thing he needed to do was get her out of his lap. Then take a very long cold shower. Then—then he didn't know what.

First things first.

Carefully, and not without a little grimacing and wincing on his part, he managed to get them both up and out of the chair. When he laid her down on the bed, she didn't rouse at all. In fact, she rolled to her side and curled up, face nuzzling into the pillow. *Like she'd just nuzzled into my chest.*

Yeah, don't think about that. He debated on taking her jacket and shoes off, but figured escaping was the better part of valor. He shook out the quilt folded over the footboard of the double bed and draped it over her. Then stood for another thirty seconds, watching her chest softly rise and fall, before finally kicking his ass out of his own guest bedroom.

He glanced at the clock over the stove as he walked into the kitchen, surprised to discover it was past midnight. *Awesome.* He'd lost an entire evening. Not to mention dinner. He debated throwing something together, then remembered there was nothing to throw. Not to mention it was hard to think about food when he had a raging erection distracting the ever-loving hell out of him . . . and the warm, soft woman responsible for it was curled up in bed down the hall.

Swearing under his breath, he headed out of the kitchen toward the stairs up to his bedroom, but paused, looking back down the hallway. He told himself he just wanted to make sure she wasn't going back to nightmare land. But she'd been deeply asleep when he'd left her—like the very exhausted woman she was. He climbed the stairs, thinking he'd figure out what the hell to do about all of it in the morning.

At the moment, there were more pressing . . . needs that he had to tend to. He trudged into his bedroom, peeling out of his uniform and kicking off boots as he went, then flipped on the shower in the master bath. At the last second, he slid the faucet to hot instead of cold. He stepped in, closing his eyes as the hot water beat on the tight muscles in his neck that came from ending a long day by sleeping in the guest room chair. Then pooled some thick body wash in his hands . . . and took care of his other stiff muscle. No need to let that go to waste, he figured, groaning as he leaned back against the tile wall, stroked himself, and let himself imagine how the evening could have ended if she'd been awake and lucid when she'd started kissing him. At least he'd get something out of the wasted night.

Logan jolted awake to the sound of the old copper pipes groaning and rattling in the walls as water flowed through them. The first strands of thin morning light illuminated the faded wallpaper on his bedroom walls as he lifted his head from his pillow. Why was water flowing through the pipes downstairs? His gaze flew to the clock even as he was already tugging off the sheets and comforter and sliding bare feet to the cold, hardwood floor. It was just before six. And somebody was in the downstairs shower.

He sank his weight back into the mattress, sitting on the edge of his bed, and palmed his forehead. "Oh. Yeah."

Feeling the twinges of a headache, he finally pushed off the bed and pulled on a sweatshirt, then dug out a pair of jeans, surprised at how rested he felt. He'd slept like the dead. He tugged his zipper up, then paused . . . remembered the shower, and rolled his eyes. *Seriously, how pathetic is it that you slept like you got laid when all you got was a hot kiss and a soapy hand on your*—a shriek echoed through the old house, cutting off the rest of his thought.

It immediately occurred to him that that shower hadn't been used in—*oh shit.* He took off downstairs, hearing the pipes groan again as the water was shut off. Then they kept groaning.

"Alex!" he shouted, taking the stairs two at a time. "Alex, get out of the shower! Those pipes are probably rusted out." He slid to a stop in front of the closed bathroom door and smacked his palm on the warped wood panel. "Alex, it's not safe, you really need—"

The door opened—well, after a firm yank, it opened—

and Alex, wrapped in an old bath towel, hair dripping wet, with tear-tracked makeup smears spread farther out from the blast of water she'd apparently taken to the face, stood there . . . with a wrench in one hand and a piece of copper pipe in the other. "What you really need is a new fitting, a washer, and some Locktite. But that should hold it for now." She held out the wrench and the rusty copper pipe until he silently took them from her hands. "Does *your* shower work?"

"It does."

She calmly wiped her dirty hands on the faded navy blue towel she was wrapped in, then with a dignified air, pushed the sodden locks of hair back from her face. "Upstairs?"

"End of the hall, through the bedroom on the right."

"Thank you." Head held high, shoulders very squared, she moved past him and walked directly and quickly to the stairs, dripping all the way.

He heard the pipes groan and rattle on the second floor a few moments later.

He stood there for another ten seconds, then finally shook his head and walked to the kitchen. *Coffee.* That would help make sense out of this. Or, at the very least, kick out the little throb at the base of his skull. And the not so little one in his pants. *Jesus, Joseph and Mary, McCrae, you're not sixteen. Get a damn grip. And despite her grand entrance the day before, Alex MacFarland is no fragile, wilting flower, either.*

It surprised him a little when he caught his reflection in the old metal toaster a moment later to discover he had something that looked like a smile on his face. "And what's funny about this? Nothing."

He put two more slices in the toaster when the first two popped out. Scraped the black off them, then grabbed butter and blueberry preserves from the fridge and set them on the small cherrywood table tucked into the bay window alcove. It was one of Eula's, actually, and had been in his family longer than he'd been alive. By the time the water up-stairs shut off, he had two cups of coffee and a pile of scraped toast on a plate. He sniffed the carton of milk still in the fridge, then, satisfied it wouldn't kill either one of them, he set it on the table along with a small bowl filled with sugar packets.

"Coffee?" came a hopeful voice from the doorway.

"And toast. Sorry, I'm out of eggs. And . . . food."

"No, that's good. More than good."

He'd picked up the coffeepot to take it to the table, then almost sloshed all of it onto his feet when he turned and got his first look at her. His first real look. She was wearing the same jeans and pullover she'd worn yesterday, or he as-sumed so. She'd had her coat on the day before. But they were definitely hers and not his, so . . . *great deductive reason-ing there, detective.*

That wasn't what had made him almost drop the coffee-pot. It was what she did for those jeans and that pullover. He'd felt her body, of course, all curled up against his chest and pushing against his—"How do you take your coffee?"

"Hot." She pulled out a chair and sat down, and he no-ticed that, while she seemed okay, alert and somewhat rested, she wasn't making eye contact.

Her hair had been toweled into a soft mass of chin-length, deep auburn curls that did amazing things all clouded around those deep-sea blue eyes. Without all the black mascara streaks, her cheeks were smooth, pale—maybe too pale, as the flush from the shower stood out a bit too starkly—which made her eyes, free of any makeup, ut-terly luminous. And then there was her mouth. Pink, soft, and surprisingly full when not pulled tight at the corners. How had he not noticed that?

Probably because it had been dark when she'd claimed his mouth like he'd been a dying man who'd requested one fi-nal kiss.

Yesterday, she'd looked like woman on the verge of collapse. Actually past that verge, since she actually had collapsed. Now she looked all dewy and soft with eyes that reached right down inside a man and—*yeah, don't go there.* Too late. The part of his body he'd like her to reach right down inside and grab sat up and said good morning.

Suddenly, he realized why she probably wasn't meeting his gaze. Come to think of it, he didn't know exactly what to say about what had happened last night, either. And not just the kiss. That might have left a lasting impression on his too-long-neglected libido, but it was the wrenching sobs and the nightmare that had followed him to sleep the night before. He had a suspicion she was more upset about that part of the evening's events.

He set the pot on the table and took the seat across from her. "Alex, listen, I—"

She held up a hand, stalling him.

He watched, bemused, as she closed her eyes and took another long sip of coffee. She made a little moaning sound as she swallowed. "This is . . . really good."

"Cop coffee sucks. So I learned early on how to brew—"

She held up her hand again. He raised a brow, but held his tongue while she took another sip. Another little sigh, a little shudder of pleasure that made his body react as if she'd just done a pole dance on the kitchen table, and he was all done waiting.

Not sure whether he was more frustrated with her, or his damn reaction to her, he put his mug down. "Listen, we need to talk about—"

She opened her eyes and pinned him with a very direct gaze, which, as it turned out, was far more effective than the talk-to-the-hand gesture in shutting him up. "Okay, so there might not be enough coffee in the world."

"For?"

"For me to get over that voice of yours. It's really . . ."

She trailed off, shook her head, then took another fortify-
ing sip.

"Deep," he finished for her, fighting the oddest urge to
smile. *Sex-god Voice.*

Did she remember saying that? Did she remember any of
it? She was a lot . . . different today. Now that she wasn't
fighting the combination of exhaustion and a sugar crash,
she was calm, collected, and surprisingly direct.

Although, when he remembered the kiss the night before, maybe that last part shouldn't have surprised him all
that much. "I know. But it's the only one I've got."

"Well, it's . . . something." She started to take another sip,
then paused with the cup halfway to her mouth.

Remember something? He hid the beginnings of a smile behind his coffee mug and took a sip of his own. He had no
clue how he'd thought she'd behave this morning, but he
was pretty sure this wasn't it. But what the hell did he
know? At least she didn't look so haunted or fragile. Of
course, she was ducking his gaze again, so he couldn't really
tell for sure.

"About yesterday," he started.

"I'm very sorry for all of that. More than you know.
Trust me, I'm usually more professional. Or at all professional."

She lifted her gaze to him, and it was like getting poleaxed, every time.

"What?" she asked. "Your expression," she clarified. "Is
something—?" She reached up and felt her cheeks, her hair.
"I couldn't possibly look any worse than I did yesterday."

"You're fine." *More than fine.* "You were fine then." At
her arched brow, he lifted his mug again. "Okay, so you
might not have been at your best, but I gather it had been
a rough couple days." *Weeks, months.* "We all have them."

"We do, and it has, but I've never gotten myself into anything like that." She lifted her coffee mug in silent salute,

a hint of a wry smile kicking at the corners of that soft mouth. "You were the lucky one to witness the first." She took another sip. "I sincerely do apologize. And I realize that I'm probably the last person you want to trust with the restoration, but—"

"Not true."

She looked at him, clearly surprised.

"Well, not the *last* person, anyway."

Her brows pulled together for a moment, then she hiked up one of them in a *oh no you didn't* look, before ducking her gaze and taking another sip. Only he was pretty sure that had been a smile, not a scowl, he'd caught before she'd looked away.

He smiled himself, thinking this was quite possibly the most bizarre morning he'd ever had. Following one of the strangest evenings he'd ever had. At least she couldn't say she hadn't made a memorable first impression. "To be honest, I hadn't actually thought about hiring anyone."

She glanced up. "Wait, what? Are you not restoring the tower? Fergus said—"

"If you knew him, you'd know that my uncle will say any number of things to get what he wants, with or without letting anyone else know if his plans will trample theirs. He's pretty sure he's always right."

"And is he?"

"Frustratingly often."

For the first time—well, with her alert and lucid, anyway—he got a real, all the way to the eyes smile. It packed a pretty good one-two punch when combined with all that deep-sea blue.

"You're looking at me funny again. I have jelly on my chin or what?" She touched her face again.

She had no guile about her at all, something he found himself liking. A lot. But Christ, those eyes were enough to kill a man, or drown him, or both. He took a sip of coffee, then another. "Yeah, there isn't enough coffee."

She looked at him more closely, sizing him up. "For?"

"To get over your eyes. They're really . . ." He trailed off on purpose.

"Blue," she said at length. "I know. But they're the only ones I've got."

They both grinned at that.

He put his empty mug down, then turned it in his hands as he spoke. "I have to apologize, too. About Fergus and about the trip—where did you drive in from?"

"Thunder Bay. On Lake Huron. Michigan."

"Ah. Wow."

"Right." She set her mug down, too, all business. "Why don't you want to do the renovation? Fergus mentioned you have a town tricentennial celebration coming, which is pretty impressive, by the way. And he mentioned the lighthouse is closing in on its bicentennial. What better time? If you don't mind my asking. If you start now—"

"I'm putting the labor into the house. The tower will have to wait."

"Is it funding?" she asked, quite directly and without sounding nosy. "Because I know a number of ways to raise funds and get—"

"The tower is privately owned. By me. Well, by my family, and I'm not interested in taking on any kind of partnership or working with an organization to restore it. We've been down that road in the past and it's not—" He broke off, waved his hand. "The particulars don't matter. And I'm very, very sorry to have caused you what has obviously been a big inconvenience. I'll be happy to reimburse you for all your travel expenses, gas, hotel, food. Whatever. And apologize again for—"

"No need," she said, studying him for another few seconds before draining her mug and setting it on the table with a little push. "I understand."

"You do?" He didn't know why he was so surprised. Or why he wasn't more relieved. He guessed, despite her initial appearance yesterday, she struck him as someone who didn't back down easily. "Good. If only Fergus had talked to me first—"

"You would have shot him down. So it's no wonder he didn't. But that's none of my business. And, actually, this is on me. We always research any project before coming out to see it. I didn't this time. If I had, I'd have known you were the owner, not Fergus, though he is family. I would have spoken to you directly before making such a long haul."

Logan wondered again about her story. Echoes of her nightmare continued to resonate inside him, and he recalled the condition she'd gotten herself into. He was pretty sure she'd hauled more stuff with her than someone would who was just being hired to do restoration work, regardless of the duration of the proposed assignment. She'd said "we" when referring to her company, and yet she was alone, and Fergus had made no mention of any other MacFarland being involved. Son, brother, father, or otherwise.

He had been privy to such a private thing as her fears or her grief or . . . whatever had provoked that nightmare with her father playing some role in it, and felt awkward asking about her business, her background.

Fortunately, he didn't have to. Her credentials didn't matter. He wasn't hiring. Anyone.

"Well," he said at length, "regardless of how it came about, or who should have done what, it happened, and I'd like to do what I can to mitigate any further inconvenience."

She ducked her chin for a moment, but not before he caught the *if you only knew* expression that flickered through her eyes. "Not necessary," she said, taking a breath and meeting his gaze directly. "Appreciated, but I can take care of myself." That wry smile kicked up again. "Yesterday's episode notwithstanding."

He tried, and failed, to ignore the memory of what it had felt like when she'd nipped his lower lip, when she'd kissed him with that wry mouth, those soft lips. And wondered what it would be like when she had all her senses about her. Like she did now. He was pretty sure it might kill him. And he'd die smiling.

"Okay." He paused to clear his throat. And tried not to shift in his seat hoping for a more comfortable fit to his jeans. She hadn't made a single mention, or even hinted at the things that had happened once he'd brought her back to the house. And given how straightforward she'd been about everything else that morning, he'd thought she probably would have. So he could officially just tuck all that away, filed under "interesting, but never to be repeated." It might take his body a bit longer to get the memo, however.

"If you need a place to stay for a few days until you sort out your schedule—"

"That won't be necessary." She gave him a brief look that let him know how ridiculous he'd sounded. *Sort out your schedule?* Like a project the size of Pelican Point wouldn't have been a major undertaking. She had no other schedule.

"I'm sorry, that was—I'm sorry." He sighed and pushed his chair back. "The offer stands. You can stay here until you figure out what you'll be doing next. Fergus told me yesterday that he'd promised you the keeper's cottage, which was right decent of him, except I doubt it's habitable. No one's even cracked the door open in . . ." He trailed off, then abruptly stood and went to the sink to rinse out his mug.

"In?"

"A long time. But the guest room is yours if you want it. I'll see to the shower problem." He ran the water over the mug far longer than necessary, trying to keep his thoughts in the moment and not on the keeper's cottage, the past . . . his past, and how they tied together. Failing.

He hadn't thought about that part of his past, about Jessica, the many lazy afternoons and chilly nights they'd spent in that cottage, in such a long time, he was surprised that it could still snatch at him the way it did. Probably just the odd direction his life had taken in the past twelve hours. Combined with that kiss.

"That's not necessary," she said from a spot just behind him.

He felt his skin react in awareness of her proximity, and thought that her refusal was probably a good thing. Definitely a good thing.

"Can I ask one favor? Then I'll be out of your hair. Or I will be as soon as I change my flat tire." She stepped next to him, leaned in and put her mug under the still running water.

He put his on the drain rack and stepped aside, but only a step—because he couldn't figure out why she stirred him up so effortlessly and he wanted to. It had been a hell of a kiss, sure, but, end of the day, just a kiss. And because he was apparently a glutton for punishment. "What favor?"

She turned the water off, then fiddled with the handle when it continued to drip. "You need a new washer and a . . ."

"This whole house needs a . . ." he said.

She shot him a brief smile. "I'm pretty good with a wrench."

"So you've shown. I—"

"I'm sure you're just as handy with one. You also have a full-time job. One that I'm guessing probably keeps you busy a lot more hours in the day than a normal nine-to-five would."

"All true, but—"

"Don't worry. I'm not angling for a job. You said you

weren't hiring. Someone else will be. I had a split-second thought to offer a trade while I find that someone, but never mind. It—I'm going to go."

"I wasn't going to ask you to work in exchange for room and board. I meant what I said. You're welcome to stay until you sort things out."

"Appreciated, sincerely, but I had a different trade in mind."

His body stood right up and saluted at the first trade idea that sprang to *his* mind. Given it was highly doubtful that was what was on her mind, he shoved that thought away.

She ducked her chin, and for the first time, the tiny hint of the vulnerability that he'd seen yesterday crept in.

"What's the favor?" he asked, hearing the quiet in his voice, wondering how she did that to him so easily.

She seemed to shake off the momentary dip and looked up again, but not at him. She was still facing the sink. "You know what, it's not important. I really should—"

"Alex. What's the favor?" He heard a short sigh.

"I'd like to go out. Look at the tower."

He couldn't see her eyes, but there was a different kind of tension, one he couldn't explain. Only it wasn't between them. Just within her.

She cut him a quick sideways glance. "For myself. No hidden agenda. No hard sell."

He started to ask why, not because he cared so much as because his natural curiosity had him poking at the reason for the tension. Then he noticed her hands on the edge of the counter were trembling. Slightly, but it was there.

As if she felt his gaze, she pressed her palms flat, then lifted them, rubbing them on the sides of her pants. She took a breath, turned to him. "Like I said, it's really not important. I've overstayed my welcome as it is. Do I need to call someone to get out to my truck?"

He shook his head, caught up once again in those stormy

seas. "It's out front. Tire's fixed." He'd peeked out the window and seen it earlier.

When they'd first gotten in the truck to head to the Point, Logan had called Fergus. He must have gotten old Earl to get it done sometime last night. While they'd been sleeping in the chair. Her all curled up and soft and warm in his arms. Before she'd kissed him like a house on fire.

She clearly didn't remember any of it, whereas he couldn't seem to forget it.

He broke their gaze and walked over to the table and started clearing. "I'll take you out to the lighthouse. Not much to see, I'm afraid. It hasn't seen a helping hand in quite some time." He knew it was nothing to be embarrassed about, just as he knew thoughts of his past, of Jessica, shouldn't be bothering him the way they were. He thought it was likely Alex's nightmare more than her kiss that had stirred up those old emotions. And even older memories.

"I can find my way around. You probably need to go in to work. I don't want to keep you. You've already done a lot more than you should have had to." She was over by the door leading to the mudroom with the whole kitchen between them. "You can lock the house before you go if you like. I just want to see the tower."

"I doubt it's safe. No one has been in it for a very long time. The wind is up and the rocks are dangerous."

"I don't know what Fergus did or didn't tell you about MacFarland & Sons, but it's safe to say I've been around one or two towers in my lifetime. Most of them aren't exactly situated in easy-to-get-to places. By comparison, from what little I saw of yours yesterday, it looks remarkably accessible. No boat required, no shaky or icy bridge." She said it without arrogance or sarcasm, simply stating fact. "I realize the situation yesterday might lead you to believe otherwise, but I can take care of myself. Want me to sign a waiver or something?" When he didn't respond right away, she pushed off the frame. "No problem. You've been more than kind, Chief McCrae. Thank you for the hospitality and the coffee. I'll get out of your way."

"It's Logan." He looked up when there was a continued pause.

She'd already turned to go, then seemed to physically shake off whatever she'd been thinking. "Thank you. Logan. Just let me grab my coat and boots."

"Alex."

She stopped, but she didn't turn around. And there was that tension again, only at least a little of it was between them.

He couldn't have said why he did it. He never invited trouble. His job brought it right to his doorstep; no need to go courting any personally. But he crossed the room anyway, and took a set of keys off the rack pegged to the wall above the counter, right next to the door. "Here."

She looked over her shoulder.

He held up the keys. "Small one is the side door to the keeper's cottage. Don't use that, it's boarded shut inside. Big one opens the front door. Or would have. It's probably long since warped shut. Middle sized one opens the door to the tower, but I imagine that's in even worse shape."

"I didn't get a chance to look and couldn't see from my position yesterday, but are the main house and cottage connected?"

"No. The house sits back inland, closer to the trees. The cottage is between the house and the tower, rocks on one side, open ground on the other, pretty much exposed, which is why the main house was added later. Tower is out on the promontory, about twenty yards past the cottage. There's a brick path between each, but it's not in the best shape. The weather really takes a toll out here. The old oil house is off to the side on the north."

"Oil house is still intact?" She nodded approvingly. "Original housing?"

"Close to it. In about the same shape, though. The tower is granite block. The beveled square shape was a big part of why the maintenance has been so overwhelming. The tower and the keeper's cottage were built in 1821. The cottage is shake shingles over wood frame, slab base, all done by hand back then. First part of the main house, the part we're standing in, was built in 1863. The parts that branch off either side, forming a windbreak of sorts, were added on over the years, but nothing new, structure-wise, since 1919. Just renovations to what was already built."

"So the newest addition is still going on a hundred years old."

He nodded.

"When was the tower decommissioned?"

"1933. One of my ancestors on my dad's side—my grandfather with a lot of greats in front of his name—was the first keeper, and every keeper after was a McCrae, so the family stayed in the cottage and the house after the tower went dark, working first with the town council, then with various other organizations, trying to find a way to save it, preserve it. For various reasons—war, history, politics, economy—all of those efforts failed."

"When did your family buy it outright?"

"With the help of an inherited trust started by one of the townsfolk—a wealthy older woman who summered up here her entire life and had always taken a particular liking to the lighthouse established it as part of her will when she passed away—my grandfather bought it in 1971. There have been renovations, upgrades. Some good and not-so-good changes to the interior, walls added, fireplaces sealed over." He smiled at the aggrieved expression that briefly crossed her face. "As someone who has spent a good amount of his spare time removing said walls and unsealing those fireplaces, I agree."

"What's the square footage now?"

"The main house adds up to around 4500 square feet, give or take."

"Unusual structure shape, or so Fergus told me. With the additions."

"Main house is two stories, the additions off either side are one. No cellar, but an attic over the back side of the second story. Detached two-car garage, which is mostly storage shed now. Five bedrooms total, two up, one down in the main house, then one in each of the side additions. Three and a half baths total. There's also a library or study on the far side of the living room, a formal dining room through there"—he nodded toward double doors leading off the far side of the kitchen—"which isn't used these days, a closed-in veranda across the central back of the house facing the cottage and the water, and a lot of random spaces, especially in the additions, that aren't currently dedicated to any particular use. Fergus is right. The additions seem to have been designed in a way that accommodated the rocky ground, so the resulting spaces were often more curious than useful."

She nodded, and he could see her mind working, filtering, processing. He realized then, despite being perfectly willing to answer her questions, it was probably less than thoughtful to go on about the place. If restoring lighthouses was her livelihood, her passion, than sprinkling the details around was probably tantamount to teasing. So he left it at that and didn't detail the cottage space or tower.

"It's impressive really. And a lot on your plate." She didn't look at him, but kept her gaze on the keys in his hand. "Thank you. For sharing all that. I-I don't need those." She nodded toward the keys. "I just wanted to take a look. Outside is fine."

He put the keys on the counter. "Okay."

"Okay."

Instead of relief, or pleasure, or whatever it was she'd

wanted to get out of looking at the tower, he felt her tension ramp up even higher. "Is it?" he asked, when he knew what he really needed to do was walk away. Shower and dress for work, close the door on this . . . whatever the hell it had been, and move on. "Is it really okay?" he clarified when she lifted her gaze to his. "You seem . . . I don't know. I'm not prying. But yesterday you . . . well, you weren't in great shape. So . . ."

She held his gaze and the silence stretched out one beat, then another, and it was the wrong damn time to remember how she'd tasted. How she'd bitten his bottom lip, pulled it between hers. He realized his gaze had dropped right to them. He jerked it back up again, but not before she noticed. And if those deep pools of luminous blue had been storm-tossed before, when the pupils punched wide, it was like a vortex had opened up in the middle of them . . . and threatened to suck him straight in. He had no chance to hold his breath, no chance to save himself.

"Alex—"

"I need to—should—go." The words had been all but choked out. She didn't pause; she left the kitchen and walked down the hall toward the guest bedroom.

And Logan had to ball his hand into a fist by his side to keep from reaching for her and dragging her right back. *To do what?*

A dozen different instinctive responses leaped to mind. All of them primal. He took the stairs up to his bedroom instead.

When he came down again twenty minutes later, showered and ready for work, prepared to convince her she really should stay until she was steadier and had things sorted out, she was already gone.

Chapter 4

A lex pushed open the door to the Rusty Puffin. She realized she didn't owe Fergus McCrae anything, not a
good-bye or an explanation, since he hadn't truly had the
power to hire her in the first place. She should be mad at
him, she supposed, but she was too tired to be mad. As
she'd told Logan—Chief McCrae—it was her fault for not
doing her due diligence.

She'd been too grateful to leave Thunder Bay and Michigan, once and for all. There was nothing left there for her
except painful memories. She'd figured she'd have a good
long time at Pelican Point to figure out where she wanted
to go, where she saw herself starting over, and maybe even
what she wanted to do with her life when she got there. By
the time the job was done, she'd know if Pelican Point had
simply been her next lighthouse . . . or her last one.

Except there wasn't going to be any Pelican Point
restoration, so she needed to regroup. Despite having zero
appetite as the strain of further indecision and uncertainty
was gnawing away at her, she needed to eat. As good as the
coffee had been that morning, it wasn't sitting well. As she'd
passed by the Rusty Puffin and spied an older gentleman
heading inside, she figured she could kill two birds with
one breakfast biscuit.

She wasn't even sure the place served breakfast, but she

imagined Mr. McCrae could point her in the right direction of someplace that did.

The front door was locked, which answered the breakfast question, but before she could turn away, the same older gentleman—Fergus McCrae, she presumed—appeared through the porthole window with a big smile. A moment later, he was ushering her into the pub.

"Welcome to Blueberry Cove, Miss MacFarland."

"Hi, and thank you. How did you know who I—"

"I noticed your truck out there, name on the side. And you did manage to make something of an entrance yesterday, lass."

She felt her face warm, but the older man's eyes were a twinkling blue under bushy gray eyebrows and above a charming, mischievous smile, making it impossible to feel any real embarrassment.

"You don't need to open just for me."

"What I need to do is apologize." He gestured to the stools lined up in front of the bar.

"That's okay," she said, though it was good of him to say so. "You were just trying to do something for the town. I understand."

"Oh, I'm not apologizing for me. I'm apologizing for my nephew."

That made her pause. And smile. "Well, I appreciate that, but he's already apologized."

Fergus frowned at that. "He didn't hire you." He didn't phrase it as a question.

"No, he didn't. I'm guessing my grand entrance, as you called it, didn't exactly inspire confidence. Can't say as I blame him."

From behind the bar, Fergus poured them each a mug of wonderful smelling, fresh coffee. She took a sip and hummed a little. Good coffee apparently ran in the family. He pushed a small bowl of creamers and sugars across the bar, but she was quite happy with the dark brew just as it was.

"You look to be in better spirits today." With his stout frame, bushy beard and brows, and charming Irish brogue, Fergus reminded her of an oversized garden gnome.

"Your nephew was a gracious host," she said, flushing a bit as she recalled waking up in a strange bed, snuggled under a thick quilt, still fully dressed like a small, innocent child. Her dreams, on the other hand, hadn't been remotely innocent or childlike. She was almost grateful for the spigot popping off in the shower. A short spray of icy cold water to the face had done wonders to clear those steamy images from her brain.

Not that he hadn't immediately put them right back in there. Coming to her rescue, or trying to, anyway, then looking anything but official and chief-like in that old hoodie and faded jeans, slung all low on his hips. And, dear Lord, but that voice of his. She wasn't too certain that, wielded properly, the vibration of that baritone alone wouldn't make a woman clim— Alex coughed and ducked behind her hand for a moment, mortified to be thinking of this man's nephew—the chief of police—like she was. *And right in front of him, for God's sake.* One night of sleep and a decent cup of coffee might be a start, but she clearly had a long way to go.

"So, are you saying it was that wee spot of trouble you had on the way in that made him decline your services?"

Alex had just taken a sip of coffee and almost choked all over again, thinking of the services she'd offered in her dreams. "I don't know. He said he's focusing his resources on restoring the house first, and that the keeper's cottage and tower are a bit lower on his list. I know how involved renovation would be on a light station the age of that one, and how costly it is, so I understand the need to prioritize.

He needs to live in the house, whereas the lighthouse . . ." She let the rest trail off with a lift of her shoulder.

That was the problem with most of the decommissioned lighthouses left to private interests. Unless there was a desire to turn them into some source of tourist income, or in the rare case, to make them into personal living quarters, it was a whole lot of money to put into something that was otherwise, essentially just a rather oversized lawn ornament. An ornament that needed constant upkeep and maintenance, given its location was rarely, if ever, in a guarded, sheltered spot.

To her, it was about preserving history. A very unique slice of history. And she wasn't alone. Lighthouses inspired all kinds of deep and powerful emotions in a broad range of folks, even the ones with no personal history or association with them. For her, it was, and had always been, very personal.

Her grandfather-with-many-greats before his name had also been a light keeper. He'd done as much of the maintenance himself as possible in those days. His son and daughter-in-law had taken over for him eventually, and his grandson after him, who was keeper when their tower had been decommissioned. The grandson had used his renovation skills, learned at the hands of his own father and grandfather, to do what he could to sustain it, then had put those skills to use helping out with the restoration of other light stations. When his two sons had joined him, MacFarland & Sons had been born. Now it had all come down to Alex, who was the last of the line.

Fergus grumbled something under his breath, then grabbed a white apron and quickly tied it around his stout frame. "Here I sit, bending yer ear and not offerin' up anything to go with that coffee. I can fire up the grill. What will ye have?"

"Please don't go to any trouble. Actually, I was hoping

you could direct me where to go to grab a bite before leaving."

"Was that your only reason for stopping by then?"

"I wanted to thank you for the opportunity, for trying to make it happen, and let you know that I understand the situation." She smiled. "And I figured a pub owner would steer me right when it came to a place to eat."

That elicited what could only be described as a jolly, whiskey-edged laugh. "Och, so you've heard my reputation with the grill here. Or lack thereof. Unfortunately, my cook doesna' start work for a few hours yet."

"No, no, nothing like that and it's okay, truly. I meant what I said about not going to any trouble."

"It's the least I can do, seeing the trouble I put you through, coming all this way for naught. And you claim my Logan was a good host, but if he couldn't be bothered to feed his guest—"

"No, he . . . well, he tried. If what you say about your lack of cooking skills is true, then it seems your nephew might not have fallen far from the tree." At Fergus's raised bushy brow, she added, "Let's just say I was thankful he stopped with a plate of toast. I'd hate to see what he'd do to a carton of eggs."

That set Fergus off on a gale of laughter. Wiping the corner of his eye, he leaned on the bar and patted her arm. "We're a pair, we are. Last of the McCrae men in the Cove." He winked. "Good thing we each have other."

She smiled, but felt a bit flustered all the same. "I probably shouldn't have said that. You both make an amazing cup of coffee."

"Oh, on the contrary. It's a right breath of fresh air ye are. Folks walk around like the sun rises and sets on the man. 'Tis true he's done more than his share of good for our wee village, and that after sufferin' more than his fair share of bad. It's thankful we are that he stuck by the town, made his home here, when most probably would have left and not looked back. But that's not to say it wouldn't be good to have someone give him a bit of a nudge, now and again."

Fergus's comment about Logan's past left her understandably curious, but her smile deepened as she recalled how the local police chief had seemed a bit surprised by her . . . less than fawning demeanor that morning. "Well, while I might have been happy to help you out with that, you'll have to find another nudger."

Fergus simply held her gaze, smiling. Those sky blue eyes of his sparkled quite merrily, which only served to underscore the whole gnome thing. "You know, one of the skills I do claim to have is being a pretty good listener."

"I appreciate that. I do," she said. He seemed like a lovely man, charming and good-hearted. His manner was something of a balm after the more tension-filled moments she'd had with his nephew that morning. And the day before. She slipped off the stool. "I should probably be going. Thank you for the coffee. If Chief McCrae—"

"Logan," Fergus said automatically, much as his nephew had.

"If the restoration project ever makes it to the top of the list, I hope you and he will keep me in mind." She had no idea what she might be doing by then, but one thing she'd learned from her dad was to cover all her bases. Thinking about him made her heart squeeze. She kept thinking she'd get used to it, or that at some point the memories would change to something more comforting, less painful. But if that time was coming, it hadn't arrived yet. And, for whatever reason, this morning she felt particularly vulnerable.

"After you came all this way," Fergus said, "and with the dual centennial anniversaries looming, I honestly thought he'd reconsider and do what the town wants him to do."

"In that case, maybe my grand entrance was more of a

factor. I am sorry for that, by the way. I've never fainted before. We've always prided ourselves on our reputation."

"I know you're a professional. I did my homework before contacting you. Your family has built quite a legacy in the restoration business. I'd ask how it was you came to focus on lighthouses, but I read the story on your website. Still, I imagine it's a far more complex tale when personally told. I'd have enjoyed hearing it from you. You come from good stock, Miss Alexandra MacFarland."

She nodded and the twinge in her chest tightened. "Thank you." She ducked her chin briefly, determined not to get teary-eyed again. Now that she'd let the waterworks start, she was having a hard time controlling them. In fact, she'd been surprised when she'd woken up that morning, just how puffy and stuffy she still felt after her little jag on the off-ramp. Even her throat had felt raw. She assumed it was just the cumulative effects of exhaustion coupled with the unfortunate fainting episode. Still, the solid hours of sleep she'd gotten had been a timely godsend.

Fergus was looking directly at her when she looked at him once again, and there was unmistakable emotion clouding his eyes as he spoke. "I don't want to say the wrong thing. I know it hasn't been that long for ye, lass. But it's sorry, I am, about your da."

Tears sprang to the corners of her eyes and there was no stopping them. She could only nod, then nod again. "Thank you," she finally said, her voice throaty again as she dabbed away the tears.

"It's a good thing, that you mean to continue. In some form or fashion, anyway. Family is important. Passion, and being passionate, equally so. You've the true luck of the Irish to have been able to combine them as ye all have. I didn't know the man, but reading up on the work you've done, that he's done, as well as your grandfather, and his father and uncle and whatnot before him . . . I can't help but think how proud he'd be, how proud they'd all be, taking everything that has come before, and putting it forward to continued good use." Fergus put his hand on her arm. "I'm sorry, lass, I didnae mean to bring ye any additional heartache." He squeezed her arm. "We're each an amalgamation of all those in our lineage. All of them are standing strong, supporting who we are, who we can be. They are in our blood and in our bones. You might feel alone, but you never will be, never can be. You're the sum of all that came before ye, dear Alex. And you'll carry them with you, wherever you go. They are part of you. I've told Logan the same thing. But my nephew . . ." He trailed off, shook his head. "Well, he's an idiot for not seeing what I see plain as day. Something he would—should—understand better than most."

Alex dabbed again at the corners of her eyes and her cheeks with the back of her hand, then forced a smile outward. It was clear Fergus McCrae was a dear man, indeed, and she appreciated his kind words, his wisdom, hard as they might be to hear. "And what is that? What do you see?"

"That both of you have a love and a need to tackle a new project, to keep your hands busy while your hearts heal. Doing the one thing you connect with best can bring you closer to finding your way there. I know it. If Logan had shut off his head for more than a minute and let his heart see for him, he'd have seen the same." Emotion was thick in Fergus's voice, the brogue serving to make it all the more poignant. "I know where ye are, lass. I've been there myself. And Logan, puir lad, has been there more than once, for all his young years. His project is taking care of the town . . . and keeping his commitment to maintaining Pelican Point as best he can. For you, the project would be yet another old beacon, a crumbling tower, in dire need of your wise and caring hand. In return, it will let ye pour all of the confusion, the grief, the questions yer having into her as you work your way through it and out the other side. As it happens, we've got ourselves a tower in need of some attention. Seems to me we'd all come out ahead on that equation."

Alex didn't know quite what to say. He'd caught her completely off guard with his deeply insightful wisdom. She wasn't sure how deep his knowledge went into her recent past, beyond knowing that her father had died. Not that she'd kept it a secret in any way, but she hadn't announced she was the only MacFarland left, either. She wasn't sure what digging Fergus had done, because nothing about her father's death was on their business website. It wasn't that she didn't want to pay tribute to him, to the work he'd devoted his entire life to, but how did one share that without appearing to be working the tragedy for the purposes of commerce? In point of fact, she hadn't even looked at the site, much less updated it, since the accident. She hadn't been sure there'd be a business left to tend to.

The accident had made the local papers, at home in Michigan and in British Columbia, where it had happened. She supposed something about it would probably come up on an Internet search. She'd never looked, and never would.

"I-I don't know what to say. I—thank you. For all the kind words, the wisdom, the advice. For trying, making the effort. I know your heart was in the right place." That was clearly true, and she was glad she'd made the stop on her way out of Blueberry Cove. It didn't help her figure out what she would, or should, do next, but it did help her put the loss of this job in a more comfortable perspective. And maybe more, once she'd had time to give his words some proper thought.

"I hope you don't mind my speaking my thoughts. But I needed ye to understand that it wasn't just a random thing, my ringing you up. And while my nephew might be willing to toss it off as the whim of an interfering auld man, I'm no' so willing to let him." The more emotion he allowed in, the deeper his brogue became.

"Mr. McRae, I'm grateful. More than you know," she said, meaning every word. "Your confidence in me is . . . well . . . humbling and inspiring. But I have to respect Chief—Logan's—decision in this."

Fergus gave her arm a final little pat, then surprised her with a quick wink and a right devilish grin. "You might, lassie, but I don't. If he's going to treat me as a meddling nuisance, well then . . . a nuisance I shall become."

"Oh, Mr. McCrae, please—"

"It's Fergus to you, lass. And I'll only ask ye this. Do you want the job?"

She thought about . . . well, everything. She hadn't walked out to the tower before leaving, but she'd taken a good long gaze at what she could see from the drive before heading out. It wasn't exceedingly tall as towers went, no more than forty feet. The jutting rocks and position on the point had naturally provided a goodly percentage of the necessary height for the focal point of the beacon. The squarish shape was actually uniquely charming in design, with framed-out windows on the side she could see that she assumed were repeated on the front and far side, as well. They would bring light into what would otherwise be a dank, dark interior, keeping the occupants from experiencing the same suffocating feeling that many towers had, though requiring significantly more upkeep. The black lantern housing and gallery at the top completed its day mark and, even from a distance, it wasn't hard to imagine the damage the weather had inflicted on the structure over the years of neglect.

A little research would tell her everything she needed to know about the light station, both the tower and the outbuildings. She'd have typically done that and much more before meeting whoever was in charge of its maintenance, much less accepting any contract offer. But none of that had mattered. Timing and distance were all the selling points she'd needed.

Her reasons for wanting to see the tower hadn't been about cataloguing any of those particulars, either. She'd wanted to see it, up close and personal, for a far more basic reason. She'd wanted to feel the yearning, the excitement, the finger-twitching, soul-stirring need to dig in, to fix, to restore.

She'd be lying if she said those were the things she'd felt when she'd looked up at the lantern gallery. Fear, trepidation, stomach-clenching nausea . . . those were the emotions that swirled inside her. For the first time, she'd wondered if perhaps Logan's decision hadn't been the wisest one.

What if it wasn't just a matter of *if* she wanted the job? Staring at it, hands trembling as they gripped the steering wheel, she'd been forced to wonder if the greater concern was would she have been able to actually *do* the job, even if she were hired?

Not only was it moderate in height as lighthouses went, the location was in as protected a place as she was likely to find. All lighthouses were exposed to the elements as part of their inherent function, but for many, that meant being positioned in fairly dire and challenging locations, from the tips of long rocky seawalls, to the ends of ice-encrusted bridges, or located out in the water, accessible only by boat and only then with extreme caution.

Pelican Point, however, was situated on an easily accessible promontory, the entire light station located on the same open stretch, all in close proximity, with the tower accessible on foot. The cottage and tower sat in the open clearing on the promontory itself, with the main house behind them, backed by forest that all but hugged the rocky point from just above the shoreline. If she was going to face her worst fears, and have any hope of conquering them, of getting the answers she needed . . . Pelican Point would be the safest, easiest place to do it.

Then there was its owner. Logan McCrae. What would it have been like, working with him? All but living with him while she did? Even if the keeper's cottage could be made serviceable, it was all the same property. How would it be working with someone . . . and wanting him? At least in the physical sense. Needless distraction? Or possibly a much needed diversion while tackling all the many things she had to work through?

"Yes," she heard herself say. "I do. I want it."

"Then let's see what we can do about that."

"Mr. Mc—Fergus, I don't want to stir things up or cause problems."

"Och, darlin' what's the point of drawing breath if not to stir things up every once in a while? And trust me, the Cove will be thrilled to see action being taken, so there are no obstacles there. We've only to persuade one man. I've a good feeling, if you'll let me talk to him, the tide will turn."

Alex felt the tide in her stomach pitch, but worked to maintain an even, confident smile and tamp down the panic. It was one thing to work through her issues on some rural, rustic site, reporting back to those in charge of the place as the job unfolded. The thought of doing the job under the close, watchful eye of the owner—an owner who'd made it clear that, left to him, she wouldn't be there—not to mention carrying the hopes of an entire town on her back as well . . . maybe she wouldn't think about that until she had to.

"Why don't you head on down to Delia's and grab a bite. It's down Harbor Street, right across from the docks. Winter is coming and you'll do well to put a few pounds on that mite of a frame of yours or the wind will pluck you right off that tower."

She felt her face go stone white and the bottom of what stomach she did have drop right out.

Fergus's expression was immediately stricken. He ducked under the bar, and came straight to her, took both her arms. "Och, but I'm a right bloody fool, I am. Should be whipped for speaking before thinking. An expression is all it was. I'm so very sorry. I didn't mean to—"

Alex shook her head. "I know. I know you didn't." She took hold of his arms, intending to step back, show she was fine, only she held on to those thick forearms for another moment, until she could be certain that was the truth. It took a moment longer to forcibly switch gears away from the past, away from visions of watching her father falling from the lantern gallery rail to the rocks below. She knew better than to close her eyes, so she focused on the first thing she could find.

Her gaze latched on the beautifully hand-carved, wood sign hanging behind the bar, which matched the one perched atop the small building, each featuring the name of the place. "Why did you pick puffins?" she blurted out, desperate to get back to the here and now and not caring if she sounded a bit manic. "Why not Rusty Pelican? Wouldn't that make more sense? Blueberry Cove is on Pelican Bay. Puffins are cute, like penguins, right?"

She felt the tension ease from his arms. The concern was still there in his eyes, though the corners crinkled up a bit as he spoke. "Well, the pelican has more than gotten his due now, hasn't he?" Fergus patted her arms, then tucked one through his and walked her over to the door, where several framed photos lined the walls. "Actually, I hail from County Kerry, in Ireland, along the coast. Grew up with a view of Puffin Island and the Skelligs, both home to that fine feathered friend." He motioned to the top two photos, which had engraved brass plates on the frames, announcing the names of their Irish locations.

"My first summer here, naught much reminded me of my homeland, until I saw the puffins had come to roost out on Sandpiper Island. It was as if they'd come all the way here to wish me well." He motioned to the bottom two photos. One of Pelican Point with the lighthouse in the background, and the other was labeled Sandpiper Island. The latter showed puffins lining the rocks. He lifted a shoulder, and Alex saw there was a bit of mist mixed in with the twinkle. "So, it was simply the natural thing to do."

She wanted to tip her head, lean on his shoulder. It also seemed the natural thing to do. And the ache that came with the need, the longing to do the very same thing again with her own father, tightened like a fist around her heart. But for once, she was able to keep her focus outward and simply be thankful for the contact, for the comfort. She squeezed Fergus's arm and gave in for a moment, briefly touching her head to his shoulder, then slowly sliding her arm free. "That's a lovely story. Thank you for sharing it with me. And these photos are beautiful. Did you take them?"

"I did, aye."

"They're really well done. You should consider making prints and selling them, unless that's something you already do."

"Oh, it's a hobby, is all it is. When I see something that moves me, I like to keep it with me, and photographs allow for that, even when the memories here begin to fade." He tapped his temple. "I give them as gifts when the subject matter calls for it, but I wouldna' ask money for them." He shot her a wink. "Would take all the soul out of it. Not to mention the fun."

Alex smiled and felt the pressure in her chest ease. Fergus

had a rather infectious joy in him. No matter what happened with the tower, she was glad she'd come by and met him. After all the events of the past year, legal and personal, she'd been resistant to deal with new people, with anyone really, just wanting to hole up inside herself, insulate herself from everything and everyone.

But Fergus was easy to talk to and had found his way past her usual barriers without even trying. As had his nephew, although in a very different way. She even found herself wondering why Fergus had left Ireland for Maine, surprised at how much she'd really like to talk with him. She wanted to hear more about his story, but didn't feel it was her place to ask. Especially as she was leaving, not staying. "I think it's a lovely tribute. All of it. The name, the photos. Makes the place here as unique and charming as its owner."

Fergus let out a laugh at that, the mist clearing from his eyes as he slipped a beefy arm about her shoulders and gave her a quick squeeze. "You're a charming one yourself, Miss MacFarland. Of course, a good Irish name doesn't hurt your case with me any, either. You'll have to tell me about your people someday, and where they hail from." He patted her arm, and smiled so sincerely, she covered his hand and squeezed back. "Blueberry Cove will be happy to add you to its hardy little clan."

"Fergus, your passion for your adopted home and the people here, your nephew, all of it, is equally charming, but I don't feel right, ganging up. Maybe we should respect your nephew's wishes."

"I'll strike this bargain with you. All I ask is that you spend the day introducing yourself to the Cove. I'll speak with Logan, and then you come back to the Puffin this evening after the sun has set. You'll get a sense of the people, as well as the plot, as they say. And we'll see what we see." Eyes twinkling quite merrily, he smiled. "Do we have ourselves an agreement?"

Her smile deepened. "You make it hard to decline."

"Then don't."

"Okay." She lifted a hand before he danced a jig or something. "But here's my only stipulation. If he's not receptive, then that's where it ends. I don't want to be held up as part of some organized town lynch mob or anything. He was very kind to me yesterday when I—well, when I had a bad day. This morning as well. I don't want to repay that kindness with confrontation."

"Understood."

Alex eyed him a bit warily. She didn't know Fergus that well, or at all, really, but given his determination to change his nephew's mind, she wasn't entirely certain he wouldn't apply the same wiles to her, if push came to shove. "Okay." She put her hand out. "Then we have an agreement."

He took her hand by the fingertips and bowed his stout frame with surprising grace over her hand. He pressed a fast, polite kiss to the back of her knuckles. Then winked at her as he straightened. "Never shake a hand, when you can kiss one."

"Why is it I have a sneaking suspicion I just struck a bargain with the devil?" She said the words with a pretty spot-on imitation of her great-grandfather's brogue, perfected by her grandfather and father after him, even though both had been born on American soil. Her efforts earned a hoot of laughter from Fergus.

"I'm no saint, lass," he assured her, grinning. "But I could be your guardian angel. And we all need one of those from time to time."

Chapter 5

"Now, Mrs. Darby—Eleanor—we'll get it taken care of. I'll send Randall over. He'll get it out of—no, I'm sure you don't need to spray it with—Mrs. Darby? No spraying! We don't want to antagonize—yes, yes, I realize he started it. Just . . . now listen to me. Leave the raccoon alone and I'll get Randall right over to take care of it for you. I'm sure it's more afraid of you than you are of it at the moment." Logan pinched the bridge of his nose. *Lord knows, I am.* He hung up and buzzed his desk sergeant.

"Yes, Chief?"

"Don't put Mrs. Darby through to me again. Today, anyway. Even if she bullies you. You can take her, Sergeant. You're armed."

"I'm not sure bullets would work on her, sir. Maybe a wooden stake and some garlic?"

Logan choked on a bark of laughter. "Just get Animal Control over there ASAP, will you? Get Randy if you can. Tell him to take the critter cage with him."

"For the raccoon, sir?"

Logan shook his head, but couldn't keep the smile from spreading. "I believe that's the only one we have the right size for, yes."

"I'm on it." Sergeant Benson clicked off.

Logan pulled the stack of files across his desk, wishing not for the first time that there was less paperwork in police work, and was debating a third refill for his coffee mug, when Fergus strolled in.

Logan immediately hit the intercom buzzer. "Barb?"

"I've got Darby back on line two. Your pick. Sir."

"Never mind." He clicked off the intercom and grumbled, "I'll take Door Number Two."

"I might be a wee bit ahead of you in years, boy-o, but I'm no' deaf as yet."

Logan put his empty coffee mug back on the desk, wishing he'd been a bit faster on the draw. Given the gleam in his uncle's eye, a healthy dose of caffeine was only the beginning of what he needed. "Please take a seat," he said to the already comfortably seated Fergus. "Let me clear my schedule."

"Auld Missus Darby let that raccoon get in? Figured it would happen at some point." Fergus shook his head. "Ye know she's feedin' the damn thing, doncha?"

"She's not feeding—" Logan broke off and frowned as Fergus held his gaze, lips twitching, seeing the truth in his uncle's eyes. "She's feeding it? What the—why would she do that? She hates the damn thing. And how would you know?" Logan's expression went slack. "Please tell me you're not—" He immediately lifted a hand. "Never mind. I don't want to know. Not a single detail."

"No, I'm not. I might be an old fool, but not that big a one." Fergus visibly shuddered at the thought. "A man would have to be blind, deaf, and—it doesn't bear thinking. I know she's feedin' the damn thing because Owen was in the other night for a short brew and mentioned she'd asked if the cat food she gets from him would be dangerous for small wildlife animals."

"She threatened to spray it with furniture polish. She's probably trying to poison it, not nourish it."

"Well, all I'll be sayin' on the matter is I've seen the size dish she keeps on her back stoop. If it's a cat she's feedin', remind me to steer clear of the docks behind her place in the wee hours. Thing'd be the size of a cougar by now. I wouldn't be surprised if she's got one of them, too."

Logan rubbed his palm over his face, then pushed the topic aside, quite certain that his uncle was about to replace it with something far more irritating. "What brings you by?"

"Alex MacFarland stopped in to see me on her way out of town early this morning."

Logan had been anticipating this argument, but was caught off guard by that tidbit of information. "She did, did she? I'm guessing she was none too happy to have dragged all of her worldly possessions halfway across the country for a job you weren't in the position to hire her to do."

"Actually, she was looking for some breakfast because apparently you couldn't be bothered."

"She said that? I wasn't expecting company, but I did make coffee and—she does realize that asking you for advice on good cooking is like—"

"Asking you for the same? I might have mentioned that." Fergus's smile faded, and his expression turned more serious. "She wasn't complaining. In fact, she said she was grateful for all ye did. She was quite embarrassed by what happened yesterday."

"She said as much." Logan looked back to his folders, uncomfortable. "It was understandable, under the circumstances. I don't hold it against her."

"Ah, so she told you then. About her business. About her father."

Logan's gaze jerked back to his uncle's. The wrenching pleas for her father during her tumultuous nightmare and the sobs that wracked her afterward echoed clearly through his mind. In fact, the whole night had played through his mind more than once since he'd arrived at work. As had the morning's events. The nightmare provided such a strong contrast to when she'd given him that blistering kiss. Combined with visions of her smacking that wrench into his palm, all business, despite being wrapped in an old towel, her face and hair still dripping from the broken pipe blast. That had just been in their first twelve hours together. He'd been trying to forget all of it since he'd come downstairs to find the house empty, not liking at all that it felt that way. Empty.

"Ah," Fergus said, a glint in his eye as he studied Logan's face. "So, she didn't tell ye. What circumstances were you talking about then?"

"Just that she'd been traveling a long distance, hadn't taken care of herself. She was pale, a bit hollow-cheeked. Bonnie thought she might have recently gotten over being sick and was probably anemic. She wanted her to go in for tests, make sure, but Alex didn't want any part of that." Logan wanted, badly, not to know anything about the real whys and wherefores that had caused Alex to pass out, literally, in his arms, but he knew from the look in Fergus's eyes that he wasn't going to be that lucky. If he were being honest with himself, he'd also admit that it wasn't going to take Fergus pushing the point to keep Alex MacFarland in his mind.

"You didn't talk to her at all, then, did you? About her qualifications? Her work history? It's remarkably impressive, given her age."

"First, she wasn't in much shape for that—"

"Yesterday, maybe, but there was no need to give her the bum's rush out the door this morning. She came all that way, the least you could do was—"

"I offered her the house, Gus. I told her she could stay as long as she needed, while figuring out her next step. She chose to leave instead. And I didn't need to know her references or her qualifications, because I'm not investing the trust in the lighthouse when it's taking everything I have to keep the house from falling down around me. The same house that provides the roof over my head."

"Then maybe it's time to consider getting some help. With the house, and . . . all the rest."

Logan didn't want to admit it to Fergus, but he'd thought about doing exactly that. For the main house, anyway. Blueberry Cove was hardly a hotbed of crime, but Alex had been right that there was still a constant stream of peace-keeping issues that kept him busy far outside normal business hours. Small towns also had small police forces, which meant even as chief he still shouldered a fair share of working directly on any issue that might come up, as well as taking on the larger political role of working with the town council and the mayor. And more of the same on the county and, at times, state levels.

The thing about living in a place where you could name every single person who resided in it was that folks felt a direct kinship of sorts. With that connection came a heightened sense of trust and faith that he'd be there for them, come any crisis. He valued that, was humbled by it, but when that individual bond was multiplied by the number of residents in the Cove . . . well, he was only one man. But he did what he could, putting the needs of the folks who relied on him first.

That meant the house out on the Point had become like the old family member whose needs were constantly moved down the list, neglected because family could be counted on to understand. Like a family put too long on the wait list, the house was getting more and more unforgiving, and if he didn't find some kind of solution, he might find himself out on the proverbial street.

"The house . . . has been a challenge," Logan said, not wanting to give Fergus even a toehold in the conversation, because he wasn't going to relent on the tower. "I haven't been able to put as much time and effort into it as I'd hoped and the list is, admittedly, getting a bit daunting." He lifted a hand before Fergus could launch what was sure to be a well-thought-out campaign to get him to reconsider his stance. "But if anything is done, it should be the house first, the tower after. I understand about the tricentennial and the lighthouse's bicentennial, but as nice as it would be for the tower to be restored, the end result doesn't help us or the town. The folks that come to look at lighthouses still see it on the harbor boat tours. Even restored, we can't open it to the public."

"Why not?"

Logan's eyes widened. "Because I live there and don't want to encourage people to be tromping around my property and through my house. I'm the chief of police, as well as a private citizen. Neither one of them think that's a great idea. We get enough interlopers every year as it is, who think simply because it's a historic building that it's open season to go wherever they like."

"To be fair, it's relatively rare, comparatively speaking, for lighthouses to be privately owned."

"Which is why we posted a sign. For all the good it does."

"Is it the funding then?" Fergus asked.

"I just got done telling you that I won't be selling tickets to my living quarters, so—"

"I don't mean about the lighthouse, or the keeper's cottage. You've recently taken a bigger role in managing the trust. Are we in worse shape there than you've let on? If that's so, ye need to come clean with me."

"No, it's okay. But it doesn't earn what it used to. Growth is slow, sometimes negligible. We're damn lucky it didn't go the other direction. I'm hopeful we can be more aggressive in finding ways to grow it without taking too many risks, but that will take time. What's in there now—

we'd wipe it out just to renovate the tower. And then what? It won't stay renovated. Over time, the winds, the sea, the weather, will hammer it all over again. True of the cottage as well. If we can get a healthy part of the house up to par, that would be the wiser investment. I guess I kept thinking if I maintained the place by doing as much of it myself as I could, then eventually we could start a modest campaign on the cottage and tower. But I have to admit . . . I'm losing that battle. I should have admitted defeat sooner and I should have been more aggressive with trust management. It's not my forte, but—" He broke off, pinched the bridge of his nose. "I'm sorry."

Fergus reached over, gripped Logan's forearm, squeezed, then held tight. "Yer doin' the best with what ye have. I dinnae blame ye, laddie. You've been dealt a tough hand, and not just once. I know ye just wanted to find peace, simplicity, and let things work at their own pace. I understand that, as ye well know. I could have pushed harder, but I guess I wanted to believe it would all resolve itself, too."

"It's the McCrae legacy," Logan said quietly. "Left to me to oversee. I should have done better with that."

"Yet another burden for you to take on," Fergus said. "As I see it, you've never shirked a one of them. As ye said, yer but one man." He leaned farther over the desk and cupped Logan's cheek with his other hand. "Even a lad as stubborn as yourself knows when it's time to ask for some help."

Whatever argument Logan thought he'd been prepared to mount, Fergus had wiped out with that one quietly stated declaration. It wasn't as if they hadn't had the discussion before in some form or other. But that was before any actual steps had been taken, and other people had been involved. Alex MacFarland, specifically. He understood now why Fergus had done it.

"I might not have, but you did," Logan said, feeling the weight of every single one of his forebears as if they were sitting directly on his shoulders. It was ironic that he could single-handedly carry the entire town of Blueberry Cove on those same shoulders, and do a pretty damn good job of it, yet fail the single branch of his own ancestral tree so utterly. "It's a monumental task and will continue to be one. I'm not even sure, frankly, where to begin. And that's talking about the main house."

"That is why I stepped in to help ye out a wee bit. It's what family is supposed to do. And I've been just as lax, so the fault lies equally with me."

Logan sighed and held Fergus's gaze squarely. "What is one single woman going to do?"

"Have you bothered to even look at her credentials? Do a search on her background in this business?" Fergus didn't wait for the reply as they both knew the answer to that. "She's done this her whole life, and her father, grandfather, great-grandfather, and more before her. They know a thing or two or three about what it takes, and that includes raising the funds to see it done."

"She might have mentioned that," Logan allowed.

Fergus's brows climbed halfway up his ruddy forehead. "Did she now? And you what? Dismissed the golden goose out of hand?"

"That's just it. There is no golden goose, no golden eggs. I didn't follow up with Alex because I've done that legwork in the past, although it's been years. I know there are ways to raise the funds, and each and every one of them comes with a price. The main one being that I lose control over the property and how it's utilized. That's something I'm not prepared to relinquish. It's the reason we McCraes bought the damn thing to begin with. It's our home. It's been our home for two hundred years."

"You've asked for a place to start and I've handed you one."

Logan wanted to say part of the reason he'd put off hiring out was it would begin a never-ending parade of sub-contractors and workers on the property. After putting in a long day making himself personally available to every single person in the Cove, he didn't want to face another army of people when he went home at night. He wanted time to himself. Needed it. It provided balance, a retreat, separation between his professional life and his personal one—as much as he had one anyway. He knew it was also because of those other burdens Gus had mentioned, but it wasn't hiding. It was simply . . . finding a way to live. He'd been settled and comfortable with his life for some time.

He didn't say any of that, suddenly realizing there had been a cost to that approach, after all.

"So maybe we start with the house, invest a bit of what we've got while leaving enough behind to earn us more capital over time," Fergus suggested. "We get some man-power in there . . . and when that burden has been lifted somewhat, maybe dealing with the lighthouse won't feel as daunting. Maybe we can tackle it in stages, or possibly find some solutions that won't include giving up control over how it's used. At the very least, it's worth a discussion, isn't it?"

"Yes, okay. But your timetable, the tricentennial—"

Fergus lifted a hand. "It was a leverage point, that's all. I needed something—anything—to get you to pull your head out of your arse and look at the bigger picture, and not just the four walls and the roof falling down over your own head. With enough help, the house could be done in-side twelve months, eighteen tops. Perhaps our gift to the town wouldn't be a fully restored, operational tower, but the promise that the work has begun on it. We can consider it our gift to the Cove. And to our own legacy."

"I'll . . . think on it."

Fergus pushed to a stand. "Why don't you think on it down at the pub, say, seven o'clock?"

Logan's gaze narrowed, and he realized he'd just been played by the master. "What's happening at seven o'clock? I'm not facing some kind of impromptu town meeting, Fergus. I'll discuss this with you, and I'll work on it in my own time, but I'm not bringing in the town to pass judgment on what will or won't be done, or give them so much as a single vote in this. It's not their legacy, or their burden. It's ours. And that burden is heavy enough without putting me at their mercy along with it. Your idea to present the restoration to the town as our personal gift is fine. After the fact."

"Are ye quite done with yer bluster, Mr. Blowhard?"

Scowling, Logan restacked the folders on his desk, then finally pressed his hands against his thighs. How could family feel so . . . restorative, so bolstering one moment, and so incredibly infuriating the next? "I'm done for the next thirty seconds. Or as long as it takes for you to tell me what you've done now."

"Ye need to trust me, lad. We need help organizing this operation, and we happen to have someone in town who can help us with that very thing."

Logan lifted his gaze, brows narrowing. "I thought you said she stopped by on her way out of town. Alex MacFarland isn't the solution. She's gone. But I understand and agree it was the right idea. In general. We'll have to look elsewhere for—"

"She did stop by, yes. And she was heading out, aye, mostly thanks to your complete lack of insight and imagination." Fergus slapped broad palms to broader thighs, and there was far too much mischief in those blue eyes to bode at all well. "However, I might have persuaded her to stick around a bit longer. See if I could talk some sense into that hard head of yours, before scrapping the effort she'd already put into getting here. And don't go saying a single word. It was almost as hard to talk her into staying as it's been to get you to consider listening to what she has to say. I swear, you're both too hardheaded and prideful for your own good. I figure you'll either be the best team ever . . . or kill each other inside the first fortnight."

Logan leveled a steady gaze at his uncle. "Sounds like the only one in danger of any bodily harm is standing in front of my desk."

Fergus chuckled at that. "Och, I've faced down fiercer than you and lived to tell." He reached in his shirt pocket and pulled out a business card. "Take a few minutes over lunch and do a little look-see." He tossed it on Logan's desk. MACFARLAND & SONS RESTORATION was embossed across the front in black ink, with an engraved red and white striped lighthouse next to it and all the pertinent information printed below. "She's the real deal. And she needs this as much as we need her."

Logan looked from the card to Fergus. "What is that supposed to mean?"

"You're the policeman. Do a little detective work."

Visions of the previous night, of Alex's state of mind, flashed through Logan's mind. "Fergus, the last thing we need is someone with problems of her own—"

"The only thing we need is someone who is as passionate about making this happen and as dedicated to seeing it through as we are. I know it's not a simple matter of throwing money at the problem. I know it will turn your life upside down for a wee bit. You'll need someone who won't walk when the going gets tough."

"What makes you think she'll stick?"

"Because she needs this. Her reasons might be different from ours, but the outcome is all the same. We'll both get what we want."

By the time Logan walked into the Rusty Puffin that evening, he honestly didn't know what he wanted.

His talk with Fergus had definitely sunk in. He agreed it was time for some changes to be made in how he was handling . . . well, everything. But he wanted time to think, consider, and do some research regarding what steps he wanted to take, how best to tackle them, and with whom. He needed to make certain the choices made and the steps taken were the ones best suited to get the desired results with the fewest risks. He understood, at core, it was really just his own foolish, egotistical way of saying he wanted to make the decisions, not have them shoved down his throat.

For that reason, and because he'd been honest in saying he was unsure about taking on someone who had her own issues to grapple with, he'd wanted to toss out the business card Fergus had pushed on him. But as the afternoon had worn on and he hadn't been mercifully called away to deal with anything immediately pressing, the echoes of her nightmares, her matter-of-fact dealing with him that morning . . . and the tension he'd felt when she'd talked about wanting to see the lighthouse . . . all of that had continued to pop up in his thoughts until he finally caved and did some Internet searching of his own. The hope had been that finding out more about her would give him the perspective he needed to be objective. About her, about Fergus, about all of it.

He was going to take immediate steps to start work on the house on a broader scale. He knew how to go about hiring on subcontractors and didn't need Alex for that. He also was going to stand steadfast against dealing with the lighthouse. For now. Heading into winter was not the time to be dealing with that. Maybe the following spring, or summer, when the house repairs were well underway, he could hire someone to come in and do a prospectus on what all would be required. It didn't all have to happen at once. He was going to recommend that Alex find herself another restoration contract as they wouldn't need her services, not for some time anyway.

At least that had been his plan before he'd gone and looked into her background. He'd been prepared to find something tragic involving her father, but he hadn't been at all prepared to discover she'd been there with him on the tower the day he fell to his death. And that she'd been the one trying to save him . . . only to have him literally slip from her fingers.

He wished he couldn't imagine that or what it would feel like. Except he could. All of it. Every harrowing second of it. His experience had been different only in that it had taken place on the water, and the fall had been from a boat. And it hadn't been his father. It had been his fiancée.

In his case, there had been no photographs, and the news stories had been local and brief. It was sad, tragic, and had devastated every person in his small town. But it had been an accident, nothing nefarious or negligent. And since Blueberry Cove was still largely a fishing town, it wasn't the first, or the last, sad loss at sea they'd experienced.

Alex hadn't been so fortunate to be able to grieve privately. The accident had caused quite a stir. In the wake of the tragedy, the owners had had the gall to file a suit against Alex and her company, blaming them for cutting corners and being at fault for her father's tragic death. Alex had claimed the exact opposite was true. In the end, after much litigation, there hadn't been enough proof one way or the other, and the suit had been dismissed by the judge. But the protracted battle had tangled Alex in its grip, preventing her from moving forward, either with her business or her personal grieving.

He couldn't believe she was as together as she was, seeing as the lawsuit had only begun a little more than a year ago and ended far more recently. He'd been some version of a zombie or a ghost, barely stumbling through the rest of that summer. The better part of his senior year in college was simply a blur to him, something he'd done by rote as grief and guilt consumed him.

He'd made choices that following summer, changing directions, deciding that feeling so helpless was simply unacceptable. He hadn't been able to save Jessica, but he could be there to help someone else. Honor her, and work through his own doubts about himself, about his worth, and what was important, by dedicating himself to others. He'd come home . . . and joined the Blueberry Cove police department.

Part of what helped him decide were all the McCraes who had come before him, who had worked so hard to establish a legacy they could be proud of. Alex knew something of that. MacFarland & Sons had started over a century ago, and had continued on until it was just Alex and her father. And now . . . it was just her.

The difference was, when his parents had died, Logan had had his grandfather and his sisters, and later, when tragedy had struck again, he'd had his siblings and Fergus. For that matter, he'd had the entire population of the Cove holding him up, supporting him, believing in him. He'd always had a foundation of love and support throughout his life, through tragedy and triumph. When Alex had lost her father, she'd had . . . no one.

Part of him wanted to know what in the hell she thought she was doing, essentially moving herself lock, stock, and trailer to some small coastal village in Maine, taking on a job the size of Pelican Point alone. But another part understood the need to reconnect . . . to bury herself in the one thing she knew and understood as a way to heal, to get beyond, to find, fix, move forward. He couldn't rightly blame her for taking the first thing that had come her way.

It left him exactly . . . where? He honestly didn't know.

Fergus waved him over to the bar. He nodded, but took a moment to scan the pub interior, looking for Alex. He said his hellos and patted arms, nodded, and otherwise acknowledged every person he passed on his way over to Gus. He liked the sense of community, the warmth and security of feeling so connected. But there were times when he really wished he could just be a guy walking into a bar for a cold beer where no one knew his name or tracked his every movement. Tonight qualified as one of those times.

"She didn't stick around?" Logan asked as he reached the end of the bar. What he should have felt was relief. So, it didn't help much when he felt quite the opposite.

Fergus slid a tall glass of ale across the bar. "She stuck. She got held up is all."

"Held up where? The only people she knows here are you and me."

"That might have been true this morning, but you know how the Cove can be."

There was no retort for that, because Logan did indeed know. He just hadn't thought of Alex as the type who would easily fit into new environments. He pictured her telling him very directly, politely, that he could take his offer to house her while she scrambled for more work and shove it. She was memorable, he'd give her that. Maybe even the kind that would grow on a person over time, but inside a single day . . . he didn't really see that.

"So, where, exactly, did she get hung up?"

"Boathouse. Talking to young Monaghan about something or other."

"She's with Brodie?"

Fergus raised a brow at the edge in Logan's tone, but kept wiping down the bar. "I heard something about him discussing some ideas he had on a remodel, but that's all I know." He spared a glance at his nephew. "Don't worry. I'm sure she'll put your concerns first."

"I wouldn't be so sure about that. I fired her, remember?" Logan didn't get into the part about how he wasn't planning on hiring her back. It hadn't occurred to him that she might stick around the Cove, anyway. Her business was in lighthouse restoration. And he was the only one with a lighthouse. So what the hell was she doing with Monaghan? And why did it piss him off?

He sipped his ale and tried not to look at his uncle, who had a knack for mind-reading. Logan was fairly convinced that's how he knew what he knew. Logan recalled Fergus's comments about Alex and him needing help. He'd initially assumed Fergus had meant she needed the work and Logan needed work to get done. But now that he knew about her father, and that, as far as he could tell, she hadn't worked a restoration project since his death . . . that would mean her first time back on a tower would be Pelican Point. Was that why she'd wanted to go out and just look at it? Was she even ready to get back on the horse, as it were? Would she ever be? Her nightmares suggested otherwise. As did the fragile condition she'd let herself get into. She was still grieving. She'd barely had time to bury the man and set his estate to rights, much less deal with the legal woes she'd faced in British Columbia.

The more he thought about it, the more convinced Logan became that his initial plan to let her move on was still the right decision. He set his glass back on the bar. "Might be a better choice for her, anyway. MacFarland's experience isn't just with the lighthouses; they've done almost as many keeper's cottages and the like. She'd be able to manage pretty much any kind of restoration project, I'd imagine." *Or would be able to if her head were screwed on straight.*

"So, you looked her up then." Fergus tucked the bar rag

in his apron pocket and gave Logan a considering look. "If it's pity you're feeling, don't let that guide ye. You wouldn't have stood for that after Jessica died. I imagine Alex feels much the same."

"How do you know what she feels? It's entirely different, what happened with me and Jessica. It was Alex's father, for God's sake. He was all she had left."

"Different in some ways, yes. In all the ways that count? Not really. All I'm saying is let Alex find her own way. Don't go making choices for her."

"The choices I'm making are for me. For us, the family. She hasn't been on a tower since her father died. She's grieved herself literally to the point of collapse, which I don't hold against her."

"Wise, given we all recall the shape you let yourself get into that summer and most of the following year. Understandable as it was."

Fergus could be blunt to the point of brutal, but Logan could handle that. "I also wasn't trying to head out on a fishing trawler anytime soon after that, either, if you recall. Took me several years until I knew I was ready. Do we really want to find out if she's ready to handle something like this the hard way?"

Fergus started to move away as calls for drinks were coming in from the other end of the bar, but he paused and looked his nephew right in the eye. "Sometimes, if moving forward is what you're after, hard is the only choice available. Would ye rather she pine herself into the ground next to him, then, lad?"

"No, of course not. But you're saying don't make decisions based on pity and I'm saying maybe what's smarter for us is to hire someone we know can handle the job."

"So you are planning on hiring someone then, are ye? Well then, that's one step forward for you, isn't it?"

"I—" Logan paused, and it was enough time for Fergus to walk to the other end of the bar, leaving him to stew in his own juices . . . probably just as his uncle had planned.

"He's right, you know."

Logan's gut tightened, but he turned on his stool and faced Alex MacFarland squarely.

She stood barely two feet behind him, dressed as she had been that morning, but with a bit more color in her cheeks. In some ways, she still looked too slight and too haunted. In other ways, she looked every inch the wrench-slapping, "shove-your-offer" stating professional.

One tugged at his heart, the other tightened his gut. One he might have been able to ignore, or at least walk away from. But together, they felt like a two-fisted punch that left his ears ringing a bit. "Listen, that was—I'm sorry. I didn't know you were standing there. I know it sounded callous and that's not what I meant." *And thanks, Gus, for cluing me in.*

"No need to apologize for speaking the truth. As you see it, anyway. And I'm pretty sure it's exactly what you meant. No need to pretty it up on my account. Contrary to my arrival yesterday, I'm really not a fragile flower. The business I've dedicated my life to is hardly soft or sweet, nor are the men I've worked for and with. And whose respect I've busted my ass and more than a bone or two, to earn. But earn it I did."

"Alex—"

"Let me finish. I wasn't hiding anything. Your uncle knew all about my . . . business situation. In fact, I was surprised he hired me as readily as he did."

"You were?"

She nodded. "If I were a prospective employer, I'd be concerned about me, too. I don't take offense at what you said. It's smart business."

"But you came out here. You took the job. Or were willing to."

She nodded.

"Why?"

She searched his eyes for a moment, but she didn't falter in her answer. "Because, like Fergus said, I have to find out somehow, and there's only one way to do it. I was straight with him, and he with me. So I figured if I was going to try . . . it seemed like as good a fit as any. I didn't know about you."

Logan ducked his chin for a moment. Her gaze was more penetrating than his uncle's had been. A feat he hadn't thought possible. She'd completely disarmed him with her matter-of-fact candor. She wasn't bragging, nor was she blowing smoke. She was being bare-bones honest with him. It was hard not to respect that.

But it didn't change his mind about hiring her.

"I didn't fire you because of . . . anything having to do with you. I didn't know about your company, or the . . . events of this past year . . . until today. I fired you because I'm not going to restore the lighthouse." He lifted a hand. "Fergus knows this, and he agrees."

That got a small lift of surprise out of one eyebrow. "What about the house and the cottage?"

"I conceded defeat on the house. The cottage will have to wait."

Her mouth curved a little . . . which surprised him. And also had the unfortunate result of reminding him of exactly how her lips had felt on his the night before. Despite her directness, he still couldn't read her. How could she not remember *anything* about the previous night?

"And?" she asked.

"And I'm sorry. Again. I can hire locally for the work I need done. Your specialty is lighthouses, so it seems better to . . . let you get on with that. I will eventually work on the lighthouse and I'm happy to keep your card until then. I can even promise you first offer when the time comes."

"Thank you," she said, with no trace of sarcasm, apparently accepting the offer as sincere. Which it was. He liked that she expected nothing less.

"No problem. I did read your family's work history. It's impressive. I'm not surprised Fergus hired you on the spot. He has good instincts."

"And you?"

His eyes widened at that. "What do you mean?"

"You're the chief of police, so I assume your instincts are pretty sharp."

"I'd like to think so." He studied her face, and wondered if she played cards. If so, she probably cleaned house in poker. "But they're not infallible."

"Given my arrival yesterday, and what you learned about my family today . . . if you were going to start work on the tower now, would you take a chance on me? Seeing as I'm here and all."

Logan immediately retreated. He might not be able to read her, but he was quite certain he could read a setup before he walked into it. "Point's moot, isn't it?"

"Humor me."

"Why is my opinion important? You don't know me any more than I know you."

"Actually, we know each other exactly the same amount."

Logan's mind went immediately to that kiss, to the way she'd smiled and called him Sex-god Voice. He would have sipped his ale to buy time, if he hadn't drained it already. He wasn't used to someone calling him out like she did. It . . . well, it rattled him . . . more than he liked to admit. "And how is that?"

"Your opinion is based on spending about twelve hours with me, give or take. And reading my work history, about which there is some pretty extensive information. My opinion is based on spending those same twelve hours with you, though I concede I was unconscious for more of that time than you were." Her lips curved again, and damn if it didn't make his palms itch. "The rest of my opinion is based on spending today in your town, talking to the folks who rely on you to keep the peace and keep them safe and sound."

"And?"

"And they respect you. Your uncle respects you, so your opinion carries weight. I'm an expert at what I do, so my opinion carries some weight. If you were hiring for the restoration of Pelican Point, would you hire me?"

"Based on what I knew when you left this morning? No. Based on what I knew when I walked in here? You'd have had your work cut out for you, but you'd have had the chance to plead your case."

She looked bemused and, if he was reading her expression properly, intrigued by his blunt response. The fact that she handled straight talk as readily and easily as she dished it out had him feeling exactly the same.

"And now?" she asked.

"Now? I'd probably have hired you. Only I'm not sure if it would be because I thought you could do the job, or out of curiosity to see if you would succeed." He did smile then. "I could always fire you again if you proved me wrong."

She poleaxed him by smiling back. A full-out grin, in fact. The way it lit up those deep-sea blue eyes of hers made the impact like another double-fist punch straight to the gut. Or . . . somewhere in that general vicinity.

"Then I have a proposition for you."

He blew out a sigh, more disgusted with himself for letting his guard down than disappointed in her for taking advantage of it. "Yeah, that's not going to happen."

"You're not even going to listen?"

"I will." Logan looked over his shoulder to find Fergus standing behind the bar, wiping down glasses.

Logan had been so wrapped up in his little tête-à-tête

with Alex that he'd completely tuned out the general hub-bub of the rest of the bar. Something he had never done, and didn't think, given his training, he would have been capable of even if he'd wanted to. But he had. So much so, that he realized the entire place had gone collectively silent. He could hear the squeaks being made against the glass Fergus was steadily wiping. He gave a quick scan of the room, and found every head in the place was turned toward them. *Jesus, Joseph, and Mary.*

Logan turned back to Alex. "You seem to have me at a distinct disadvantage here."

"How could that be when you hold all the cards? I'm certain, after what I heard today, the fine townspeople of Blueberry Cove will respect your decision."

Logan wouldn't be too certain of that. He might not be able to read her, but he could sure as hell read the room. The barely tempered, unmitigated glee he'd noted on most of those familiar faces said it all. Just exactly what in the hell had she been doing all day, anyway?

He shot a glare at Fergus, who was whistling, the picture of innocence as he wiped down the perfectly clean bar.

"At the risk of being lynched by those very same fine townspeople"—he leveled a direct gaze toward them as he did a slow, steady scan of the room, which cowed not a single solitary one of them—"go for it."

To her credit, she didn't look smug or even entirely confident. In fact, if he wasn't mistaken, for the first time since she'd faced him that night, she looked almost . . . nervous. Was it because she really wasn't sure of her own scheme? Or because she wanted it that badly?

"Let me do the project analysis I'd have done before taking on the job. I'll waive my normal fee, and you'll get a detailed report on the restoration needs and costs for the lighthouse, the cottage, and the house. It's information you're going to need no matter how you proceed. I am well aware, as you said, that you're quite capable of hiring subcontractors who can tell you what's wrong and what needs fixing. But even the newest part of your house is a hundred years old, the cottage and tower twice that. It's not necessarily a simple matter of getting someone to slap new shingles on it. If you want it renovated, sure, hire whoever and let them have at it. But restored is a different story. You have to know who can maintain the integrity of the original structure without destroying it in the process.

"There's also the matter of making sure you have someone who knows about the new advancements that have been made in restoring homes and buildings like yours, which will bear lifelong exposure to extreme elements. You can do what's been done before, then keep doing it over and over again, or you can look at new options that might reduce the need for constant heavy maintenance. You can also take a significant chunk of time you don't have and educate yourself on all that, or you can hire someone who's already an expert and move on without delay and without making costly mistakes—which I promise will happen. Because no amount of off-the-cuff research is going to double for the information someone who has spent a lifetime in the industry already knows."

He waited a beat to make sure she was finished, wishing he wasn't as impressed as he was irritated. "You're saying you're willing to give me the benefit of all of this hard-earned knowledge free of charge?"

"Does your original offer still stand? The one you made when you fired me?"

He assumed she meant a roof over her head while she figured out her next move. Knowing what he did now, he could imagine her financial situation was likely not very secure, and he hadn't forgotten that part of Fergus's original offer had been a roof over her head, albeit the sagging one of the keeper's cottage. "It's not open-ended, but for a reasonable amount of time, yes."

"That's all I ask."

He tried to ignore the weight of every single gaze in the place. "What's in it for you?"

"Worst case? Time to secure my next contract."

"How do you plan to support yourself while you're doing all that free project reporting and contract negotiating?"

She sent a glance down the bar. "Some people find my skill set more valuable than you do."

Logan followed her gaze to find a grinning Brodie Monaghan hoisting a beer in her direction to the hoots and catcalls of everyone else in the place. More surprising, he spied Eula March seated alone at a small two-top by the front door. He couldn't recall ever seeing her in the pub before. His gaze snagged briefly on hers, and while he couldn't have said she smiled, there was something . . . knowing . . . about the look she sent him.

Her words from the day before came back to him once again. *Change is coming. Be open to it.*

He looked back at Alex and felt that little ripple sneak up his spine and lift every single hair along the back of his neck. *Damn it, Eula.*

Before he could find the words to tactfully shut down Alex's little scheme, she smiled. "And best case? I can take care of myself long enough to provide you with the opportunity to realize why you should have hired me in the first place."

Chapter 6

She was an even bigger idiot than she'd thought. In the course of a single day, she'd managed to do the two things she'd sworn not to do. She'd put the weight of the expectations of an entire town on her admittedly less-than-stable shoulders . . . and she'd pissed off the only guy she needed on her side: the one she wanted to hire her. "Oh yeah, you're totally ready to take on a new job. Handled that like a real pro."

The thing was . . . she had to be ready whether she truly was or not. Her other options were that there weren't any other options. Her bluster and bravado in the pub the night before aside, doing a loft conversion on an old boathouse for Brodie Monaghan did not a side career make. She was hopeful that would lead to other small jobs around town, enough to keep food in her belly and gas in her truck while she did her prospectus for Logan, but since she was fairly certain Brodie was a somewhat controversial new resident, she wasn't sure his hiring her was going to help her street cred with the longtime locals.

Alex sank down in the overstuffed chair in the corner of Logan's guest room, which was her room for the next few weeks or so, and dragged her duffel bag over to her feet. It was barely past seven in the morning and she could already hear the wind howling outside the bedroom window. She rummaged in the bag and dug out a freshly laundered pair of faded old work jeans, a long-sleeved tee, a plaid wool lumberjack shirt, then tossed another long-sleeved tee on top for good measure. Two thick pairs of socks, cotton bra, and clean underwear completed the stack. She eyed her closed bedroom door, wondering if her host was up and about.

The night before, he'd informed her the door to the house was unlocked, then left the pub for parts unknown. She hadn't seen him since and had headed back to Pelican Point shortly thereafter.

After spending the better part of an hour unhitching and parking her trailer with only the moonlight to guide her, fingers and nose numb from the steady winds, then carting in the bare minimum of personal stuff, she'd gone straight to the guest room. She had no idea when he'd come in. Or if he had.

That led her to wondering whether he was involved with anyone. No one had mentioned it to her during her mini-tour of Blueberry the day before. Considering that every last person she'd come across knew she'd stayed with their police chief the night before, it seemed like something that might have come up. He had to be, if not the most eligible bachelor in town, certainly one of the most visible ones.

Not that it mattered. Not that she cared. It was just . . . well, it would be good to know if she might be inadvertently pissing off some significant other just by being present in the police chief's personal orbit. At least, that rationale sounded pretty plausible to her, so she was sticking with it.

She'd been awake since before dawn, but, for once, not for the usual reasons. In fact, for the second night running she'd gotten a decent amount of sleep. The previous night wasn't too much of a surprise given how the day had gone, and she'd still woken the previous morning feeling raw, achy, and emotionally wrung out. But this morning . . .

well, her throat wasn't raw for the first time in as long as she could remember, so she hadn't cried in her sleep or worse. Her head wasn't all cottony, and she almost felt . . . rested.

As a lighthouse restorer, she'd spent more nights in places with the hum of a steady wind rattling the windowpanes and the sounds of waves crashing on rocks than not, so it wasn't the setting. Maybe her collapse had been her body's way of saying that it simply couldn't sustain that protracted level of grief any longer. Maybe she'd finally, literally wrung herself out. If that meant no more nightmares, too, then hallelujah, strike up the chorus.

Maybe the fact that she was finally taking a personal step forward, officially putting the year of tragedy, pain, and transition behind her with actions instead of wishful thinking was part of it, too. She sure hoped so.

"Maybe tonight I'll go back to the Sex-god Voice dreams." She smiled at the thought. Not that she had any designs on her potential future boss other than to get him to hire her . . . but the dreams she'd had about him sure beat the hell out of the nightmares she'd been dealing with. At least she knew her libido wasn't totally disconnected from utter lack of use. She zipped up her duffel and shoved it between the nightstand and the chair, thinking at some point she needed to unpack and get a few more of her things from the truck, but she would work up to that.

Her thoughts drifted to her other boss, the one who was actually going to pay her. Brodie Monaghan was a testosterone-fueled, walking testament to just how beautifully packaged the male of the species could be. Always grinning, he was an innate charmer, ready with a laugh, a wink, and the kind of constant flirting she suspected came so naturally to him, he wasn't even aware of doing it. His fresh-off-the-boat Irish brogue didn't hurt him any, either.

He was completely at odds with the dark-haired, brooding, tough guy she was rooming with. Of course, truth be told, nothing, not even Brodie's charming lilt and infectious laugh, affected her like Logan's reverberating baritone had. Even when he wasn't all that happy with her, the sound of his voice was like a velvet caress, stroking every one of her libidinal nerve endings. Brodie Monaghan might make her blush . . . but Logan McCrae made her wet.

"Aaaand, we're all done thinking about that," she stated, pushing out of the chair and heading resolutely to the bathroom down the hall. The same one that had given her the chilling wake-up call the morning before. She'd come prepared. She put her stack of clothes and zipper tote with her shampoo and other essentials on top of the old wicker hamper, then turned to face what she suspected would be one of the easier Pelican Point challenges. She'd already parked her tool belt and a few other odds and ends she'd picked up in town the day before in the small tiled room when she'd come in the night before.

Owen Hartley, at the hardware store, had been quite helpful, and she'd already made a note about setting up a time with him to go over cost projections. Walking into his hardware store had been like stepping back in time. She could have spent hours there, days even, and not been able to fully catalog and appreciate all of the myriad bits and bobs he had tucked in every nook and cranny of the old clapboard building. While one of the larger local suppliers might be able to beat him on price, nothing was as valuable as a shop owner who knew his customer base and the kinds of things they were likely to need. Quite probably, he would be a perfect source for the vintage pieces of hardware she would otherwise have to hunt down from her Internet and other business contacts.

He'd already proven his worth on that score with the replacement pieces for the old pipe coupling and antique spigot contraption attached to the claw-foot tub. What Logan really needed was to have the shower wall torn out and all the pipes completely redone. She could see water spots and other issues with the tile and the ceiling. But that would have to go in her project report. For now, all she had to do was make it functional so she could take a shower without fear of being coldcocked by a flying faucet.

Still wearing flannel pajama pants and her dad's old Packers jersey a half hour later, Alex had used up her go-to list of swearwords and was getting creative as the old pipes continued to create a new issue for every one she solved. "I just want a hot shower, you ancient copper, crumbling piece of patina-crusted—"

"You could have just asked," came that velvet baritone from the doorway behind her. "I'd have let you use mine."

Her first thought was that yet again she was not showing him her best side. It wasn't just her choice of colorful vocabulary, but also the fact that his present view was of her pajama-covered backside. Yeah, at some point, her karma really needed to swing the other way.

"If I'm going to be staying here"—she gritted her teeth as she tightened what she hoped was the last copper fitting, silently praying the pipe she was attaching it to didn't crumble under the pressure—"it seemed to make more sense to go ahead and get this one working."

With one final turn of the wrench, it was on. She clambered to her feet, brushed her hands on her pj's, then sent up another prayer as she turned on the water spigot. The pipes shook, they shimmied, they groaned, and she was about a half second away from covering her face with her hands, just in case . . . when a steady stream of water came shooting out of the tap. "Aha! And *ha* again!" She danced a little jig, then pointed her wrench at the pipes. "See, you're not the boss of me. Told ya."

The deep chuckle behind her made her close her eyes tight. In her glee, she'd forgotten he was watching.

"Do you always make it so personal?"

"The pipes started it," she said, but couldn't help the little smile that kicked at the corner of her mouth. She turned to face him. "But I ended it."

"Only after the pipes won a few rounds, from the looks of it," he said, his gaze taking in her wet hair and the soaked front of her jersey.

"Hence the trash talk and end zone dance," she said, as if that was a perfectly reasonable reaction.

He shook his head, but that mouth of his still had more upward curve than frown, and the very idea of him laughing and smiling made the only dry parts of her start to get completely different ideas.

"Well, you might want to take advantage of what hot water there is. I'm making coffee."

"Black for me." She smiled as she stepped forward to close the door. "No toast."

"Suit yourself."

She closed the door behind him, then leaned against it. She could blame the shaky legs on having been stuck in a crouch position for the better part of the last thirty minutes, but she knew that for the lie it was. Damn but the man was potent. And she hadn't missed that little wry glint in his eye at her toast jab. He had a sense of humor in there somewhere.

He hadn't been kidding about the hot water time frame. Luckily she'd gotten the suds out of her hair because she barely got the chance to do a quick scrub over the rest of her before hot went directly to icy cold. She was soapsuds free when she got out, but one giant goose bump as she pulled on fresh clothes. *So, a new water heater goes to the top of the list.*

Even the steam from the mirror had cleared before she got her shoes on. She groaned inwardly at the loveliness that was her towel-dried hair and pale face. She might have felt somewhat refreshed, or at least less exhausted, after the past two nights in Logan's guest room bed, but it wasn't really showing up in her face as yet.

"A hot meal or ten would probably help out a little," she muttered at her reflection, realizing she was actually hungry. Starving, in fact. She'd gone to Delia's the morning before, as Fergus had recommended, and while it had smelled heavenly, her stomach had been too jumpy to do justice to more than a bowl of oatmeal and some unburnt toast and jam. But it had been a start. And a good one. She'd been so busy roaming around the town, she hadn't grabbed anything else until later that afternoon. And though the half a ham sandwich Brodie had offered had been good, part of it was still wrapped up on the passenger seat of her truck. She'd felt better by then, but had still been too nervous at the thought of the pending confrontation with the police chief to be able to eat much.

Now that that was over and she was still in Blueberry Cove, and with another night's sleep under her belt she felt . . . well, not invincible by any means . . . but pretty sure she could do breakfast some serious justice. That meant going back into town to Delia's, she supposed.

She tugged a comb through her hair, thankful she had enough natural wave to keep it somewhere between stringy and springy, and brushed her teeth, but there was little point in doing anything else. Not that it mattered what she did or didn't do with her hair and face. Her reluctant host might make her lady parts sit up and beg for a little attention, but she sincerely doubted that any part of her had come even close to having the same effect on him. So, no point in being tempted to girly herself up. She'd tried that the day she'd arrived, and everyone knew how that had turned out. Scary, streaky clown face.

She left her toiletries on the sink, then wrapped her damp pajama bottoms and jersey up in the bath towels and headed to the kitchen and the mudroom beyond, where she'd spied the washer and dryer when she'd come in the night before, only to stop when the most heavenly scent filled the air. "I'll throw in free breakfast prep if you'll show me how you make your coffee."

"Won't be necessary. I make it every morning anyway." He glanced over his shoulder, then did a double take.

"What now?" she asked, looking down at herself.

"Nothing." Toast popped up and he dropped the randomly burnt squares onto a plate. "Sure you don't want any, Mrs. Bunyan?"

She smirked at the crisply pressed uniform covering his back and tried not to notice the breadth of the shoulders it covered. Or the narrow hips where the shirt was tucked into pants that showed off a pretty fine looking butt. "No thanks, Mr. Chief of Police. I have to head into town, so I'll grab something at Delia's. I figure I'll pick up a few things at the grocery while I'm there. You don't mind if I put them in your fridge, do you? I'm assuming there's plenty of room."

"Knock yourself out," was all he said.

She watched him move between coffeemaker, toaster, sink, and fridge for another couple seconds, wishing like hell he looked more troll-like, like his attitude that morning, and less godlike, like his voice. "Listen, I know how it looked last night at the pub. I honestly didn't plan for the whole town to be in on our conversation. In fact, it was the last thing I wanted. Fergus asked—"

"It's done, right?" He turned to face her, cradling a heavy coffee mug in one broad hand. "No point in rehashing it."

"Okay." So, he wasn't going to sulk about it, but he wasn't going to pretend he was happy about it, either. That was fair.

"How long will it take?"

"What, my report? A few weeks, weather permitting, three probably, to get all the inspections done and the information for the estimates I'll need after that."

"And if you weren't also tied up with whatever Monaghan has you doing, then how long?"

Her eyes widened at that. "Listen, if you don't want me here, I can find somewhere else to stay while I put it all together."

"I didn't say that. You'll be tromping all over the place, anyway."

"Yes, there is all that tromping. I can pitch in for water, electricity, coffee—"

"Also not necessary. Like I said before, we dragged you cross-country, the least we can do is house you while you get your next project lined up. How long will it take if you just focus on the one thing?" He lifted a hand to stall her response. "I can pick up some groceries and if you need gas—"

"I can handle gas and I can feed myself," she said, trying not to grind her jaw too tightly.

"How long then?"

"Ten days to two weeks minimum. I won't know until I start looking. I could give you a better estimate by the end of today or tomorrow. The work I'm doing for Brodie is on a flexible schedule. If you're in that big a hurry to—"

"You've got seven."

"Seven what?"

"Days." He pushed off the counter, snagged the keys he'd offered her the morning before from where they still sat on the counter and tossed them to her. "After that, you're on your own."

She snagged them in her fist. "Wait—!"

He turned at the doorway. "I'd suggest you focus on the house first, as that's the only part of all this that I'm going to spend any money or effort on. If you have any time left over, it would be a good idea to spend it looking for another lighthouse to fix." He turned away again.

"Chief McCrae—"

"Logan," he said, looking back from the hallway.

"Chief McCrae," she repeated, coming to stand in the kitchen doorway. "It's not like we signed a contract. I can be packed up and out of here—"

"We made a verbal agreement. My word is as good as any signed document. Not to mention I had over half the town there as my notary. You've got a week. I don't need anything overly detailed, broken down to minute cost projections. I just need to know the basics ranked from biggest problem to smallest, and a general ballpark figure of what it will set me back. I can take it from there."

"So you're saying that no matter what kind of work I put in on this report, you're not hiring me to do any part of the restoration. That's been decided?"

"That was decided yesterday when I fired you. I agree with Fergus that I can't get on top of the repairs needed on the house without hiring outside help, but I've got a long list of folks who have lived here their whole lives who could use the work. If and when we need more specialized help on the tower, as I said, I'll keep you in mind."

"Then why am I bothering to do this report if you're not even going to be open-minded about my recommendations?"

"Don't ask me. It wasn't my idea." And with that he took his heavy uniform jacket off one of the hooks fixed to the wall beside the mudroom door and slipped it on. He tucked his uniform hat under his arm and snatched his truck keys off the small table beside the coatrack. "Leave the place unlocked. You're on your own for supper." After a quick blast of cold air when he opened the side door, he was gone.

"Have a nice day," she called out with fake cheer, then

scowled as she turned back to the kitchen. He'd suddenly been in such a big hurry to get away from her that his mug of coffee and plate of toast were still on the countertop. She picked up a piece and crunched it, made a face, and put the bitten piece back on the plate. "I'd have left it behind, too."

She finished her coffee, then picked up his mug, freshened it with what was left in the pot, and sipped it as she scooped up her pile of damp laundry and went back to the mudroom. Thankfully the washer and dryer looked as if they'd been built in the current century, so getting her clothes clean wouldn't require a tool belt, just detergent.

She got the load running, made a mental note to pick up a small bottle of laundry detergent—far be it from her to use any of his precious resources—and went back to the guest room to retrieve her coat, gloves, knit hat, and work binder. She caught sight of herself in the mirror over the antique dresser as she turned to leave. "Okay, so maybe you earned the Bunyan crack," she told her reflection. "But he can bite me on the rest of it."

Ignoring her traitorous body for apparently thinking a few little bites from the local police chief would be a good thing, she pocketed the keys to the cottage and lighthouse and set off outside to do her first once-around. "We'll just see who you think is best suited to do this job."

She had a harder time ignoring the sick knot that twisted in her gut as she looked up at the lighthouse lantern, which she could see above the pitch of the main house roof. "It's just a walk-through," she murmured. *Dipping a toe in. Flexing a few atrophied muscles.* That was all. No one said she had to take the job. At the moment, her main motivation was simply getting him to offer her the job. She could always turn him down. "In fact, I might enjoy that."

Smiling, she turned her back to the headwind, pulled on gloves, hat, zippered up her jacket to the chin, then propped the bottom edge of her old-school aluminum clipboard, the same one her father and grandfather had used, against her stomach . . . and took that first step.

She focused on the house, keeping initially to the front and side perimeters. The tower, even the cottage, would have to wait. She didn't bother trying to convince herself it was because Logan had ordered her to document the house first. She'd dipped her toe in, but still . . . baby steps.

The structure was sprawling, with additions attached as he'd described, based more on the property allowances than for aesthetic appeal or, in some cases, true functionality. The original part of the house was a two-story, standard salt box, rectangular deal, with painted shake siding and a wood shake roof. The front faced the long driveway and the encroaching forest that ended pretty much at the front door. A narrow patch of pine-needle-covered ground between it and the large paved turnaround area at the end of the drive took up most of the space between the house and the detached garage.

The keeper's cottage was essentially a single-story box with dormer windows set in a drop-sided, wood shake roof situated beyond the center of the back of the house. The lighthouse was directly in front of the cottage, which put it prominently out on the point.

From either side of the main house, running along the uneven, rocky shoreline, were the additions to the building. Not wings, exactly, but it was a close enough description. She examined where she could get close enough to poke, prod, or dig, making a constant stream of notes. Most of the shakes on the protected side of the house weren't salvageable as far as she'd seen. They would need to be replaced. She expected the shakes on the roof were worse and could only hope they hadn't been neglected so long that significant damage had happened inside, in the attic and beyond. The window frames were slightly better, though the seals on most of the glass panes were cracked or shot, as was some of the glass, so they'd have to be replaced, but she'd assumed as much as windows were often the first things to need work.

All in all, considering the age of the place, it wasn't as bad as it could be. It was salvageable and with the proper materials, Logan should have no problem if he wanted to use local contractors. It would just be a matter of getting a few tests run, then getting work estimates. From what little she'd already seen, the interior was going to be the far more involved project and possibly require more specialized skills. If Logan had been tearing out walls and unsealing and restoring fireplaces, neither of which was a simple, easy task, then it was anyone's guess what else had been done to the place over the years. She already knew that the linoleum flooring in the kitchen covered some beautifully hand-laid wood flooring as was evidenced by the same flooring in her guest room, which needed work. She had no idea what awaited under that linoleum, or what sins or past damage it might have been put down to cover up. That Logan had kept up with all he had, given the size and age of the place, was impressive. That he'd done it while working full-time and then some was downright miraculous.

Still, if he had any hope of making headway before things went from bad to worse, he needed help. It was beyond the ability of any one man. Or woman. As overwhelming as it seemed, if he could get the exterior up to par, safe, and sealed, then he could take a more measured, one-problem-at-a-time approach to the interior. "Starting with those damn pipes."

She placed a call to Owen and set up a time to meet with him later. She wanted to talk to him about contractors and some of the vintage hardware they'd need. She made additional notes to contact a few of her people to see what her best bet was for protecting the new shakes, as she'd need that for the cottage as well. There had been recent innovations in the industry, and having been out of the loop for a year, she knew she was likely behind the curve a little. She knew who to call to catch her up, though she dreaded the initial round of calls she'd have to make. It meant rehashing the events of the previous year and everything that had happened since, over and over, which was painful and awkward and all-around hard to even think about, but once she started, it would get easier.

She prayed it would, anyway, because she needed to get the word out that she was back. Eventually, she'd need to build a team again, and so had to set the wheels in motion sooner rather than later. She didn't want just anyone. She wanted the people who had worked for MacFarland & Sons before. Many of them had done so exclusively for years. She was excited . . . and a little shaky . . . at the idea of officially putting things into motion. Okay, a lot shaky. But she had to start laying the groundwork if she really wanted to make this happen.

Jittery at the thought of it, and wishing she hadn't had that second cup of coffee, after all, she continued her survey. *Baby steps, remember?* She discovered she couldn't get around the addition jutting to the south of the main structure as it was built almost to the edge of the jumble of boulders that continued all the way out to the shoreline. She'd need different equipment and gear to get an exterior look there, probably coming down from the roof. It would also make any renovation on that side a major pain in the ass.

When she traversed back around the entire place to the north side, she saw that a wide expanse of cleared property ran between the addition on that side and the waterfront. Most of the grounds surrounding the house and the cottage were fairly rocky, strewn with more outcroppings than grass or smooth ground, but the strip between the addition and the water's edge was mostly grass with only a few outcroppings of rock. A lot of work had to have gone into clearing that, but the payoff was well worth it. She turned and looked at the glassed-in veranda on the back section of the main house and the storm-glass windows that pretty much comprised the entire waterfront side of the addition. The views from any perch inside would be spectacular.

The briny scent in the air was stronger on that side, probably because the house blocked a good share of the headwind. But it was still pretty breezy and the mid-November air had a healthy nip to it. She wouldn't be surprised if snow came soon. Actually, she was a little surprised the ground wasn't already snow covered.

She walked across the open expanse, toward the water's edge. The drop-off was about twenty yards or so from the back of the building, and, like the rest of the point, it was mostly a huge jumble of boulders. As she neared the edge she saw most of it had been framed with a stacked stone wall. Or at least part of one, anyway. On closer inspection, she realized it was being newly unearthed from what looked like decade upon decade of heavy vegetative growth. Maybe longer than that. She guessed it was Logan's handiwork she was looking at as she examined the painstaking care that had been taken to preserve the structure of the wall. It would add a great deal to the charm of the place when it was completely restored, not to mention a valuable breakfront.

She turned and surveyed the property from her vantage point, seeing it as it would be with new shakes, glistening new windows, and a fresh coat of paint. She couldn't see much of the cottage from where she stood as it was blocked by trees, but she could see the top of the tower jutting above them. She finished a complete turn, looking once again at the restored section of the centuries-old, hand-stacked wall. The man did good work, she thought, curious to see what all he'd done inside the house, as well.

She smiled as she spied an intentional break in the wall.

She stepped through it, delighted to find that it led to a path of sorts, winding down through the rocks. There appeared to be an inlet below, created by the breaker the point provided. Despite the winds, it looked relatively calm, sheltered as it was. She couldn't see the area where shoreline and path met, as the rocks obscured her view. She'd have to go all the way down the path to find out what lay below— a pier, or docks, a boat, or boathouse. If so, Logan hadn't mentioned them. But that exploration would have to wait until later. Still, there was something about knowing there was direct access from shore to water to open sea that brought her an unexpected level of calm.

It didn't take a rocket scientist to figure out why. Although she knew, intellectually, that the fall to the rocks from the lantern gallery had taken her father's life brutally and swiftly, and nothing could have prevented that outcome, the added horror of not being able to get down to where he lay below, of having to wait for helicopter support in order to get his body lifted out, had been agonizing. There was no direct access to the water or shoreline from their position up on the cliff's edge promontory, and the rocks and wave action were too dangerous for a water approach. Somehow, the knowledge that someone could get to the shore, to the water, if the unthinkable happened, took a bit of the edge off the ball of sick fear she carried constantly tucked in the back of her mind.

As she stood there, gazing down the pathway, a stray thought struck her that if she fell, there was no one left with any personal connection to her to suffer. Rather than depress her, the realization filled her with an odd, but surprisingly invigorating sense of . . . well, of freedom.

She understood, intimately, the risks that went with loving someone, of being so tied to a person that you couldn't imagine your life without them. Her father had been her lifelong hero, her rock-solid support, the person she knew, without doubt, was always in her corner, always had her back. But he'd been her father. He'd had her heart from her first breath. She hadn't chosen to love him. She simply always had.

Now, however . . . now she had total control over who she gave her heart to. And whose heart she took responsibility for.

As long as the answer to both of those remained no one, then she was as invincible as she could possibly be. If anything happened to her . . . the only one who would truly suffer was her. If she never allowed anyone in, then she couldn't be touched by anything unthinkable happening to someone she cared for, ever again.

She turned with a very specific destination in mind, cutting across the back of the property behind the house, going toward the cottage, until she could look at the lighthouse directly. From her location on the north side of the point, she could view it in all its glory. She imagined the view from the water was stunning. The lighthouse was both traditional and unique, with its windows and beveled corners, while still being majestic and proud. Now that she was closer, she could also see just how direly it was in need of some tender loving care to restore it to its full former glory.

And finally—*finally*—she felt that familiar tingle in her fingertips. The thump in her chest, the buzz that danced along her spine, and tickled her curiosity. It made her feel almost dizzy. And only partly in relief. She'd be lying if she said all those things weren't still accompanied by that queasy knot in her gut. But, oh boy, it was a lot easier to take that part in stride when those more familiar feelings were there, too, to help balance it out.

She continued walking until she was well out into the

open, away from the trees and the shadow of the cottage and the main house. There, feeling the tower standing guard at the periphery of her vision, she tipped her head back and looked heavenward. *It took me a while to figure it out, Dad. I'm sure it's been hard for you, watching me flounder. I know that's not what you'd have wanted, that you expect better from me.* "But I think I understand now," she said out loud. "I think I know where to begin. And that's all it takes, right?"

She tucked her chin as the wind picked up and froze the tip of her nose. But while there were tears gathering at the corners of her eyes, there was a smile on her face. And it felt good. So damn good.

She palmed the set of keys she'd stuck in her pocket and set off for the exterior side door that led to the keeper's cottage before she lost her nerve. The cottage and the main house were done in traditional New England white, although the house had a pitched roof with inset dormers and the cottage had a flat roof top, with pitched sides and dormers. It was a bit of an odd little thing, stuck as it was between sprawling house and majestic tower. As she neared, she saw that it was in far greater disrepair, more weathered than the house, being out in the open as it was, and not entirely even-framed any longer. Clearly, time hadn't been any kinder than the elements, as the foundation wasn't level and the roof, at least the part that she could see, had an odd slant to one side.

Her heart sank a little as she acknowledged that it was quite probably not even close to habitable, and possibly only remained upright at all due to a well-built frame. Even that was possibly suspect. "Poor baby," she murmured, running her hand along one window frame, seeing the rot and disintegration of the exterior casement. Two hundred years was an admirable life span, especially under some of the harshest conditions. With the size and constant input of time and money required by the main house, it was no wonder that the cottage had been left to fend for itself. But it didn't make it any less sad. "Well, if we can save you, we will."

She remembered Logan saying the side door was boarded from the inside and went around to the front, then took a second to recall which key he had said went with what door. She slid the largest key into the lock, but it wouldn't even go in all the way, much less turn the knob. She pulled it out and bent down to peer into the key slot. No obvious blockage. She took out a small wire tool with a pick on one end and a tiny brush on the other and worked first one, then the other into the slot. A little rust and a lot of corrosion. Salt air and steady wind was brutal on pretty much any surface; wood, stone, metal, any alloy.

She tried the key again, and though she was able to get it in all the way, the tumblers weren't going to budge. She'd have to take off the knob entirely, possibly take the door off the hinges. She sighed, knowing seeing the inside was not a priority at the moment; Logan had made it clear the cottage and the tower were low on his priority list. That only increased her determination to get in there and check the place out. One way or the other, she was going to get inside the cottage.

She turned and looked at the lighthouse again, from the closest to it she'd been. She swallowed, flexed her fingers, heart still thumping. *And I'm going to get inside that tower, too.* She wanted to test herself now, find out what her limitations were going to be, how big the mental obstacles. She had no doubt they'd be many and none of them small, but she was ready to at least find out what it was going to be like, instead of just imagining what kind of demons she was going to face.

She made herself another vow: if there was any way possible to make it happen, to make him see her potential, her value, she was going to be the one to get this job. Not a year from now, or five years from now. "But one week from now." She swallowed. Hard. It might have been more of a gulp. "Yeah, so we might have to work on that deadline a little."

Tomorrow, she'd start early. With her camera, ladder, and a handful of other necessary tools, she'd begin the slow process of documenting and running tests, along with all the general poking and prodding.

At the moment, she had a different to-do list. With her clipboard under her arm, she headed back around the house, intent on going straight to her truck and heading into Blueberry Cove to find the county offices so she could look up the various drawings and plans that had to have been made and filed over the years. If she was lucky, they'd have records in some form or other dating back to the initial plans for the lighthouse, cottage, and house. She could probably save herself some time and ask Logan for them, but she preferred to handle it on her own. Then she'd head over to Delia's for some lunch and free Wi-Fi and start the due diligence on the property she should have done before ever leaving Thunder Bay, as well as her initial reach-out to her contacts.

She knew she should call rather than reestablish contacts via e-mail, but it was an easier start, and for most steps in this project, easier wouldn't be an option. She wasn't going to beat herself up too much for taking the easy route first. She'd be making calls and talking to people directly, soon enough. Hell, she'd talked to more people in the twenty-four hours since she'd been in Blueberry Cove than she had since the conclusion of her court case.

She'd also hit the library and see what old publications they had on New England architecture. Sometimes libraries were the best resource around, along with used bookstores. Maybe the Cove had one of those, too. She'd make a stop by Brodie's boathouse and start the punch-out list, then another stop by the hardware store for the chat with Owen, who probably knew a specific thing or ten about the McCrae property and lighthouse. Then the grocery and back to the Point by dinner. Big day.

Logan had said she was on her own for the evening meal, but she thought maybe she'd get the fixings for her grandfather's chili and some cornbread. If she was going to try to wrangle a few extra days out of him, she wasn't above working it so the house smelled delicious and there was a hot meal bubbling on the stove whenever he got in.

Feeling lighter of mood than she had in so very, very long, she changed direction and opted to head inside first for a quick change of clothes. She'd never been one to dress for anything except comfort and practicality, but the Bunyan remark was still floating around the back of her mind, so perhaps something a little less lumberjack might not be a bad thing for her trip to town.

Rather than go all the way around to the mudroom entry, she tried the side door to the north addition and smiled when it opened with little more than a shove. Warped wood was a continual issue on coastal properties, with the constant damp, the salt spray, and the wind. There were short-term fixes, but over the long haul, wooden things like doors and window frames needed regular replacement. Most folks had long since shifted to synthetic products to avoid such costly repairs, but despite Pelican Point being privately owned and therefore not restricted by any National Historic Registry limitations, the McCrae family had clearly wanted to preserve it as close to its original state as possible.

She had other ideas on some cost-saving compromises Logan might be willing to make as she tugged the door closed behind her. Then she turned toward the wall of windows that lined the exterior wall of the addition. "Oh . . . wow."

She'd been so very right. The view of the lighthouse, the expanse of bay that spread out beyond it, and the curve of the little harbor town of Blueberry Cove nestled in and around Half Moon Harbor was breathtaking. So much so, she hardly paid any attention to the drooping ceiling, the watermarks below every window, the rotting frames, and the cracked and loose panes of glass that were rattling constantly with the wind. All of that was fixable. And all worth any price for the sheltered viewpoint this room provided.

Though she'd only lived there for short periods of time between jobs, the MacFarland home base had always been on the shores of magnificent Lake Huron, specifically in Thunder Bay. In addition, she'd spent most of her adolescent years and all of her adult ones working on lighthouse sites all over the United States and Canada, and even a few in the islands and in Europe. By their very nature, all the sites were coastal, and had afforded her a lifetime of some of the most beautiful views ever to be seen. "And this one is right up there," she murmured, already imagining how much more impressive it would be from the top of the tower. The shudder of unease that accompanied that thought wasn't unexpected, but it also wasn't as crippling as it had been before.

Before she'd felt the familiar tingle again. Before she'd wanted it again.

So what if her fingers were trembling as they gripped the clipboard, and sure, her knees might even be a bit shaky . . . okay, more than a bit. But she was smiling as she made her way through the long windowed room, then worked her way through a rabbit warren of smaller rooms toward the main section of the house. *I* can *do this,* she thought. *More important, I want to do this.*

She opened another door and found herself at the landing leading up to the second story in the main part of the house where Logan's bedroom was, and where she'd showered what now felt like a lifetime ago. She opened her clipboard and quickly sketched out the overall shape of the house perimeter, then blocked off rooms as she saw them in her mind's eye. It would be good to have the record of how it was now, to match up to whatever plans were on file with the county. She thought about grabbing her camera, but her sketch was detailed enough for the time being.

She glanced up the stairs. She knew Logan's bedroom was up on the right, with one of the three full baths as the master, but she had no idea what the rest of the layout was.

What the hell, why not? It would only take a quick walk-through to get the basic lay of the land. She put her clipboard down long enough to take off coat, hat, and gloves. She checked her boots. No mud or dirt clumps. *Okay, then.* Clipboard open and at the ready once again, pencil poised, she headed upstairs, intent only on doing a rough sketch of the second floor. The real examination would start the next day.

The previous time she'd come through here, she'd just wanted to grab her stuff and get the hell out, but even then, she'd noticed his bedroom.

The door was open, so she stepped in, made a quick sketch of the layout, the two recessed dormer windows that faced the front of the house, thinking she'd have done something with them, utilized them better. Logan's height and the slant of the roof angling toward the dormers was probably why he'd left them empty of any furnishings. He'd have to all but fold himself in half to tuck in there. Even custom shelving wouldn't have been all that practical for someone so tall.

He might have put a small desk on the short wall be-tween the dormers—though, privately, for herself, she'd have put an antique dressing table there. Then, in the al-coves themselves, there could be custom-built shelves for books or knickknacks. "Or both," she mused. A bench seat built in under the windows, storage underneath for quilts and throws, topped with a thick, cushy pad and a few comfy throw pillows.

Smiling at that visual, she took a quick look around the rest of the room. He was a big man, long-legged, broad-shouldered, and his bed reflected that. King size with a whole-log frame, it was clearly a custom piece, and worth every penny. "Now who's Paul Bunyan?" she murmured dryly, but sighed as she ran her hand along the heavy beam footboard and stared at the virtual sea of thick mattress, the tangle of white linens with a heavy, marine blue down comforter piled on top, as if he'd spent a restless night. Her mind went to other, far more pleasurable ways the bed linens could end up in that kind of tangled heap and she found herself pressing her thighs together against the rather insistent ache that started between them.

She'd spent more than a minute or two in his shower the morning before picturing him naked, sprawled across that sumptuous expanse. And, so okay, maybe he hadn't been alone. In her imagination.

Today, that was the last thing she could allow herself to imagine. Any possibility that she could use her attraction to him as a distraction from her other issues had died when she'd put him on the spot in front of his entire town. Of course, he hadn't been real thrilled with her when she'd passed out all over him, either. And goodness knew he'd made it quite clear his opinion of her today was even more dismal. So, she could cross out indulging in an office fling.

He didn't have to be attracted to her, or even like her. He just had to respect that she could get the work done and that she was the one for the job. Despite the excitement she'd begun to feel about getting back to work again, she still had no idea what obstacles lay ahead for her, what the reality of working another tower would truly be like. However, proving herself to Logan McCrae was all kinds of motivation.

She just hoped she didn't win the battle only to lose the war. Last night had just been a skirmish. The true campaign had started today.

And time was a-wastin'.

Rather than head down the hallway to check out the remainder of the second floor, she found herself wandering over to the dormer windows. Even at five-foot-five, she had to duck her head, but the twin dormers, with their double-sash windows and cutout eaves, would make charming little alcoves. The windowpanes were a little clouded from years of salt spray covering the exterior of the hard-to-reach windows, but she could see enough to note that they faced the front of the house, with a view across the tops of the thick pine forest that hugged the coastline.

She backed up a step and sank down on the side of his bed, sketching the room as she'd envisioned it, the sitting table, the bookshelves, knowing it was utter folly, but also knowing if she got the images on paper, then they'd be out of her head, freeing her mind up to focus on the real matter at hand.

When she was done, she clutched the clipboard to her chest, and gave in, just for a moment, to the temptation to lie back on the bed. It was like lying on a cloud. Her eyes drifted shut, an entirely new series of images taking over . . . those broad shoulders, big hands, deep voice . . .

"Something I can help you with, Goldilocks?"

Chapter 7

Alex shrieked in surprise, leaping straight off the bed and grazing the side of her head on the edge of the alcove eave. "Ouch! Dammit!" Crouching, hand to her head, she turned to find Logan standing just inside the door between his bathroom and the bedroom, wrapped in nothing more than a damp, forest green bath towel. Had she been so lost in her thoughts she hadn't heard him in there? "Sorry. I didn't know you were home. Why are you home?"

"Why are you lying in my bed?"

"I wasn't. I mean, I was, but just for a moment. I was . . . sketching."

"Sketching." He nodded toward her head. "Are you okay?"

She rubbed at her forehead, happy to see there wasn't any blood when she lifted her hand away. "Yeah. I'd be more worried about the wall; I have a pretty hard head. Don't say it," she warned.

She shifted the clipboard she was still hugging to her chest, looking at her sketches of the alcoves . . . and, more to the point, not at half-naked Logan. "Just taking a few minutes to get the layout of the house on paper. Then I was going into town to look up the architectural drawings and any other plans filed with the city."

"You could have just asked me."

She made herself look at him—which was hard, because part of her mind and pretty much every part of her body was still back in that giant sea of soft linens and thick pillows. With him. Naked. Which was so much easier to visualize now. "I—" She paused, cleared her throat, and dammit, looked down at her clipboard again. But his body matched that voice. And she was only human. "This morning when you left, you made it pretty clear that you were merely tolerating me. You definitely had no interest in helping me. Plus, you have your job, and I have mine. I'm perfectly capable of doing this on my own. I know you don't believe that. That I'm capable. But I am."

"I never said—"

"You didn't have to. Sometimes actions speak louder. In fact, they almost always do—which is why you have no faith in me, and, frankly, I wouldn't, either, since my actions so far include having a less-than-professional-looking vehicle that breaks down practically in your driveway—"

"It was a flat tire."

"Trust me, it could have easily been complete engine failure. It failed off and on all the way from Michigan. And it was driven by a tear-streaked woman who immediately up and fainted on you."

"Well, when you put it like that."

She caught the corner of his mouth kicking up in an ever so slight grin and wished she didn't admire the comeback as much as she did. It was exactly the kind of thing she'd have said.

"Saying it was aberrant behavior and far off the grid of who I am is fine—not to mention true—but you don't really know that. The breaking down and the fainting is all you really know of me. So I'm taking this opportunity to show you the rest of my act."

He lifted one brow. "By playing Goldilocks?"

She gave him a look that said *really?* and continued. "I

explained what I was doing. But if that's what you honestly think, then I guess that makes you the grumpy papa bear?"

Now it was his turn for the *what gives* hand gesture. "Why is everyone suddenly calling me grumpy?"

"Have you heard you? Not exactly lightness and sunshine. I mean, it can't be easy being police chief in a small town where you know everybody's business and have to get in the middle of it on a regular basis, so I get it. Unless you're normally a regular barrel of laughs and it's just me bringing out the worst. Which, I suppose, is also a fair assumption." She looked down, shook her head, and blew out a breath. "Yeah. This is so not how I saw this next part going."

"And what way was that?"

Her brain went immediately to how it had been seeing things just a few moments ago, before she'd been so rudely startled. She shut that right down. *All business, all professional, that's how. Why don't I start now?* "Doing my job, doing it well. Just as I always have. Somehow you have a knack for continually finding ways to catch me at my worst."

"I see it more as stumbling over them, but okay. I'm not doing it on purpose."

"Neither am I." With a cleansing breath, she squared her shoulders, forged a bright smile, and faced him squarely. "Let's try this. I'm going to let you get back to"—her gaze skipped down to the towel and jerked straight back up again—"whatever it was you needed to do. And given I'm under a pretty strict deadline that only a grumpy person would consider reasonable, I'm going to get back to what I came here to do." *And ignore how much more he does for damp terrycloth than I do.*

Okay, so maybe she hadn't exactly pulled off that bright and sunny part as well as she'd hoped. But he rankled. Standing there, all sex-god perfect with the voice of a fallen angel. Damp, dark curls clinging to his forehead, the perfect amount of manly man-hair matted to his quite beautifully muscled chest, and, worse—far, far worse—those topaz eyes of his that reached right past every barrier she was rapidly throwing up against their too-insightful-for-their-own-good power. Not to mention an attitude that she really didn't think she'd earned. Much.

Added to that was the fact that while he was all effortlessly godlike, she stood there looking like a pale-faced Mrs. Bunyan, sporting several layers of shapeless tops inspired by the winter lumberjack collection, complete with matching ever-so-not-flattering clunky black work boots. The backs of her legs clad in well-worn denim were pressed against his very big, very manly, ridiculously sexy bed made for sex, and not just any sex, but deep-into-the-mattress take-me-like-you-mean-it sex, the kind she was never going to have, at least not in that bed and not with him. So, it was clear why she was a bit off her game. Not to mention that just the thought of the deep-into-the-mattress thing had her heart pounding like she'd just run up the side of a very steep hill. She made a mental note: *more food, less caffeine.* She really should have forced down the toast.

He didn't respond. But he didn't tell her to get the hell out of his house, either, so she took that as a win and turned to exit the room before he changed his mind or before she lost what was left of hers.

She got as far as the foot of the bed.

"That's not all of you I know." He said the words so quietly that she realized hers hadn't been.

She'd been shooting for sunny, confident. Strident was probably a better description. *Okay. A lot less caffeine.* She turned, looked at him. "I'm really not sure I want to know what else you think you know about me," she said more quietly and quite honestly. "What I do want is more time. This house is . . . well, it's amazing. Just its endurance alone, the history it's been through."

Warming to her subject, she found a source of much needed distraction, something that wasn't about his naked body and her wanting to jump it, and she let the words flow. "It's such a strong testament to you and all the Mc-Craes that came before you. I want to find a way to make this work, not because you deserve it or because I do, but because this house deserves it."

She stepped closer, feeling the tingling in her fingertips, across the back of her neck, down her spine. It was familiar, like an old friend. It was excitement for her work, and she latched on to the comfort of something she understood. "The keeper's cottage is . . . it's breaking my heart. I don't even know its full story, and it breaks my heart, sagging and struggling to remain strong . . . yet failing all the same. And your lighthouse. It's proud, Logan. It makes me want to know its secrets and its stories, and I want to give it the chance to tell them to another generation. You couldn't possibly know what that means to me personally, to feel that, to want that, but I can promise you that you won't find a person more committed to finding a way to make it happen. To making it all happen."

He stood there, staring at her, saying nothing. His expression unreadable, but his eyes searching, and his chest rising and falling, perhaps, just a little bit faster.

She almost opened her mouth to apologize for making such a dramatic, emotional plea. She was a professional and she was damn good at her job, despite the fact that, with him, she seemed determined to appear anything but. She'd never once begged for a job and she'd be damned if he would make her feel as if she had to do so now. But there was a lot riding on this, more than even she'd realized until she'd opened her mouth and all of that had simply tumbled out straight from her heart. She'd overcome far worse than being denied a contract, but she'd never once wanted one as badly as she wanted this one. Something about the epiphany she'd had out by the stacked stone wall was beating inside her, fueling a rebirth of confidence. Moving forward was painful, and hard, and downright terrifying, but in every possible way it still beat the living hell out of staying where she'd been for the past year.

"Let me do my job, and give me the time to do it right. I know that means you have to put up with me being under your roof, but you're about to have workers climbing all over the place, so, by comparison, having me here will be a cakewalk. I'll be lost in the crowd, so to speak. I'll stay out of your way as best as I can. But I'm here. And I can do this. I'm damn good at it. Let me stop telling you and start showing you."

He held her gaze for another long moment, too long; then she saw his chest move, heard the low escape of a long, steady breath. "Part of what else I know about you is that you are cocky, stubborn, even a little arrogant."

She took the comment in stride. "It's not arrogance when you can back it up."

"Big words."

Okay that dig was harder to take. She hated that those two little words had the power to ping her the way they did. But he knew. He knew about her father. Knew she hadn't been up on a tower since his death. Knew she actually might not be able to do it, despite what she was saying. Knew just how big, in fact, those words were.

And then he was standing right in front of her. "Alex. That was—you're right, I haven't been happy about this, any of this, and I've said as much. Bluntly. But that wasn't—I shouldn't have said that. I'm sorry."

"Don't ever be sorry for being honest." She made herself look up at him and meet his gaze. "You're right. They are big words. Huge words. The biggest. But I wouldn't have said them if I didn't believe they were true. If I didn't believe in myself. And I do. I do now."

She was stunned to see the corner of his mouth kick up ever so slightly. He thought this was *funny?* Maybe she'd been wrong about his sense of humor.

"Who are you trying to convince?" he asked. "Me? Or you?"

The mad went out of her before it even worked up a good head of steam. He was frustratingly rational. "Both," she said, with maybe a little huff afterward.

"More honesty. I respect that."

"So do I," she said, hearing the grudging note in her tone. She really wanted to be mad, or at least seriously annoyed. It would make it easier to sustain her energy. She was quickly realizing just how drastically she'd allowed the stress of the past year to take a toll, not just physically, but mentally. Her instinct was to hide that from him, hide any weakness, with bluster and bravado, then work like the devil to do whatever it took to get herself back up to speed, so he'd never have any doubts. Except he already had doubts. Big ones. Because he already knew her weaknesses. She'd laid them all, literally, right in his lap.

"Did Fergus tell you about Jessica?"

Surprised at the sudden topic change, she looked up at him again, into those eyes. And found him staring deeply into hers. The combination of that intensity and that velvety smooth baritone all but rippling over her skin made her throat get all tickly. It might have made her thighs quiver, too. He was standing too close to be having those thoughts and have him not see how they were affecting her. She shook her head, not trusting her voice at that moment.

"The other part of what else I know about you is that maybe I have more insight into what you're going through and how it feels to take the steps you're taking than you know."

Her eyes widened. That was pretty much the last thing she'd expected to hear him say.

It was his turn to momentarily avert his gaze. He took a breath and looked back at her. "Seeing as we're being cheerleaders for honesty here, I'll also admit that that was why I was somewhat abrupt with you this morning."

"Somewhat?"

He lifted an eyebrow at that, but it made her want to smile. What was it Fergus had said? That his nephew could use a good nudge every once in a while? She was finding it came quite naturally to her to want to help him out with that. The thing was, Logan nudged back. Though, much as she hated to admit it . . . maybe she needed it, too.

"Okay, maybe more than somewhat. It was just . . . you remind me of . . . well . . . of a lot of things. Things I don't think about anymore because I don't have to think about them. Things that—" He broke off, then seemingly made himself hold her gaze. "Things I thought I didn't think about because I had overcome them. When, in truth, I didn't think about them because they still have the power to bother me. A great deal more than I wanted to know they did."

"I didn't mean to dredge up old memories. Especially painful ones."

"Of course you didn't. You didn't even know. Your first night here, I didn't know about your past, about your father. And you still shook me up. Just the idea of you being here at all meant I'd have to deal with the tower and the cottage, and I'm not talking about costly renovations, but about the other reasons I've found every excuse in the book to put off dealing with them."

"And all of that has to do with . . ."

"Jessica Tate. My late fiancée."

Alex's lips parted in a short gasp, and she felt pain—sympathy pain, but very real nonetheless—for his loss. "I'm so sorry," she whispered.

"It was a long time ago. More than ten years. It's not a fresh wound. Or at least, it hasn't felt that way in a very long time. What I realized was that it hasn't felt that way because I've been damn good at not thinking about anything that could make me remember."

"You said the cottage . . . the tower . . ." Her eyes widened. "You didn't—she didn't—"

"No, no." He cupped her shoulders with his hands, real concern etched all over his face. "I'm sorry, no. I didn't mean for you to make that connection. They were very special to her, to us, but more to her. In a sentimental way, which I wasn't. Not then, anyway. But they weren't the reason she died."

"It's okay. It doesn't matter, not really. I mean . . . any circumstance when you lose someone you love, no matter the cause . . . they're all equally terrible. You don't have to explain."

She felt his hands tighten slightly on her shoulders, only she wasn't sure whom he was bolstering just then, her or himself. She thought maybe they both could use it, so it didn't really matter.

"I want to. Or maybe I need to. So you understand what I know about where you are. She didn't fall. She drowned. We were on her father's fishing trawler. It was summer, and we were both home from college, working for her dad. We got caught up in a summer squall. She was trying to help save the catch we'd just pulled in and got caught in the nets. The storm was fierce, the waves were cresting over the boat. She was dragged over before we could do anything about it. We tried to pull the nets in to get to her, but it was too late."

"Oh, Logan, that's awful! I—" She reached up to cup his

cheek with her palm, instinctively needing to soothe the very real pain she saw in his eyes. She didn't even realize she'd done it until he moved his head and she felt the bristle of his morning beard brush against the tender skin of her hand. She pulled it away. "I'm so sorry," she said, not bothering to clarify exactly what for. She was just . . . sorry.

"As I said, it was a long time ago. And yet, to be honest, I haven't been up in the tower since. Or in the cottage. We spent a lot of time together in both. It was a place we could go and be alone. It was never a draw for me like it was for her, and it's been falling apart for so long, no one really went up there anyway, even back then. I told myself it was just not something I'd have done anyway. But . . ."

"It's all part of it. I know about how twisted up it can be, and not entirely rational."

"More to the point, it was two years before I could go out on a boat again. Any kind of boat. So, in that way . . ."

"You know about me," she finished. "What that tower represents. The horse I have to climb back up on."

He simply held her gaze and she saw the truth in his eyes. "I guess I really didn't want to know what you were dealing with, because it meant I had to deal with what I knew, and why it made me feel the way it did, and all the other tangled parts of my own loss."

Before she could say anything, he lifted his hands from her shoulders, and she felt suddenly bereft.

"But that's on me. In all the more obvious ways, I have moved on. It happened a lifetime ago and almost feels like it happened to someone else, in some other life."

Alex sighed. "I'm still sorry I stirred it all up again. I don't know what I'll feel like in two years, much less ten, but I imagine being reminded of how I feel right now isn't something I'm ever going to welcome."

"Still, it's not an excuse. At the very least, I should have been sympathetic, empathetic, and instead I've been . . . resentful." He paused, then shook his head. "It was selfish. And now I feel foolish."

"Don't ever apologize for feeling. Good or bad, it's what makes us human."

"Famous quote?"

"One of my dad's." She smiled. "He was a big one for never holding anything in. He could read me like a book, and he made it his business to drag out any problem I might have, big or small."

"He sounds like a good man."

Her eyes sheened a little, but she was still smiling. "The very, very best. Of course, I'm a little biased."

"You should be. Sounds like he earned it."

She nodded, not trusting herself to say more. She'd cried enough in front of this man. Still, it struck her that it was the first time she'd spoken out loud about her father in a fond, reminiscent way. It was a little sad, because it felt so . . . past tense. But it also made her feel, well, not good, but . . . better, healthier, for being able to speak the words and honor him fondly, proudly.

She blew out a breath and smiled through the ache inside her chest. "He'd have been so angry with me . . . for keeping it all in like I have and for making myself sick with it. I guess I just . . ." She trailed off, shaking her head.

After a moment, Logan said, "Just what?"

"I just didn't have anyone to tell. Or at least, no one I trusted to hear me. No one I needed to tell. It sounds pathetic, and I don't mean it that way. It's just the truth."

"I know. It's your new reality," he said quietly.

"Yeah." That he got it—got her—intimately was clear. Disconcertingly so. It forced her to reassess entirely what she thought of him, who he was, and what he was made of. "It's an adjustment. A transition I obviously haven't handled well."

"You're doing what you can, the best way you know

how. It's a lot and it's all on you. You two weren't just father and daughter—you had a family business together.
When Jessica died, I had a family—hell, a whole town—
behind me, and I floundered pretty badly. I didn't do well
at all when I went back to school. Stopped playing sports,
everything. Cost me a full semester and would have cost me
my degree if I hadn't finally pulled myself together. My
family didn't hold it against me. Nor did hers. Their love
and solid support was a big part of why I was able to finally
move forward." He held her gaze, searching her eyes. "I
didn't know the man, but if he was half of what you say, and
I'm guessing he was all that and more, then your father
doesn't hold it against you, either."

She felt tears prickle again and moved to brush them
away, but he beat her to it. Using the side of his thumb, he
caught them before they fell. His skin was warm, a little
roughened.

"Sorry," she said, the word throaty with emotion.

"Don't ever apologize for feeling," he said, and there
was kindness in his tone as he echoed her father's words.
"Something I picked up from someone smarter than me."

She sniffled a little inelegantly. "Thank you," she said,
then added a watery, wry laugh. "God, I'm so tired of crying. I never used to cry."

"That changes. In its own time." He ran the side of his
thumb down her cheek and along her jaw. "After my parents died—I was seven—my grandfather told me each tear
shed is a tribute two times over. Once to the ones you lost,
and a second time as tribute to how deeply you loved and
were loved in return. And what a blessing that is. It took me
a while longer to truly appreciate that, but he was right."

"Sounds like we both knew some pretty smart people.
I'm sorry. About your parents. That's . . . a lot."

"It was like losing my whole world. But my grandfather
was a larger-than-life kind of man, and he made it his busi-

ness to become our whole world, while making sure we still honored our parents. My sisters were younger, and they don't remember them. They just remember all the stories. But I do. He made it . . . well . . . not okay, but he helped it to make sense. He was there when Jessica died, and Fergus was there by then, too. I knew I could trust them because we'd been through hard things together before. And that helped. A lot. Did you—do you—have . . . anybody?"

She shook her head. "My mom died when I was little. Pneumonia. I was only four, so my memories . . . it's probably like your sisters. I'm not sure what might be a direct memory or I remember because their stories—my dad, my grandfather, my great uncle—were so vivid."

"Cousins, distant or close?"

She shook her head again. "My dad raised me, along with his dad and his uncle. I was—" She broke off, surprised by the smile and the ease with which it came. "I might have been a handful."

"No," he deadpanned, but there was the most delightful gleam in those eyes. It was downright dazzling.

"I might have also been spoiled." She put her fingers close together. "Wee bit. But I started working with them as soon as I could swing a hammer. They might have kept me somewhat in a protective bubble, but on the other hand, I was a pretty worldly kid. I traveled all over and met kids from everywhere, but most of my time was spent with adults. We took jobs here, Canada, overseas. It was . . . well . . . it was pretty much awesome. I loved it."

"It's an education I imagine only a few ever get, but, yeah, it sounds pretty incredible."

"I never went the traditional college route. Heck, I never really went to school. I mean, I did spend time in this one or that depending on where we had our jobs. In the end, I just studied and got my GED at sixteen, mostly because it was important to my dad, then called that a day. I knew my life's path and I loved it. Everything about it called to me."

"I can see that." With his thumb propping up her chin, her gaze drifted from his eyes to his mouth. She felt the oddest flutter in her stomach as an echo of a memory floated through her mind. About not just wanting to bite that bottom lip of his, but of actually doing it. Then doing a lot more. That had been a dream, right? One of her Sex-god Voice dreams. Hadn't it?

She blinked, glanced away, and grabbed at the thread of their conversation. It was easier, less confusing than . . . whatever it was she was kind of remembering. Not to mention all of the things he was making her feel.

"After—after the accident, when it was over and it was past that horrible day, I was suddenly dealing with everything that came next. It was all so abrupt and it felt so . . . rude and intrusive. I just wanted to be left alone to make some sense out of it. Only there was no sense to be made. I wanted to curl up and die, or find someplace I could go where I didn't feel so much pain. I didn't even know a person could feel so much pain, not like that.

"But I couldn't leave, and there was nowhere to go, anyway. There were things that had to be done right away and decisions to be made. So I shoved it all inside. After his funeral, from that day on, I didn't cry.

"I was numb at first, when everything started to unravel about the accident, all the legal stuff. That was almost a relief. I just focused on the decisions and the avalanche of other things that had to be taken care of. The lawyers, the lawsuit . . . God, it was all so awful. But it did one thing. It made me mad. And angry was a far easier thing to be than devastated, so I clung to that. It was an emotion I understood, one I could willingly grab hold of. I couldn't cry, couldn't let myself feel anything except anger, because if I let one part of me even start to crack, it would be like a rock striking a windshield, and I'd just shatter completely. If I started crying . . . how would I ever stop? If I let myself go, give in to that crushing vise grip of grief, wouldn't it just squeeze my heart to a stop? And, even scarier . . . did I want it to? If for no other reason than to end the pain?"

As soon as the words were out, she regretted giving voice to them. There was opening up, and there was being vulnerable, but it was not the time or place for that. She'd been lulled by their shared tragic background, but that didn't mean he wanted to hear—

"Stop it." He framed her face with his palms, tipped it up to his.

She blinked and looked into his eyes again. Shattered topaz, she recalled thinking, when she'd fainted into his arms. That was the perfect description. "Stop what?"

"Pulling back every time you begin to let go. Never apologize for feeling."

She wanted to duck her chin, to duck him, but she couldn't. He wouldn't let her do either. "You're a very frustrating man, you know that? Annoying, too."

"You wouldn't be the first to say so." There was a smile in his voice and a curve in those lips.

Lips she found herself staring at again.

And then he was shifting closer still, so that their bodies almost brushed together. The broad palms he'd pressed against her cheeks moved until strong fingers were weaving through her hair, urging her to tilt her face upward even more. "Talk about frustrating," he murmured, and his gaze dropped to her lips.

It had the positive effect of making her forget everything they'd been talking about . . . but the less positive result of making every nerve ending in every sexual part of her body and even some she'd never thought of as particularly erogenous stand up and cheer. "What is?" she whispered, once again having fleeting thoughts—memories?—of what his mouth tasted like . . . as if she knew. For certain. Not from a dream.

"Wanting you," he said, his voice so deep he might as well have rubbed those words directly across her bare nipples. "Knowing I shouldn't."

Her entire body gulped. "Why shouldn't?"

"Because it will complicate things." He let his head drift closer, his lips even closer still. "And I don't need complicated. I already have complicated. But it's the kind I can handle. You . . . you're a whole other kind."

Her pulse was thrumming so loudly in her ears, she almost couldn't hear him. She continued to stare at his mouth. "Can I—can I ask you something?"

"I'm pretty sure at this moment you could do almost anything and I wouldn't say no."

She would have laughed at that, or at least smiled, but she wasn't feeling flirty, she was feeling . . . confused. "That night . . . that first night . . . when I fainted. I woke up in your guest bed. You had to have put me there. Right?"

He nodded, his pupils shooting wide as he glanced into her eyes.

She swallowed hard—twice—at what she saw there. Naked desire. Emphasis on the naked part.

"I did," he said, his voice black velvet on sandpaper.

"Did we—did I—do . . . something? Inappropriate? I'm sorry, I was pretty sure it was a dream, only now I'm . . . not sure."

"What are you not sure of?"

"I-I remember wondering about kissing you." Her gaze darted to his. "I was delirious, remember."

"Of course." Those beautiful lips tilted, and the glimmer of humor in his eyes set off the topaz like a match striking a spark. "After all, no sane woman would want to kiss me."

It was hard enough hearing his voice go all gravelly with

want, but add in that wry humor and she was a goner. "I didn't mean it like that. But, did I—I mean, was that all I did? Wonder about it?"

"Maybe this will refresh your memory."

He brought her lips up to meet his, then moved into the kiss by sliding a hand down her back, then wrapping it around her waist and molding her body to his. He kept his other hand woven through her hair, cupping the back of her head, urging her mouth more fully against his as he took hers slowly, intently, in what had to be the most thoroughly decadent kiss she'd ever experienced.

One she knew instantly she could never have dreamed. She had kissed him. And he'd let her. But he wasn't done refreshing her memory as yet, and she found she was in no hurry to stop him.

If his voice had been enough to make her body vibrate with need, the deep groan he made as she opened her mouth under his almost made her come. Her clipboard clattered to the floor as she gripped his bare shoulders, digging fingertips into the thick muscles as he lifted her to her toes when he took their kiss deeper still.

And when she thought she might pass out from how fast her heart was beating, he left her thoroughly kissed lips and moved along her jaw, alternately kissing, nipping.

"You didn't—we didn't—before," she stammered breathlessly. "I was—I woke up dressed."

"No, we didn't. I might have let you kiss me and I might have kissed you back, but you were in no shape for more. Nor was I, to be honest. You surprised the hell out of me."

"You . . . you didn't tell me."

"If I thought you'd remembered, I would have apologized. When you didn't, I thought it was better to leave it be."

"Apologized?"

"You didn't know what you were doing. I did." He tilted her head, giving him greater access to that sensitive spot where her neck curved into her collarbone. "It was just a kiss. A hell of a kiss, but that's all. I probably shouldn't have let it go that far."

"And now?" she gasped, gripping his shoulders.

"Do you know what I thought when I came out of the shower and saw you lying on my bed?"

She couldn't make a single noise, so she shook her head.

"I thought I dreamed you." He nipped her earlobe. "That first night, you kissed me like I was the last man on earth."

She shuddered, pleasure rocking through her as his hand slid over her bottom and cupped her to him.

"That's what you did to me that night," he said, his voice dark and thrillingly velvety as he kissed the side of her neck. "I needed a cold shower, only there wasn't one cold enough for that. So . . . I took a hot one instead."

She clung to him, helpless, not caring as long as he didn't stop touching her, using that voice of his like a live vibrator against every oversensitized inch of her skin. The feel of him, the sound of him, and now those images of him, steam rising in the shower, him hard, erect, needing release . . . because of her. She squirmed against him, making him groan.

"I can't get in that shower without . . ." He held her more tightly against him and, heaven help her, she rocked against the hard length of him, barely covered in that damp towel. "And then there you were. In my bed."

"So inviting in all this lumberjack plaid," she panted, gasping as he continued his sensual assault, reaching for something, anything . . . rational. Anything sane. This was . . . off the charts crazy.

"Layers," he said, not slowing down, not letting up.

"Begging to be peeled off." He lifted her completely off her feet and carried her to the bed, wrapped torso to torso. "I'd have used my teeth. Gladly."

"Logan—" She didn't even know what she was asking. She didn't want him to stop. She wanted to yank that towel away, wanted him to claw her clothes off. Wanted . . . Just blessedly, mercifully *wanted*.

He laid her on the bed and came down on top of her, dragging them both into the middle of that sea of mattress as he climbed over her. He found her mouth again, kept her lips molded to his with his hand fisted in her hair as the arm he still had wrapped around her waist pulled her up into his body.

She moaned against his mouth, already arching against him. There were so many reasons why they shouldn't be doing this, going so far, so fast, except she couldn't think straight, couldn't think at all. Didn't want to. She just wanted to revel in feeling something so intense, so all consuming, something that, for once, wasn't pain.

"I want you," she said, owning her part in what was happening. She felt him jerk against her and it was . . . exhilarating. "Layers," she gasped as he ran his hands between them, covering her breasts with those broad, warm palms, rubbing fingertips over her tight nipples. Fingertips she'd felt on her cheeks. She knew they were a little rough, knew they could make her come if she could feel them directly. "Take them off."

She didn't have to tell him twice. Still kissing the side of her neck, he moved his lips along her collarbone as he unbuttoned the plaid wool shirt. She moaned as his mouth closed over her nipple through the layers of T-shirts and bra, squirming under him, wanting them all to magically vanish.

"Stop . . . wriggling," he breathed, then yanked her shirts from the waistband of her jeans and up and over her head in a single, very satisfying tug that made her feel sexy, desirable, and more than a little wild.

He didn't waste any time peeling her out of her bra. Before she could spend even two seconds worrying about what he thought of her naked body, he was showing her . . . with his tongue, his fingers . . . and making her do a lot more than wriggle. Panting, moaning. She might have screamed a little. Okay, a lot, but damn, the things he was doing to her . . . and that was just her nipples.

And then she was toeing off her boots and he was unbuttoning her jeans and she was having a hell of a hard time keeping her hips still, the anticipation almost killing her. His palms almost framed her entire waist, holding her where he wanted her, making her feel utterly claimed as he moved his mouth below her navel.

He didn't toy, he didn't tease. He peeled off jeans, panties, socks in one smooth slide, before working his way up the inside of her calf, across one knee, over to the inside of another thigh, until he found—

"Oh. Oh!"

She'd have grabbed his head, fisted her hands in his hair much as he'd done hers, only he needed absolutely no guidance, no urging onward. And she was too busy gripping the sheets like a tether to reality. He made her hips jerk, her back arch, and her teeth grind while he wrenched—not teased, not cajoled—*wrenched* an orgasm from her that rocked her so hard she might have seen stars.

As soon as she could form credible thought, she reached for him, wanting his weight on her body, and to feel him fill her while she was still so sensitized she was pretty sure a mild breeze could send her over the edge all over again.

He was more than happy to comply. A man who knew what he wanted, and hallelujah, it was exactly what she did. She didn't question it, she dug her fingernails into his shoulders and pulled him up on top of her.

Once again, he needed no urging. He kissed her shoulder, her neck, bit her earlobe, traced his tongue along her jaw. His oh-so-very talented tongue, making her quiver all over again.

"Now. Now!"

"Your wish," he growled, his voice so deep it was just a velvet buzz saw. "My command." He pulled her thighs up to press against his hips, still nipping, kissing, licking, until she was jerking under him, so close . . . so damn close. . . .

"Dammit." He paused and started to move off her again, looking toward his nightstand. "I don't think I have—shit."

"We don't need—I'm—the pill. You?"

"Police. Tested. Annually."

"Thank God."

He chuckled against the slick skin along the side of her neck. A moment later, he was jerking her thighs up higher, urging her heels to lock behind his hips. He didn't have to urge her twice.

"Hold on," he groaned. "Hold on tight."

And, oh, that voice. Turned out it *was* enough to make her come, and she started to shudder, started to fall apart again.

"Wait for me."

Then he was finally, finally where she needed him to be. She wanted to hurry him, wanted him to fill her in one hard thrust, take her the rest of the way home, shoot her to the stars. But ready as she was, he was . . . big. So he pushed, then lifted her up, and pushed again, tilted her hips . . . and thrust the rest of the way in, with one satisfying growl.

She'd groaned in utter, exultant pleasure the entire time. Nothing had ever felt like this, nothing had ever felt like him. He filled her beyond what she knew, what she'd ever experienced. "Yes!" *Oh, hell yes!*

And then he began to move.

"Don't . . . stop," she ground out, arching with every thrust.

He found her mouth, and their tongues danced, thrust, moved, in the same rhythm as their bodies. She shouted, he growled, they panted, gasped, groaned. He moved faster, she dug in her heels, her nails, and urged him on, commanded him on. He lifted, drove, drove again and again . . . and she peaked again, shuddering, crying out, shaking, clinging. Reveling, soaring.

Then he was driving, climbing, climbing higher, thrusting harder, and she was with him every slick slide, every groan, every gasp, clenching him, holding him, pushing, pushing . . . taking . . . until he shuddered his way through a guttural, shouting release that made her feel like she'd just won the lottery, discovered Santa was real, and seen God, all in one.

They clung to each other like shipwreck victims, floating, floating, trying to find something solid, something whole to hold on to while attempting to suck in air, find their breath . . . struggling . . . and not caring. Finally he rolled off her to his back. They lay there, side by side, trying to find their way back down to earth, to reality.

"That was . . ." she breathed.

"Yeah . . ." he panted.

Still working for every breath, Alex stared at the ceiling, the cracked plaster, the water stains, for once not cataloging repairs or mentally fixing any of it. When she could finally speak, she said, "So . . . for one, I'm not going to tell you how professional I am. Ever again." She let her head roll to the side and looked at him. "I can say, the person I used to be would never have just up and . . . frolicked. Not like that. And never with her boss."

"Frolicked, huh?" Logan looked at her, his dark hair all mussed, perfect mouth curved in a knowing smile, eyes that said way more than words ever could. He knew . . . too much. Because he knew her.

It made her heart pound all over again.

"I know who I used to be." She looked back at the ceiling again, willing her heart to slow down, or just stay in her chest. "But I realize now I have no idea who I am in my life, part two."

He could have done or said so many things. Or nothing at all. What he did was slide his hand across the tangled sheets and find hers. He wound their fingers together, pressed his palm against hers, just like that. Simple . . . except it felt anything but. It was an entirely different intimacy, that connection, palm to palm, pulse to pulse where their wrists crossed. Making her feel more than just physically naked . . . or sexually connected. It felt like . . . a bond. And a lifeline . . . to a person, one person, who knew her. *Knew* her. Was it true? Did she have a person now? Someone in her life, her new life, who understood? Who would listen if there was something that needed to be said?

She didn't even dare think it.

"Maybe," he said at length, his voice more gravel than velvet now. "Maybe it's time you found out." He pressed his fingertips to the back of her hand. "Maybe it's time I did, too."

His words made her heart catch. This was all so much. Too much? In part, it was overwhelming, definitely. But in part it also felt . . . just right. That part scared her a lot more.

His cell phone buzzed and his hand left hers as he rolled to get it. "Yes, Barb." There was a pause, then he sighed and cleared his throat, finding his police chief voice. "No, no, I can handle it. Yes, I'm sure. Give me ten. Thanks."

Alex didn't wait for an explanation. She didn't need one. The truth was, despite what had just happened, they weren't really in each other's personal lives. She might not know who she was in this new life, but she did know who she wasn't. She rolled over and slid to the far side of the bed and silently dug around for her clothes, pulling them on as she uncovered them.

Maybe what her new life was about was just taking things as they happened. Making choices as they came up. Living in the moment, as they say. No regrets. Then continuing onward, until there was another choice to make, another moment. No planning for a set future because she knew all too well the future didn't always go as planned.

Was that what she wanted? Would that be enough?

He kneeled behind her on the bed, but didn't slide his arms around her.

She was grateful, despite the fact that five minutes ago he'd made her shout through her third orgasm, then she'd made him climax so hard she knew she'd be feeling it for days. She was pretty sure any twinge, any residual muscle ache would make her smile—which was when she knew she'd be okay. With that anyway.

One new thing learned.

He leaned in and kissed the spot between the curve of her shoulder and the curve of her neck. He rested his mouth there for another second, but didn't say anything. Then he moved away, rolled off the bed, and walked into the bathroom.

She let out the breath she didn't realize she was holding. What was that kiss about? She'd been okay. They'd given in to their animal attraction. They'd had sex. Wall banging, crazy hot sex. But . . . sex. They'd bonded over their similar pasts, which meant she felt . . . safe with him. Accepted. Respected. And that was enough. She wasn't going to be the Girl Who Wanted More.

So . . . what *was* that?

A kiss good-bye? Wait for me later? Thanks for the great lay? *What?*

She discovered her second thing. In this new life, she

wasn't going to be content to consider, to endlessly ponder, or worry. Life left too many things unanswered. So when there was an answer to be had, well, dammit, she wanted to have it.

With two T-shirts on, one inside out, and one sock in her hand, she got off the bed and walked to the bathroom door. Okay, so maybe half-stalked, half-staggered was a better description. She didn't want to be get-crazy-after-great-but-meaningless-sex girl, either. She just wanted a simple answer. *What did he expect?* She needed to know that, so she could decide if it was what she expected, too.

She took a calming breath as she lifted her hand to knock on the door. *See? So civil, so polite.* Not at all crazy-after-sex-girl.

Before she connected knuckles to wood, he opened the door, fully dressed in a fresh, crisp uniform. If he was surprised to find her standing there, half dressed, he didn't show it. In fact, his gaze locked on hers, and she got as far as thinking *damn, you're so beautiful,* before he yanked her into his arms and kissed her senseless.

"That's what I really wanted to do," he said gruffly. "When you moved away, turned your back. In case you were wondering."

"I wasn't—" *Wow, that was some kiss.* It took her a moment to recalibrate. Her toes were still curling.

"I didn't turn my back on you. I was just—" She broke off because she wasn't sure what she'd just. Not really. He'd gotten a call to go into work and she'd rolled away to leave him to it. Great sex, but just sex. Clean and simple. Except it wasn't going to be either, apparently. That was fine. Obviously, no matter what she'd wanted to believe, just sex, clean and simple wasn't really for her, either. Or she wouldn't have stalked over to the bathroom door in the first place.

"I get it," he said. "I was supposed to give you your

space. I didn't want to. So . . . I compromised. You frustrate the hell out of me, and I'm all done with being frustrated. So, this is what I wanted to do. Pretty much from the moment we stopped doing it. You?"

She was still reeling from the kiss and the declaration. Both of them had been—well, there was only one word to describe it. *Possessive.* And damn if she didn't learn a third thing. She liked it. When it was him doing the possession anyway. "Me, yes. Uh, too. Me, too."

"Good." He kissed her again. He took his time, sliding his hand under her hair, tilting her mouth up to his, and backing her up against the wall before sinking into the kiss as if he had all day, even though he clearly didn't. He kissed her until her knees were jelly and stars were twinkling in the periphery once more. And then he was gone.

She slid a little until she was sagging against the open doorframe of the bathroom, hand touching her mouth, lips so tender, feeling like he'd just touched her in places everything that had come before hadn't come close to touching. She shifted her head and looked at the bed. The sexy sex bed made of sex—where she'd just enjoyed some of the very finest of its kind. And she smiled. "Well, one thing I'm not, is frustrated."

She took a few moments to use his bathroom to clean up, hell, to brace herself against the sink until she could stand up, then tortured herself with images of what he looked like in his shower, all hot and steamy and naked and aroused, doing . . . what he'd said she made him want to do . . . which made her want to do . . . a lot of things. And none of them alone. Back in the bedroom, she had barely uncovered one boot and was digging for the other when she heard her cell phone chirp. Her cell phone never chirped. Who would be texting her? Who even had her number? Fergus, she supposed. Oh, and Owen. And Brodie. How had that even happened? She hadn't even been in town that long.

She wanted to bask a bit more, okay a lot more, but new life or old, apparently one thing didn't change. Life was determined to move along at its own pace, whether she was ready or not.

She finally unearthed her phone, but didn't recognize the number associated with the text. She did, however, know who'd sent it.

About the prospectus, it read.

She sat cross-legged amidst the tangle of linens and comforter on the floor next to his bed, smiled, and typed: Yes?

It takes as long as it takes.

Her smile spread to a grin. Okay. Thank you.

There was a pause, then: Include tower and cottage.

Her heart thumped, part nerves, part excitement. Okay, mostly nerves. With shaky fingers, she typed: Okay. I'm glad. Thank you for trusting me.

That part was never in doubt.

She was still sitting there, grinning like a loon, when she heard an engine start up outside. She half crawled, half stumbled over to one of the alcoves, careful to keep her head ducked. She knelt in front of the window, looking through the clear part of the pane, down at the side driveway as his SUV slowly backed out and turned around. He paused as he turned, looked up. Their gazes met. She didn't smile, neither did he. She didn't wave. He didn't nod. They just . . . looked. And there didn't have to be anything else.

Then he drove off.

And she watched him until his taillights disappeared. "Alexandra MacFarland, what has just happened to you?" She shifted around and leaned back against the window. "Welcome to your life, part two," she murmured.

Then she crawled out of the alcove . . . jumped on his bed, and danced.

Chapter 8

Scowling, Logan entered the police station, the front of his uniform shirt soaked clear to the skin for the second time that day. It was forty-two degrees outside, for crying out loud.

"Again?" Sergeant Benson took in the state of his uniform, rightly guessing that Eleanor Darby had nailed him once more with her gun. Her high-powered, super-soaking water gun. "Sir, you do know that your gun has real bullets in it."

"Yeah, well, I'm pretty sure you were right. Garlic and a stake, maybe." He wasn't laughing this time. "She took a sniper position from her bedroom window. That's what she called it. Sniper position. Are we sure she's lived in Blueberry all of her seventy-nine years? She wasn't CIA? FBI?"

"Just be happy she's not NRA." Barb followed him into his office. "Chief, why don't you go on home for the day? Except for Eleanor and that damn raccoon of hers, it's been quiet."

"Can you believe that?" Logan demanded, still working off his mad. He hung his jacket—which had still been damp from the earlier assault and was now soaked—on the back of the door, then plucked at the front of his sodden shirt. "Now she's claiming it's a pet and she's shooting at Randy with that damn gun."

"And you, sir. Twice."

He leveled a look at Barb, but she didn't so much as blink. One of the many reasons he'd never joined in the Thursday night poker game she'd started up a few years back with some of the officers and a few other locals. Alex, on the other hand, would probably fit right in.

"I just wish I knew what the hell has gotten into her," he said. "Yesterday she was trying to mace the damn thing with furniture polish and oven cleaner. Do you think maybe it's some kind of Alzheimer's?"

"What I think is that she watches way too many cop shows. You should get Randy to trap that thing at night when she's in bed—they're nocturnal, right?—before it up and bites her. He can cart it over to the next county and release it. She'll just think it wandered off."

"And then she'll find some new way to waste our time. Remember when she was convinced someone was sneaking into her house and rearranging her doll figurines? The woman needs a different hobby. Why can't she knit or sew? Like other women her age. Something safe, noncombative, that doesn't require firearms."

"I knit. And I sew. Sir."

Again, Logan leveled a look at her.

"Her family has all moved away," Barb said. "Husband passed what has to be almost nine years ago now. Maybe she just needs something more in her life."

"Well, she's a little too late to enroll in sniper school and I don't think a life of crime is a good alternative. I still say it might be time for her to have a little chat with her doctor. At the moment, though, we have to do something about this damn raccoon. Before you know it, she'll have it on a leash walking it around the harbor, scaring folks half to death and starting a rabies scare."

"I'll call Randy and tell him to trap it tonight. Why don't

you go on home before you catch your death of cold? I can handle things here, call you if there's a problem."

"Make sure you tell Randy he has to wait until the damn thing isn't on her property so she doesn't get him for trespassing. I'm not too sure she's not nocturnal, too. And I'll stay on. I know we're short-staffed with Nate being gone for his sister's wedding."

"Speaking of sisters, one of yours called today. I left the message on the desk."

Logan lifted a quick glance her way, but she didn't look particularly perturbed, which meant it wasn't Fiona; nor did she look worried or concerned, which meant it wasn't Hannah, either. He made a mental note to call Fi and get an update on Hannah. He was a little worried about her, too, and being the middle of the three girls, Fiona was the one who kept track of them all. "Kerry?" he guessed, referring to the youngest of his three siblings as he slid files around on his desk, looking for the phone slip. "Is everything okay? You should have texted me or had her call me on my cell."

"Told her that, but she was in some big hurry. Didn't sound like anything bad. In fact, she sounded pretty excited. Said it wasn't something she wanted to say in a text or leave on voicemail."

"Okay, well, that's good." When the comment was met with silence, he glanced up. "Isn't it?"

"I'm sure it's not my place to say."

Logan rolled his eyes. All three of his sisters had gone out of state for college, and never really made their way back, but they all kept in touch with him, often through Barb. Fiona had been the last to leave permanently, and that had been . . . wow, seven, almost eight years ago. She'd been in New York City ever since and had just launched her own design business in the Village. Hannah was a lawyer and lived just outside DC in the historic town of Alexandria. Kerry . . . well . . . the baby of the family was also the family nomad. She'd taken off at seventeen, and other than the occasional pit stop between adventures, was the sibling he saw and heard from the least. A wandering gypsy, Fergus called her. But a happier gypsy he'd never met. "She's still in Yosemite? Doing the guide thing?"

"Winter is coming, so I'm thinking probably not. I think they close most of the trails in the off-season. I'm not sure. She didn't say."

Logan gave up looking for the slip and dug out his phone instead. "Well, she must have said something." When Barb hedged, he said, "Come on, spill."

"You know she was seeing that park ranger for a time."

"Kerry's relationships usually last as long as her interest in whatever job she's latched on to." He looked at Barb. "Why, is something different this time?"

His desk sergeant merely lifted a shoulder. Then, when he narrowed his gaze, she said, "Well, you didn't hear it from me, but, as you know, I've got two sons, both married, and three granddaughters, also all married. So I know when a girl sounds like she's thinking about wedding bells."

"Engaged? Kerry?" Logan started to laugh. "Oh, that poor guy. What's his name? Steve something? Tom?" He noticed Barb wasn't smiling. "Oh, come on, you know she'll bail before they ever walk down the aisle." When Barb continued to stare, his smiled faded. "What, are you saying she eloped? You think Kerry got married?"

Barb shook her head. "But I suspect she'll want to be."

His gut clenched. He gulped. "Pregnant?"

"You didn't hear it from me." She turned to leave the office.

"Hold on there! You said wedding bells. Where did you get a baby from wedding bells?"

She looked back. "Sometimes the baby comes before the I do's. What else would get that girl down the aisle?"

Logan sank down in his chair. He stared at his phone. When had he lost control of his nice, steady, understandable life? When?

"I'd call Fiona first," Barbara said.

"I was going to anyway," he said absently, mind spinning. The baby of the McCrae family . . . having a baby? It didn't compute. Kerry was a happy soul who always landed on her feet somewhere, but it was one thing for her to pack up and go anytime and anywhere the mood struck her. She'd long since proven she could handle herself. Not that he didn't worry about her anyway, all the time. But that kind of life wasn't any way to raise a child. Last he'd spoken to her, she certainly hadn't sounded like she was planning on slowing down anytime soon, much less settling down. "What do you know about this Steve character? Is he going to stand by her? Do we want him to?"

"I could say something about it being a sad commentary that you need to ask me these things—"

"Barb, you know I only half listen when Kerry talks about her latest lust interest. They're never serious. I do listen when she talks about whatever work she's doing. It's always struck me that she's a lot more passionate about the jobs she takes on than the men she dates. So, do I need to run a check on this guy?" He was already turning the computer monitor toward him.

"Already did. That's the top file there."

Logan looked up. "He has a file? What the hell has he done?"

"Nothing. Straitlaced as they come. Hard worker from what I can tell. Been with the park service pretty much his entire adult life. Eagle Scout."

Relief made him a little giddy and he laughed. "Kerry went for an Eagle Scout?"

Barb lifted an eyebrow. "My Evan is an Eagle Scout."

Logan sobered. "Right. I didn't mean—it was more a comment on Kerry than on—"

"Timothy Stevens. That's his name. Top of the pile there. Why don't you grab it and head home? I'm sure with the project report thing happening out at the house, you have a lot of things you need to get your hands on. So why not go ahead and take advantage of—" She broke off suddenly and stared at him. She seemed to be at a sudden loss for words, then just as suddenly snapped her mouth shut and turned to the door.

But not before he'd seen the smile peeking around the corners of her mouth. "Sergeant?"

"So much paperwork. Better get back to it," she said over her shoulder, bustling out. "I'll call Deputy Dan and get him to come in early. Go home."

Deputy Dan was actually Officer Daniel Baker, but even at twenty-five, he was so fresh-scrubbed, apple-cheeked, and peach-fuzz-faced, Barb had nicknamed him Deputy Dan his second day on the job and it had stuck.

Logan didn't care about covering the rest of his shift; he wanted to know what that damn smile was about. Hell, he wanted to know a lot of things, starting with that was going on with his baby sister. But that's not where his thoughts were lingering at the moment.

With everything else going on, it should have been easy to back burner what had happened at the house that morning. But quite the opposite was true. Almost in defiance of everything else going on, his thoughts had never strayed far from Alex. At the moment, he was thinking that if he went home, and she was there, getting to the bottom of the Kerry and Timothy story would, at best, not happen right away. In fact, just thinking about that made him shift in his seat as his body enthusiastically put in its vote on how it would like to spend the evening.

The thing was, now that he was back in town and back at work, he'd had a chance for the fog to lift a little, and wasn't sure what he hoped would happen when he finally went home. Or what he hoped wouldn't happen.

Suddenly, staying at the office took on another layer of appeal. "No need," he called out. "I have a fresh shirt here. Eula didn't get my pants wet this time."

From her desk just outside his office door, Sergeant Benson murmured something that sounded an awful lot like, "No, but it looks like someone did," but the radio squawked just then and a moment later he could hear her talking to Randy.

"No," he muttered. *Not possible.* Barb was good at reading people and situations, but no way had she'd figured out . . . anything regarding how he'd spent a part of his morning. How could she have? He hadn't said a word . . . and he seriously doubted Alex would have made a peep.

Her goal was to get the restoration job on Pelican Point, and being viewed as professional was key to that. The last thing she'd be doing was flaunting a personal relationship with him. In fact, her first instinct had been to roll away and grab her clothes.

So despite her enthusiastic response to his parting kiss, he wasn't all that sure she was interested in a relationship with him. That annoyed him no end, which in turn worried him. He wasn't sure he wanted one, either, so why in hell was he pissed off that she might not? God, he hated complicated emotional shit.

It was exactly why Logan went to great pains to keep his personal life just that. Personal. Private. It meant not having one at all in the Cove. Not that he had much of one anywhere, but he wasn't the hermit Fergus made him out to be. Not exactly, anyway. And he wasn't a monk, either. When he wanted to . . . socialize, he generally found it a lot wiser to do so when he needed to go away on business, either to the county offices in Machias, or the state capital in Augusta.

That brought up the whole thing about how, exactly, he wanted to handle what was happening with Alex in terms of the rest of the town. Once one person got wind that there was something more than a business agreement going on between them . . .

He massaged his forehead, then pinched the bridge of his nose as reality came crashing in. "Seriously, what happened to quiet, simple, and predictable? How did I coast along for ten, twelve years, only to lose it inside of forty-eight hours?"

Not wanting to know what was happening with Randy and the raccoon situation, and possibly better off not knowing what Barb thought she knew about Kerry or . . . anything else . . . he closed his office door and flipped the blinds in front of the glass pane that comprised the top half of the door. He opened the supply closet door in the corner of the small office and pulled down another dry-cleaned uniform shirt that was folded and pressed, sitting on the top shelf.

He'd have to go without a T-shirt, and the seams scratched like hell, but it was only a few hours. He quickly unbuttoned his wet uniform shirt, slipped the badge off the above-the-pocket panel, tossed the wet shirt on the chair, and put his badge on the fresh shirt. He'd just peeled off his wet T-shirt when his intercom buzzer went off.

"Chief?" Barb used the intercom only when she was trying to give him a chance to duck whoever was outside his office.

He could think of only one person who it could be and groaned. *Eleanor Darby.* He hoped like hell she didn't have that damn critter with her. He stepped over to the blinds and peeked through.

Alex? She looked . . . he didn't know her well enough to know what her expression meant. She was chatting politely and calmly with Barb, smiling briefly, but there was something in her eyes. Tension, worry, *something*.

Without thinking, he immediately opened his office door. "Alex, what's wrong?"

Alex had been standing in front of Barb's desk talking with her, but looked up when the door opened. Her eyes widened. "Do you ever have your clothes on?"

Behind her, Barb's eyebrows climbed halfway up her forehead, followed by a far-too-gleeful smile.

Logan stepped through the door. "Come in here." He took her wrist in a gentle but firm hold and shuttled her directly into his office, closing the door behind her and snapping the already closed blinds shut again for good measure. "Is there a problem? With the house? Or . . . something?"

He pulled on his clean uniform shirt and made quick work of the buttons. He started to automatically loosen his belt so he could unbutton his pants to tuck the long tail of the shirt in, but stopped. He wasn't sure which was more awkward, that after a single roll in the hay he was already so comfortable with her that he didn't think twice about unzipping his fly and half undressing? In his office, no less. In the police station, with the all-knowing, all-seeing Yoda Barb sitting watch? Or that he'd stopped and stood there with his shirt hanging out, like he was suddenly so uncomfortable around her he couldn't tuck his own damn shirt in.

It was moments like these that made him embrace his bachelorhood with renewed enthusiasm.

"Please, don't be modest on my account," she said dryly.

Feeling beyond ridiculous, he loosened his belt, unbuttoned and unzipped his trousers just enough to be accessible, then finished the job in record time. "Why are you here? Is everything okay?"

"Nothing is wrong with the house and I'm . . . fine. I came in to get copies of the plans and work permits that have been filed at the county offices over the years, then grab a bite at Delia's and do some research." She lifted the old canvas duffel pack she had slung over her shoulder, indicating she had her laptop and whatever else her research required. "Delia has Wi-Fi."

"So do I."

"Yes, but I don't have your access code, and I didn't want to bother you after having just told you I wouldn't be bothering you."

That was just it. She wasn't bothering him at all . . . except just her talking was hot and bothering him. He took a seat behind his desk, thinking he'd revealed enough for one office visit.

"Did you have problems getting the house plans from the county? They should all be public record, but I can call over there if that helps. I know some of the oldest records might not be there. There's a whole file in the keeper's cottage—"

"You have things stored in there?" She seemed incredulous at the idea.

Logan frowned. "It was the keeper's cottage. They stored lots of things in there. It was their job."

"No, I mean that you still store things in there. Logan, when I said it wasn't in good shape, I wasn't kidding. I'm not so sure it's even restorable, and I'm not talking just sagging roof and some structural issues, but—when was the last time anyone was in there? Does it have functioning electric? Has anyone looked at water damage, because that roof—"

"Whoa, whoa. The answer is . . . I don't know. Well, yes, it does have electric. The house, cottage, and tower all do. But I'm pretty sure it's not turned on. As to the rest, I'm not sure."

She gaped at him. "How long have you been solely in charge of the place?"

"Since my grandfather passed when I was twenty-seven. So, seven years. I told you, I haven't been in either the tower or cottage since college." He saw the flicker of apology cross her face. She knew why he hadn't gone back in there.

"But as to when the last time my grandfather was in there, I honestly couldn't say. He was forever puttering with the house, the property. For the better part of the last twenty years of his life, it was his full-time job."

He could see her do the math, and figure that had been from about the time his parents had died, which was exactly right. But she didn't ask. "So, it's been at least seven years. Logan, we should really get in there."

"Okay."

That caught her by surprise. She'd apparently been ready to lay out her argument, but went silent for a moment, then nodded. "Okay. Thank you," she added sincerely. "You don't have to do anything. I will give the exterior a thorough inspection first, determine how best to go in as safely as possible, and figure out what we need to do before we enter so it doesn't collapse on our heads."

"Whatever you think is best."

That earned him a wry smile, and he found himself smiling as well.

Alex raised her eyebrows. "Maybe I should have gone the Goldilocks route sooner."

He grinned at that. "I didn't say that, and I hope you know what happens between us doesn't impact the work you're doing. Anything else I say right now will likely get me in trouble. It may have been a while since I was in a relationship, but with three sisters, I know a no-win setup when I hear it."

Her expression went from teasing to . . . well . . . to blank.

"I did it anyway, apparently. What did I say?"

She snapped out of it and pasted on a smile. "You have

three sisters? Before you just said sisters, but I didn't know how many."

He wanted to rewind and ask her what he'd said to bring that look to her face, but figured that was another one of those no-win situations, so let it go. "I do. All younger. Hannah is next, she's two years younger, a lawyer, works in DC. Fiona is two years behind her, just started her own design firm in New York, and Kerry, the baby, is eighteen months after her and . . . well . . . I'm not sure where she is right now. That's also on my list today."

"Is everything okay?"

Some of his concern must have shown on his face. "She called earlier, had some exciting news, but I wasn't here."

"Oh. Right." Alex's cheek's became the most intriguing shade of pink. "Sorry. Well, not *sorry,* sorry, but sorry you missed her call."

He found himself smiling at that. She didn't strike him as the blushing type. Far from it. "I'll catch up with her later. It's all fine. Kerry doesn't just have nine lives. We're pretty sure she's immortal, so whatever it is, I'm sure she's got it figured out. She always does."

It was Alex's turn to grin. "Who are you trying to convince?" she asked, an echo of his question to her earlier that day.

He sighed, letting out a half laugh. "Good question. I think she might be pregnant."

Why on earth had he gone and told her that? He barely talked family news with Barb, who was not exactly a surrogate mother by any stretch, but the one who knew the most intimate details about his family simply because she made it her business to know. His sisters knew she was his watchdog, and since he wasn't always great at keeping up with them, they made it their business to keep in touch with Barb.

"And . . . that's not a good thing, I take it? You look a little . . . green."

He rubbed a hand over his face. "I don't know what it is, to be honest."

"Do your other sisters have kids?"

He shook his head. At her clearly amused smile, he said, "What?"

"You've never been an uncle before. You're nervous."

"Of course I'm nervous. But not about that. Hell, I hadn't even thought about it that way." *Dear God. He might be an uncle.* "It's just—you'd have to know Kerry. Of the three of them, let's just say, she wasn't the one I thought would make me an uncle first. Actually, on second thought . . . hell. I don't know. I guess at our age, it's probably strange none of us have kids yet, but it just . . . hasn't worked out that way. So far, anyhow. I kind of keep on forgetting we're all getting older."

"How old are you? Oh, right. Thirty-four," she answered herself. "If your grandfather passed seven years ago—I did the math."

"Yes. Kerry just turned twenty-eight."

"That's not too young or so old. You or her. Not these days. A lot of women are getting careers going, that kind of thing, couples getting more established, settled, before starting a family. I think it's smart."

"Because you know so many normal couples and normal career women?" He'd said it teasingly, and was relieved when she took it that way.

"Point taken, but still, it sounds logical, right?" She studied him, then smiled again. "This has really gotten to you, hasn't it?"

You're getting to me, he wanted to say.

When she smiled spontaneously with that teasing lilt to her lips, it lit up her entire face. Her eyes actually sparkled.

He found himself completely dazzled. It didn't help that she'd changed out of her lumberjack look to jeans so old and soft they molded to her legs, brown leather lace-up boots, and a thick, cable-knit, dark blue sweater that made her eyes look impossibly bigger. It was all topped with a canvas coat that was open up the front. He could see how nicely that sweater accentuated curves he was on intimate terms with. Her hair was a jumble of waves and curls, which he'd like to think was a result of how they'd spent the morning. He had to dig his fingers against his thighs to keep from rounding the desk and sinking his hands in them all over again.

"It's my baby sister we're talking about," he said, struggling to stay on the conversational track. The rest of him had quite gleefully gone to another track entirely. "She might be twenty-eight chronological years old, but to me—"

"She's your baby sister."

"Exactly."

Alex laughed.

"What's so funny? I'm a caring older brother. Is that so hard to believe?"

"More like a freaked-out older brother, but it's equally endearing. You've been so tall, dark, and stoic since you first strolled up to my truck window." She tilted her head. "It's good to know you can get flustered. I was beginning to think you were Mr. Invincible."

He leaned back in his chair. "Tall, dark, and stoic, huh?"

"That's what you took away from all that?" She laughed again, easily, guilelessly.

Any part of him that hadn't leaped completely to life, did so then. Even parts he didn't know could do that.

"It's easier to focus on what you said than the part about Kerry."

"The part where you're flustered, you mean?"

He pushed his chair back and stood, then came around

the desk. He eased a hip on the corner of his desk and reached out, took her hand, and tugged her closer. "You know what flusters me?"

She let him tug her closer still. Teasing smile on her face, she simply shook her head.

When she was between his knees, he put his hand on her hip, but kept the fingers of his other hand woven through hers. "You. This."

Her smile faded, and a hint of what he'd seen earlier crossed her face. Her cheeks turned the lightest shade of pink. She wanted to be all cosmopolitan about this whole thing, and she was probably a lot closer to pulling that off than he'd ever be. But the thing about Alex that grabbed him most was the many facets of her that were woven in with that confident devil-may-care, in-your-face swagger.

They'd first met when she'd been, ostensibly, at her worst. Vulnerable, defenseless, grief-stricken. Since then, he'd seen her angry, passionate—both in and out of bed— teasing, playful, laughing . . . as well as confident and ut- terly confused. She was at a crossroads, trying to make sense of her life, and of who she'd become because of happen- stances well beyond her control. He knew more about that than maybe even he'd been aware, so he got it. He *got* her. It was intoxicating and terrifying in equal measure.

He felt her fingers reflexively tighten in his. "I'm not sure I know what *this* is," she said at length. "I thought we were just going to sort of . . . wing it."

"We are."

"You said *relationship* earlier. That it's been a while since you were in one."

Ah. So that's what had caused her sudden blank look. "That's true."

Another thought crossed his mind, and he was surprised at the strength of the pinch he felt. And the jealousy. He wasn't the jealous type, usually quite the opposite. Mr.

Casual was a far better moniker, at least in regard to how he conducted his relationships, if you could call them that. Yet, right from the start, nothing about Alex MacFarland made him feel remotely casual. "You're not involved with anyone. I mean, I assume since we—"

"No, I'm not in any kind of relationship. I wouldn't do that. I'd be offended that you even thought it, but we're kind of going about this thing backwards and I know you don't really know me or my character."

"I believed you when you said you weren't the type who'd have . . . frolicked," he said, liking that the word brought a smile to her lips again. "But you—some people are content with being more casual, and that's really what I was asking. I guess."

Logan rubbed his thumb over her hip, wanting to tug her fully between his legs. "I'll go first. I am casual. Usually. I don't date women in Blueberry. I grew up with almost all of them, and it's just . . . being in a high-profile job here, I prefer to keep my personal life separate—which means somewhere other than the Cove. Because of that, anything serious is . . . challenging."

"You said you didn't want anything complicated. I understand. Neither do I."

"I'm honest and straightforward. I don't lead anyone on."

"Consider me unled," she said.

He thought he heard relief in her voice—which kind of pissed him off—which, in turn, annoyed him. And upped his nerves, right along with it. It had been a long time since he'd been in a relationship. If it meant more bouts of confusing and conflicting emotions, he couldn't rightly say why he thought it was a good idea to change that status.

He cleared his throat. "I'm not—I'm usually pretty good at communicating. But I'm not making myself clear."

"So just say what you mean."

"Okay." He pulled her closer then. "As long as we're . . .

winging it together . . . I won't be having any casual, un-complicated, straightforward, unled sex with anyone else. I don't do that."

He could see her throat work as she swallowed. "Neither would I. Do I. I mean, I won't. Either."

He couldn't help it. He grinned. "Now who's flustered?" Perversely, that calmed him immensely.

"It's been a while for me, too. Relationships, I mean. But this isn't . . . I mean, it's not really . . . that. Right? We're just . . ."

"Winging it," they said together, then laughed.

"I don't know what it is or isn't, and I don't need to la-bel anything. I just wanted to make sure you knew where I stood."

"So, we're good then."

With one tug he pulled her fully up against him and slid his hand up and into those curls, cupping the back of her head, finally doing what he'd ached to do since he'd pulled her into his office. Hell, since walking away from her in his own bedroom. "Oh, I thought we were a lot better than good."

"Me, too," she said against his lips.

He'd meant to kiss her and let her go. He just wanted to taste her, even though his body wanted a whole lot more than a taste. But it turned out one kiss wasn't enough, so he dipped in for another, then another still. And in some part of the back of his brain, he knew the very last thing he should be doing—even with blinds drawn—was to be es-sentially making out with . . . well . . . anyone . . . in his of-fice.

As police chief, he did his best to conduct himself in as professional and responsible a manner as possible. Because everyone knew him so well, it was the only way to estab-lish the respect the job demanded. He was accessible, ap-proachable, friendly, and wanted every and anyone to feel they could come to him if they had a problem that required his help. But there had to be a line between being the friendly police chief and being a buddy.

Alex lifted her head and he liked—a lot—the way those dark blue eyes of hers got all stormy and darker when she was aroused. "I—uh, I should probably let you get back to work." She swallowed again and he watched her throat work . . . and wanted to bite it. Then lick it. Then bite it again.

Yeah. He'd better get his head back in work as well.

"Don't—ah." Wow, his brain felt like scrambled eggs. "Don't go into the cottage or the tower until I can go with you. Okay?"

"Okay. Are you sure? Because you don't have to."

"Certain. I don't have a problem going in either. I just haven't had any need to. Until now. Now I want to."

She held his gaze, and the depth of what moved between them was equal measures provocative and disconcerting.

"Okay. Thank you." She looked at him, and he thought she was going to ask him something, but she seemed to think better of it. She started to step back, but he stood and kept her in his arms.

He kissed her again, then smiled against her lips. "Remind me to kiss you like that every time I need to ask you to give in on something."

She punched him lightly on the chest, making him laugh. "I might be stubborn, but I'm not stupid. I wouldn't have gone in the cottage or the tower without some help." She smiled at him. "I know. It's shocking that I actually can be professional."

"Yes," he said, then laughed at her affronted expression and dropped a hard fast kiss on her mouth to close it again. "And no. That's what gets me. I never know what to expect."

"I thought that frustrated you."

"That, too."

She held his gaze, studied it, then him.

"What?" he asked.

"Well, as long as we're being cheerleaders for honesty . . . you seem to truly get me. That's a little scary. Maybe a lot. But comforting, too. I didn't expect that."

"Me, either."

That confession surprised her.

Surprised him, too. Something about her made it easy— too easy—to say whatever popped into his mind. Probably because he knew she wouldn't ask for explanations, but would simply accept what he said. She wouldn't wheedle or make demands. Or assumptions. If she wanted to know something, she'd ask. Maybe she didn't want to know anything. But he wanted her to. That was the scary thing for him. He did get her. Part of her anyway. It made him want to know more. For the first time, maybe ever, he wondered how he'd feel if she didn't want the same from him.

His intercom buzzed again, startling them both. "Sorry to interrupt, Chief, but we've got a hostage situation."

Alex's eyes went wide and she stiffened. "Hostages? Oh, wow!"

Logan merely reached across his desk and pressed the button. "Does this hostage situation involve a very large water gun and a senior citizen with remarkably good aim?"

"It does, sir."

He sighed and swore under his breath. "Who's the hostage?"

There was a pause. Then Barb said, "The mayor. And pretty much the entire town council. Sir."

He let his chin rest on his chest for a moment, then said, "Okay. Give me a minute."

"Will do, sir."

Alex started to scramble out of his way. "Hurry. That's horrible. Do you have, like, a SWAT team or something?"

"Never had a need for one. And we won't now. Water gun," he reiterated. "Not one with bullets."

"Still, if he's crazy enough to storm city hall—I was just there!"

"Not he."

He didn't think Alex's eyes could get any wider. "A woman? An elderly woman took a gun into city hall?"

"Water gun." He did wonder how she'd gotten it past old Avery. The security guard wasn't exactly spry, but he'd have to be blind to have missed it. The damn thing she'd aimed at him today was the size of a small bazooka.

"My guess is she just wants them to pass some ordinance that says she can keep her damn raccoon. We'll get it all settled. Hopefully without any shots fired. I'm running out of clean uniforms."

Alex opened her mouth, closed it again, then burst out laughing, anyway. "That's why you came home this morning? Because an elderly woman shot you with a water gun?"

"A very big water gun. And she was in sniper position. I didn't see her."

Alex just grinned. "Sniper, huh?"

His face grew a tiny bit warm. "You laugh, but if you see a woman walking a small raccoon, steer clear. That's all I'm saying."

Alex was still laughing as she moved toward the office door.

"Hey, wait a sec," he said. "What did you come in here for? Wasn't it about the plans? When I looked out and saw you, you seemed . . . I don't know . . . worried about something."

Her laughter faded, but a hint of the smile remained. "See? That's what I mean. That's going to take some getting used to."

"What is?"

"You reading me."

"I'm a trained professional, too, you know."

She grinned. "Good to know we're behaving so responsibly, too. It wasn't anything—well, it might have been. But I can talk to you about it later. I was going to stop by the grocery and pick up stuff to make my dad's chili. Some cornbread. There will be plenty. Heats up easy, so it's good leftovers whenever you get in."

She didn't ask when that would be, so he didn't offer. It didn't change the fact that he wished she had. But they were winging it. So he winged. "Okay. That sounds good. Thanks."

She nodded, then ducked out.

And just like the house had felt empty that first morning when she'd taken off . . . his office seemed to echo a little bit, as well. He sank back down on the corner of his desk.

Winging it. A new concept for him. Especially when the woman he was winging it with also happened to be living with him.

Not sure what he was feeling, but knowing *flustered* didn't even begin to cover it, he grabbed his hat and his still damp jacket from the hooks behind the door and jerked it open. At least he knew what to do about the hostage situation.

"Good meeting? Sir?" Barb beamed a particularly knowing smile at him.

"Don't start," he said, which only added a twinkle to go along with the smile. "Did you call Dan? You might want to get Thomas out there, too."

"Do you really think it's going to take three of you?"

"No. But I want to impress upon Mrs. Darby that this isn't the sort of thing we take kindly to. Just because she's getting up there in years—"

"Hey now."

"—doesn't mean we're going to treat her with kid gloves.

You wouldn't expect to be, right? Well, she's proven she's not exactly a wilting, fragile flower, either. Senile, maybe," he muttered under his breath as he headed for the station door.

"I heard that," Barb called out behind him. "Oh, and Chief?"

"What?" He turned back, knowing half his annoyance was really just a cover for the pulse-thumping panic rising inside him as he was forced to acknowledge that the woman who had so effortlessly turned his head was also quite probably going to turn his entire life upside down. Actually, it felt like she already had. Barb had probably called half the town already.

"You might want to check your uniform shirt before you storm the fort. Missed a button."

Yeah. His nice, quiet, predictable life was doomed. "Be open to change, my ass," he muttered as left the office and climbed into his truck.

Chapter 9

Alex flipped the bacon over with a fork, making a mental note to get a pair of tongs next time she went into town. Maybe Logan had some on his grill. Was he the kind of guy who grilled? Toast popped up and she beamed at the perfectly golden brown color as she moved it to a plate. She dropped two more slices in, then, turning back, she dumped chopped mushrooms, onions, and peppers into the scrambled eggs she was making in the other skillet. Next up, grating some cheddar into a small bowl to sprinkle on top. It was day one of her new eating-actual-food-for-meals campaign. No more burnt toast and coffee for breakfast. Or lunch.

She'd slept well again. That made three nights in a row now. She was getting regular sleep, and now there would be regular meals. Life was getting better. Except for the part where she had no idea whether or not regular sex was also going to be part of it.

Logan hadn't come home the night before, but they were winging it. No rules, no expectations. Other than there would be no sex with other people while they were having sex. Crazy, head-spinning, spine-melting, toe-curling, the-kind-you-read-about-but-never-thought-was-real sex. The exact same kind of sex she had kind of sort of been hoping to have again . . . last night.

She understood he was police chief, and handling a hostage crisis. And doing whatever else a police chief did. She was doing a job, too. She'd stayed up half the night documenting the interior of the main house, from warped floorboards to water-damaged crown molding. She'd made lists of the obvious structural issues and had even pulled up a corner of the kitchen linoleum. And wished she hadn't, as it had added a whole new column to her list. She'd gone over the architectural plans she had for the house so far, and working from the oldest to the most current, she'd started to build a history of the place, noting what had been done and when. Sadly, when it came to upkeep and maintenance, it was more a question of how much hadn't been done, ever, and not just during Logan's time at the helm.

None of what she'd discovered in the house had been a good omen for what was likely going on inside the more neglected keeper's cottage. She wasn't sure why she already felt such an attachment to it. Maybe it was because the cottage was easier to tackle than dealing with all the emotional landmines the tower was sure to bring with it. In the end, she wanted to see both reclaim their former glory, and the more she learned about their history, the more personal it felt.

On most jobs it was the thrill and the challenge of the work itself that engaged her. She'd always had a healthy respect and a great deal of admiration for the towers she'd worked on, their architecture, their history, the steps it took to honor both and how gratifying it was to be a part of the restoration process. But this time it felt different. Probably because Pelican Point represented her return to the world she loved, the only one she'd ever known. It shouldn't be surprising that she felt a more personal connection because it was a more emotional project on so many levels. Nothing that had come before could ever match that.

Some part of her knew it also had to do with Logan, his

story, and his past. The more she learned about him, the more personal he was beginning to feel to her, too.

She'd stopped working long enough to make the promised chili and cornbread, then, when it appeared Logan wasn't going to show, she'd ended up working while she ate, eventually storing the leftovers and cleaning up, which had only served to uncover more issues that would need repairing.

The freezer part of the ancient fridge didn't work properly, not that it had been an issue for the sole bachelor living there. The man's idea of stocking fridge and pantry began and ended with a bottle of wine, two loaves of sliced bread—each half gone—blueberry jam, a jar of super crunchy peanut butter, a few boxes of pasta, and canned cheese. She didn't even want to think about how those all came together on any kind of regular basis. Clearly, he was eating out or ordering in because he was in great shape, and no genes were good enough to make up for such a dismal diet.

"You're one to talk about dismal diets," she murmured as she worked the eggs and other ingredients with her spatula. At least that was one thing she could change. Sleeping soundly still felt more like a lucky gift, but one she hoped would keep on giving as she got the other parts of her life more stable. She wasn't sure what those "other parts" were going to entail, not entirely anyway. She'd told herself that maybe her uncertainty about her relationship with Logan would provide the exact distraction she'd hoped for, after all. By comparison, it made the work feel comfortable and familiar, the one known entity in her current universe.

She'd come close to texting him several times during the evening. Partly because she'd wanted to know when or if he'd be home, but also because she'd wanted to know what was going on with the situation at city hall.

She hadn't been in town long, and yet she'd already come

to know a number of people. She'd seen and chatted with Fergus, Delia, Brodie, and Owen at the hardware store on a few occasions. They'd all made her feel welcome, chatting her up as if they'd known her for ages—which meant she knew a lot about other folks she hadn't even met yet.

How she was in the Cove was different from how she normally was on jobs. Normally, she had her father and crew members to keep her company. They had been her world, so she hadn't connected with the locals, not in any lasting sense. Given how often she'd moved around, it had made sense to stick with those who'd moved with her. That had always been enough. More than enough. But now that it was just her, she found herself engaging in conversation instead of simply listening to it going on around her.

She'd been surprised to discover she'd worried about Logan as the evening had stretched into night. It was morning, and still no word on what had happened, if he was okay, or when he'd be back. Not that she really thought he'd been in any danger. He certainly hadn't seemed all that concerned about the situation. More annoyed. Still, she'd like to know how things had gone. Or, more to the point, she'd like it if he wanted to share how things had gone with her.

Winging it apparently wasn't going to include that kind of thing. She got that, too. She was sure it was life upheaval enough for him that she was living under his roof. And working there. Yes, they'd had sex. And yes, they'd made it clear they wouldn't be having sex with anyone else as long as they continued to have sex with each other. But that didn't mean they were a couple—one that texted and kept in touch and told each other where they would be and when they'd be home and how their day had gone. That wasn't them. They weren't even really a *them*. Or an *us*.

So she hadn't texted. Or called. If he'd wanted to keep her informed of his whereabouts, he had the means to contact her. He was a grown single man doing whatever it was he always did. And she was a grown single woman who could certainly sleep in her own bed, and fix her own dinner, and her own breakfast.

So what if she was also a grown woman who'd risen with the sun because as soon as she'd opened her eyes that morning, she'd wondered if he was upstairs sleeping alone. Alone and probably naked in that amazing, sexy sex bed made for sex. With his Sex-god Voice that grew deeper when he was aroused, and that body of the gods that could perform amazingly devilish things to numerous parts of her anatomy. And all of that tangled up in those soft cotton sheets, sprawled across that sea of mattress. A mattress she knew felt as wonderful as she'd imagined, lying on it on her back with him on top of her, driving every hard, pulse-pounding inch of himself into her very willing body. Making her scream, making her come, making her—

She had leaped right out of bed and found something else, dear God, to distract her from those indelibly imprinted, highly detailed images.

To that end, she'd taken apart the ancient toaster and replaced one heating coil and rewired it with a new electric cord. Then she'd fixed the wonky burner on the stove, and, feeling cocky, had even gone another round with the bathroom plumbing. This time with the leaky faucet on the sink. She'd won, thankyouverymuch. She was feeling pretty accomplished. Her industriousness had taken her mind off the rest of it for whole seconds at a time, win-win. She didn't even really care if Logan had already gone to work without even leaving a note. Or some of his amazing coffee in the coffeepot.

They were winging it. That's what winging it people did.

Presently, she was whisking the scrambled eggs in the skillet so hard, she was leaving marks. She gently laid the spatula down and grabbed the next round of toast as it popped up, then took the nicely crisped bacon strips off the old cast iron griddle one at a time, letting them drain on the stack of paper towels she'd set up. So what if she'd made enough for two people? Especially if one of them was really big and ate like a grown man? She could always reheat the eggs and the bacon for breakfast tomorrow. Or make a sandwich later. "That's what winging it is all about, baby!" she exclaimed, tossing the last piece of bacon on the stack with a little flourish.

Her gaze tripped over the empty coffeemaker. She had ice cold orange juice, just the way she liked it, already poured and waiting for her, so there was no need to glare at the empty pot. At some point later on, she'd get him to show her how to make his kind of coffee. She'd looked, but hadn't found his bean stash or grinder. If she was really missing her morning coffee that much, she could get some later in town. Maybe Fergus had a pot on. He probably knew what had happened at city hall, too.

She sank a hip against the counter. *Okay, okay.* What she was really missing was the guy who made the coffee. *Dammit.* She sucked at winging it. "Pathetic, that's what you are."

"I don't know about that. I'm pretty sure this is what heaven smells like. Is that bacon?"

Alex spun toward the door. Her erstwhile coffeemaker and partner in winging it stood in the doorway in full uniform. But it wasn't a first-thing-in-the-morning crisply pressed uniform. It was . . . well . . . she didn't know quite how to describe it. But there was nothing crisp about it. The stubble on his handsome cheeks was well past five o'clock shadow, too. Unless it was five in the morning shadow when you hadn't been to bed the night before. Which, he clearly hadn't.

"What happened?" she asked. "Are you just now getting home?"

"The town councilmen and mayor are fine. The city

municipal building security has been restored. And the raccoon has been relocated." He looked utterly exhausted.

She tried not to smile, much less snicker. "I'm afraid to ask, but what about the water gun wielder?"

"Successfully disarmed."

"Behind bars?"

"Out on bail."

Alex's mouth dropped open. "You arrested her?"

His eyebrows lifted, even as the rest of him sank against the door frame. "You just asked if she was behind bars."

"I was joking. You said she was a senior citizen. How old is she?"

"It's not about age."

"It was a water gun."

"It was a water *bazooka*. Given the escalation of aggression in a short period of time, we had concerns that it might be a . . . a gateway weapon."

Alex couldn't contain the snicker any longer. "You mean to harder water weapons? Like what, a fire hose?"

"No, to the kind that shoots bullets instead of water." He blew out a long, weary breath. "I'm glad this amuses you, and at some point in the very distant future, we might all have a good laugh over the events of the past eighteen hours. But at the moment, I'm tired, I'm hungry, and a little out of sorts for being put in a position where I had no choice but to arrest a woman old enough to be my grandmother. That's why I'm just getting in. I stayed for her arraignment this morning to be sure she made bail."

She looked at him more closely. "And possibly helped her out a little with that?"

"I can't." He glanced away. "Not directly, anyway."

Something shifted in her chest. Trying to ignore it, Alex slid the skillet with the finished scrambled eggs to a cool burner and turned the hot one off. She moved a few steps away from the hot stove and leaned a hip on the counter, putting her a little closer to Logan. What she wanted to do was fold herself in his arms and hold him up a little. But she didn't know if they were doing that sort of thing. "I'm sorry. I can't even begin to imagine what it's like, doing what you do. And doing it for people you know. I wasn't making fun of the work, just the circumstances, but that's no excuse. Was anyone hurt?"

"I think our collective pride took a pretty good wallop. It's a good bet Teddy and the rest of the council won't be letting us forget that anytime soon. Especially Ted."

Hearing that name brought her thoughts back to the reason she'd stopped by the police station the day before. As a newcomer to town, she hadn't been sure it was the right call to make, and after she'd left the station without discussing it, she'd more or less made up her mind to let the matter drop. But seeing the look on Logan's face when he'd said the man's name—no love lost there—made her reconsider. She'd felt the same way after knowing the man for all of five minutes. "Are you talking about Ted Weathersby? He's like . . . what? The grand pooh-bah of the league of extraordinary town councilmen or whatever it's called, right?"

That got a hint of a smile out of Logan. "I will pay you large sums to never ever let him hear you call him by that name. He would have it printed on shirts that he'd make the entire council wear." Logan's gaze strayed to the counter behind her. "I will pay you even more money if you'll agree to part with even a piece, or ten, of that bacon."

"I made plenty. Eggs, too. And toast. There's juice. I couldn't find your coffee beans." She hadn't meant that last part to sound at all like a pouty accusation, but a hint of it might have been in her tone.

"I don't grind my own coffee."

"You have to. That coffee is too amazing not to be freshly ground. Besides, you told me you made your own."

"Yes, but it comes already ground. I found two flavors I kind of liked and discovered that when I mix them together, they're perfect."

"So, you make your own blend—that amazing, wondrous tasting coffee—by . . . mixing commercially ground coffees?"

He lifted his head from the doorframe at her surprised tone, a smile hovering on his tired face. "I'm pretty sure it's not illegal."

"No, it's not. I just—I've had coffee all over the world, and I'm not saying I'm a coffee snob—"

He smiled. "Oh, you don't have to."

She made a face at him. "I am complimenting you, be nice. I was going to say that your coffee is too incredibly rich and aromatic and full-bodied and perfect to be some off-the-shelf ground stuff you mixed together like a kid mixes box cereals."

"Which is why snobs shouldn't be so . . ."

"Snobby?"

"I was going to say close-minded and overly self-important, but you said it more succinctly."

She bared her teeth in a fake grin. "I also said I made plenty of bacon and eggs, but maybe I misjudged."

His smile grew, even though it wasn't remotely contrite. "Present company excepted."

She realized why she'd missed him so much even though she hadn't known him long enough for it to make any sense. Even exhausted, sleep-deprived, and understandably a bit cranky, he was sharp, willing to engage, and kept up with her pretty effortlessly. He also made her smile. Often. She couldn't begin to explain how something so simple felt so huge without sounding like Overly Clingy Girl, so she kept that part to herself. It made her smile, anyway.

She turned and picked up a large metal serving spoon she'd gotten from the crock full of utensils on the counter to scoop up the scrambled eggs. "Do you want to go take a shower while I put all this together and on the table?"

"Once I go upstairs, I don't plan to come down again until I've slept enough hours to feel human."

He angled off the doorframe and stepped into the kitchen, but she held him at arm's length with the as yet unused metal spoon. "You can use the shower in the hall, then." She smiled. "I fixed it. Sink, too, if you feel like shaving."

He stared at the spoon, then at her as if he couldn't comprehend being told he couldn't come into his own kitchen.

"No offense," she added, "but I just spent the past half hour creating all these delicious aromas you said smelled like heaven, and while, up to this point, I have always found your aroma equally delicious, this morning . . . it's a little . . . well . . . off-putting."

"Oh. Yeah." He stopped. "That's probably the furniture polish. And the oven cleaner. I guess I've gotten used to it."

"Furniture—" She waved the spoon. "I probably don't want to know."

"Smart call. Why don't I go shower."

"Great idea." She beamed. "Thanks for thinking of it."

It was his turn to aim a fake smile her way. To which, she batted her eyelashes and waved her spoon in bye-bye fashion.

She squealed when, like lightning, he snaked out his hand, grabbed the end of the spoon and used it to yank her up against him, then claimed her mouth in a kiss so hot and steamy the spoon clattered to the floor. She wasn't even aware of the smell of oven cleaner until he lifted his head and smiled.

"I'm a sucker for eyelash batting. What can I say? The coffee is in the plastic cocoa container in the cupboard next to the mugs. Keep the bacon warm."

"O . . . kay," she said weakly, sinking against the doorframe space he'd just vacated. *Wow,* she mouthed as she waited for her knees to regain enough strength that she could trust them to support her the few steps it would take to get back to the stove. It was a miracle she'd kept her eyes from rolling back in her head. "And I don't even care if I smell a little like really old lemon Pledge with a side of oddly clean, wild forest creature."

She did go change into a fresh T-shirt, and was just moving the freshly brewed pot full of heavenly smelling coffee to the hand-painted tile trivet on the kitchen table when she heard him come back downstairs. The downstairs bathroom might be functional, but fresh clothes were upstairs.

Clad in old gray sweats and a forest green sweatshirt so faded and worn she had no idea what the decal on the front might have once said, he was still toweling his damp hair when he paused in the open doorway. "One more second."

She heard him in the mudroom-slash-laundry room rustling around, cupboards or drawers opening and shutting; then he was back, sans damp towel, but with towel-tousled damp curls clinging to his forehead and neck, his still unshaven face, and sleepy eyes framed by those ridiculously gorgeous eyelashes, the sum total managing to exude every bit of the gorgeous he'd been born with.

"I wish I could do that," she said as she set plates with napkins and silverware stacked on top at their respective places at the table. "But I've already proven, oh so dismally, that I can't."

"Do what?" He scuffed by her, barefoot and clearly not all that physically refreshed despite the shower. It was still all she could do to keep from leaning in as he passed behind her. He smelled like soap and shampoo and manly man.

"See, that you have to ask is even more annoying."

"Minefield question," he decided as he took his seat and poured his coffee.

She tilted her head, thought about it, then nodded. "Probably."

"Then I pass." He crunched a piece of bacon, groaned in appreciation, and spooned eggs onto his plate. He took a bite of eggs and another bite of bacon, then paused long enough to close his eyes in abject pleasure. "I can almost forgive the past eighteen hours for happening. This is really good."

"Thick cut. And fresh. Blueberry Cove has an actual butcher shop," she marveled.

"Yes, I know. But I've never known Sam's bacon to taste like this."

Eyes still closed, he finished off the bacon strip, enjoying each bite in a way that made her squirm a little in her seat, wishing he was enjoying her like that. Wondering when he would again.

"Well, I might have doctored it up a bit. Sort of like maple cured ham, only with bacon. Your little grocery had those incredibly adorable little handled jugs of maple syrup that came right from trees here in your own county."

He opened his eyes long enough to take another strip of bacon off the plate and pick up his coffee mug. "I know that, too." He took a bite, groaned, then sipped his coffee, eyes shut again. "For a worldly person such as yourself, you seem easily impressed."

"Given the fact that you're making a sex face over a piece of bacon, I think we're even."

He cracked open one eye, but it was the accompanying sleepy grin that made her wriggle a little more in her seat. "What, exactly, comprises a sex face?"

She picked up a piece of bacon, bit into it, and did her best Meg Ryan "I'll have what she's having" *When Harry Met Sally* reenactment. Then, instantly composed, deadpanned, "You know, like that."

"Wow, that good huh?" He took another bite. Sighed a little. "You might have a point."

Alex snickered, making his grin sleepy and sexy. She

picked up her coffee and tried really hard to stop thinking about how wonderful it was going to be when they ended up in his bed again. Or across the kitchen table.

They ate in silence for a few moments, helped themselves to more eggs and bacon. He was on his third piece of toast when he noticed. "Hey. It's not burnt. How did you do that?"

"By replacing the heating element and old frayed cord. God only knows what kind of voltage was going through that thing. I figured since you didn't just replace it that it meant something to you, but it's a miracle the cord didn't catch fire or the whole thing didn't explode."

"I did intend to replace it, but it's been here since before I was born and . . . I never got around to it. I don't eat at home much."

"No," she said with mock surprise.

He sent a sleep-slitted glance her way over his second mug of coffee. "Most mealtime hours I'm in town, so it just makes sense. Plus, cooking for one . . ." He just let that go with a shoulder shrug.

"Speaking of which, there's chili in the fridge and corn-bread in the pan on the counter with the foil wrap on top. Help yourself."

He opened his eyes then, catching her gaze directly as he cradled his heavy mug in his hands. "I should have let you know I wasn't going to make it back last night. I'm sorry. It was—"

"No worries. You don't owe me any explanations."

"You said you were cooking, and—I should have let you know."

She lifted a casual shoulder. See, she could wing it. "So, were the mayor and the council folks trapped there all night?"

"It got a little . . . complicated. But that's mostly on Teddy."

"Weathersby. Yeah. I met him yesterday when I was at city hall."

Logan's gaze sharpened a little. "Did he give you any problems?"

"No, I wouldn't say that."

Logan's gaze narrowed. "What would you say?"

She toyed with her mug, debating on how much of her initial visit to city hall she wanted to relate. Most especially the parts that involved Ted Weathersby. "He was there when I went to get the plans on record for Pelican Point. Before I say anything else, you two aren't close friends or anything, right? Because it's none of my business what's going on between you two."

"We grew up together, played high school football on the same team, but no, no one would characterize us as buddies."

She paused to see if he would elaborate, but when he didn't add anything, she went on. "He just struck me as kind of . . . well . . . he comes across as that guy who is always trying a little too hard." That was putting it kindly. Too kindly. Ted Weathersby was a self-important ass who thought his title came with certain liberties. The kind of liberties that no one was entitled to, no matter who they were. "My grandfather used to use the word *smarmy*. I don't know that I ever really got what that was, but I'm pretty sure Ted's the kind of person he meant. Maybe it's a politician thing. Always on the campaign trail."

"Teddy has been on that campaign trail since birth. And trying too hard is probably as apt description as any." Logan paused and sipped his coffee as if debating on saying anything further, then finally asked, "Did he say anything about the restoration project, or you working for me? Did he get in your way?"

She shook her head. "He was just really interested in why I was there. Very . . . chatty." Actually, he came across like an overly confident, egotistical, narcissistic lounge lizard, but she didn't see any point in going into that much detail. "He made it seem as if he was pretty tight with the chief of police and was quite happy to see you were finally making some headway out on your 'historic property' as he called it."

"He's been pushing to get Pelican Point tied in to the tricentennial celebration. Not so much for the town's sake, but because it would make him look good to claim responsibility for it when he campaigns for reelection next year."

"Then let him come up with the money for it," she retorted, liking the guy even less.

"We've had that discussion, trust me."

"So, I'm guessing my taking that stand at The Rusty Puffin didn't help you out much. Was he there that night? I didn't stay to talk with anyone other than Fergus for a brief moment."

Logan nodded.

"I'm sorry."

"Nothing to be sorry about. The thing with Teddy is, he's always seen himself in direct competition with me. For anything. Mostly it was sports when we were in school, but he could turn anything into a sport. And he keeps score. For life."

"Sounds incredibly annoying."

"Can be, but it's a known quantity, so you just learn to deal with it."

"He said your family was a cornerstone of Blueberry, back to its inception." She smiled. "Is this one of those Hatfield-McCoy things with your two families?"

"No. Weathersby is third generation, so his family has been here a while, but they're not historic in the way he's talking about."

"Maybe that's what sticks in his craw."

Logan shrugged. "Maybe, but we can hardly change the

choices our ancestors made as to where to live and build their lives. I can say that I know he places great value on holding a position of prominence in town, and that being in a position of power is central to his identity."

"Is Blueberry Cove bigger than I thought? How much power does he have? Is his extended family political?"

"No. And the Cove is exactly what it appears to be. A small town with very deep roots in the state's history. But that can be said of a lot of little towns dotting our coastline. Ted is nothing if not proud to be a big fish in our very small pond. He's made it clear he wants the mayor's job and that he has designs on state politics and more."

"Will he make it, do you think?"

"I don't know. I do know that when I am involved in police business on a county or state level, his name has come up. Not always in a good way, but I'm not sure if that's a good or bad thing in politics. So . . . who knows? His wife is very determined to help him get there, and if anyone can make that happen, it's Cami Weathersby."

"He's married?" Alex snorted in disgust.

Logan had been about to take a sip of coffee, but paused. "Why is that a surprise?"

It surprised Alex how quickly his attention went from being halfway to Mr. Sandman to alert and intently focused. "What? Oh, nothing. Weathersby was just . . . really friendly, if you know what I mean." She shrugged it off, just as she had done the day before. Right after wishing she could take a quick shower to get the slime off her skin. "It goes hand in hand with the smarmy personality, I guess. Maybe he sees it as friendly small-town charm. Who knows?"

"How did you see it?"

She studied Logan, then figured she'd gone that far, so what the hell. "As some guy trying to use his position to impress me so I'd be flattered by his attention. It didn't and I wasn't. But I guess his intent came across enough that I'm surprised to hear he's a married man. Or, more to the point, that he'd so openly flirt with someone right in the middle of city hall."

"I'm sorry you had to deal with that. With him."

She gave Logan an amused look. "I'm going to have to continue to do so if I want to get this project underway, so it is what it is. I've worked in a male-dominated field my whole life, with men who have the kind of off-the-charts testosterone levels it takes to do what they do and who think nothing of wielding their masculinity like the proverbial Neanderthal club they think it is. Trust me, Ted Weathersby was not a problem in that regard. It was more . . . uncomfortable . . . because I am new to town, He is in a place of power here, and I didn't want to inadvertently step in the middle of something I didn't understand. Or piss off anyone who would then complicate my job. So I just sort of . . . skirted around it. And him."

Logan drained his coffee, then set his mug down. "He lays so much as a hand on you, you have my permission to handle him the same way you'd handle any of those other Neanderthals you worked with."

She smiled, amused at the edge to his tone. Amused and, if she were being honest, turned on a little. Maybe more than a little. "What makes you think I didn't welcome those other Neanderthals' moves?"

He arched a brow. "Really?"

"Well, I could point out that you picking me up and tossing me on your bed yesterday didn't exactly seem to turn me off."

He closed his eyes. "I walked right into that minefield, didn't I? I'm too tired for lose-lose debates." He opened his eyes, though, and she was surprised at their intensity. "So I'll just say this. If you don't want Ted Weathersby breathing all over you, or if he ever does anything that makes you feel even slightly uncomfortable, you have the permission of the chief of police and the owner of Pelican Point to handle him however you see fit."

"Thank you," she said, meaning it. "Not so much for the permission, but for trusting that I could take care of myself."

Logan pushed his chair back and stood, stacking his dirty dishes and mug so he could carry them to the sink. "What I didn't say was that if I ever see him making you even remotely uncomfortable, I also have permission to handle him however *I* see fit."

Her eyes widened a bit, and she tried not to wriggle in her seat. "Most of the time that Neanderthal attitude is not effective."

He paused in his stacking. "Most of the time," he repeated.

"Most. But I think I just realized that it's not so much that the caveman club is being wielded"—she smiled up at him—"but more a matter of which caveman is wielding the club."

Rather than look annoyed, he surprised her by chuckling. "You're the damndest woman I ever met."

She stacked her dishes and stood as well. "Yeah, but in a good cavewoman or bad cavewoman kind of way?"

He took both stacks of dishes and put them right back on the table, then stepped around it with that surprising grace and speed of his, and, before she could react, much less guess his intent, he'd hoisted her up and over his shoulder. "In a 'I'm discovering I really like a good bad cavewoman' kind of way."

After her shriek of surprise at his little maneuver, she was too busy laughing to do more than thrash her legs and beat ineffectively on his broad, caveman-like back as he carried her out of the kitchen and headed toward the stairs.

"You're exhausted," she told him. "You need to sleep."

"I seem to have gotten my second wind." To prove it, he

took the stairs two at a time, wrapping strong arms around her legs and waist to keep her from bouncing.

He climbed on the bed as he slid her off his shoulder so she landed flat in the middle of it. He followed her right down.

Since it was exactly where she wanted to be at that moment, she didn't waste time pretending otherwise. She slipped her arms over his shoulders, around his neck, and pulled his mouth closer to hers. "You know, every time we end up here, the longer it's going to take for me to finish that report."

"Oh darn."

"Yesterday you couldn't wait to get rid of me."

"Yesterday, I think we've established, I was an idiot. Or I started the day as one. I'd like to think I've redeemed myself somewhat since then."

He closed the distance between his lips and hers, but just as she was relaxing in anticipation of what she knew was about to come—namely her—he paused and lifted his head. Then he surprised her further by pushing the hair from her face and looking quite intently into her eyes.

"It just occurred to me. When you came by the station yesterday, was that right after you were at city hall?"

"Yes, but—"

He brushed his thumb over her lips, which made her hips arch, but did stop her from continuing to talk. "Did he really make you that uncomfortable? I'm not doubting you could take care of yourself, but it's my job to make sure people can conduct business wherever they see fit and not be made to feel . . . infringed upon in any way." He pressed his thumb down gently when she would have responded. "Let me finish. I wasn't really completely forthcoming when I said that Teddy makes a competition out of things between us. Usually it's town business . . . because I don't give him any other avenues to try and beat me."

Her eyes widened. She pressed a kiss to his thumb, then shifted her head so she could speak. "Are you saying that if he knows we're . . . that he'll come on to me as some kind of twisted game of—he's married!"

"Yes, well, both Weathersbys are a bit . . . challenged . . . when it comes to being faithful to their vows."

She was pretty sure her eyebrows couldn't climb any higher. "This is common knowledge? Well, that explains a lot about him being so bold yesterday, but—wow. How does he expect to get anywhere in politics if—wait. Never mind. Gah. I guess if you're open about it, it can't be considered a black mark. Especially if wifey is on board with the whole thing." Her mouth dropped open. "Do you know wifey? I mean, of course you do, but do you . . . you know . . . *know* her?"

"If you're asking if I ever slept with Cami Weathersby—"

"I didn't mean while she was married. I honestly didn't— you don't strike me as—I never thought—"

He stopped her with a kiss that was carnal and claiming.

She was pretty sure he didn't know any other way, but there was something else there. Something that was just . . . honest and sincere and well . . . theirs.

"No," he said, when he lifted his head, leaving her breathless all over again. "I haven't. Before or during." His smile was slow and sexy, more so because he was clearly tired and tousled. "And thanks for the vote of confidence. You'd be right, by the way. There's a lot more to that story."

He leaned in and nipped her bottom lip, making her gasp and wriggle under him. "Since you're going to be here for a while, and I'm hoping that's here in Blueberry and here"— he moved his hips on hers—"as well, you should probably know the history." He found her hands, wove his fingers through hers, then slid their joined hands up over her head, stretching her taut beneath him, and taking full advantage of that position by nuzzling her head to the side so he had access to the sensitive skin along the side of her neck. "But I really don't want to talk about it right now."

"Mmm," she hummed. "Talk about what?" she asked, all innocent. She smiled as he nipped her earlobe and gasped in surprised pleasure when he rubbed his thumbs over the racing pulse point on her wrists.

"Exactly." He left her hands resting over her head, and slid his warm, broad palms down her arms and along the sides of her torso, slowing long enough so that his thumbs took their sweet time rubbing over her tight nipples. She was still groaning and writhing as he stripped her naked and got himself the same way.

He was doing the most incredible things to a spot just above the inside of her ankle while his hands—his oh-so-clever hands—traveled back up her legs.

As she pressed her head back into the mattress and arched her hips up to meet his questing fingers, her last thought before her eyes rolled back in her head was *so, maybe this whole winging it thing might work out, after all.*

Chapter 10

Logan closed his office door behind him and paused by Barb's desk on his way to the station door. "Dan just radioed that he's on his way in, so I'm going to head on out."

Sergeant Benson's smile was approving . . . and a bit too twinkly. "That makes a full week now that you've gotten out of here at a decent hour. Nice to see you're finally getting a little balance. Sir," she added when she caught his very direct gaze.

"I told you. Alex has scheduled meetings with the first round of subcontractors all this week. So I need to get out here before it gets dark."

"She moves fast. I'm glad you're helping her with that." Barb's expression remained the picture of innocence, but that twinkle in her eyes said otherwise.

Logan refused to bite. It was the only way he stood a chance. "She has a good way to go on the final report, but we're in agreement on some of the basic needs on the exterior. She has received the results of the tests she had run, so I want to get going on them before we get any further into the winter season. By the time the weather really turns, I'll know where I want to start on the interior."

"Sounds like you two have found a pretty good rhythm." She kept her smile steady. "Working together."

Logan knew he was up against a pro, so there was no

point in trying to glare her twinkle into submission. "We've got two appointments this evening, and the same tomorrow and Thursday. I want to be there to make sure we hire not only who's best suited, but, in some cases, who I know needs the work."

"I think that's great. I know folks here are grateful for the work and you for looking out for their best interests. They tell me so all the time."

"Nice to hear. Thanks." He popped his hat on his head and zipped up his coat. "Any emergencies, you know where to find me."

"Actually, sir."

Logan ducked his chin, bit back a sigh, then turned back to face her. "Yes?"

"It's Ted Weathersby."

"Isn't it always?"

She didn't bite, either. She also knew better. "Yes, sir. He's left three messages today asking me to remind you of the council meeting this evening."

"I'm well aware. He's been informed I won't be attending. There isn't any business on the docket that requires my input."

"Not as police chief, but he's going to talk about the Pelican Point restoration project. I know he's asked Alex to be there, too."

Logan's gaze narrowed. "You know this because?"

"Because he made it a point to tell me he'd talked to her. Now, don't go getting all bunched up over it," she told him. "From what I've seen, Alex has absolutely no problem keeping him in check. In fact, if I knew her better, I'd swear she actually enjoys it."

"How so?"

"She just doesn't take any of his nonsense. You know how he is. She's all smiles and polite as she can be, but he doesn't gain so much as an inch with her." Barb grinned.

"Between you and me, it's hard not to like that. Most folks feel pretty much the same about her, from what I've heard."

"Most folks?"

"Well, you know how Cami Weathersby and her klatch can be. But generally, from what I hear, Alex is pretty well liked." Barb reshuffled and restacked the folders on her desk. "I'm not saying it has anything to do with the way she stood up to you back when she first arrived in town, but then again, I'm not saying it didn't."

Logan also knew to sidestep a potential minefield altogether whenever possible. "If she has people's respect, it's because she deserves it. How do you know how she's handling Weathersby? Or that she's had to at all?"

"Well, I ran into her at Hartley's the other day. She was chatting up Owen, asking him stories about the house and the tower. You know how much he loves our town history. They were bonding over kerosene lamp generators and something about iron lanterns or some such. I gather they were talking about the lighthouse. Anyway, I was over on the feed store side picking up that newfangled kind of kitty litter he got in. Looks like little blue and tan beads or something. I was skeptical, but do you know that stuff is downright amazing? I mean, you just dump it out and it takes care of its own—"

"I'm sure it does. Weathersby?"

"Right. Well, he came in while Owen was ringing me up and Alex was right there, still chatting, and you know Ted, never saw a conversation he couldn't make all about himself. He started going on about how glad he was to see you were finally taking all of his advice on the restoration project and how Alex should consult with him on the work she plans to hire out as he knows everybody who is anybody. Insinuated he might even call in some special favors, help her out, if she was, you know, nudge-nudge, interested. You know how he is."

Logan felt the muscles in his cheeks flex. "I do, indeed."

Barb kept her tone light and gossipy, but Logan didn't miss the way her gaze latched right on to his, alert to so much as a flicker in his expression. To look at her, it would be quite easy to believe she was just a guileless grandmother of six, unless you knew she'd also been a police officer for more than half her life—which translated to almost all of everyone else's life—meaning she likely knew more about every last person in town than even their closest kinfolk did.

"Alex wasn't having any of that," Barb went on. "Smiled, pretty as you please, and put him in his place in a way that made him not quite sure he'd heard her just right. She'd said her good-byes and was pulling out of the side lot before Ted realized he'd just been set down by a pro. You know what I mean?"

Logan had expected to be pissed off by wherever the story was headed. Instead, he found a smile kicking at the corners of his mouth. "Yes, I believe I do."

"She's something. A fresh breath, that's for sure." Barb's smile was well on the knowing side even when he finally narrowed his brows. "Not that we needed one. Sir."

He didn't miss the smile that hovered as she went back to stacking files.

And she didn't try to hide it. "Did you ever get hold of Kerry?"

"Two voice mails and a text message saying she'd call later this week. We keep missing each other. I think she must be guiding a trip or something. Have you heard anything? I haven't had the chance to call Fi, but—"

"Fiona hasn't talked to Kerry, either, but said if she got through before you did, she'd call."

"Good. Keep me in the loop, okay?"

"I always do." Barb's smile was affectionate when she added, "Sir."

His smile softened then, too. Their partnership was long and enduring, but while he had to be on his toes pretty much every second or she would run more roughshod over him and the rest of the station than she already did, he honestly didn't know what he'd do without her. Professionally or personally.

"Okay, I'm out of here. Who's on the desk tonight? Is Velma back?"

"No, she's still down in Philly. I set up a rotation to cover for her. She'll be back next week." Barb smiled. "New grandbaby. You can't blame her for taking a little sick leave along with her paid leave."

"No, you can't. I can't recall when she's ever taken a sick day. Put the paperwork on my desk." Velma Simon had been on the night desk for eighteen years, still a rookie compared to Barb. She'd been around longer than Logan had been on the force, and he had great respect for her abilities and work ethic. "I'll sign off on it."

"I thought you'd say that." Barb beamed and picked up the folder on the top of the pile on her desk. "Already taken care of, sir."

Logan smiled as he gave a slight shake with his head. "Thanks. Tell Dan when he gets in to check with Owen about that problem he had last week with the back entrance to his store. Someone definitely tried to jimmy the lock. He replaced it, but he's talking about putting up a camera or some such. Motion detector. I don't know. Apparently Dan's uncle is in the home security business in Bangor. Maybe he can give him some basic ideas that won't cost too much."

"Good. Great. I know Owen will feel better if he does something. You know he's been kinda jumpy as, well, as a raccoon on Mrs. Darby's porch, ever since Lauren went off to college in the fall."

Logan gave her a mild look at the Darby reference, but she didn't so much as blink.

"He worries about her being so far away, such a big campus, big city. Between you and me," Barb added, "I don't think he has the first idea what to do with that empty nest of his. I think that's why he spends all his time at the store these days."

"I'm not sure I'd be any better at handling either one. I remember how it felt when I got back from college and Fi left for school, then Kerry took off for parts south and west. And I was just the older brother. Owen raised Lauren by himself, so it's a pretty big transition." Logan made a mental note to stop by and see Owen. Barb's previous comments had reminded him what a lighthouse buff Owen was, so maybe getting him out to the Point when they finally went inside the tower would be something of a much needed distraction for him.

"He mentioned that Lauren wasn't coming home for Thanksgiving next week, staying to study for midterms or some such, he said. I know he was pretty disappointed about that. But I heard she'll be back in a few weeks for winter break, so that'll cheer him up some."

Logan smiled. "Good. That's good. I'd better get on the road."

"Have you made plans yet?"

"Plans?"

Barb sighed. "Thanksgiving. Just a little more than a week away? Are the girls coming home?"

"Well, I'm guessing no for Kerry, and Fi said she's got a new client who's pretty demanding, but will be great for word of mouth, so she's out. Hannah . . . I hope she comes up, but it sounded doubtful in her last e-mail. Some case she was trying that looks like it's going to run through the holidays. She said she'd let me know."

"You cooking?"

He smiled. "You kidding?"

She laughed. "I hear Alex knows her way around a stove.

Delia said Alex gave her an idea on how to do something different with her meatballs. Maybe you two could sweet-talk her into keeping you from eating frozen dinners and watching football at the Puffin like you did last year. And the one before that, if I recall correctly. Pitiful, if you ask me, especially when anybody in town would be happy to have you at their table. Shouldn't spend Thanksgiving alone."

"I didn't. I was with family. Was a nice day off, is how I remember it." He lifted both hands in surrender when she fixed him with a stare. "But I'll take it into consideration. Maybe we'll see if Owen wants to join us."

"Well, now isn't that just the nicest idea." Her expression softened instantly into one of pride and appreciation.

Deciding to cut out while he was ahead, Logan nodded. "See you tomorrow."

But he had only made it two steps when the station door opened and in sailed Cami Weathersby. Petite, blond, always dressed smartly, with hair done and makeup applied so masterfully, he'd always thought she could easily be the stand-in at a wax museum and no one would ever tell the difference.

"Chief McCrae, I need a minute of your time." She wasn't asking. Camille Winstock Weathersby never asked. She informed . . . for as far back as he could remember. And they went as far back as two people could go. They'd shared the same nursery school teacher.

Logan swallowed the urge to use very unprofessional language and merely gestured to his office. She stalked past him—Cami was a champion stalker, something to do with the fact that she always had heels on, probably even back in nursery school—and breezed right into his office as if she owned it. In Cami's mind, that applied to pretty much any-place she chose to inhabit. Of course, given how much of the town her family owned, more times than not, she probably did.

Logan shared a look with his desk sergeant, who rolled her eyes as if to say, *That one. What are you going to do?*

But Logan knew the one person who was well aware of Cami's dual nature when it came to him was also the very same one seated outside his office door. And he was ever so grateful for it.

"Thirty seconds?" Barb asked, meaning how long was she to wait before buzzing him with an "emergency."

"No need." He'd had enough of both Weathersbys. Cami had picked the wrong day to play whatever her new game was going to be about.

He entered the room, left the door open, and walked around to his side of the desk. He didn't sit. "I was just heading out. What can I do for you?"

"It's about this restoration business," she said, the words clipped, clear disapproval in her tone—which was exactly how she played it anytime there were other ears listening in.

He watched her debate on whether or not he'd let her get away with closing the door, but apparently one look at his expression had her opting to leave it open. Smart choice. But then, Cami was many things, but stupid wasn't one of them.

Designer purse dangling from one arm, she clasped her hands in front of her in a deceptively polite demeanor, keeping her shoulders squared, chin level as she spoke. But with her back to Barb, she let her gaze wander up and down his body like a jungle cat looking for its next meal.

When Logan had first come home from college and joined the Cove's police force, she'd already been engaged to Teddy. She had taken great pains to make it clear to any and everyone in town that she held Logan responsible for the death of her best friend and future maid of honor, Jessica. She'd also made it clear to him in private that she'd be quite willing to listen if he was of a mind to persuade her to forgive him. If it involved maybe ripping her sensible lit-tle dress off of her body, all the better.

Her aggressive and confusing game used to disconcert and unsettle him, not to mention piss him off. But he'd always known, at core, the player was a viper. He'd also known better than to confront her. The Winstocks had been wheeling and dealing in the Cove forever, not as long as the McCraes or the Monaghans, but far longer than Weathersby's kin and most everyone else's. They'd made their fortune early, invested it wisely; in addition to owning their fair share of the Cove, they had been one of its wealthier and therefore more politically influential families for more generations than most could recall.

Hence Teddy's early determination to hook his claws into the current generation's available Winstock heir. Logan hadn't quite understood what she saw in Teddy, but maybe she'd realized early on that his political aspirations combined with her money could eventually propel her beyond being big fish in the Cove pond to a state level lake or even a vast national ocean. It had never once occurred to him that she and Teddy actually loved each other.

In all the years that had passed since, his opinion re-mained unchanged.

Keeping his gaze on hers, Logan made it clear he was not only unmoved by her little display, but bored by it as well. "I'm not sure what the restoration has to do with my being police chief, but as this isn't police business, you'll have to excuse me."

Cami quickly recalibrated and stepped right up to the opposite side of his desk. "It's not news how I feel about you personally, Logan McCrae, given my loyalty to my dear late friend, but I can certainly keep my professional inter-ests separate from my personal ones. You know I always put the needs of our good townsfolk before my own."

That wasn't just a minefield, it was the equivalent of stepping on a nuclear bomb. But he wasn't stupid, either. "If there's a point to this, I have an appointment to make, so please feel free to skip straight to it."

Her perfectly plucked and penciled eyebrows lifted, or as much as they were able to anyway. He thought he'd been calm and polite, almost ruthlessly so, as he always was with her, but perhaps, given the personal nature of her husband's antics this past week where Alex was concerned, he'd allowed a bit of an uncustomary edge to creep into his tone. He'd learned the best way to disarm the ticking time bomb that was always Cami's latest mission was to refuse to acknowledge there was a bomb in the first place. Annoyed her no end.

It also, apparently, turned her on, which was an unfortunate side effect. Unsurprisingly, she recovered quickly. "My point is, you know the town council is pleased that you're finally moving forward on their recommendations, and we'd like to discuss—"

"I'm moving forward for the sake of the property," he said before she got any further. "If that pleases the council, it's a happy coincidence, and I'm glad." He leaned his palms on the desk. She'd made an uncharacteristic mistake thinking she could trump him on his turf. "However, how I choose to go about working on my property, including who I choose to do that work, will be exclusively my decision. It's not up for council discussion. Nor is the time frame in which the work will be completed, or which part of the property will be restored first, second, or last. Nor will your husband or anyone else on the council be claiming any sort of responsibility for the restoration taking place as some sort of campaign asset. I already made this very clear to Teddy, so there was no need for him to send you with a personal message."

Fire lit her dark brown eyes, but not in a way anyone would describe as warmly. "I am not my husband's errand girl. As usual, you're so caught up in your personal issues with me, you're blinded to the bigger picture—which is that this town wants to help you."

"The council's help comes with strings attached. No, thank you. Now, if you'll excuse me." He gestured to the door. "I believe you can see yourself out."

"I'm not sure what you think I've ever done to you to warrant such rudeness. Although I'm sure I make you uncomfortable as a constant reminder that you're walking around a free man, while our poor Jessica never had the chance to see her graduation, her wedding day, her—"

"Enough, Camille." His sharp tone surprised a moment of silence out of her. He never reacted to her very calculated digs, and he knew he needed to rein it in, but dammit, he'd had just about enough. "I have no personal problem with you. I have no personal issues with the council. I've made that clear to you, and to Ted. I believe Alex has made that clear to him as well." At the mention of Alex's name, he caught an uncustomary flicker in her expression. *Ah.* Now he understood. Ted was making a spectacle of himself with Alex and Cami was annoyed. So this little visit was to give herself a chance to even some kind of private score.

"Word is Alex MacFarland is doing a lot more than restoring your falling-down relic of a house."

It wasn't often Cami made any miscalculated moves, much less two in one visit. Because when he grinned in the face of her tactless insinuation, she was clearly caught off guard. "Frankly, Camille, I don't care what the word is. Now, if you don't mind." Logan nodded toward the open doorway.

Clearly livid, but smart enough to know when to cut her losses, she turned to leave, then paused at the door and looked over her shoulder. He absently wondered if she practiced that move in the mirror at home.

Eyes steady, expression smooth and flawless once again,

she gave him a smile of her own. "Well, perhaps you would care more if you knew that she's been spending every spare moment—and possibly a few more that she should be spending doing her job for you—with Brodie Monaghan. He won't shut up about her. I'd say he's completely smitten. I do know tongues are starting to wag."

Logan had no idea what he'd expected her to say, but that wasn't it. While the insinuation didn't affect him any more than her first one had, she must have seen something flicker in his expression. And that's all it took.

Her smile spread, as much as it was able to, anyway, revealing a row of perfectly matched and blindingly white teeth. "She's flaunting her connection to the police chief all over town, trying to score favors so she can lowball this proposal she's putting together, so you'll give her a contract. All the same while, she's taking care of her personal interests behind your back, but right under the noses of everyone else. Quite the piece of work you're harboring under your roof." Cami slipped her purse farther up her sleeve. "I'd watch your back if I were you, Chief McCrae. You're making a fool out of yourself, and, because of your position, the town as well. Maybe people will finally see what I've known all along—that they should have never trusted you with this job in the first place."

And then she was gone, leaving a chill in the room and the faint scent of Chanel in her wake.

Logan waited until she'd exited the building, then tucked his hat back under his arm and left his office, closing the door behind him.

"Sir, she's just—"

"Sergeant, I'm very well aware of exactly what she's just."

"A woman scorned will say whatever she can to draw blood."

"She's not scorned, I never—"

"She's perpetually scorned where you're concerned. And thank goodness for it. Sir," Barb added, when he merely continued to stare at her. "Only now she's got a new target to aim for. If she thinks for a second it's made you vulnerable in some way—"

"I don't pay attention to her nonsense, you know that. I haven't before, and I certainly won't now."

"Yes, sir. But what I meant was, if she thinks she's found a chink in the armor, she'll exploit that chink directly, if you know what I mean. While Alex has handled Ted with admirable efficiency, we both know Camille is a Winstock and plays on an entirely different level." Barb held up her hand briefly to stall Logan's reply. "All I'm saying is, you need to give Alex a heads-up. Explain the town dynamic so at least she has some sense of what's going on around her." Barb folded her arms on her desk. "And fair warning on what might be coming straight at her."

The sun was just beginning to dip over the trees behind the Point as he pulled in his driveway. Alex's old truck was there, as were three other pickups. Two had company names on the side that he recognized as the subcontractors he was supposed to be meeting with. The other truck, if he wasn't mistaken, was Brodie's.

Wonderful.

Shutting out a replay of Cami's snide little scene in his office didn't keep him from wondering what the hell Brodie was doing out on the Point. Logan climbed out of his SUV, and since he was already late, didn't bother going inside and changing out of his uniform. He trekked around to the north side of the house, where they were supposed to be meeting to discuss the roof and the windows and do some preliminary talks about the cottage. If he'd been much later, the twilight would have deepened to the point that getting anything productive done would have been impossible.

He found himself pausing as he rounded the back corner of the house and spotted Alex standing out in the middle of the open grassy area, ever-present clipboard propped against her stomach, while she watched—his gaze scanned away from her to the house—two men clomp around on his roof. Another was out by the cottage on his hands and knees, looking at something along the back wall. He recognized all three men. None of them was Brodie Monaghan. Maybe he'd been wrong about the truck and Cami had gotten under his skin more than he wanted to admit.

His gaze shifted back to Alex. She was wearing green fatigues tucked into black work boots, a thick dark blue hoodie, and her heavy canvas coat over it all. She also had what looked like one of his knit caps pulled down over her ears. There was nothing even remotely alluring about her getup, and yet, she had his full and complete attention. Watching her in her element—taking copious notes while she shouted back and forth with Wade up there on the roof, smiling, laughing, but keeping things on point— grabbed at parts of him that had nothing to do with regular sex and a whole lot more to do with a very different set of needs he'd avoided thinking about for a very long time.

She'd only been in the Cove and under his roof for a little over a week, but the change in her was remarkable. It wasn't that the shadows and the remnants of grief weren't still there, but it was easier to see past them when she smiled. He could almost see her brain working a hundred miles a minute on whatever restoration issue was on her mind at any given moment, just like it was now.

She hadn't been kidding about being very good at what she did. In fact, the amount of information she'd put together had blown his mind—the breadth and depth of her knowledge on how best to approach the repairs, in what order, and in a manner that was not only fiscally responsible for him and the trust, but also with an eye toward layering the repairs in a way that would allow any number of new technologies to be applied. All of it would reduce the need for constant maintenance and upkeep while preserving and respecting the origins of the property as much as possible.

He owed Fergus a call and another apology. He'd been so caught up in creating a stable day-to-day existence for himself, he had truly let the family down, current and past. And he was beginning to realize how much he'd been letting himself down. He should have been exploring options and staying on top of things far more than he had—with regards to the property and himself. Steady and stable were good things to strive for, but he was beginning to realize that in his attempt to minimize risk so his personal life wouldn't be turned upside down again, he'd also removed any chance for his life to be turned upside down by something good.

Eula had told him to be open to personal change and he'd more or less smirked at the idea, thinking he was as open as the next guy. And yet, in one week's time, he'd come to realize just how entrenched and closed off he'd let himself become. The question was . . . what was he going to do about it?

The answer to that had been one he'd been grappling with all week.

It was one thing to acknowledge there was a problem— one he sincerely wanted to tackle—and another thing entirely to actually take the steps required to make some changes.

Wade's shout interrupted his thoughts and he looked back up to the roof. "Whole thing's gonna have to come off down to the frame, if you want the truth of it."

Wade's brother Scotty came across the roof from the other side. "Miracle one of us didn't go right through. Did you check for water leaks? Is there attic space?"

"I'm still working on that," Alex called up to him.

"We've got water damage in all of the exterior walls, but nothing coming in through the ceilings in the upper level rooms. There's a crawl space attic on the back side of the main house. I've been up there, but I haven't gotten any indication there's been water or anything else coming in through the roof directly. I think Logan's been really lucky in that regard. Mostly, the leaking seems to be under the eaves and around all of the windows. And there's a definite issue with the pipes."

Before Logan could assimilate the idea that he was going to have to replace more than just the shakes on the roof and that this fell into the *lucky* category, Hank had clambered to his feet and was calling Alex over to look at something along the foundation wall next to the side door of the cottage. Logan couldn't hear all of what Hank was telling her, but from the sudden sag to her shoulders and then the rapid scratching of pencil to paper, he assumed that whatever it was, the word *lucky* wasn't part of that particular assessment.

Realizing he'd been standing in the gathering shadows at the corner of the house for the better part of the last five minutes watching Alex work, he figured it was time to join the conversation directly.

Another voice chimed in before he'd taken a single step. "Have you been up in the tower yet? It's quite the proud sentinel, isn't it then?" The musical sound of his lively brogue was joined a second later by the man himself as Brodie Monaghan came around the far side of the lighthouse and crossed the grass toward Alex. "We had a lighthouse out on Dunagree Point near where I grew up in County Donegal. Never been up in one, though. Is she still seaworthy? Can we take a look?"

Logan stepped from the shadows then, fingers clenched, his protective instincts a bit more evolved than he'd realized until that moment. He told himself it was simply a by-product of wanting to protect Alex from anything that would trigger those harsh images and memories. But looking at Brodie smiling, all engaging and charming, and Alex standing there, seemingly relaxed despite the abrupt shift in subject matter, he wasn't so sure there weren't a few other emotions at play. Ones that weren't all so altruistic in nature.

Damn Cami and her insidious gossip. Logan would have never gone there if it hadn't been for her planting the seeds. Why the hell was he letting it bother him? He had no claim on Alex. Not really. They'd had sex a few times and had agreed they'd keep that exclusive to each other while it lasted. But it would certainly be easy for her to end that agreement as swiftly and easily as she'd entered into it in the first place. Maybe her short time in Blueberry had been more restorative than he realized. Maybe she wanted to embrace a broader scope of things in her newfound life. And maybe that scope included Brodie Monaghan.

"And maybe you're an even bigger idiot than you thought," he muttered, and walked across the yard.

Chapter 11

"Not yet," Alex told Brodie. "It's not a priority at the moment." She congratulated herself for maintaining a steady hand on the clipboard, a steady note to her voice. Admittedly, it was a bit easier to do with Brodie's megawatt smile and dancing green eyes providing a distraction from the tower looming behind him. But she could feel it standing watch over her—as she had every single minute she'd been out there. Mostly it felt good, comforting . . . as long as she didn't think about going up inside it.

"I imagine watching the sunrise from the top is quite a spectacle."

"It is."

Alex's gaze jerked to her right. She hadn't seen Logan approaching.

"Sorry," he said to her. "I got held up at the last second."

"Not to worry," Brodie told him, giving Logan a hearty, open-palmed slap on his shoulder. "From the looks of it, she's got things well in hand."

Logan's gaze shifted to hers. "So I see."

Alex wasn't sure what was going on behind Logan's enigmatic gaze, and she wasn't quite certain she wanted to. She was pretty sure it might piss her off.

"Wade and Scotty have done the assessment on the roof," she said, shifting the clipboard so he could see her notes.

"It's pretty much what I thought, but thankfully, not worse. So there's that." She nodded toward the side of the cottage. "Hank's looking at the foundation and the exterior. He's done some restoration work locally and knows his stuff. The good news is, despite the sinkage and resulting pitch issues, it's salvageable and the frame is sturdy." She flipped up several pages on the clipboard and tapped on a drawing she'd made earlier. "The bad news is that everything else is pretty much . . . questionable."

Logan lifted his gaze from the drawing and met hers. "Questionable," he repeated. "Meaning what, exactly?"

"We won't know for sure until we look inside, but saving any part of it means a total renovation. Stripping it down to that sturdy frame and slanted foundation and rebuilding from scratch. I can get a second opinion, but—"

"What's your opinion?" he asked.

"That Hank's right, and your money would be better spent following up on his initial assessment than paying for another one."

"Then go with that." Logan glanced away from her and looked at Brodie, who was standing at Alex's other elbow. "What brings you out to the Point? Your expertise is boats, right?"

"That it is, Chief." Brodie's grin was easy and open— which meant either he was oblivious to the tension Alex could feel all but choking the air between the three of them, or was doing a damn fine job of not letting it show.

She wished she could say the same, and tried not to fidget.

"I'm not here in a professional capacity. I came out to give Alexandra a lift back into town. We've our own business to discuss and I thought it would be nice to do so over dinner." His grin was guileless, but Alex realized there was indeed more going on when he added, "Give her a break from doin' all the cooking. All work, no play, our Alex. Of course, I've always said the best work is both."

Alex thought about exactly what kind of play she'd been up to with the man she was ostensibly working for and felt the flush begin at the base of her neck and start a slow but steady crawl northward to her cheeks.

Unsure of exactly how she'd come to be the center of what felt like a very awkward and quickly escalating situation, she took a step back and hugged the clipboard to her chest like a shield. Favoring both men with a cool smile, she said, "I need to go talk to Hank, set up a meeting with him and Owen to nail down some quotes." She looked at Brodie. "I have the quote and schedule already done for you. It's out in my truck. I appreciate the offer of dinner, and I'm sorry you came all the way out here, but Logan and I have several hours of work ahead of us tonight and a lot to go over and decide on before our next round of appointments tomorrow, so that's not going to be possible. But I appreciate the gesture."

"Some other time then," Brodie said, his smile steady as ever as he took her refusal in stride. "I'll meet you out by your truck."

"Give me ten minutes." She turned to Logan. "Did you have any particular questions for Hank?"

"Not until we go over things. I'll go talk to Wade and Scotty. I think they're off the roof now."

"Good, thanks." She gave both men a polite nod. "If you'll excuse me."

It took significant will not to look over her shoulder as she went around the corner of the cottage Hank had disappeared around moments before, probably continuing his assessment. *What the hell had that been all about?* She wasn't blind or dumb—she realized Brodie had been making a play. He'd been making a play since the moment she'd first met him. But she was pretty sure he was simply wired that way. He seemed like the easy-come-easy-go type, so she doubted her refusal of his dinner offer would set him back. In fact, she wouldn't be surprised if he had a dinner replacement lined up before he got back to Blueberry.

What was more disconcerting to her was that, even with Brodie's surprise appearance and his always sunny, flattering, overt flirtation, her thoughts had never strayed far from the man in uniform she'd just left standing on his side lawn.

After the initial and quite tempestuous first few days spent in each other's company, the opportunity for more frolicking hadn't occurred. The first day—and night—or two, she'd figured Logan's long hours away from the house had been work related. But two nights had become four, then six. Added to that was the fact that no matter what time she'd woken up, coffee had been brewed and waiting for her in the kitchen . . . and his truck had already been gone from the driveway.

Most nights he'd come home at what seemed like a normal time, changed clothes, then headed out to work on the stacked stone wall until dark. If she happened to be somewhere in the house or outside where their paths would cross, he'd say hello, ask how things were going, if she needed anything, then would go on with what he was doing.

His version of winging it, she gathered.

She'd put something together for dinner, for which he'd thank her whenever he wandered back in. Then he'd fixed a plate and disappeared into his study with nothing more than an absently delivered, "If you need anything, let me know."

Last night she'd eaten in town at Delia's and left him to his own devices for the evening meal, then had come in and gone straight to her room to finalize coordinating the information she knew the contractors would need for the first round of appointments, all the while telling herself that it was pretty obvious things had moved too far, too fast, and he was gently, but firmly putting some distance between himself and the woman he'd allowed to live under his roof.

She got it. She even knew she should be grateful that at least one of them was being clearheaded about it. Apparently, he'd decided that even winging it came with too much potential for complications. She wished—desperately—she could agree with him on that, but just thinking about him made it quite clear that her body was not at all happy with the sudden return to drought time.

Their only commitment—made in the heat of . . . frolicking—had been to not frolic elsewhere. So, she supposed, other than the formality of inquiring whether that agreement no longer required enforcement, there was nothing whatsoever stopping her from taking Brodie up on his next offer. He'd be exactly the type for a no-strings, short-term fling, and she had very little doubt that he would make it a fun adventure . . . if that's what she really wanted.

But it wasn't Brodie's dancing eyes and promising grin she saw when she closed her eyes at night. She knew she should be grateful Logan had given her something new to dream about. Her subconscious didn't even have to work all that hard. She didn't need to embellish or fantasize . . . all she had to do was remember what it had truly been like.

"You're just being perverse, wanting what you can't have."

"Well, missy, I wish I could tell you otherwise, but truth is, it's a miracle this place is still upright."

Unaware she'd spoken her thoughts out loud, Alex ducked her chin to hide her sudden blush as Hank continued his poking and prodding along the front of the cottage. He was focused on where the footing met the shake siding.

Clueless to the fact she hadn't been paying the least bit of attention to him, he moved to a spot next to the small, sagging front stoop, pulled the end of one loose piece out, and pointed to the exposed frame behind it. "See here? Original foundation. See those nails? Handmade. Every piece here was measured and cut exact to fit. Don't see workmanship like that anymore. Takes too much time."

He moved the shake back into place and gave it a little pat. "But that's why she's still upright." He pushed his floppy, dark blue wool captain's cap back on his forehead and pushed the few thinning strands of white hair the wind kept catching away from his ruddy face. "It's all gonna have to come straight down to the frame. And you're going to need folks who know what to do with this kind of foundation. Can't just let anybody with a hammer have at it." He peered through one of the salt- and wind-blasted windows. "Can't see much of what's inside, but you'll want to take care getting in there. Front door will be your best bet, though you'll have to take it off at the hinges to get in. Then shore the doorframe before taking a step inside. You find anything in there worth storing for the duration, would be wise to make a plan now for where you're going to put it. All that'll have to get done before we start takin' her apart. Won't be able to start work until spring after the weather turns, so you have some time. If you want my company to do the work, I can put together a quote for you. I got some recommendations on who you can get in to help with the specialized work. Not from the Cove, but local enough to be day laborers. We can go over scheduling, labor. You'd be smart to get this contracted now, so come spring you know you have things set to go. Otherwise other opportunities come up." He lifted a beefy shoulder. "Folks'll take 'em when they can get 'em."

Alex's thoughts moved mercifully away from Logan and back to the job at hand. "I understand. That's why I have

you out here now. The plans said the shakes were last replaced in the seventies. Just patch jobs done since then. I
know that was over forty years ago, but I had hoped more
of it would be salvageable."

"Forty years in most places is doubled out here on the
Point, with the effects of the weather and nothing to shelter the cottage other than the tower. Even then, winds
moving north to south whip right through the passage between tower and cottage, so—"

"No, no, I understand. I know what the weather can do,
but even so, this is much worse degradation then you'd typically see in under a half century. Have there been more
record storms than normal? More unusual or dramatic temperature swings? Warmer than usual weather can actually be
more corrosive than the deep cold. I haven't done a weather
chart yet, but—"

"Nothing that out of the ordinary, I don't think. I've
lived here all of my sixty-five years, so I'm a walking
weather chart," he added with a deep chuckle. "What I
think is that substandard material was used last time, trying
to shave some of the cost, but it allowed the weather to get
in. Now the Chief is paying the price for decisions made by
a past generation. Happens all the time."

Alex had lost track of what he'd said after the term *substandard material*. Not that it was at all surprising. Switching to low-grade shake shingles wasn't in any way the same
as switching to low-grade support iron and untested con-
nective hardware that wouldn't hold up under harsh weather
conditions. No one was going to die because one of Logan's
relatives had decided to put up cheap siding. But with the
lighthouse looming over her, literally a breath away from
where she was standing, it was a trigger she couldn't nim-
bly sidestep.

Hank kept rambling, then finally realized she wasn't following him as he was pointing to the rotting window frames and weather-cracked seals. "You okay? You look like you've seen a ghost."

She swallowed past a particularly large knot of emotion and nodded. "Fine. It's—getting dark. I really appreciate your coming out."

Hank nodded. "Happy to. There's a few more things I want to check out while there's still a little light left."

"Okay. I'm going to go catch up to Logan." Alex turned and headed back around to the side of the cottage and main house, hoping her abrupt departure hadn't seemed rude. Fortunately, Hank didn't strike her as the kind of guy who paid much attention to social niceties.

Logan was still talking to Wade and his brother. Brodie was nowhere to be seen.

Oh, right. Her truck. The quote for the job he'd hired her to do. "I'm heading out front," she said as she neared Logan. "Do you need anything else from me regarding the roofing on the house? Hank said we'd have to take the cottage down to the frame, so we'll need to talk about that. But if everything is good here, then I'm ready for a roof estimate." He didn't say anything, so she turned to the brothers. "I already gave you that info on the specially treated shakes I want you to use, but I'm open to your recommendations on what to put under it."

Wade and Scotty nodded, smiles spreading on both of their faces. "We'll get on it."

For his part, Logan just held her gaze. She couldn't read his expression and the growing gloom didn't help. There were floodlights on the side of the house, but they hadn't been triggered on as yet.

Annoyed, she kept her gaze on Wade and Scotty. "Good, good. I'll look forward to receiving your quote." She clasped her clipboard close and continued on toward the driveway without another glance at Logan. She supposed she needed to just up and admit to herself that she needed to talk to him and put what was bugging her directly on the table. She wasn't cut out for winging it, after all. Not with him, not with anyone. She might have had a summer romance or two in her early twenties while on jobs in other countries, but this was not anything like that. Hell, she didn't even know what *this* was.

She was an adult, in charge of her own company, albeit a company of one, and that's where she needed to focus her energies. The best thing to do was to officially end whatever they weren't actively having anymore and move on to a strictly business arrangement. She realized that he'd likely assumed they'd already done that, but because she really didn't know how they'd gone from playful, toe-curling *frolicking* to his pretending she didn't exist, she wanted it stated clearly, so there would be no ambiguity. Then maybe he could stop hiding in his study in the evenings and they could manage to eat breakfast at the same time in the same room on occasion.

Given the intensity that seemed to naturally exist between them, it was definitely for the best. It had only been a week since the last time they'd ended up in bed—or the shower, as had been the case—and she was already spending way too much time thinking about him, worrying about what was or wasn't going on between them. If that were true this early on, she could well imagine what would happen if she stayed intimately involved with him for any real length of time.

Besides, even if she wanted to risk that, wanted to go for it all . . . there was no future in it. If she got the contract to manage the restoration project for all three buildings, which was looking more and more promising, it was still a short-term situation. A year or two at best. Then it would be on to the next job. That was the nature of her work.

Logan didn't have to come out and state that his life was

in the Cove. That much was clear. His roots were deep, and she respected him and envied him for it. She also admired him for continuing onward in the place he loved, despite the huge losses he'd suffered. The last thing he'd want was someone who was already set up to leave Blueberry Cove.

If they nipped things in the bud, kept their relationship business only—"Yeah, maybe I'd have a chance in hell of not falling for him anyway," she muttered. She was trying to work the math on what it would take for her to relocate to a place in town—maybe she could lease out a little loft space or even just a room—while overseeing the restoration, when she walked straight into Brodie.

"Earth to Alexandra," he chuckled, reaching for her arms to help her get her balance. "Ye work too hard, lass. Head always filled with numbers and lists on top of lists." He pushed her knit cap up where it had slid over her eyebrows, then bent down to peer into her eyes, his own merry green ones twinkling with mischief. "Sure and I can't talk you into a quick bite? I promise no' to keep you too long."

"Brodie, it's nice of you to offer, but—"

"Take him up on it if you'd like." Logan stepped out of the darkness and walked to the driver side door of his SUV, which was parked directly behind hers. "I've been called back to the station." He opened the door, climbed in, then glanced over at them, which was when she realized how it must look. She was all but standing in Brodie's arms.

She wasn't sure what it was, pride maybe, stubbornness, but she didn't pull away or try to explain. Besides, what business was it of his anyway? He'd made his position pretty clear over the past week.

"Make whatever appointments you feel necessary," Logan told her. "And contact Owen, get him out here tomorrow as well if you can."

"Owen? But why would—"

"He's the closest we've got to a lighthouse expert in the

Cove. We've got some answers on the house and cottage. Tomorrow we'll start dealing with the tower." His gaze shifted to Brodie. "Find out if she's still seaworthy." Then he closed the door and started up the engine.

Her mouth was still hanging open as he backed out, turned, and drove off. She looked back at Brodie to find him studying her.

"Is there something more between you two then? Other than business?"

She worked to mentally regroup from Logan's sudden appearance to the announcement that she'd be expected to go inside the tower. Tomorrow. *Well, we'll see about that.* "Just business," she said flatly, hoping he didn't hear the slight tremble in the words. The tremble of fear . . . and fury. "But I'm here to work, so—"

"All work and no play, lass, no' a good thing, no' a' tall."

"It's a big job and it's important to me." She mustered up a smile. "Like you said, the best work is both. I need—to focus."

He rubbed her arms, then gave her a wink as he tugged at her knit cap, and let her go. "Aye, that I can see."

"Let me get your quote." She fumbled with the door handle, swore under her breath when it stuck, then finally got it open. She snatched the estimate sheet from the passenger seat and handed it to him. "Go over it, ask me to clarify anything that doesn't make sense or seems out of order. I'll be in town around noon tomorrow, so I can come by then and we can set up a start date and go over what will need to happen before the laborers get started."

He was still studying her with that perpetual sunny smile of his. But a closer look at his eyes said he probably saw a lot more than his devil-may-care disposition would seem to indicate. "I understand about work and focus, but if it's no' a flirtation you're up for, perhaps you'd accept something else instead."

She lifted an eyebrow. "Such as?"

"The offer of friendship. We're both new to the Cove. Couldn't hurt to have an ally who's not otherwise umbilically attached to the place."

She simply smiled at that.

"Och, now you've gone and hurt me feelings. Ye think I can't be but a friend?"

"I think if I honestly asked you to give me a list of female friends you'd never gotten into bed or at least tried your damndest to, it would be a very, very short list."

He hooted out a surprised laugh at that, and she laughed too. He was . . . infectious. And pretty damn easy on the eyes. Another time, another place, maybe she'd have reconsidered. Or at least been more open to his playful, flirty banter. But her plate was full enough, and more confusing emotions she did not need.

"A woman who speaks plain and direct," he said, when his laughter subsided. "You have my full admiration, lass, that you do." He picked up her hand and gave the back of her fingerless glove a loud kiss. Then looked up through thick lashes and winked. "And ye'd have been right about that list, too. But that doesn't mean I'm no' up for being re-formed." He straightened, let his fingers trail lightly over her bare ones, before letting her hand drop. "If there was a woman alive who could do it, my money would be on you."

She laughed again. "Thanks, but I already have a full-time job."

That set him off again and they both laughed until she had to put her hand to her waist to help catch her breath. "Go on with ye now," she said in perfect imitation of her grandfather's brogue. "I'll see you tomorrow."

He clutched his heart in dramatic fashion, then gave her a smart salute, and thankfully did as she asked. The floodlights came on as he was pulling out. She framed her forehead with her hand and blinked a few times to adjust her vision, then lowered it in time to see Hank, Wade, and Scotty headed across the drive as well.

"I'll have some information for you by beginning of next week," Hank said, then handed her a sheet of paper. "I'll need to make some calls, get some numbers, but that's a base list of the work that needs to be done. Let me know if you're interested in continuing."

"Logan said he wanted to hire local where we can, and I couldn't agree more. We do have a few other quotes to discuss and there may be some overlap we'd have to work out, but if you all are open to working with me on that, then I know I'm interested."

Wade and Scotty shared a quick grin and Wade handed her a sheaf of papers, too. "Same as Hank. We need to crunch some numbers, but that's the outline. Let us know when you want to talk schedules and money." Scotty elbowed him at that last part, but Wade just grinned. "She's okay. She gets business talk."

"I do," she assured them. "I'll be in touch in the next day or two. Thanks, you guys, for coming out and getting going on this. I appreciate it."

"Oh, our pleasure. This being one of the oldest places on Pelican Bay, it's an honor and privilege to get to work on it. I imagine anyone else you get out here from the area will tell you the same. It matters to us, seeing this place preserved," Scotty said. "Please tell the chief thanks for considering us."

"I will. I know it means a lot to him, too. I should warn you, I'm not sure if that will be the case with the lighthouse. Hiring local, I mean," she told them, figuring it best to get the word out on that sooner than later. "Some of that work is specialized and I'm not sure we can find the right experts locally."

Hank lifted his hand. "We understand that. Wouldn't

know the first thing about what to tell you to do with that monstrosity. Wish you the best with it, though. If you need anything basic—wiring, electric, plumbing, what have you—well, we can help you with that."

She smiled, relieved that they already seemed to know that part of the job wasn't likely to be up for grabs. "Good to know. And thanks." She shook hands with each of them, then waved as they climbed in their trucks and headed out.

She walked back up to the house and paused to look up at the looming shadow of the lighthouse tower on the far side of the cottage. She felt immense relief at how well things were going so far. She was very grateful to Logan for making it clear to the local contractors that she was heading up the job and had the power to hire—and fire. That he'd given her his blessing had clearly held major sway. Any issues she feared might crop up, either because of her gender or her being the new face in town, hadn't happened. So far, anyway. She was hopeful that the project would continue on as it had begun.

She went in through the mudroom door, thinking she'd heat up some of the spaghetti and meatballs she'd made two days before, which reminded her she needed to e-mail Delia her dad's meatball recipe. She smiled, thinking of the trim, outspoken, forty-something redhead who ran the local diner. Delia served locals, tourists, dockworkers, and fisherman alike with the same direct, no-nonsense flair that almost always included her opinion on all manner of things personal and professional. The first time Alex had eaten there, she'd had to hide her constantly climbing eyebrows behind the monitor of her laptop, but Delia, of course, had noticed anyway, and called her straight out on it.

Blushing to her roots, Alex had stammered an apology, then complimented her on making the best seafood omelet she'd ever tasted—which had been the truth—after which Delia had laughed, then parked herself in the booth across from Alex and proceeded to grill her like a hard-boiled police detective from one of those late-night cable shows. Since then, Alex had been welcomed like a native—which also made her fair game for any of Delia's observations or advice.

Alex had taken in stride the wiggled eyebrows Delia had served up along with her world famous chowder, laughing along as she'd been teased about the exact nature of the work she'd been doing for Brodie Monaghan. At the time, she'd figured it couldn't hurt if the town was thinking there was something there as it would keep the attention off what was actually going on out at the Point. Except nothing had been going on there, either. She wondered if perhaps the teasing had spawned talk of an entirely different and far less flattering nature.

It wasn't until she was seated at the small kitchen table, laptop open, notepad by its side as she worked through a bowl of spaghetti, that it struck her that Logan hadn't been wearing his uniform when he'd left. He must have gone in and changed right after she'd left him, before being called away. Conveniently keeping them apart for yet another evening.

Of course, if there was chatter making the rounds about her and Brodie, then surely he'd have heard about it. She'd like to think he had more sense than to believe idle gossip, or at least come out and ask, but she honestly didn't know him well enough to know how he'd handle it. She supposed it depended on who had told him what. Nor, she reasoned, did he know her well enough to know what kinds of choices she would make. Not really.

However, they had an agreement, so she hoped he'd expect her, at the very least, to terminate what was between them decisively and directly and not just let him assume she'd done so simply because he'd gone out of his way to steer clear of her for the past week. She propped her elbows on the table, pressed her face against her hands, and groaned. "Why does this have to be so complicated?"

"It doesn't. Or it shouldn't be."

She startled, then clutched her heart and grabbed her glass of wine before she sent it flying to the linoleum covered floor. "Holy—you scared me half to death. I didn't hear you come in." She steadied the wineglass, then looked over to where he was leaning in the doorframe. He was wearing a soft blue button-up shirt tucked into jeans that had long since made themselves perfectly at home on his long, lean, larger-than-life frame. Add to that a pair of worn leather hiking boots and a worn leather bomber jacket, and she wanted him so badly it made her teeth ache. "I thought you got called back into work."

"I lied."

That surprised a wide-eyed look from her. "Why? Where did you go?"

"I promised Fergus I'd get into town more often. Get a life he thinks I don't have. With good reason, I suppose."

"So you were at the Puffin? Why didn't you just say— never mind. It's not my business."

"You didn't go to dinner."

"No, I never planned to." She gestured to her plate. "I'm a good cook. Apparently the whole town knows."

"Delia mentioned you owed her a recipe. I'm guessing that's the source of the rumor." At Alex's questioning look, he added, "She stopped in the pub as I was leaving."

"You didn't stay long."

"It wasn't where I wanted to be."

She was still annoyed with him about the weird tension with Brodie and about the one-eighty his interest had taken since the beginning of the week. She didn't owe him an explanation, and yet she heard herself say, "An evening out with Brodie Monaghan wasn't where I wanted to be, either." A little of the irritated edge crept in as she added, "I'm having enough trouble with one boss as it is."

"I'm not your boss. Not in any way that matters. No one questions your expertise. If you do this project, it's because you're qualified."

She lifted her wine glass toward him. "Thanks." Then another thought struck her. "Is that why you've been hiding out? Because you think folks will assume I earned this job some other way? If they're going to talk, they're going to talk. I'll earn respect for the work from those who matter, and the rest, well, they can bite me. But your mileage apparently varies on that."

He eased off the doorframe and walked into the kitchen, leaning against the end of the counter a few feet from where she sat. When he crossed his legs at the ankles and folded his arms, she had to work not to squirm in her seat.

By any measure, Brodie was a good-looking guy with an easy charm and a confident manner that said he probably knew his way around a woman's body. At the moment, there was nothing easy or particularly charming about the man standing before her. Yet, with nothing more than a brooding look, he managed to short-circuit every nerve ending in her body to the point where she could barely sit still. It took more effort than she wanted to admit to casually turn her gaze away from his and back to her monitor. She would have sipped her wine again, but she was afraid she'd snap the stem in half.

The silence grew; then he said, "I don't know what to do about you."

She went still, then set her wine down and put her trembling hands in her lap, twisting her fingers together so he wouldn't see. "You don't have to do anything with me. Other than let me do my job."

"Oh, I know what I want to do *with* you."

Dear . . . God. Did he know how easily he was dismantling every brick she'd so carefully laid in that protective wall she'd spent all week building?

"And yet, you've gone out of your way to have *nothing* to do with me." She made herself look directly at him, shoulders level, chin straight. "I thought you said you were done with being frustrated."

"Turns out there are different kinds of frustration."

"Such as?" She turned, folded her arms, crossed her legs, mirroring his closed-off posture. And thought she saw a muscle in his jaw twitch. His throat might have worked a little, too.

Ah. So she wasn't the only one being affected. *Good to know.*

She held his gaze, then wished she felt more triumphant when he was the one to look away first. With his gaze on the toes of his boots, he finally said, "You make me want more."

That wonderfully deep voice of his, with that rough edge to it, was like a live wire, stroking every inch of her skin. Add in that hint of confusion, and she lost any hope of maintaining her brief hold on the upper hand. "You could have had more. I wasn't the one hiding in my study all week and leaving before the crack of dawn so you wouldn't have to risk being in the same room with me for breakfast. If this is about some perceived—whatever it is you think I'm having, or want to have, with Brodie—I've told you, even though I don't owe you any explanation, it's professional. Nothing more. Not for me."

His gaze flicked up to hers and the hanging light over the kitchen table caught and reflected the heat in those golden eyes. It made her pulse twitch and her heart pound as if she'd suddenly come upon a wolf in the woods. She wasn't too sure she hadn't done just that.

He shook his head. "I'm not talking about sex. With me or anyone else."

That caught her by surprise. "Then what are we talking about?"

He held her gaze for another long, intense moment. Then, just when she thought her skin might start to sizzle, he shifted his gaze toward the ceiling, and abruptly pushed off the counter and walked to the door. "That's just it. We're not."

"Logan. What the—" Swearing under her breath, she stood. "Wait."

He paused, then looked back.

"If you're not talking about wanting sex, then what is it you do want?"

"I wish to hell I knew." He smacked his palms on the door frame, then walked through. As he was crossing the living room, he added, "That's what's so damn frustrating."

Acting on impulse, before she could think better of it— why start now?—she went after him. She caught up to him at the bottom of the stairs and grabbed his wrist.

By the stunned look on his face, he'd been so lost in his thoughts, he hadn't known she was behind him. "Alex, don't—"

"Too late." She let his wrist go, but didn't step back. "I'm done with all this enigmatic bullshit. I'm also done watching you hide in your own damn house. How do you think that makes me feel? I don't want that. Not for you. Not for me. If you want a strictly professional relationship, then just say so. We're grown adults. We can certainly behave accordingly. Just because we had sex, it's not like we can't respect each other's boundaries and keep our hands to ourselves."

She'd forgotten about his lightning-fast reflexes. One second she'd been standing behind him, giving him a piece of her mind. A split second later, she was pinned against the wall of the stairwell without so much as a breath of room between her body and his.

"That's just it. Maybe I can keep my hands to myself. But I know I don't want to." She'd never heard his voice that low, that heated.

She could barely hear her own voice above the echo of her pulse thrumming in her ears. "Then why are you?"

His gaze dropped to her mouth as she spoke, and there was no hiding the trembling. And it wasn't from fear. Far from it.

"I told you. You make me want more."

More. And then she realized. *More than sex.* She'd been caught up in being so sure that's all he wanted, so worried that she'd be the one wanting more, that it hadn't occurred to her . . . She looked into his eyes, and feeling as if her heart was going to pound straight out of her chest, did the scariest thing she'd ever done. She said, "So?"

If she'd thought his eyes were molten before, they were nothing short of volcanic now. He took her face in one broad palm, cupping his hand around her chin, his fingertips brushing the pulse in her temple. He drew his thumb over her lips, then guided her mouth to within a breath of his. "So, if I take more . . . I'm not sure I'll want to stop."

She was shaking with need, with the knowledge that the promise in his words, the intent in his eyes, the possession in the way he held her, sent a dark thrill through her that no amount of rationalizing would enable her to deny she wanted . . . badly. And yet her defense mechanisms, shaky as they were, kicked in, anyway. "I'm not . . . here to stay."

"Well aware." He pressed his thumb on her bottom lip and the shudder of pleasure that rocked her had her pressing her thighs tightly together.

Her voice was raw, needy, even to her own ears. "We— we don't need more loss. In our lives."

She saw the frustration, the flicker of pain, of regret. The idea that he was struggling as much as she was only made her feel closer to him.

"That's why I've become a hermit in my own damn house."

She was locked in his heated gaze, wanted his mouth on hers, his hands all over her. She wanted him to peel her clothes off, feel those hands on her bare skin, that mouth, his tongue, caressing her, electrifying her. She knew what he felt like—warm, big, strong—moving over her, pushing into her. She'd never wanted to feel anything so badly as she wanted to feel that, to feel him, inside her again.

But then what?

"I could—move out," she whispered, the very idea making her throat ache. "I . . . was thinking about it earlier." She felt the tremble in his fingertips, unsure whether it was truly him, or her. "To help us keep . . . a professional distance. I-I thought that's what you wanted."

"Is it what you want?"

She reached up then, her own fingers trembling as she stroked them along the side of his face, feeling his body jerk against hers as she traced the outline of his ear and brushed through his hair. He shuddered as she drew them across his bottom lip; she saw his throat work. His jaw was so set, she thought his teeth would grind to dust. His body was hard and unyielding, pressed up against hers.

But what she saw in his eyes, past the desire, past the frustration . . . the confusion and the vulnerability . . . made her own throat tighten with an emotion she couldn't put a name to, didn't dare to. She couldn't speak, so she just shook her head.

"Then what do we do, Alex?"

What he wanted was clear, but it was that thread of real confusion, of . . . fear . . . that undid her. "I wish there was an easy answer. I really do."

Chapter 12

He wanted to be angry . . . at something, at someone . . . for putting him in the last place he wanted to
be—wanting something that came with the very risk he'd
done his best to avoid.

Alex understood. *We don't need more loss.*

Perversely, it was because she understood his frustration
that he was being drawn in even more deeply. He wanted
to discover all he didn't know about her. What he did
know, that elemental connection they shared, had created a
bond that had been instant, specific, mutual. It rendered the
element of time completely meaningless. The connection
felt so . . . certain. It made wanting to know more about
her feel exciting, the thrill of discovery, something to look
forward to. Trusting that everything else was the proverbial
icing on the cake. Icing he wanted to lick off slowly and
over a great deal of time . . . layer by delectable layer.

It was a right pisser, as Fergus would say, that anything
should stand in the way.

It isn't fair.

Thinking that made Logan feel ridiculous. He knew better than anyone that fairness was a meaningless construct
when applied to life. He could be angry all he wanted, but
it didn't change the fact his life was deeply rooted in Blueberry Cove. Everything that held meaning for him was

there. Even if he willing to give it up . . . Alex's life involved moving from job site to job site. He couldn't fathom
a role he could play in that kind of life. Similarly, she was
just rediscovering her own life, taking the reins of her family legacy, following her passion, doing what she loved,
which was as deeply rooted in her as the Cove was in him.

It took considerable will to stay in the moment, that very
specific moment. With her. Everything inside him wanted
to buck reality. But he gentled his grip and willed his body
to relax, knowing he needed to step back.

That last part . . . that was going to take a little longer.
He lowered his forehead until it rested on her hair, breathed
in the scent of her, and, just for a moment, soaked in what
it felt like to know there was someone so perfectly suited to
him.

She . . . matched him. Intimately, intellectually, emotionally. She drove him crazy in ways unbelievably good and incredibly challenging. He wanted to be deep in her personal
space as often as possible. In private. In public. In life.

He wanted to kiss her, *never stop kissing her,* even as he
knew he had to find a way to shift them to where they
needed to be. He needed to say . . . something. A personal,
intimate good-bye to the promise of more. Just as he knew
there was no way he could taste her now, or ever again, and
be able to walk away.

"Logan—"

"I'll help you find a place," he said, squeezing his eyes
shut when he felt her entire body go still.

He lifted his head and found her gaze. It felt like the
hardest thing he'd ever done, staring into those sea-blue
eyes and seeing the want and the pain swimming together.
Knowing he was the root of both. He couldn't believe he'd
finally found that next step in his life . . . and he couldn't
take it. It felt like the cruelest thing. Hadn't he had enough
of cruel? Hadn't she?

He took a deep breath. "I can work with you. But I can't live with you. We'll—*I* won't be able to—"

"I know." Her words were hushed, emotion thickening her voice. "You don't have to explain. I . . . I already knew."

He watched her eyes go glassy and pulled her into his arms, hugging her close. He pressed his cheek to her hair, then his lips. "It's not what I want."

"I know," she said roughly. "I thought I could . . . wing it. Take what we could get. Be okay with that. I . . . I can't. And hearing that you can't either—I didn't know that. Didn't know you felt . . . Now that I do . . . it just . . . makes it even . . ." She shook her head and he pressed his lips harder against her hair.

He lost track of how long they stood like that.

Later, he'd wonder how in the hell he'd let her get in so easily, so swiftly, and so deeply. He'd convince himself that he'd just spent too much time alone and had been ripe for the picking, that—*was a crock of shit is what it was.* Any other time, any other woman, maybe he'd have pulled that off. But not Alex. He'd only been ripe for her . . . because she was the only one he'd wanted to pick him.

"I have to—I can't—" She didn't finish, but gently pushed at him, disentangling herself. Keeping her gaze averted, she stepped around him. "I'll—while you're at work tomorrow, I'll pack up."

She paused after turning away, but didn't look back.

He watched her take a breath, try to square her shoulders, steady herself. Her struggle made him want to put his fist through something. She shouldn't have to be the strong one all the time, handle every goddamn thing alone, carry it all. He hated that he'd added to the burden she carried.

"I can handle the appointments tomorrow. I'll leave my notes in your study or on the kitchen counter. And I'll get—" She took a deep breath then, chin up, eyes straight ahead. "I'll get Owen to go up in the tower with me. He'll love that."

The one who should be punched was Logan. "Alex, you don't have to go up in the tower tomorrow. I was pissed off and frustrated when I said that. Seeing you with Brodie, laughing, even though I had no right to feel . . . anything. I was an ass for saying what I did. Especially that. Deal with it when you're ready. I don't—"

He blew out his own breath, swore under it, then shook his head. "The job is yours. The house, the cottage, the lighthouse. I know you can handle it. You're damn good at what you do. And it needs to get done. Just . . . make your recommendations and whatever else you need to do, and we'll find a way to make it happen. All of it. However it works best."

He saw her shoulders slump, and he couldn't tell if it was in relief . . . or defeat. "Unless you . . . if you think you don't want to deal with . . . any of it."

She shook her head, started to speak, then cleared her throat. "No, it's—I want the job. I'm already . . . invested. It feels really . . . personal. I didn't—I wasn't sure—" She broke off, ducking her chin. "I wasn't sure I'd ever feel that again, so, if the job is mine, then I need to—want—to see it through. Okay?"

"Yes. Absolutely. Whatever. Just tell me what, when, how."

She sucked in another breath, then looked over her shoulder. Her eyes devastated him. It should have been a happy, positive achievement for her, a major step forward . . . and all he could see was what it was costing her.

"Thank you." She looked like she was going to say more, but then she gave a little shake to her head and looked away while blinking back her tears. "Good night, Logan."

She turned and crossed the living room toward the kitchen.

He realized he was clenching the knob on top of the stair railing so hard it was a miracle it didn't grind straight to sawdust. He made himself relax his hand, his fingers, then rubbed his palms on the sides of his pants. It was that or go after her, pull her back into his arms, and ask her to stay. *Ask, hell . . . he'd beg.*

"Good-bye, Alex," he said quietly, then climbed the stairs before he lost what courage he had left.

Stupidly, Logan tortured himself by getting online and doing a little more research on Alex's family history. His rationale was that the more he could cement in his mind what generations of her family had accomplished in their specialized field, including all of her personal contributions to that impressive and important body of work, the easier it would be for him to establish the professional boundaries he knew they needed to maintain.

He did a little more digging into her father's death. The controversy over faulty building materials and the lawsuit brought by the owner of the tower blaming Alex's company for substandard work, essentially blaming her for her father's death, pissed him off all over again.

He couldn't imagine if he'd had to deal with something similar after Jessica's death. There was no question that it had simply been a horrifying accident. Camille's ridiculous blame campaign notwithstanding—she'd simply felt Logan should never have let Jessica work alongside him and her father in such a dangerous job in the first place—he'd suffered guilt enough for not being able to save her, and that was with the support of the town, including Jessica's own father.

He couldn't fathom facing the kind of nasty inquiry Alex had been subjected to. It had come from someone far more powerful, with greater resources, and connections in the Canadian courts, who was apparently looking to deflect the blame from himself. Alex had shown remarkable strength and resiliency, not only in persevering and getting through it, but emerging victorious in getting MacFarland & Sons acquitted from any and all culpability.

Logan hated that there hadn't been enough evidence to countersue the owner, whom everyone—including the judge—seemed to think was truly at fault. It explained a lot about the shape Alex had been in when she'd arrived . . . and was still in, despite getting herself back to a steadier, healthier routine.

The more digging he did, the more he realized all she'd lost and the more his heart broke for her. It was literally *just her.* One truck, one job. She had no place to go back to. At least, nowhere that felt like home. Except maybe whatever lighthouse she was working on. And they represented terror and tragedy to her now.

He wondered if she had aspirations to eventually return MacFarland & Sons to its former glory. He smiled faintly, thinking if there was anyone who could do it, it was the woman sleeping one floor below him.

Eventually, he shut down his laptop and hoped that sleep would come, giving him a break from the hamster wheel of thoughts and emotions that wouldn't stop spinning through his mind. All he could think about was her. Her past, her present . . . her future.

When he first heard the cries, the sobbing pleas, he thought he'd awakened from his own dreams, his own nightmare, reliving some fugue-like mixture of Alex's past and his feelings of helplessness as he stood on the sidelines. Once he'd shaken off the sleep, he'd realized it wasn't his nightmares that had woken him up. But hers.

Half asleep, he knew that going to her was all kinds of unwise, but there was no way in hell he was going to lie there and listen to her suffer through one more minute of pain. As he pulled on the first pair of sweats he found and headed downstairs, he wondered if this had been happening to her all week, and he'd just slept through it. She looked so much better than that first day, he guessed he'd just thought . . . *what, asshole? That she'd miraculously gotten over it? With a freaking lighthouse staring her down every single day?*

His gut clutched at that, and he knew he was worse than an ass. He was an idiot. Likely his own selfish, stupid jealousy and frustration, all but ordering her to go in the tower tomorrow, had triggered the damn flashback. It didn't matter that he'd recanted later, or that he'd apologized. The seed had been planted. Who knew how much of the evening she'd spent thinking about it, worrying about it, while he'd been essentially hiding from her. *Coward.*

"Daddy, don't! *Please!* Don't let go!"

Logan thought his heart would squeeze itself dead listening to the plaintive, wrenching, begging note in her voice. He knew how her father had fallen through the lantern balcony railing when it had given way, how only his grip on the side of the gallery ledge . . . and his daughter's own hand . . . had kept him from falling to the rocks below.

"Help! Somebody! Anybody! *Help me!*" She was shrieking in terror and anguish, reliving the moment that defied living through once, much less over and over again.

He forced himself to slow down after taking the stairs three at a time, so he wouldn't burst into her room like a wild man and make the nightmare worse. Heart pounding, breath coming in gulps, living the horror with her through every wrenching sob, he wished he could somehow take it from her. He turned the doorknob with a shaky hand and stepped quietly into his guest bedroom.

His eyes already adjusted to the dim moonlight, he saw her hunched under the covers, sobbing as if the tears were being ripped from her heart. Working solely on instinct, he climbed in bed behind her and carefully, gently, put his hands on her arms. "Shhh, Alex, it's okay."

He eased her from the fetal ball she'd curled in and turned her toward him. "It's just a dream. Come here." Tucking her against him, he cradled her to his chest. "It's okay. You're here now. It's over."

The tears continued to fall, but she clung to him as she cried.

He wasn't sure if she was awake or still fighting dream demons, and he didn't know what else to do but hold her. He stroked her hair, whispered to her, and rocked her.

"I couldn't hold on," she choked out, the words barely understandable. The fear, the terror, and the grief were utterly palpable. "I couldn't hold on."

His throat constricted and tears formed at the corners of his own eyes. "I know. I'm so sorry. I know." He kissed the top of her head, then nudged her face up and kissed her temple, wiping the tears away with the side of his thumb. "Alex." He kissed her cheek and the soft spot in front of her ear. "It's over. You're here. It's okay."

Her hands slid around his neck and she clung to him, burying her face against the bare, heated skin on the side of his neck. "It will never be okay. I can't—get past it."

He wrapped his arms around her and rolled to his back, keeping her curled up on him. He kept stroking her hair, kissing her forehead, wishing like hell he could take her pain away and make it his. "You will get past it," he told her in hushed tones as her tears slowed. "It takes time. But you will."

She slid her hand down over his bare chest, pressing it over the thumping beat of his heart. Turning her face into the crook of his neck, she said nothing more as she struggled to get her breath back.

He held her, knowing he would continue until the end of time, if that's what it took. Eventually he felt her relax;

her breathing, though still hitched, finally slowed, becoming more even as she fell fully back asleep again. Peacefully, it seemed.

He kept her wrapped in his arms, sheltered against his body, and stood guard as she slept. It was all he could do, and it felt like so damn little.

"What am I going to do about you?" he whispered, pressing a gentle kiss to the crown of her head. She made him want to give her shelter always. To be the home base she didn't have, the foundation on which to rebuild. In a way, he supposed he was all those things. Except he'd have to do them, be them, at a distance. Once her foundations were rebuilt, she'd fly away from the nest. From him.

Chapter 13

A lex hiked her pack up higher on her shoulder and held her clipboard closer as she ducked down to look through the second-story dormer window. Outside, the early winter sky was a luminous gray, but it felt more cocoon-like than foreboding, providing a protective cap over the tranquility of Half Moon Harbor. She wished she could will the stillness of that smooth, peaceful surface into her. If only she could be like the boats tethered to the docks and those dotting the harbor and the bay beyond—just bob gently along the surface of life.

Though the setting around her was quiet and composed, nothing seemed capable of slowing the stormy onslaught of jumbled thoughts and emotions tumbling around inside her head. She felt off balance, as if the ground was constantly pitching and rolling beneath her feet, only all on the inside. She'd taken the job in Blueberry Cove because she'd wanted—needed—a steady, sturdy place to land. A safe, uncomplicated harbor where she could find her way back to her passion, to the work she loved. Or say good-bye to it forever. A potentially tumultuous time, but one she'd at least have a merciful chance to explore alone, at her own pace, with no one but herself to contend with as she sought out those answers. She hadn't thought that was too much to ask, or expect.

She'd never been so wrong.

It was tumultuous all right, but so much more than she'd anticipated. It wasn't just about her any longer. She hadn't planned on Blueberry Cove opening its collective arms and pulling her in. She hadn't counted on Logan McCrae making her feel things she'd never felt, want things she'd never known she could have. It all seemed like too much . . . and there was no place to hide. She couldn't retreat from her own thoughts, which included all the feelings the town itself and the people in it had evoked, as well as the emotions and desires Logan had so effortlessly stirred inside her.

Added to all that, she'd woken early to tear-streaked cheeks, puffy eyes, and a raw throat, and had felt an immediate sense of defeat, of failure. She'd known the nightmares would return at some point . . . periodically, anyway. There was no way they'd miraculously disappear overnight, but still . . . it had felt like a giant step backward. That on top of an already monumentally confusing and emotionally charged evening with Logan—which was likely why the dream had come back in the first place. Her defenses had not only been down, but weakened to the point that she wasn't sure how to rebuild them again . . . or if she really wanted to. It seemed an exhausting way to go through life, constantly on guard, constantly worrying.

The nightmares, the pain, and the terror had been a stark reminder of why she'd built those walls in the first place. It was all fine and good to lower them to allow the positive things in; the sizzle of desire, the excitement of feeling wanted, and of wanting in return. Being unguarded also allowed the rest in. The confusion, the pain, the frustration of having to make choices—complicated, bewildering, nerve-rattling choices—that had no perfectly right or wrong answers.

The one thing about leaving Thunder Bay that had felt so good was the relief of knowing those kinds of choices were finally behind her. All she'd thought about was how big a relief it would be to get back to work, where the answers were a lot more cut and dried—see what was in need of repair, assess what it would take to fix it, then find a way to make the numbers line up, and do the work. Gratifying work that provided a wonderful feeling of personal accomplishment, but without any challenging emotional entanglements.

Her only fear in taking the Pelican Point job, or any job, had been whether or not she would be able to recapture the passion she'd had for it, experience once again what it was like to see something that was broken . . . and know she could fix it, restore it to its former glory. Her one hope was that by doing that again, she'd finally find the way to heal and fix herself.

How was it that Logan McCrae had come into her life, providing her with the means to do exactly that . . . only to bring with him an even more confusing and challenging set of conflicts and questions to figure out than she'd started with?

She had memories of him being there for her again last night, of him holding her, rocking her, soothing her. She'd thought it had been a mixed-up part of the dream, adding bits and pieces from that first night . . . except his scent had been on her pillows when she'd woken up. He had been there, had held her, soothed her. She had no idea how long he'd stayed or when he'd left. She did know that there had been no torrid kiss, and she knew it was wrong to wish there had been . . . along with everything that would have likely come afterward.

Saving herself from a nightmare by reigniting the incendiary passion that came so naturally to them would have been an even bigger mistake. She knew she should be thankful he'd been there to help her through it . . . and equally thankful he'd had the strength, the control, to leave before she'd woken up. She wasn't sure, in his place, she'd have been as strong. But knowing what she should feel . . . and acknowledging how she actually felt . . . were going to remain two distinctly different things, no matter how much she tried to browbeat her subconscious mind into accepting the only workable solution.

"So, what do you think? Will this work for you?"

Alex spun around as Delia came into the small loft space. "Yes. It's perfect. Thank you. Are you sure it's okay? You said you don't have a regular tenant."

"I wouldn't have offered to let you become one unless I'd already made up my mind about you." She walked past Alex and stood in the corner of the open area that comprised the kitchen. "It's basic, but functional," Delia said, gesturing to the tiny four-burner stove, short counter, sink, and fridge. "I know the table only seats two, but anything bigger and you can't really move around."

She pointed to the two doors on the front wall opposite the pair of dormer windows. "Bathroom is through the door on the left. Just a small, stand-up shower, no tub. Closet is on the right. Coats, clothes, it all has to go there, I'm afraid. But it's a decent size. One of the former tenants built some shelves underneath the hanger rails and added some little square canvas baskets to hold socks, underwear, and the like. Sort of an open dresser type arrangement. There's a place for shoes in a hanging rack on the back side of the door."

The main area of the room held a soft blue couch and a small antique walnut coffee table that had seen better decades. A mismatched, round, oak end table was angled between the couch and a high-backed, overstuffed red chair. There was a standing lamp on the other side of the chair and an old brass and stained-glass hurricane lamp on the end table for lighting. A ceiling fan with a single light in the center hung over the kitchen area.

"Couch folds out to a double, but it faces the windows, so you have the view to make it feel a bit bigger. Radiator heat, though you might want to get a little space heater for when the temperatures really dip. No central air in the summer, but you won't really need it. Just crank out the dormers and set a fan in one to circulate the breeze coming off the water. Always cools off at night. We've got the Wi-Fi downstairs in the diner, so you'll have it up here, too. No television though, sorry. If that's something you need, we could talk about trying to figure something out. There's a radio around here somewhere. It's a good idea to keep it tuned to the weather. Especially this time of year. Keep flashlights and fresh batteries, too." She came back to stand next to Alex. "Not much, I know, but—"

"It's just right. And I appreciate it, Delia. More than you know."

"Well, you might not feel that way when you realize there's going to be folks underneath you at all hours, yammering on and such. I know it sounds quiet now, but we're just done with the breakfast crowd. You'll see what I mean come lunch. I come in early—and by early I mean no later than four—to get started on the day. We open at five to feed the fishermen and anyone else crazy enough to get up at that hour. We're here until nine in the winter, but the nights are quiet on the water this time of year. Come summer, that all changes. We're open all the way to midnight and there's always something going on down on the docks and out on the water. There'll be plenty of noise, but you get used to it."

"It's okay. Noise won't bother me." Privately Alex thought it might be a good thing. The sounds of talking, laughter. She'd get enough silence out on the Point, and probably too much time to be inside her own head.

Alex's gaze shifted back to the harbor, and Delia's followed hers. "You're also right close to the Monaghan's boathouses and docks," she commented, about as subtle as an anvil. "Just down there." She pointed. "You know, I rented this place to Brodie when he first got here. I guess he's holed up somewhere on his property now, though I can't see where. He lived on one of his boats for a bit, but that's docked and wrapped for the winter now."

"He's renovating the boathouse on the far end of his property into living quarters," Alex told her. "That's the work I'm doing for him. He's more or less camping indoors there at the moment, but he needs to get something more solid before it gets really cold."

Delia had folded her arms and finally shifted her weight a little, glancing back to Alex. "Why'd you let us all believe there was something going on between the two of you?"

Caught off guard, it took Alex a moment to regroup, but in that same moment she knew better than to say anything less than the truth. "It was easier."

"Easier than . . . ?" Delia gave Alex a considering look with her shrewd hazel eyes. "I'm guessin' it has something to do with why you're working out on the Point, but needing to find a place to live here in town."

"I have Brodie's remodel, and a lot of what I'll be doing for the Point restoration will require me to be here, so it's six of one, half dozen of the other." That was true enough.

Delia turned and faced her. "It's the lighthouse, the man who owns it, or a bit of both." She kept her gaze steady on Alex's, so Alex was pretty sure she could see the answer as clearly as if she'd stamped it in bold black letters on her forehead.

"Why do you think it's the lighthouse?" Alex asked by way of reply.

"Honey, we all know about your family, your dad. Couldn't be sorrier, by the way." Delia reached out, rubbed Alex's arm, then gave it a solid squeeze before folding her arms again. "We're a small town and you're big news, especially this time of year when things are quiet. Have you been inside it yet?"

"No. This week. It's next on the list." Alex had thought it would be harder to say. Maybe it was Delia's no-nonsense plain speaking, but it helped.

Delia cocked her head. "You ready? You don't look it."

That surprised a laugh out of Alex. "Yeah, well, if I wait until I'm ready, they'll need to hire someone else to do the job."

"Would that be the worst thing?"

Surprised again, she looked straight at Delia, and the words tumbled out. "Yes. I want that lighthouse. It's my project." The truth in those words still stunned her a little.

Delia grinned, stunning Alex again with how completely it transformed her face. She'd seen the diner owner laugh often, but it had been more of a raucous thing. Alex knew Delia was only in her early forties, but the cheerful, beaming smile of approval knocked a full dozen years off her.

She gave Alex a slap to the side of the shoulder. "Now that's what I wanted to hear. A little grit in there."

"I've got plenty of grit," Alex said, affronted and amused at the same time.

"Oh, when it comes to dealing with our police chief or the head of the town council, you're all ready to do battle, yes sir. I'm guessing we'll find out you sent Brodie home last night, tail between his legs, too. Was probably good for him to experience rejection." Delia barked out a laugh when Alex gaped.

"There's nothing that happens in the Cove I don't hear. Anything I miss during the day, Fergus picks up on the night shift at the pub. Anyhow, it's good to know you've got some of that fire in there for yourself. From the looks of ya, you'll need it."

Alex knew the nightmare and the crying hadn't helped her out there. She half snorted, half spluttered a laugh. "Thanks. I think."

"I'll let you get settled." Delia dug in her apron pocket. "Here's the keys, though during the winter, I don't expect you need to worry much. There's a baseball bat behind the door if it helps you sleep better."

Alex just grinned. "It might."

Delia hooted a laugh at that and headed to the door that led to a narrow set of steps running down the rear of the building to the parking lot. "We get bad weather, I'll remember to ask Charlie or Pete to salt and scrape the stairs for ya. I forget, just take that bat and pound it on the floor."

Still smiling, and feeling oddly more settled and less rattled as Delia went on, Alex said, "Okay."

Delia turned at the door. "You have plans for Thursday?"

"Thursday?"

"Thanksgiving. You've heard of it?"

Alex nodded, her smile turning dry. "A rumor, yes."

"This your first one?"

It took a moment for Alex to catch on. Delia meant her first one alone.

Alex shook her head. "Uh, no. My second. But I was in Canada last year. They don't celebrate the holiday." Not that she'd have been all that aware of it if they had. Her father had died the end of August and by Thanksgiving she'd been gut deep in the lawsuit.

"So . . . plans?"

"No. No, I haven't. Lost track, I guess."

"Well, you do now. I do a dinner here every year. For folks who don't have a family." Delia grinned. "Or want to escape the one they do have."

"Oh, that's okay. You don't have to—"

"I don't do it because I have to. I do it because I want to.

Same reason I just invited you. Boy, do you make everyone work this hard?"

"Hard at what?"

"Being your friend?"

If Delia had slapped her, Alex wouldn't have been any more shocked. Or hurt. "That wasn't my—I didn't mean that. I just—"

"You just try and keep out of anything that's not business. Otherwise, you prefer to stay invisible. It's what you try to do, anyway. I understand that when life gets real big and real hard, it's a tempting thing to do. I've been there. But you're here now. And we all see you. So . . . since you can't hide, I say why waste energy you clearly don't have back yet, doing something that won't get you anywhere, anyway?"

Alex just stood there, mouth open. She finally managed to snap it shut. But the best she could manage was, "Okay."

"Okay, you'll come to dinner? Or okay you'll stop being such a shrinking violet when things get personal?"

"I—yes. To dinner. But . . . I don't shrink. Do I?"

"Like I said, when it's business? No. You're up front and ready to go. But let anyone try to get past the business end and show an interest in you personally? Then? Oh yeah, you're a shrinker."

"But—"

"Case in point." Delia aimed a finger at Alex's chest and the clipboard she was hugging. "You're either making notes on that damn thing or clutching it to your chest like some kind of shield. Put the armor down every once in a while. You can't be working all the time."

Alex looked down at the clipboard she was, in fact, clutching to her chest, and made herself lower it.

"And next time you're downstairs to eat, close your damn laptop and talk to people. They like you. Or they want to.

They respect what you're doing out on the Point. Work that and make a few friends. You've heard of them, too, right?"

Somewhere, Alex found a smile, and it even felt real. "I've heard rumors."

"Well, despite being lousy at it, you've already found one." Delia rolled her eyes when Alex raised a brow in question. "Me, Violet. I'm talking about me."

Alex's smile spread and she felt the corners of her eyes sting a little. Delia was the oddest woman she'd ever met, but already she knew she'd gotten very lucky—very lucky, indeed—that Delia had picked her to befriend. "Thank you."

She started to hug her clipboard again—reflex action— but lowered it as soon as she realized what she was doing. "If there's anything I can do to help, let me know. With dinner on Thursday."

Delia grinned. "As a matter of fact, I wanted to bend your ear on a few ideas I had. Spruce up the menu a little. You're the only one around here who seems to understand about good home cooking that doesn't come in a casserole dish. We'll talk. If you ever can't sleep or we keep you up with the noise, there's always coffee on in the back of the kitchen. Help yourself."

"Thank you. For everything. I'm picking up a check from Brodie today, so I'll give you first and last as soon as I—"

Delia waved her silent. "We'll figure all that out. Relax. I know where you live."

Alex smiled at that. "Okay." Again the clipboard came up, and again she made herself lower it. Then, with a decisive flourish, she tossed it on the couch.

"There you go!" Delia crowed. "Baby steps, but violets don't sprout and bloom in one day, now do they?"

"I guess not. But they're hardy little flowers, you know."

"That I do. But then, I don't have patience with weak, fragile things." Delia turned to the door once more.

Alex hesitated, then blurted out, "Can I ask you one thing?"

Delia looked back. "Shoot."

"You said you knew what it was like. Wanting to be invisible. I—it's none of my business, but—"

"Oh dear Lord, you are going to take some work. Honey, when it's between friends, it's all your business. Don't apologize for wanting to know me better. Hell, I know all about your business and we haven't even talked much yet. Fair's fair, right?" Delia laughed. "Of course, you might wish you'd never asked. But that's also how it works."

"So . . . what happened?"

"Well, the long version will require a few adult beverages and some time to kill. The digest version is I married my high school sweetheart right after graduation. Henry Cavanaugh. Fisherman. His folks were first generation here in the Cove. He worked for Blue's—longtime fishing company based in the harbor. I helped my grandmother run her restaurant. Not this one. It was on the other side of the harbor. We weren't going off to college. Our lives were here and we knew where we were headed, so he wanted to start a family right away. My grandmother was starting to do pretty poorly, health-wise and I was all she had. I had an older brother, but he joined the military when he was twenty-one. Got himself killed in the Gulf War. So it was just me. I decided to hold off having a family, help Granny. Henry decided he didn't want to live his whole life stuck here. He wanted more. He got a job offer, industrial fishery in Alaska."

"You didn't want to go?"

She shook her head. "I used my Granny as an excuse, and I would have stayed for her alone—what was she going to do without me? But truth be told . . . this is where I want to be. I don't have the wanderlust. I don't know how you do it, traipsing all over the world, one job to the next. I know it sounds all glamorous and exciting, but to me . . . it sounds exhausting. I'm more of a rooted person. I need my roots, home, stability. Henry didn't. And seeing as I hadn't given him any babies to stick around for, well, he took the job offer."

"He just . . . left?"

"He might have done a little begging. And maybe I should have at least tried it. He said roots were where you planted them, but I didn't want to start over. Frankly, I didn't think he'd stick it out there. Figured he'd be back."

"So . . . you regret not trying?"

"Not moving away, no. I don't regret that part. But not honoring him enough to even consider trying? Yeah, that kept me awake at night for a good long while. Who knows, maybe I might have caved, chased after him. Then our restaurant caught fire. No one was hurt, but Granny didn't have it in her to start over, and the loss sent her downhill a bit faster. So, I started up this place, moved her in with me, and . . . I stayed. Divorce papers showed up eventually. I signed them." Delia shrugged. "Granny died six months later."

"Did you think about going out there? Once she was gone. See if there was anything left to salvage?"

Delia shook her head. "He remarried five months after I signed the papers. Already had a baby on the way when Granny passed. He kept in touch with the family he fished for here. They told me. To his credit, he stayed out there. Still there, far as I know. He found his place. Maybe it was because his roots weren't that deep here that he didn't feel what I felt. Maybe it was never going to be his place. His folks up and moved out there, too, once he started giving them grandbabies. Somewhere out in Washington State, I think, last I heard, which has been a long time now.

"But the Cove, well, this here is my town. Fifth generation I am. I was born here, my brother was born and buried here, my mom, too, and Granny. Never knew my dad. After Henry left me . . . well . . . I suppose I tried to be a bit invisible, wondering what folks thought of me for not going with him. But there's no hiding in the Cove. There were a few who whispered, but there were plenty more who supported me for staying and taking care of family. Then I was divorced, Granny was gone, and none of that mattered anymore. Or it shouldn't have. I could hardly go back and change my mind then anyway, you know?"

"Delia—"

She raised a hand, palm out. "Don't get maudlin. I'm nineteen years past being maudlin. The bottom line is, I didn't want to go anywhere before he left, and to be honest, I didn't want to go anywhere after he or Granny left. I'm a root person, and my roots are here. I need the Cove. It's part of what I am. It just took a while before I gave myself permission for that to be okay."

"Did you ever—" Alex broke off, already humbled and moved by Delia's openness. She shouldn't pry further.

"Did I ever find another man?" Delia asked.

When Alex nodded, Delia continued. "Honey, I know this feels like a great big revelation, but there isn't a single person in this town who doesn't know that story. Or for that matter who doesn't already know yours. In my case, most of them lived through it with me. Just as they lived through Logan losing his folks in that horrible crash, then him losing his fiancée. We've also been there to cheer the good times. It's not just tragedy that binds us. Bonds are forged through time and shared experiences.

"Sure, we know every last thing about everybody else. It seems intrusive, and it feels that way at times. But it's also like a kind of big security blanket. To think that a whole town can know every last thing about you, and you're still welcome, still valued, still loved. No matter what." She grinned. "Beats even a dog for unconditional love. And you don't have to walk it twice a day."

Alex laughed at her analogy, even as Delia's words made her think. "I guess so. Thanks for sharing with me, anyway. That might not be a big deal to you, but for me . . . it is."

"I can't claim to know what it's like, living out there with no security net like you do. Maybe the thrill of it and the uncertainty is as addictive to you as the steady foundation and security of community is necessary for me. I expect I'll figure it out when you share some stories about your adventures. We're all curious, by the way. So start talkin' already." Delia smiled. "Who knows, you might surprise yourself and end up with a few more friends. To answer your other question—there have been a few men in my life since Henry, but none I'd marry. I don't think that's in the cards for me."

"Did you want it to be?"

"Well, I married Henry, didn't I? But after Granny was gone and I had this place, it was like . . . I got to take care of everyone here. Feed them, listen to their stories. I had my family. Never really could see bringing kids into the picture, so I didn't need to disappoint yet another husband in that area." Delia's grin turned a bit devilish. "Not that men aren't good for a few other things. But when I want other needs taken care of, well, that's what summer tourists are for. They're here, they're fun, then they're gone before they can talk."

Alex laughed at that. "Smart. No muss, no fuss."

Delia laughed, too. "Well, I'm not saying that for the right man I wouldn't have minded getting a bit mussed and fussed over, but . . ." She lifted a shoulder.

"You talk like you're one foot in the grave. You don't even qualify for a midlife crisis yet. So, you never know. Could still happen."

"I was forty-two last month, but some days it feels like double that. I'm not saying never, but if it did happen? Well, let's just say it will be a bigger shock to me than anyone else, and that's saying quite a bit."

"You know what they say, life is what happens when you're busy making other plans. So . . . you just never know."

"No, I guess you don't. I mean, who expected you? But I'm glad you're here. And clearly so is our very fine and very eligible police chief." Delia wiggled her eyebrows. "Now there's a man it would be a shame to waste. How he's kept his bachelor membership card this long, I'll never know. But if he's set his sights on you, well . . . that's a life plan I'd say is worth considering, you know?"

Before Alex could even decide how to respond to that, Delia went on. "Okay, now I really have to get down there and prep for lunch rush. Meatloaf sandwiches on the menu today from last night's dinner special. Better today, if you ask me. Come down later and we'll talk turkey. And dressing."

Alex grinned, thinking it was a good thing she wanted to go along with that plan, since most likely Delia would just wear her down anyway. "Okay. I have appointments, but I'll be back before dinnertime."

Alex shivered a little as the cool air whipped in when Delia let herself out. Even after the door closed, she remained where she stood, thinking *what the hell just happened?*

It was . . . well . . . she didn't quite know what it was, or what she thought about it, but she was smiling, and her brain didn't feel as jumbled as it had when she'd left Pelican Point that morning, or maybe it was just jumbled in a new way. Whatever it was, she'd have to think about it later. The hardware store would already be open and she needed to talk to Owen.

About the lighthouse. *Oh boy.*

She grabbed her clipboard from the couch and fished out her truck keys, Delia's summation echoing through her mind the whole time. *You don't look ready.* She let herself out and used her new key to lock the door to her newest temporary home. "Yeah, well, this is apparently as ready as it gets," she said under her breath as she trotted down the back steps.

She hoped Owen's enthusiasm would add some of the calm she'd sought as she'd stared out over the harbor, or at the very least make her feel more confident about the next step she was about to take. If everyone did indeed know about her dad, maybe she wouldn't have to explain to Owen why she was going to be a wee bit shaky about the whole thing. Or a lot shaky.

Five minutes later, she was standing on the sidewalk in front of Hartley's Hardware, peering through the window of the locked front door. There was no note taped to it, and the sign clearly said he opened at nine. It was half past already.

She drummed her fingers on the back of her clipboard, then looked down, made a face at herself, and lowered the damn thing to her side. "How else do you carry a clipboard if not up against your body?"

Irritated more with herself than Owen's unexpected absence, she turned and looked down Harbor Street. Maybe he'd stopped by one of the other shops that lined the narrow road, which angled downhill to the water and wrapped around the harbor, hence the name. Her luck, he was probably back at Delia's having breakfast.

A brisk wind chose that moment to swirl down the skinny brick sidewalk, catching the papers on her clipboard. No longer shielded by her body, they were snatched right off and sent tumbling through the air like so many autumn leaves off a tree.

"See?" she grumbled, jumping around like a crazy person, trying to snag the sheets before they got completely away from her. She stepped on several and managed to grab a few from the air. Trapping them against her chest with the empty clipboard, she chased after several more, got two, but the last one taunted her halfway up a short side street, which angled uphill at a steep rise. When she finally managed to trap the last sheet under her boot, she snatched it, only to look up and see she was standing across the road from that cool antiques store she'd noticed on her first drive into town. It was kind of hard to miss.

"Mossy Cup Antiques," she read off the beautifully hand-carved sign hanging from the gingerbread trim that ran along the top of the wraparound porch. Her gaze shifted upward and she framed her forehead with her hand so she could lean back and take in the entirety of the huge, majestic oak . . . which appeared to grow right up through the center of the boxy, quaint-looking shop. From the moment she'd first laid eyes on it, she had been completely charmed by the very idea of the place, and had intended to double back, check it out more closely. Then the tire blew out and she had that whole unfortunate fainting incident—which had led to her meeting Logan and getting all caught up in . . . well . . . everything . . . and she'd never made it back.

"No time like the present." She grinned again as she caught sight of the whimsical brass croquet mallet that formed the door handle. "And further down the rabbit hole you go, Alice," she murmured as she opened the door and let herself in. A waterfall chime echoed as the door closed behind her, not loud or brassy, but musical and delicate.

The beautifully restored antique pieces, each one more unique than the last, would normally have been more than enough to snag her complete attention, but she was immediately drawn to the tree instead. Its bark was deeply grooved and knotted, the trunk thick and wide, and real, she realized, running her hand over the rough surface. Maybe it was the whimsy of the *Alice in Wonderland* door handles, but she could easily picture a little door and windows set in the massive trunk. Those little cookie-baking elves came to mind.

She stepped back so she could take it all in, imagining three or four people with arms outspread having a hard time encircling the base of the oak. It was all trunk halfway up to the apex of the open, wood-beam-supported roof, but up there it branched out with thick, sturdy limbs that extended upward through the roof via their own, specially created slots. The main thrust of the tree grew through the largest hole in the center of the roof, joining the other limbs to spread out in the umbrella of branches she'd seen from the sidewalk. She imagined in the spring and summer, when the branches were thick with leaves, they'd form something of a protective cap over the shop.

And *in* the shop, for that matter. She wondered how often the owner had to rake the leaves up in the fall, inside her own shop. Alex glanced at the restored pieces of handcrafted art and wondered how that might affect them, too.

She looked up again. From inside, the apex of the roof was too high up and too obscured by the tree itself for her to see how the windows and main central hole had been crafted so as to keep out the weather and any critters who'd like to make the tree into a home. It made her itch to get up on the roof and check it out for herself.

"Well, it's about time."

Alex turned to find a tall, severe-looking older woman standing several yards behind her. She appeared to be in her eighties, though it was kind of hard to tell. Her gray hair was pulled back in a smooth, tight bun. She wore a floral dress buttoned up to the neck, then a surprisingly charming, gaily designed shop apron over it. On closer inspection, it was actually a stitched scene from *The Velveteen Rabbit*.

The whimsy of it seemed at odds with the stern expression and tone.

Alex looked around, but when she saw there wasn't anyone else in the shop, she realized the woman had been speaking to her. "I'm sorry?"

"You should be. I'd have thought you'd have made time before now."

Alex blinked, and thought maybe her *Alice in Wonderland* prediction had been more prescient than she'd anticipated. "I—uh, I'm Alex. Alexandra MacFarland," she said, wondering if the woman might have her confused with someone else.

The older woman huffed. "I might be old, but I'm not senile. I know who you are."

Alex finally managed to gather at least some of her wits back around her. "Well then, I'm afraid you have me at a disadvantage. I don't believe we've met."

"If you'd come in when you first got here, we could have taken care of that bit of business, now couldn't we?"

Okay, she had fallen down the rabbit hole. There was no other explanation for this Jabberwockyesque conversation.

"I did see your shop when I drove into town and it's been on my to-do list. I'm sorry I haven't made it in until now." She glanced back at the tree. "It's truly magnificent." She glanced back to the woman in the apron. "I'm guessing you're the owner?"

"Eula March. You can call me Eula. And that I am. Shop has been in my family longer than the Cove has had its name. The tree is a mossy cup oak. Hence the name."

Alex smiled, charmed despite the lack of anything that could come close to being described as such in the owner's demeanor. She looked at the oak tree again. "It's . . . fantastic. And fantastical." She pressed her palm against the bark again, purely because it seemed to call to her to do so. Then, realizing that might be frowned upon—she hadn't yet looked for a sign indicating she shouldn't—she pulled her hand away.

"If it calls you to touch it, then do as it asks."

Alex glanced at Eula. "I don't know why, but you're right, it does seem to do that. Maybe it's the idea of how long it's stood here, how many stories it could tell. I can almost envision a band of faeries and nymphs and other fantastical beings living in its branches and under its roots." She let out a short laugh, feeling her cheeks warm. Despite the whimsy of the name and the very idea of the tree being there in the first place, the current March proprietor didn't strike Alex as being a remotely whimsical sort.

A look in Eula's direction showed the woman was quietly studying her, and yet she said nothing.

Alex turned away from the tree, but continued to feel it at her back, like a sentinel of sorts, a friendly one. It was . . . comforting . . . in the same way lighthouses used to make her feel.

She turned her attention to the finished pieces that were for sale. "These are remarkable," she said, completely sincere. "Each piece is unique." She stepped over to a gorgeous sideboard with a glossy surface and intricately hand-carved panels on the cabinet doors. She bent down and studied the detail, marveled over the lovingly preserved and beautifully hand polished work that made the grain in the rich cherry-wood glow with warmth.

From there, feeling the effects of Eula's focused, silent attention and the warm, protective sensation that she assumed came from being in the shadow of the tree, she moved on to a dainty, padded footstool with a beautifully detailed peacock embroidered into the fabric stretched over the pillowy top. "Do you do all the restoration work yourself?" she asked, truly curious, but also wanting—needing—to break the growing silence.

"These could be reproductions."

Alex straightened and looked at Eula. "But they're not. I know my work is on buildings and lighthouses, not furnishings, but I understand craftsmanship, and these pieces weren't made in some factory."

"Could be I find them already restored."

Alex frowned. Why was the woman being so perverse?

"Could be"—Alex nodded toward the shop apron—"except it looks like you've got a little linseed stain there on the front pocket, and if I'm not mistaken, that's four-aught steel wool peeking out from the top of the other one." She met the woman's steely gaze. "Besides, where's the joy in selling pieces after somebody else gets to do all the fun parts first?" It was a total guess, but as Eula didn't remotely strike her as a natural born saleswoman, Alex assumed the old woman didn't get her pleasure from the sale-making part of the process. Although, for all Alex knew, it was possible Eula hated everything having to do with the business and resented being stuck with it.

Eula studied her for another moment, and, not entirely sure why, Alex met her gaze and held it. Then the old woman abruptly nodded and turned away. "You'll do."

"Do . . . for what?"

"Like I said. It's about time." Eula headed to the back of the shop and with that, it appeared their conversation was over. She disappeared through a half-open, sliding panel door in the rear corner.

Alex didn't even pause. She followed right behind her, knowing she should have turned and walked out. "What did you mean?"

She immediately lost track of the conversation, because she was too busy staring, slack-jawed, at the workshop spread out before her. There were three rows of long wood tables, framed with a scattering of short benches, stools, and other wood boxes on either side.

The walls were filled with custom shelves and tiny drawers, most filled with tools, furniture parts, supplies, and other odds and ends. She assumed the drawers held hardware and things like that. The tables were covered with a variety of different antique pieces in various stages of restoration. None of which, in itself, was particularly odd or surprising.

She was standing there with her mouth hanging open because the size of the room was easily three times the square footage that could possibly fit within the four walls of the whole shop. If there had been some kind of addition off the back of the shop, she'd have seen it from the street.

"Unless you plan to help here, I've got work to do."

Alex pulled it together enough to close her mouth and look at Eula stationed on the far side of the table farthest from the panel door. She was using the steel wool from her apron pocket to work on a set of what looked like old brass doorknobs.

"I—it looks interesting," Alex said politely, though she realized she was being quite honest. "Is that why you thought I was here? That I needed a job? I—thank you, if that's the case, but I'm sorry. I already have a job. Two, in fact. This all looks amazing, though, and I'm sure I'd enjoy it."

"Then find a piece that calls to you and get to it."

Alex was surprised by just how much the offer actually called to her. In fact, had it been any other time, and any other owner, she'd have likely stepped in and taken a closer look at the work. She was truly curious about what methods Eula used to achieve the results she got. "I-I wish I could."

Though she couldn't say she was equally enthusiastic about the idea of spending any length of time holed up with Eula, she was actually sincere. "I have to meet with Owen. Then get back out to the Point. I'm going to restore the lighthouse. Along with the keeper's cottage and the main house."

"So I've heard." Eula looked up at her. "And yet, for someone so clear on her purpose, you're at a crossroad, Alexandra. And not a small one. A crossroad implies there are multiple choices to be made—meaning there are other paths you could take from that intersection." Eula's gaze traveled the room, then landed on Alex. Actually, it felt more like it pierced her. "My question is, how can you know what other paths there might be, if you don't open your eyes, look around you, and find out what they are?"

"I-I don't know." First Delia with her find-a-friend instruction manual on how to improve her personal life, and now Eula pointing out she might want to put a little more thought into her professional one. It was all just . . . too much. Too much jumble, too much confusion, too . . . well . . . just too much.

Jabberwocky, indeed.

"As much as I appreciate the offer and the insight, I really need to get back to the work I've already signed on to do. Thank you, though."

"Have you ever considered what it is about your work that draws you?"

"Making something whole," Alex answered automatically, even though she knew she really should be going. But something about Eula compelled her to respond as if she was being challenged in some way. "I like bringing it back to life."

"Ever considered what else might give you that same feeling of accomplishment?"

"You mean . . . like restoring old houses? I've done plenty of cottages, but it's not—"

"Of course it's not. Anybody can put shakes on the side of a house."

Privately, Alex knew there was a good bit more to it than that, but thought better of saying so.

"The thing is, dear, you're drawn to the unique, the one of a kind. You want something with history, with meaning. You see more than the engineering, the math. You see the qualities in what a creative mind once put together. You see where and how it fell apart, and you feel it, like a physical thing. You want—need—to make it whole again. It makes something in you whole again."

Alex stared at her, unable to comprehend how this stranger had pegged it and so . . . perfectly.

"I understand, because we're one and the same," Eula said as if the conversation was being conducted out loud on both sides. "Only I don't need to go climbing all over a lighthouse, risking life and limb, to get my fix."

Alex stared at the various furnishings on the table, already having recognized that each one truly was a unique and interesting piece. Nothing standard issue, only pieces that came from the creativity and artistry of a single set of hands. And she could see how, though the restoration process was entirely different, the satisfaction would still be very similar to what she felt in her own work.

As if Alex had said the words out loud, Eula nodded. "And I'm fortunate in that I get to have all my adventures, do all my exploring, and face all my challenges right here." Her eyes lit up in what might have almost been described as a smile as she nodded to the pieces in various stages of restoration around her. "And my playground is far more vast and varied than yours. I daresay, it's also a lot more fun."

Alex didn't know what to say to that, or why she bothered saying anything at all, since it seemed Eula was reading her thoughts anyway.

"Offer stands," Eula said. "Make time to consider things.

Instinct brought you to the Cove. It brought you here to me and to the others whose paths you've now crossed. There's always a reason. Unfortunately, we don't always take time to understand what that reason is. Or, worse, we try to apply logic to help us make sense of it. Logic, Miss MacFarland, doesn't apply to instinct."

"You're saying I should go with my gut."

"In a manner of speaking."

"But go with my gut on what?"

The old woman looked up from her work and Alex was surprised to see a hint of what might have been loosely described as a smile hovering at the corners of her thin, compressed lips. "That would be the question now, wouldn't it?"

"But—"

"I've work to do. No time for idle chatter. We've covered what needs covering. Have a good day."

Alex wanted to ask her to explain . . . well . . . a lot of things. The workroom was just the beginning. But she'd been quite clearly dismissed. "Okay. Um, thank you. Anyway. I'll show myself out."

Eula said nothing more and Alex turned and stepped back through the half-open panel door, feeling as if she was stepping back through the looking glass. As she stepped through, she could have sworn she heard what sounded like the tittering of a bunch of mice or . . . some sort of chirring noise. Maybe some tool Eula had switched on. But it was . . . odd. The sound made the hairs on her arm lift a little and her feet hurry as she crossed back through the shop. She did pause at the tree, though, and place her palm flat on the trunk for an extended moment. She didn't question why she felt the need to do it, but it made her smile, and feel . . . connected . . . in some way.

She heard the waterfall chimes tinkling as she let herself

out of the shop, then laughed at herself as she shook her head a little. "Well, that certainly got my mind off of Logan and the lighthouse situation for five minutes."

But the time had come. She needed no more distractions and headed back down the hill to the hardware store.

How can you know what other paths there might be, if you don't open your eyes, look around you, and find out what they are? Instinct brought you to the Cove . . . and to the others whose paths you've now crossed.

There's always a reason.

Alex shut out Eula's tantalizing, yet confusing comments. Her instincts had told her to restore the Pelican Point lighthouse. And, at the moment, that goal had brought her to Owen. For now, that was all that mattered.

Chapter 14

"I'm no' stayin' in for the holiday meal this year, laddie." Fergus pushed a mug of coffee across the bar to Logan. "I've decided to join the band of merry misfits at Delia's this go."

"I thought we'd do what we did last year. Maybe ask Owen to join us. Lauren's not coming home until winter break, so—"

"It's proud I am that you thought of it. Although"— Fergus lowered one bushy brow—"my guess is a certain desk sergeant probably put the bug in your ear. Aye, I can see the truth of it in your eyes. It's all for naught, actually, as Owen told me himself he plans to join us down on the harbor." He freshened his own mug. "Besides, for all I've been haranguing you to get out and be social, I figured I should take my own advice and chat with folks when they aren't payin' me for the privilege of chatting back. By the by, laddie, wantin' you to come to the Puffin to socialize doesna' mean comin' in the back door and sitting in the kitchen, brooding over a pint. It means being out here with actual people."

"I see actual people all day long," Logan retorted, knowing full well that wasn't the point. "I'll do better next time."

"Aye and that ye will, because yer comin' to Delia's with me on Thursday. Don't even bother puttin' up a squawk.

I'm no' be letting you sit out there on the Point by your pathetic, moping self, eating heated-up God only knows what and feeling sorry for yourself."

"How do you know I'd be out there by myself?" Logan asked. "And I'm not feeling sorry for myself."

"Well, you're sure looking it right enough. And the reason I know is because I spoke to Delia, who happened to mention that our Miss Alex just this morning rented the room over her place."

Lord save him from the town grapevine and his uncle's role as head grape. "And you wonder why I don't spend more time in town when I don't have to."

"Why would the lovely Miss MacFarland be needin' a room here in town when she had a perfectly good roof over her head out on the Point, I'm wonderin'?"

"It's complicated," Logan said, nursing his coffee and knowing he sounded exactly like he was moping. And maybe he was. Alex had said she was going to pack and go while he was at work. He'd quietly left her bed after daybreak to take a shower, intending to come back down and make breakfast for them both, and talk to her. About all of it. Her moving out, the lighthouse. To say the previous night had been an emotional seesaw was putting it mildly. He just wanted to clear the air, make sure they were both okay, and frankly, get a bead on just how ready she really was to tackle the tower.

If it was better for them not to tackle it together, then Owen was a good choice, and yet Logan couldn't help but feel frustrated at the substitution, at being boxed out of being there for her, even though he agreed with the reasons behind making the switch. He was annoyed he couldn't do a better job of being there for her during what would probably be her biggest test, without it threatening to undermine their attempt at a business-only relationship.

Annoyed didn't come close to describing what he'd felt when he'd come downstairs after showering and shaving, having spent the night holding her in his arms, protecting her, being there for her . . . and wondering if there truly was no way that they could make it work between them . . . only to find her already packed and gone.

"The best relationships are complicated," Fergus said. "You'd die of boredom if it were simple."

"Ours is a business agreement," Logan said, hating the truth of it. "That's all."

"Och, and you're an even bigger fool than I feared, then."

Logan looked up and met Fergus's clear, crystal blue gaze. But rather than bluster and protest too much, what came out was the truth. "That's my fear, too, Gus. But I don't see a way around it."

Fergus sighed, and his shoulders slumped a little. "As good as it is to hear you admit it, I wish I had better counsel for you." He refreshed Logan's mug, and topped off his own, and Logan let him ruminate a bit. He had nothing else to say at the moment, anyway.

"You're afraid you'll come to care too deeply, only to lose her to wherever the road takes her next. Is that the crux of it, then?" Fergus said at length.

"I already care too much . . . and she hasn't been here a month." God, it felt good to say it, to own up to the truth of it.

But rather than crow about it, about being right, Fergus looked as tormented by the confession as Logan felt. He'd have rather endured the crowing. "And Alexandra?"

Logan lifted weary eyes to look at his uncle. "She's . . . we're both fighting it."

"Well, laddie," Fergus said, as serious as Logan had ever heard him. "It seems a damn shame when a man and woman find each other as ye have, both of you acknowledging the power and goodness of it, both of you wanting what the other has to offer, especially after losing all that was dear to you in the past . . . only to let it go. Why would you not move heaven and earth to find a way to keep something so precious?" He laid a hand on Logan's arm. "It's one thing when the fates conspire against ye, taking from you what you love, without so much as giving you a say in the matter. You've both endured that particular cruelty. So forgive me if I dinnae understand how, when those same fates have seen to bless you and you've finally the power to do as you please . . . you simply give up without a fight. Is she not worth that to ye?" Fergus lifted a shoulder. "If so, perhaps you're right, and you should leave her be."

"I—it's not that. She is worth it."

"Then why did you let her move out?"

"I don't *let* Alex do anything."

Fergus's eyes picked up a bit of twinkle when he smiled. "Another reason why you should have been a bit more creative in finding a way to make her want to stay. You want out of your rut, and she seems like just the woman to keep you guessing."

"Her moving out wasn't what we wanted, Gus. Either of us. It comes down to the fact that my life is here. And my roots are deep. And hers will be everywhere but here."

"Just because Pelican Point is your heritage, doesna' mean you should be shackled by it. If life's journey calls you to go elsewhere, then look for other solutions."

"That's just it, I don't feel shackled by my life here in the Cove. I will admit you're right that I've become too comfortable with the safety and stability of my routine. I am in a rut. But I can work on that. I want to. Bottom line is, I'm where I want to be, where I'm meant to be. I love what I do, and, frankly, being responsible for the Point is probably a large part of why I am who I am. It pushed me, forced me to grow up, to deal with what's been handed to me and find a way to make it work."

"Then use what you've learned and find a way to make this work."

"I have, or I've tried to. Trust me." Logan had just spent a very long night trying to figure out exactly that. "But . . . I don't see it. Not realistically. Sure, I could give it all up, find someone to manage the Point. I know I'm replaceable as chief. It's not like I'm the only one who's ever held the job."

Fergus's bushy brows climbed halfway up his ruddy forehead. "You've considered that, have you? Well then . . ." He trailed off, then shook his head.

"Why is that a surprise? Do you think I'm so stubborn or so stuck in my rut that I'd only consider things one way? My way?"

"No, no. Quite the opposite—hearing you say it so matter-of-factly." Fergus held Logan's gaze directly. "Do you understand that the very fact that you even considered making such a monumental shift in your life is proof that you can't just up and let her go?"

"Yes, of course I do." The house had felt ridiculously empty, and Logan was dreading going back that night. He'd once embraced the quiet, the solitude, the sameness of life on the Point. Now it would just feel lonely. Distant. Apart. "But even if I chose to leave here, to follow Alex when she was done with the Point project . . . what would I do? My calling isn't hers. She might be worried—terrified even, in some respects—about having what it takes to do what she's always done, what she loves . . . but I see her love of it every day. The deeper she gets into the project, the clearer and more obvious it becomes that she's doing what she's meant to do. I think when the work finally gets underway, it will resolve any questions she has left. I'm proud of her and want that satisfaction for her.

"But, quite honestly, I don't see a role for myself in her world. The work I do restoring the Point is only gratifying because the place itself has meaning to me. Restoration, in and of itself, is not my passion or my calling. I've already found my calling. And I can't do what I do while traipsing around the world." He fidgeted with his coffee mug, staring at the dark brew as if it could magically provide him an answer. He finally looked back up at Fergus. "The only thing I could really come up with was that if I truly do care about her . . . then maybe the best way to show it is to do whatever I can to help her get back to the life she loves."

"Did it ever once occur to you to ask her to stay?"

Logan frowned. "I just got done saying that I couldn't see a role for myself in her life. But I'm supposed to be selfish and ask her to find a role in mine?"

"The work you do doesna' translate to the lifestyle her job requires. That is true enough. Why do you automatically assume the same is true in reverse?" Fergus lifted a hand to stall Logan's reply. "What I'm saying is, the life she once knew . . . she can't get back. Her family is gone. I'm betting that a large part of the satisfaction she found in that calling was doing it with her family. Doing what they loved together. Her family is gone now. And the framework of the extended family, meaning those who worked alongside them, is all gone, too. Remember, she didn't go out and seek a life restoring lighthouses. She was born into it."

"She loves it, Gus. It's in her blood, just as life here in the Cove is in mine."

"I'm not doubting that. But how much of that was because she got to do something so fulfilling with her father? Her grandfather? What is it about restoring lighthouses in particular that so fulfills *her*? What I'm saying is, there are all kinds of restoration. In fact, she's already working for you and for Brodie, doing projects that have nothing to do with that lighthouse. Does she not find some measure of fulfillment in that? Would it be enough? Or is it truly the towers themselves? Or even the vagabond life? Have you talked about that? Considered that?"

"She agreed with me that our lifestyles weren't compatible. That when this was done, she'd be leaving. That didn't sound to me like someone looking for a new life— or a different one, anyway."

"Maybe because she hasn't considered that there's a different life to be had. She's trying to get back to the one she lost . . . because what else does she know to do?" Fergus leaned his elbows on the bar. "Seems to me the thing she's truly lost isn't her passion for her work. What she lost was what made it important. Her family. They were her home, her Cove. But now . . . it will be just her. Alone. Maybe what she really needs is a new home . . . except she can't just up and go find that. Maybe she doesn't even see it. So, she's thinking she'll find a sense of belonging in her work, instead. I think we both know that that's not the same thing."

"If she thought there was something different for her, or even wanted to find something more permanent, don't you think she'd have figured that out on her own? Is that something you can ask of a person? Hey, just hang out a while longer, I'm sure you'll fall in love with the place? We're not her family, either."

"You're the closest she's got to the beginnings of one. She's been forced to start over . . . and she has to start somewhere. It sounds like she's already found a rhythm here, and in a short amount of time, to boot. A year from now, she might have roots she wasn't even aware she'd planted. My guess is she'll have a much harder time moving on than she knows. Perhaps now is the time to get her thinking about what kinds of things she might want to do here in the long term, so she can keep both. Her work . . . and her new home. She'd be welcomed here by more than just yourself. She already has been."

Logan wanted to pick apart all the flaws in Fergus's thinking, but they weren't readily visible. In a perfect world, Alex would fall in love with the Cove. If he were remarkably lucky, with him, too. She'd find a way to combine their worlds. It felt like such a huge gamble, a risk beyond anything he'd imagined. What if she didn't fall in love? With the town or with him? He was pretty sure he already knew the direction he was headed. It was hard enough to find her gone this morning. How would it feel a year or so from now, if he'd let himself not only want it all, but truly believe he could have it . . . only to watch her walk away forever?

His radio squawked just then, saving him from having to put any part of his greatest fear into words. He unclipped the receiver from his belt and pushed the button. "Yes, Barb?"

"Owen's on his way to you."

Logan sat up straighter as he automatically switched gears, relieved at the reprieve to think about something other than Alex. "Is everything okay?"

"Remember Dan was going to help him with those motion sensors? Well, seems Owen took matters into his own hands early this morning."

Oh, for the love of—"You should have told him to stay put at the station." Logan slid off the stool and palmed his hat. "Call him and tell him to meet me at his store."

"He should be outside the Puffin any second. Talk to him." The amusement he hadn't heard at first, came through now. "You're not going to believe this one. Sir."

Before Logan could even respond, Owen stuck his shaggy head inside the pub door. "Chief? Could I have a word?"

"Thanks, Sergeant. He's here." Logan clicked off and turned to Owen. "What's going on, Owen?"

Owen didn't come inside, but instead hovered by the door. "Remember that problem I had with someone tampering with the lock on the back door to my shop?" He was clearly a little anxious and looked over his shoulder a few times.

"Last week. Yes, I do. Sergeant Benson just radioed me that something happened this morning?"

"Well, ah, it turns out I didn't need that motion sensor."

"Why don't you come on in, have some coffee," Fergus told him. "Looks like you could use something stiffer, but it's early yet, so we can start with a cup of joe."

Owen looked over his shoulder again. "No, no. That's okay."

Logan frowned. "What's going on, Owen? What's happened?"

"Well, I just had this . . . inkling . . . I guess you could call it, that whoever tried to break in would come back." Owen looked out the door, toward the parking lot, then back at Logan. "So, I've sort of been staking out my own business. At night. And last night—well, this morning, actually—it happened."

Fergus hooted at that. "You should have given me a shout. I'd have brought the coffee."

"Owen, you shouldn't have taken matters into your own hands," Logan said, shooting Fergus a quelling look. "If you were that concerned, you should have called me or whoever was on desk."

"That's just it. I didn't really know for sure, so there was nothing to call about. Something has to happen, to call the police, right?"

"Well, something obviously has happened."

"That's why I'm here."

Logan shifted and looked out the door behind Owen, but

didn't see anything beyond his SUV and Owen's pickup truck parked next to it. "Why do you keep looking over your shoulder? Did you get in some kind of fight? Is someone coming after you?"

Completely unfazed by Logan's previous glare, Fergus snatched up the bat he kept behind the bar and ducked under the walk-through. "Where are they, laddie? Nobody comes into my town and—"

Logan palmed the end of the bat and snatched it from Fergus's hand. "Stop it. Both of you. Owen, for God's sake, come in here and close the door. I want to know what happened. Start from the beginning. Whatever it is, I'm sure we can work it all out."

"That's just it. I'm not sure what kind of time I have. You see, I sort of caught the intruder."

"Good on ya there, lad!" Fergus shook his fist. "That's the way."

Logan felt an instant headache pinch at the space between his brows. He couldn't have imagined his day getting worse than how it had started. "You caught him," Logan repeated. "Meaning you still have him somewhere? Or—did he get out? Is that who you think is after you?" Having no idea what the threat was, Logan moved forward, pulled Owen inside the room, and took up a watchful stance by the door to the pub.

"I don't know. I mean, yes, I still have him. I mean, her. It's not a him. It's—but I don't trust her. She could have gotten out. I mean, she broke into my store, so—"

"She?" Logan said, abandoning the door to turn back to Owen, incredulous.

"This is getting better by the minute," Fergus cackled.

Logan didn't bother trying to glare Gus into submission. His attention was completely on Owen. He crossed the room and took Owen by the arm. "Come on."

"Where are we going?" Owen asked as Logan flat-palmed

the pub door open with perhaps a bit more force than was necessary.

"To wherever it is you have your intruder stashed." Logan shook his head, not believing he was even saying those words. He turned back to Fergus, who was halfway across the room, and pointed at him. "Sit. Stay. I'll call you later."

"No fun a' tall," Fergus called out as the door swung shut behind them. "At least tell me who it is ye've captured!"

"We'll take my vehicle," Logan directed Owen. "Get in."

Once they were belted in and pulling out of the lot, Logan said, "What on earth were you thinking? Anything like this happens, you don't take matters into your own hands. You call me. Or whoever is on duty."

"I meant to. But it all happened so fast. I mean, when I parked behind the Dumpster last night, I didn't know if anything was going to happen, so there was nothing to call about. If someone did come, then my plan was to call the station." Owen's expression turned sheepish. "Then it got kinda late and I sort of fell asleep. When I woke up it was getting light out and—well, it was probably the noise that woke me. She was jimmying the lock to my back door. I was trying to find my phone—it had fallen on the floor of my car while I was sleeping—and she got in. I didn't know it was her. It was still early so it was shadowy under the loading dock overhang on the back of the shop. I just knew it was somebody. The light inside the back door comes on automatically, so I saw who it was as soon as she opened the door. And then I wasn't so much afraid as I was pissed off."

"Who?" Logan asked. "Who was it?"

"Oh! Right. Eleanor Darby."

"Eleanor Dar—?" Logan broke off, snapping his mouth shut, mostly to keep from voicing the very long string of expletives sitting right on the edge of his tongue. *What the hell?* "You should have called. Right then."

"I know. I mean, I do now But I couldn't find my phone.

It was still too dark, and it wasn't like I was worried about her overpowering me."

"She held city hall hostage a little over a week ago."

"I know, I know. That was part of it, too. I've known Eleanor my whole life. She was a customer of Hartley's when my dad ran the place, you know? I don't know what's going on with her, but this isn't like her. Or didn't used to be. She's never been the friendly sort, but this? It doesn't seem right. So . . . I'm worried about her."

Privately, Logan agreed with him. "You could have driven to the police station in two minutes."

"I didn't know what she was doing in there, so I couldn't just drive off and leave her. And like I said, I was mad, but worried about her. I figured this violated her parole—or whatever—from the other day."

"She's out on bail, not parole, but yes, this would nullify her bond."

"See? So I figured I'd just go in and talk to her, find out what's really going on. Maybe help her out in some way without getting her into more trouble."

"Well, that's nice of you, Owen, but don't ever do that again, okay? Clearly she's not using good sense if she's breaking into your store. If you wanted to help her, you should have called us. Or come and gotten us." Logan turned down Harbor Street toward Owen's store. "What happened? What did you do?"

"Well, I sort of locked her in my supply closet." Owen looked more miserable by the minute. "She's not too happy about it, either, I can tell you that."

"No. I imagine she's not." Right about then, the idea of traipsing around the globe sprucing up lighthouses with Alex was sounding incredibly appealing. "Tell me what happened after she broke into the store."

"I went inside after her, just to talk to her, but I ended

up startling her pretty badly, I guess. Her hearing's not what it used to be. She tried to attack me."

"Bodily? Or did she have a weapon?"

"I don't know if she had anything else, but I just got in a shipment for the feed store last night and it was still sitting inside the loading dock door, where we were. So she grabbed a ten-pound bag of this new kitty litter. People are going crazy over it. I can't keep it on the shelves. It has these blue beads in it that—"

"Yes, so I've heard. What did she do with it?"

"She took a pretty good swing. For an older person, she's got a strong arm. She swung that thing—surprisingly hard, like I said—and, well, I acted on instinct. Now, I would never hit a woman, you know that."

Logan privately thought that maybe where Eleanor Darby was concerned, that basic etiquette rule should be rescinded. Or at least modified.

"I grabbed the closest thing to me to block the swing, which was another bag of kitty litter, and well, they kind of exploded on impact and the beads went everywhere. She reeled back a little and her feet hit the beads and she kind of slipped and slid right into the storage room. Normally, I keep it closed and locked, but I guess I left the door open when I was unloading last night. Anyway, once she was inside, she got her balance back and she was mad as a wet cat, I guess you could say. She came at me and I just reacted and reached in, yanked the door shut, and locked it. There is no way to unlock it from the inside. I did turn the light on for her," he hurried to add. "The switch is outside the door. Then I used the store phone and called you. Only Barb— uh, Sergeant Benson—said you were with Fergus, so it was just as easy to come to you at the Puffin as it was to go to the station."

Logan pulled into the lot behind Owen's shop. "Owen—"

"I know, I know. You don't have to say it. She's not hurt or anything. And I am sorry for the trouble. But—she did break into my store, Logan."

"I know." He also knew that Owen Hartley was about as mild-mannered a guy as there was. And softhearted. Though the whole stakeout thing seemed a tad out of character, it didn't surprise Logan in the least that Owen had wanted to help Mrs. Darby. He knew Owen wouldn't hurt a fly if he could help it.

"So . . . am I in trouble?"

"You're lucky she didn't bean you with that kitty litter and knock you out."

"I know, right? She's got deadly aim for someone who wears bifocals."

"Tell me about it," Logan muttered as they both got out of the car. "I want you to stay out here until Sergeant Baker gets here. Tell Dan everything you told me so he can take that down as your official statement. I'll go in and deal with Mrs. Darby."

"Tell her I'm sorry, okay? You know she's going to want to press charges."

"She broke into your store, Owen. You have some charges of your own to file, if you want to. Let's save any more words between the two of you until we sort out what she was doing in there."

"Okay." Owen shook his head and looked pretty miserable. "You know, staking out places and going in after the bad guy . . . it all looks a lot more exciting on television."

"Most things do," Logan said, then started across the lot to the loading dock steps. He'd just jumped up on the dock when his radio went off again. "Yes, Sergeant?"

"You're not going to believe this."

"Oh, try me."

"Just got a report of another break-in."

"What? Where?"

"At Hartley's Hardware."

"*What?*"

"I know. What the heck is going on over there? Jean Reisters, who runs the little jewelry shop across the street—"

"I know who Jean is."

"Right. Well, she just called in and said she saw a woman throwing a rock through Owen's front door. Then she reached inside, unlocked it, and went in! What's this town coming to? Do you think this is some kind of gang thing?"

"Unless Eleanor Darby has started one—which, honestly, I wouldn't put past her at this point—I doubt it."

"Eleanor Darby? Oh dear Lord, is she somehow involved in this?"

"I'm at Hartley's now. Send Dan over here, will you? Tell him Owen is in the back lot by my truck. Get him to take his statement. I'll report back in as soon as I get inside and find out—"

Just then the back door burst open, and for the first time in his career, Logan palmed his gun. He immediately holstered it again as Eleanor Darby came staggering out . . . followed by Alex.

"Logan, thank God," Alex said, looking more than a little rattled. "I was just going to call you."

"You might have wanted to do that before I'd have to think about arresting you for breaking and entering."

"There wasn't any time for that. I thought someone was in real trouble."

"What are you saying?" Eleanor demanded. "Someone was in real trouble!"

Logan stepped forward. "Now, now—"

"Don't you 'now-now' me, you—"

Logan took Eleanor's arm in a gentle but firm grip. "Mrs. Darby, why don't we go have a seat and you can tell me your side of the story."

"There's no story to tell, just the truth! This whole town is against me." To his shock and utter dismay, she went from blistering fury to a sudden convulsion of tears.

"Mrs. Darby—"

Alex stepped to Mrs. Darby's other side and tucked her hand through the older woman's arm. She looked at Logan. "I can take care of this, okay? Why don't you call for some help? Or . . . something."

Logan met Alex's gaze over the stooped and sobbing Eleanor and thought of a million things he wanted to say to her. None of them appropriate for that moment. "Just help her out to my truck. Get her in the backseat. And join her. You have some explaining to do, too."

"I know. I'm sorry. Not for saving her—just that she had to be saved in the first place. Even though that wasn't my fault." Alex held his gaze for a beat longer, then they both shifted to helping Eleanor down the loading dock steps and out to his SUV.

Sergeant Baker had arrived and had Owen over by his car. Still not sure what had provoked the initial break-in, Logan motioned to Alex with his head to keep Eleanor on the far side of his SUV and Owen out of her direct line of sight. Alex saw Owen, looked back at Logan, nodded, and they maneuvered Eleanor to the other side. The tinted windows helped to further block her view of her nemesis.

Once Eleanor and Alex were both in the backseat, he handed Alex the roll of paper towels he had in his truck in lieu of the tissues he didn't have. Closing the doors, he headed back around to where Baker and Owen were standing.

He called for three additional officers, then directed Dan to take Owen to the station. Once the officers arrived, he told one of them to drive his SUV to the station and get both Alex and Eleanor's statements, then directed the other two to help secure the front and back entrances to the store.

A crowd was slowly gathering out front as word spread, and Fergus had already buzzed him twice. It promised to be a very long day.

All that taken care of, he investigated the scene inside the store, his thoughts staying focused on the younger of the two women who had broken into it that morning. Fergus was right about one thing. Alex had definitely made quite a splash in her short time in Blueberry. Today's little adventure would likely earn her a bigger spot in the locals' hearts. They loved adding stories to the Cove's long list of colorful town lore.

Whether Alex would see that as planting roots, or if she'd even consider such a thing, he honestly had no idea. But after talking to Fergus, he knew he wasn't prepared to let her go without finding out.

Chapter 15

"I told you. I'd gone by Owen's about nine-fifteen, nine-thirty, but he hadn't opened yet. I saw the antiques store up the hill and had been meaning to go in, so I went, talked with the owner, then came back to Owen's. He was still closed, no note on the door. I'd turned to go back by Delia's to see if he'd been in for breakfast or if she'd heard anything about why he might not be open when I heard a pounding noise coming from inside. Then someone yelling. I mean, the person was totally panicked. So, I guess I panicked. I had no idea what was going on in there—"

"So, you broke in and went inside alone to find out?" Logan paced behind his desk. "Do you realize how bad an idea that was . . . on numerous fronts?"

Alex shrugged. And wished like hell that watching Logan play bad cop wasn't making her squirm in her seat. She could only hope he mistook it for fear of the law. "I couldn't just stand there and I didn't think waiting around for someone to come help was a good idea. Did you hear why Eleanor broke in? I mean, it was crazy, and the wrong solution of course, way wrong, but I feel sorry for her. Is Owen pressing charges?"

Logan hadn't talked to Owen yet, and given the man's attitude earlier, he sincerely doubted it, but no one seemed to be taking the whole episode seriously. "She broke into his store while out on bail from her recent arrest."

"An arrest that was a result of the same problem that led her to do this."

"Alex, just because Blueberry Cove is a small town doesn't make the law any less specific, or the consequences of breaking it any less severe."

"I know." She looked up at him from where she sat. "She's just lonely, Logan. She feels completely alone in the world, and, well, maybe I understand that a little bit. More than a little. Not the crazy part of it, but the alone part. Add in her age and possibly—okay, probably—a bit of senility playing a factor, and really, can't there be some other solution besides jail?"

Logan lifted his hands, then let them drop to his sides. "No one wants a peaceable solution more than I do, but—"

"Good. Why don't we all sit down together and talk it through? I'm sure we can find a something that works for everyone."

"Because that's not how the law works."

She folded her arms and slumped back in her seat. "Well, it should."

He came and sat on the corner of his desk. "On one hand, I agree with you. But on the other—if we let someone barge into city hall—"

"Waving a water gun," she reminded him.

"With the intent of creating havoc, gun or no gun. When this same person breaks into a store and we do nothing but say, 'oh, well, she didn't mean it, she was having a bad week' and give her what amounts to a slap on the wrist, what's to keep someone else in town—specifically someone young and still very impressionable—from thinking they could get away with something similar because they're mad at mommy and daddy, or their schoolteacher? Except they don't pick up a water gun. Do you understand? Actions have to have consequences."

Alex didn't want to admit it, but he had a point—a very good one. "Okay," she said grudgingly. "I see your side. But does she have to be made into some kind of an example? It will humiliate her."

"Alex—"

"All I'm saying is, why can't we figure out something that will penalize her for the wrongs she committed—"

"They're called crimes."

Alex sent him a quelling look. "What if Owen doesn't press charges and you get the judge to give her community service or something for her past transgressions? She pays her dues and everyone moves on."

"Until she does it again. Then what? And what about your role in this?"

"I've already told Owen I'll pay for the damages. Obviously, I know I broke the law by breaking in, but he seems to understand that I didn't do it maliciously, but to help someone who was obviously in distress. I don't know if he'll file charges, but if he does, then I'll deal with it. I'm not looking to duck the consequences of what I did. But I'm not talking about me. I can handle that. I'm talking about Eleanor."

Logan held her gaze without saying anything, and whatever anger or frustration he'd felt when she'd been ushered into his office seemed to dissipate as the silence stretched out and he continued to study her. "Why are you so worried about her? Is it just because you identify with her being alone, or is it something else?"

"I—does it have to be something else? She's in trouble. And not just with the law. I'm just trying to do what I think is right. Did you talk to her yet?"

"Not directly, but I read Jackson's report."

"I don't know what she told him, but she talked to me

while we sat in the back of your truck before one of your officers got there. Did you know she's been feeding that raccoon for over a year?"

"What? The raccoon? What does this—"

"Did you know?" Alex asked again.

"I—I know Fergus said something about it, but I didn't pay much attention, other than it's a dangerous thing to do—which proved to be true when the thing got inside her house and she tried to mace it with furniture polish."

"Well, she wishes she'd never called you that day. You ruined everything. I mean, she panicked, but—"

"I didn't ruin anything. I sent Randy over there to get the raccoon out of her house before it bit her or she bit it. Did she mention to you that a year or two back she kept calling us over because she swore someone was coming in and rearranging her porcelain doll display?"

"No, but I'm not surprised by it."

"She's getting older, and I understand that it's—"

"No, it's not because of that. I mean, yes, she's getting older, but it's because she's older that she's alone. She didn't have children and her husband died a long time ago. She had one sister who lived in Florida who died six years ago. The only two people she could call friends also died within the last eighteen months. The dolls? That was a cry for help, I'd say. Just wanting attention. She's not the most sociable person."

Logan gave her a look that said *really?* but didn't put voice to it.

"She hasn't the first clue how to make new friends at her age, and really, where would she even try? I'm not sure she's ever been a people person. She's not a churchgoer and there isn't a community center or senior center here, so . . . anyway, that raccoon had been getting in her trash and causing her problems, and at first she did want someone to come and trap it. She even called your animal rescue guy—

Randy—about it. But the raccoon kept coming back. So she started to leave food out for it, hoping it would leave her trash alone. And it worked. After a while, she found herself looking forward to its visits. She'd watch it through the window from her kitchen when it came up and ate."

"This isn't a Discovery Channel special, Alex. Those animals can be dangerous. She—"

"She was lonely, Logan. Feeding it made her happy. Trust me, she knows very well how dangerous it can be because one morning she left her back door open while she was taking the trash to the curb and it got in her house. It scared her to death. She liked the idea of it outside, but not in her home. She panicked and called you. She didn't want to hurt it. She just didn't want it in her house."

"If she wants companionship, why not get a cat? Or five or six of them?"

"I don't know. All I know is Randy got the raccoon out of the house and it broke her heart to think she wouldn't see it again. I'm not saying it's rational or logical, but sometimes emotions aren't, and she is old and"—Alex raised her hand—"just let me finish. The raccoon came back and she wanted to find some way to make sure you wouldn't all take it away again, which is why she attacked you with water guns and later went to city hall. She wanted a license or whatever it would take to let her keep it, just not in her house. She was trying to stop it from being removed. I don't know why everything got out of hand like it did, but she was scared, Logan. Scared and old and maybe not all that clearheaded about it. Like I said, she's not a people person."

"She seems to have bonded pretty well with you."

"I don't think she thought through her actions. She just—she wanted the raccoon to come back and she knew if she went into Owen's to buy pet food again everyone would know she was up to something. Crazy as it sounds, she thought she'd just go in before he opened, get as big a bag as she could carry, leave money on the counter, and no one would know it was her." Again, Alex lifted her hand against his rebuttal. "Also wrong on so very many levels, but it wasn't a malicious act. She just . . . doesn't want to be alone."

"And again I ask, why not get a cat? Or a pet goldfish for that matter."

"She liked the raccoon because she didn't have to take care of it or interact with it or even live with it. The animal was happy to be fed and that made her happy. And feel less alone. Something counted on her, depended on her, needed her, I guess." Alex lifted a shoulder. "Surely there's some other solution to this than jailing her or fining her or both."

Logan didn't say anything, but once again held her gaze for a long, silent moment.

She gave him a wry smile. "And now you think I'm nuts for sticking up for the crazy raccoon lady."

"No. I don't," he said at length. "I think you're caring and compassionate. And trying to get the right resolution to a string of wrong actions."

Their gazes connected and she wanted so badly to stand up and let him pull her into his arms. It was disconcerting to realize how much she'd grown to need him, and yet, she knew it would have felt like the most natural thing in the world. Just as it always did with them.

She also knew they were on the same side in this Eleanor problem. He just had a different responsibility, one that had to take his entire town into consideration and not just one woman. Or two, as the case might be. She hadn't really thought about the true responsibilities he faced, and what it took to do a job like his. On the one hand, it wasn't as if Blueberry was a hotbed of crime, but at the same time, there were all kinds of things that brought troubles to people's lives, no matter where they lived. In a town the size of the Cove, not only did he know all those people personally, but with a force as small as his, she imagined it often fell to him to resolve the issues that came up.

Now she understood why he'd put off having workers out at the Point. She didn't blame him for wanting to preserve his peace and quiet, his alone time. As much as she knew the renovation had to be done, she felt bad about being the catalyst to force all that on him.

Her thoughts, the situation, the surprising strength of her feelings for him, all sort of caught up with her at once. She broke their gaze, feeling more than a little confused. She wanted the right result for Eleanor Darby. She also wanted Logan McCrae.

But she'd already made her choice regarding him. One he'd agreed to . . . with good reason. Although, with him so close, emotions in the room running high, and the tension winding tighter and tighter, the longer they talked . . . the harder it was to remember why stopping what they'd started had been such a good idea.

Alex shook off her musings. "You're right. That's exactly what I want." *Just not all of what I want.* "Surely there is some solution that will please everybody. Is there really no way we can at least try?"

"We?"

She caught his gaze again. "You. Me. Us. Whoever it takes."

A spark leaped to his eyes, and she felt her throat go dry. She wanted to tell him that maybe she wasn't just talking about Eleanor. Maybe there were other solutions to other problems, namely the one that had caused her to move out this morning. Maybe they could figure out what would be best for Eleanor, Owen, and the town. Then talk about what might be best for them.

She hadn't even been gone a full day yet and nothing

about leaving felt like the right move. It felt more like . . . hiding—as if she could pretend she wasn't having this dilemma, and it would go away. It was true she would leave Blueberry, but not anytime soon. If she felt like this now, how on earth was she going to make it through a year or more, living in the same small town as him, wanting him, wanting . . . more?

Suddenly the idea that sleeping under different roofs would solve everything seemed like the ridiculous solution it was—which meant . . . what? Walk away from Pelican Point? Leave Blueberry *now*?

If moving across town to get away from the temptation of Logan McCrae had felt wrong . . . the idea of leaving town altogether made her stomach clutch. She wasn't ready to leave yet. She hadn't done what she'd come to do. She needed the job, the work. She needed it so she could sort things out, figure out what came next.

Not only didn't she have any answers, now she had a dozen more questions.

"Alex." His deep voice had that rough edge to it. The one that always sent shivers down her spine.

And this time was no exception.

He shifted off the desk and she half rose out of her chair as if he'd simply willed her up and into his arms and she'd gone willingly, without question. Just as he reached for her, his office door opened and Sergeant Benson ducked her head in.

"Sorry to interrupt, sir." She took in the two of them and the way they had simply frozen in place. "Truly sorry. But Owen Hartley is out here. He's done with his statement and has asked to speak to you."

Logan held Alex's gaze a moment longer, then glanced at his sergeant. "Send him in."

Alex scooted around her chair. "I'll just—I can wait outside."

"He wants to talk to both of you," Sergeant Benson added.

"Oh," Alex said, surprised. She glanced at Logan, then back at the sergeant. "Okay."

A moment later, Owen stepped into the room. He was of average height, average build, somewhere in his late forties with reddish-brown hair that wasn't exactly thick or curly, but just enough of both to always have a bit of an unruly look to it. He had more the look of the quintessential mild-mannered college professor than a hardware store owner. All he needed was a set of wire rim glasses and patches on the elbows of his plaid wool jacket.

"Thank you," he said, looking nervous and exhausted. "I just wanted to—is it okay if we all sit down?" He was holding his wool cap and alternately crushing it and smoothing it in his hands.

"Sure," Logan said, motioning Owen and Alex into the two seats that fronted his desk. He took the seat behind it. "Owen, Alex and I have been talking about Eleanor, and—"

"That's what I wanted to talk to you both about. Now, Chief, I know you're going to want me to press charges, but I spoke to Eleanor just now—"

"You talked to Eleanor?" Logan shot a look through the open blinds on his office door at his sergeant, who was remarkably busy with the folders on her desk. He looked back to Owen. "I understand this is all a little overwhelming, and I'd like to caution you to take some time, let the shock wear off, then think things through clearly."

"What did you want to do, Owen?" Alex asked him, careful not to look at Logan, whom she assumed would not be happy with her intrusion.

Owen turned to Alex. "She's very apologetic to me. I was kind of . . . surprised, actually. She's usually not so . . ."

"Friendly?" Alex supplied. She reached out and put her

hand on Owen's arm. "I think this whole thing has gotten away from her, too. She was just so upset, so sad, and so scared."

"Yes, scared! I was surprised to see that, too. I mean, I know she was mad about the raccoon, about . . . well, frankly, I never took the time to find out, and I'm feeling badly about that."

"Owen," Logan began.

But Owen talked over him. "No, Chief. I realize she's never been the easiest person, far from it. I guess I just never stopped to ask myself why that would be. She doesn't handle people all that well, is all. I guess that's the nicest way I can put it. She doesn't want to make anyone mad. I think she resents a little—maybe a lot—that other folks find it easy to make friends and get along in the world. I think she counted on her husband to kind of run interference for her, and the few friends they'd made when he was alive helped her after he passed. But they're gone now, too, and I get the sense that she's feeling kind of lost. But she didn't really know how to ask for help."

Logan started to speak, then caught Alex's gaze and paused, took a measured breath, and said, "Alex has said much the same thing. They talked after she and Eleanor left the store. My problem here, Owen, is twofold. While I do feel for her situation, we can't just turn our backs to what she's done as if it didn't happen, or it will very likely happen again. I can't risk that. I can't risk it escalating to some other level of anger and defiance. I don't know who might get caught in the crossfire. Also, it's a matter of the rest of the town knowing that when people break the law, there's a consequence. Otherwise, everybody would be taking matters into their own hands. Do you understand where I'm coming from?"

Owen looked a little heartsick. "I do, Chief." He twisted his cap some more, then looked helplessly at Logan, then at Alex. "The thing is, I just can't see my way to pressing charges and putting her through more grief, not at my hands. I know she's already in trouble with the town, and what happened today will only make that trickier for her." He lifted a shoulder in a half shrug. "It just seems to me we should be finding a way to help her and I don't think more prosecution is the answer."

Alex and Owen looked back to Logan, and she knew he understood she was aligned with Owen. She waited for Logan to say something.

It was Owen who broke the silence first. "Oh, and I'm not charging Alex, either. If I hadn't done what I did to Eleanor, Alex would have never had to break the door to get in."

"I'm paying for damages," she said.

"Let me check with my insurance company first."

"No, it was my choice to do what I did." She put her hand on Owen's arm again. "We can talk about it later, okay? We'll figure it out."

"Why were you at the store, anyway?" Owen asked. "You said something about having come by twice that morning. I'm sorry I wasn't there, but I fell asleep, and then, well, you know."

Alex smiled. "It's okay." She cast a quick glance at Logan, and felt the confusion come tumbling back over what she wanted to happen with him, over what she knew couldn't happen with him. "I wanted to talk to you about Pelican Point."

For the first time, Owen relaxed and a true smile lit up his face. "I'm always happy to talk about the lighthouse."

"Actually, I didn't want to talk to you about it, so much as ask if you'd like to come with me when I go inside to see where we stand with the renovations."

Owen gaped, then snapped his mouth shut. He looked to Logan, then back to Alex. "I'd be honored," he said, beaming as if Santa had just granted him his fondest wish. "Is it okay with you?" he asked Logan, then quickly looked to Alex. "I mean, not to second-guess you."

He turned back to the chief. "But I know you're not happy with me at the moment, so—"

"Owen, I'm not upset with you," Logan said. "I'm just concerned that we handle this properly so that moving forward, it's well and truly resolved, that's all. Of course you can go up in the tower. I know Alex respects and appreciates all the history and information you have on the place. Hell, you know more about the thing than I do. Or you recall more of it anyway."

"Thank you," he said, then turned to Alex. "When were you thinking of going inside?"

"Well, originally, today, but seeing as—"

"Actually, if you think you can still manage it, I can do that. We've got the front of the store boarded up. Hank's going to fix it, but I want my insurance adjuster to take a look first and he can't come till tomorrow."

"I hadn't thought about you not being able to open for business. I'm so sorry. It's not right, you losing revenue like that."

"This time of year, it's not like I'm doing a booming business anyway. If we're going out to the Point, well, I'd have gladly closed up shop for a bit for that."

Alex wasn't too sure she was buying his explanation, but she'd have time to find a way to square things with Owen later. She was hoping he might be willing to help out with the restoration work itself when the time came, so she'd find a way to make sure he was compensated. "Well, okay then. That's great."

Owen looked back to Logan, who was looking at them, his patience clearly being tested. "Are you going to keep Eleanor here?"

"I'm afraid so. At least until we get things sorted out with the district attorney and her lawyer."

"Chief, I really want to say how much I want to find some kind of workable solution to this. I just don't want—"

"Owen, we'll figure something out. I've heard what you had to say and I've listened. Truly. Okay?"

Owen nodded, breathing a sigh of relief. "Okay. Good." He stood. "I won't take up any more of your time." He looked at Alex. "When did you have in mind?"

"Why don't you go home, get a little rest, clean up, get something to eat? We can meet at Delia's around two. That will give us a solid handful of hours before we lose the light."

"Okay." Owen smiled, bouncing a bit on the balls of his feet. "Delia's. Two o'clock. I'll be there." He stuck his hand out to Logan. "Thank you. For listening, for taking my concerns seriously. We all know we can always count on you, Chief. We know you're in our corner."

"I appreciate that," Logan said, shaking his hand. "We'll figure this out."

Owen left and closed the door behind him. Alex turned to Logan. "If there isn't anything else keeping me here, am I free to go, too?"

Logan looked at her for the longest moment, and all that tension and heat that had evaporated with Owen's arrival came roaring back, picking up without so much as a missed heartbeat.

She wanted to tell him that she was unsure of her decision to move out, that she was confused by a lot of things. But she didn't want to lead him on, or make things more complicated than they had to be. She should just stick with what they'd decided. Nothing had really changed.

"Legally?" he said, at length. "Yes, you're free to go. Owen isn't pressing charges and I doubt the DA will want to make a fuss over it as long as you and Owen are in agreement on how to take care of the damage."

And other than legally? Personally, do you want me to go? She wanted to say the words, wanted to know if he was as torn over the choice they'd made as she was . . . but she didn't. "Okay." She took a step toward the door, then turned back, but he spoke before she could.

"You settled in okay at Delia's? Is it—will you be able to make that work?"

Her heart sank. So, that was it then. He was still good with the decision. "Um, yeah. It's fine. Delia—well, she's something, isn't she? She's really been great to me." Alex remembered what Delia had said about making friends, about reaching out, and thought about Owen and the look on his face when she'd asked him to go up inside the lighthouse with her. "I'm really glad to have met her."

"She's a little . . . outspoken," Logan said, "but you couldn't ask for a more loyal friend. If she's on your side, she's a good ally to have."

Alex smiled then, even as it felt like her heart was constricting. "I was thinking the same thing. I like her. She's given me some things to consider. Not necessarily easy things, but things that bear thinking about all the same."

A look of concern crossed Logan's face. "Are you sure you're okay? Do you really want to go up in the tower this afternoon? I mean, it's been a pretty eventful morning, and—"

"I know this sounds a bit weird, but I actually feel like . . . I don't know. I guess I feel more settled somehow. Maybe it was taking action, getting Eleanor out of there. It was kind of empowering. Scary, breaking doors and things, but I did it." Alex's tone turned dry. "Don't worry, Chief, I'm not contemplating a life of crime to get my thrills. But I feel like I'm on a roll, taking more steps into Alex's Life: Part Two." She took a breath and plowed ahead. That's all she could do. "Moving into Delia's, helping Eleanor, working with Owen. Oh, and I even met Eula March today. At her shop. Talk about outspoken." She hadn't thought much about all the things Eula had said, hadn't had time really. But she knew she would. "It was . . . memorable."

Logan saw something in her face, her expression, surprising her by asking, "What did she say to you?"

"Well, I don't know that I remember exactly. I left there and went down the hill to Owen's and we all know what happened after that. She talked about my life being at a crossroads and that I need to see all the avenues leading from this spot. I think she even offered me a job. Sort of. I'm not sure, really." She shook her head. "It was . . . well . . . not spooky, but . . . thought-provoking. Like I said, I didn't get much time to think about it. Why did you ask? Is there something about Eula I should know?" Alex smiled briefly. "Are the older women in your town all a little off their rockers? Should I be concerned?"

She'd been teasing, but if anything, the heat in Logan's gaze only increased. The ache of need was instant and consuming. She wondered if that would ever go away, if she would ever be able to look at him, talk to him, without feeling that incredible yearning. She couldn't imagine it would. It wasn't just the sexual part. It was all of it. Talking, laughing, knowing he was there for her, like he had been last night when she'd had her nightmare again.

Tonight she'd be in a room over Delia's, alone, and not at Pelican Point, with him. It seemed . . . wrong. *How could she already miss someone so badly even when he was standing right in front of her?*

"No, nothing like that. Eula is . . . something of a local legend," Logan said. "And yes, she's outspoken, too. But it's not so much advice, like Delia hands out. It's not so much a warning, either, but maybe a prediction . . . although it often feels like both. Eula likes to think she has a sense of what will come to pass and she's pretty direct in making sure you know about it."

He kept his gaze so tightly on hers, she was only half listening to him, trying not to wriggle in her seat.

"She had a little chat with me recently, in fact," he added.

But Alex was already talking, struggling to keep two conversations going on in her head. The one she was actually having with Logan and the one she wanted to be having with Logan. "That's exactly it. She was like that with me, too. Telling me my future kind of thing, only . . . well, you pegged it. At the time I chalked it up to that tree and all the fantastical things it makes a person imagine, about faeries and gnomes, you know. I'm sure everyone says that. Then you add in her workshop in the back, which, wow, right? I'm not sure I even understand how that works. I'm sure I just wasn't adding up the dimensions right, but it was a surprise."

Logan's intensity instantly ramped up another notch, but it was surprise she saw on his face. Disbelief, actually. "She invited you into her workshop?"

Alex frowned, caught off guard by the edge to his tone. "Why? Is there some reason she shouldn't have? You just said she wasn't dangerous."

"No. It's just . . . as far as I know, as far as anyone knows, she's never had anyone back there. Ever."

It was Alex's turn to be surprised. "Well, I can't imagine why she'd invite me then. We were just talking and I followed her back. It wasn't any big deal."

"It is a big deal. Or will be if you tell anyone. Her workshop has become something of a legend in and of itself."

"Why?"

"Like you were saying about the tree and the fantastical things it makes you imagine, with her being so secretive about her workshop, folks naturally created a bit of lore as to what really goes on back there."

Alex smiled, amused now. "Like there really are faeries and elves and gnomes, oh my? Do you believe in this local lore?"

"No. Of course not. It's good for tourism in the summer,

so I'm not against it, but no. My work deals with logic, facts, and that's how I tend to operate as well."

"And yet . . . ?" She let the sentence trail off. Clearly Logan wasn't telling her everything.

He paused, then said, "You mentioned the dimensions of her workshop making no sense. The fact is, the building that houses the shop isn't all that big. There is no basement. And she appears to do all the restoration work on the pieces she sells at the shop herself. She has no other location that anyone is aware of. But her workshop would appear to be too small to handle some of those pieces."

"Right. I thought the same thing." Alex's smile faded as the hairs on her arms and the back of her neck prickled. "Not logical."

"Hence the stories."

"So . . . what is the reality? How does she do it? Smoke and mirrors?"

"No one knows. Nobody has been back there to tell the tale. Until today, apparently." He broke off, and she could see he was struggling with the desire to beg every detail from her, like a little boy getting a peek inside Santa's workshop.

It was pretty damn cute, actually, though she doubted he'd want to hear that. "It's killing you that you didn't get to go back, isn't it?"

"I'm . . . curious. I'd be less than human if I wasn't. I've been in and out of that shop my whole life."

"I'm here five seconds and back to the workshop I go. I wish I knew why. And I wish I could tell you it was all magical and otherworldly, but the truth is, it's a pretty basic workshop. Tables, tools, shelves lining the walls. There were a number of different projects in various stages of restoration."

"That's it?"

"Pretty much. I mean, the dimensions were off, like I said, but"—she lifted a shoulder—"I can't explain that. In every other way, it wasn't anything special."

He eyed her closely, but all he said was, "Well, I'd suggest you don't mention to anyone else that you've seen it, or you'll be hounded."

"It's really that big a thing?"

He nodded. "People really enjoy the stories. The truth would be like saying Santa's workshop was just a shed with some tools thrown about and a few really short guys helping out."

She laughed at that, even as she realized he was one of those disappointed ones and wished she had a better story to tell him. Then something he'd said earlier, when she'd been sidetracked, finally sank in. "You said she talked to you recently. What did she say?"

There was the whimsy of the shop and their talk of elves and faeries in the air, but the moment she asked that question, the undercurrent that constantly ran between them turned into a sudden riptide. The way his eyes went all hot made her pulse jump.

He didn't answer right away, as if he was debating whether he should. "She told me change was coming. And I should be open to it."

Alex went still, and every other conversation they might have been having ceased. There was only one topic between them now. "And?" She heard the tremor in that single word and wondered if he had, too.

"I met you that afternoon."

Alex's heart skipped a beat. It took her a moment longer to form words. "Did she say anything else?"

"She told me that I didn't like change, but that just because it's difficult, or challenging, doesn't mean it isn't a good thing." He held Alex's gaze for another interminable, tension-jacking moment and she thought she might melt or spontaneously combust. "She also said that sometimes the best changes need to be both."

"Logan." She didn't even know what else she wanted to

say, but she wanted him to know the idea was affecting her, too. Not just him.

"What did she say to you, Alex? Specifically. You said she told you that you were at a crossroads, and you needed to see each path in order to know which one to take. What else?"

"I-I thought you said you didn't believe the stories. About her predictions."

"I said I didn't believe in gnomes and faeries. We've all learned never to discount what Eula says. It may not make sense at the time, but it always becomes clear. Whether you want it to or not."

"Well, she . . ." Alex closed her eyes, knowing the only chance she had of recalling anything Eula might have said was if she wasn't staring into Logan's eyes, feeling the heat of his gaze on every inch of her body. What was he trying to say with this? Had he taken Eula's words to mean that the change and challenge he should be open to was the restoration? Or did he take it to mean a relationship with her? "She told me to go with my gut, not with logic. She said we were alike in that we both needed to fix what needed mending, just that I did it with lighthouses and she did it with antiques. She said it wasn't just that we wanted to do it; we needed to do it, to feel whole and like ourselves. Or words to that effect."

"You said she offered you a job?"

"I-I think so. Or maybe she just wanted company. Though she certainly doesn't seem the type who'd want that. She told me to pick up the piece that called to me and get to work. I assumed that meant she wanted me to work with her, so I said I had two jobs already. She told me the offer stood. She said something about how I had to go all around the world to do what I did, risking my life to have an adventure, but she had the pleasure of going on an adventure with every piece she restored, without ever leaving

home. And that her—how did she put it?" Alex smile
faintly, remembering. "She said she had more fun. And that
her playground was actually much bigger than mine."

She opened her eyes and was startled to find that Logan
had come around the desk and was leaning on it right in
front of her.

Being that close to him, and knowing there would never
be a time when she could just go into those arms, kiss that
mouth, feel the heat, the flames that licked at them anytime
they got close to each other . . . she wanted to close her
eyes again.

"Alex."

She'd been staring at her hands in her lap, wondering if she
should tell him what she felt, knowing it was unfair, yet
struggling with the desire all the same. She lifted her gaze to
his, but didn't risk saying anything, afraid she'd beg him to rethink their decision. He was being strong, standing firm; the
least she could do was not make it any harder on him.

"I know you haven't been here very long, but—" He
stopped, and for the first time, he was the one who broke
eye contact since their conversation began.

It took every last drop of willpower she had not to stand
up and move into his arms. "But what?"

"What Eula said to you"—he lifted his gaze to hers and
all that shattered topaz shone through his thick fringe of
lashes—"did it . . . make you think about . . . your playground?"

"I-I haven't had time to really think about what she said.
How do you mean?"

He took a long moment, and she wasn't sure if he was
going to ask her anything else; then he suddenly said, "Have
you thought about your next job? I don't mean the specific
job, but just . . . what it will be like? What that life will be
like? Now that it's just you?"

"I—" She broke off. In all honesty, she hadn't. Other

than having dreams of going back on the road, back to the work she knew and loved, she hadn't thought about the actual lifestyle, or how different it would be. Not really. "No. Not like you mean. I guess I needed to know if it was even something I wanted to do anymore. That's what I needed to find out here."

"And you did. You love your work."

She nodded, gratified and scared that he knew it to be true without asking her, just from observing her. Maybe that's why he was standing firm on their living apart.

He ducked his chin again. "What about Blueberry?"

She felt as if a light had been blown out somewhere inside her. "What about—? You mean, what do I think about it?"

"Is this what it's like when you go to a new place? You jump right in, get to know people, form friendships . . ." He let the sentence trail off and she knew what else he was mentally adding to that list. *Get involved with someone.*

"No," she said, the word a little rougher now. "I've never . . . this is different. All of it. Very different. Probably because I am alone. Or just . . . I don't know."

He glanced up at her again. "So . . . is it something you hope to do the next place you go?"

She started to respond, then realized she had absolutely no idea what to say. "I-I haven't thought about that."

He pushed off his desk and she had to hold on to the armrests of the chair she sat in to keep from grabbing his hand and pulling him back when—instead of reaching for her and taking her like he had last night, like he had when he'd come out of the shower that first time, like he always did and probably always would have, as long as they were together—he turned away and walked back around his desk.

"Will you?" he asked.

"Will I what?" she asked, completely lost and thinking that applied to far more than what they were saying.

"Think about what you hope to find wherever you go next. If you'll miss the place you left behind, the people, the life you had with them . . . or will any old town fill the void?" He sat down in his chair and she saw his shoulders slump a little. "Is it really all about the work? Will that give you everything you need? Because, if it doesn't . . . what do you plan to do to get the parts of life the work doesn't provide? Is the work alone—and working alone—worth giving up all the rest?"

Alex was trembling now. "What are you asking me, Logan? Just . . . ask me."

"I'm asking if you ever considered that place, people, and having a life outside of work could equal, or even trump your work. And, I guess I'm asking if you ever thought about switching playgrounds?"

"I haven't before. It never came up."

"Will you think about it?"

She nodded. "Logan—"

"Don't . . . say anything. Just . . . as you're working, living at Delia's, making friends like she said, and being a part of this town, involving yourself like you already have . . . think about it. That's all I ask."

She stood then, and she saw him go still. "Okay. I will."

Their gazes stayed connected and held tightly again, until she felt unsteady on her feet. She turned to the door.

"I'll tell you this much," he said, stopping her in her tracks. "I've thought about it."

"About me switching playgrounds?"

"No. About me switching playgrounds."

She turned around, certain she'd misunderstood him. "But—this is where you belong."

"I know. I agree. But that doesn't mean I wouldn't try. If I could see any way to find something that was for me, in addition to us . . . I'd try."

She stared at him. "You're serious."

"As I've ever been in my life."

She thought her heart might leap right straight out through her throat. What did he mean? Just a second ago he was wanting her to be okay at Delia's. And now—she was confused. It was . . . *maybe exactly what I want it to be.*

"Logan—"

"Just . . . think about it. Because I can't seem to stop thinking about it. Okay?"

His intercom buzzed just then, making them both jump.

"Sorry, Chief," Sergeant Benson's voice echoed into the silence in his office. "But you've got a call you need to take. Your sister, Kerry. Long distance. Very long distance."

"I'll—I should go," Alex said, opening the door. Her emotions and thoughts all tangled up in one giant jumble, she glanced back just as he punched the button on the phone to pick up the receiver. "And I will. Think about it. I promise."

She stepped outside the police station, only to realize that her truck was still parked on the street in front of Owen's store. It wasn't that far to walk, and she was dressed warmly enough, so she set out on foot. It gave her time to think about what Logan had said, about what Eula had said, and Delia, too.

What did she want from life now? Was it all about the lighthouses? She loved the work, but without her father, without their crew . . . would it be enough by itself? Or had she simply not known what else to do? If Blueberry hadn't happened, maybe she'd have never had a taste of what else her life could be. But Blueberry *had* happened. And Logan had happened. And Fergus, and Delia, Owen, Brodie, even Eleanor had happened.

When she thought about the next lighthouse . . . and contrasted the joy of tackling a new project with the reality that it meant leaving the Cove and all of those people behind . . . was the work, in and of itself, a worthy substitute for all she'd lose? Would she be content to re-create Blueberry over and over again, just to supplement the work? What kind of life was that? It was like work with no soul. No foundation. What was it Delia had said? No safety net.

"Could it be I'm a root person and I didn't know it? Or was I not one before, but now . . . without a foundation that travels with me . . . would I be happy becoming one?"

She turned up the hill from Harbor Street and immediately spied the boarded and taped-up door to Owen's shop. Beyond, her gaze was drawn back to the broad branches of the mossy cup oak tree. She looked at it for a long time, Eula's words echoing through her mind. Then she turned around and looked down the hill and out over the harbor, to where Delia's place sat at the other end of the half-moon-shaped cove that gave the harbor its name. She looked at Monaghan's Shipyard, and, though she couldn't see it from her vantage point, she looked out toward Pelican Bay, toward the tower she knew stood sentinel over the sprawling home there, and everyone tucked safely into the cove behind it.

How would it feel to leave Blueberry? A month from now? A year from now? *Hell, right now?*

The tug on her heart was matched by the knots that formed in her stomach. One was longing, one was fear.

She turned back toward Owen's shop and her truck parked beside the curb. Could she just drive off into the sunset? And then another sunset? And then another? She hadn't been too good at winging it with Logan. What made her think she could wing it with town after town? Of course, the alternative was to not get involved, to focus on the work, hang with the crew who would leave when she did, only to go off in different directions to different jobs. She glanced over her shoulder, her gaze skimming over the water back to Delia's. The truth was, she was looking forward to Thanksgiving dinner. She was looking forward to going to the Rusty Puffin. Sergeant Benson had mentioned they had live music on the weekends. That sounded like fun. She wondered if Logan would go. Would he dance?

Could Blueberry Cove be my playground?

She looked up the hill to Eula's oak tree . . . and smiled. "Well, there's one way to find out." She pulled out her phone and dialed Owen, who sounded as if she'd woken him up. Not surprising, all things considered. It made her feel a little better about asking him to postpone their tower jaunt until after the holiday. By then, hopefully, the rest of the situation with Eleanor would be settled, too. She promised him it would happen and he sounded happy enough with that. Then she headed up the hill to the antiques store and walked straight inside before she could change her mind.

She browsed a bit, and looked at the tree, trying not to study the dimensions of the store too much. She was going with her gut. Not logic.

"You're back."

Alex whirled around, and her bravado ebbed a good bit at the less than friendly welcome. "I, uh—yeah. I mean, yes. I am. When I was here before, I noticed you were working on some old brass doorknobs. I—we came up with a really great compound, my dad devised it, actually, that works wonders getting off the grime, especially in the intricate designs."

"So, what, you came to sell me some of it?"

"What? No. No, that wasn't—" She broke off. In her mind, she'd pictured this first step going so much better. "I just—I'm sure you have a method you like. But, you said, earlier . . . about me being welcome. In your workshop. I just thought maybe you'd like me to show you the . . . ah . . . the method we use."

When Eula didn't immediately jump at her offer, Alex's first instinct was to apologize for bothering her and duck out, rethink her plan. Then Delia's comments echoed in her mind. *Don't be a shrinking violet.*

Alex didn't want to be a shrinker so she straightened a little, smiled, and said, "Or maybe I can just come back there and, like you said before, see what piece strikes my fancy."

"Maybe you could," Eula said, her expression not changing so much as a flicker.

Here we go into Jabberwocky-world. Alex didn't want to play that game. It had been confusing enough talking to Logan, figuring out what he wanted. Smile still in place, but less overly cheerful, she opted for plain speaking. "I want to come back and see what it would be like to do what you do. You said the offer was open. I'm hoping you meant that."

"Why?"

Oh, for the love of— "Because I'm trying to figure out if one of the paths in my crossroad is the one that led me to your shop. I want to know if Blueberry can be my playground, too."

Eula stunned her then by smiling. Truly smiling. "Well, why didn't you just say so?" She turned and walked to the back of the shop. Without looking back, she barked, "Don't just stand there. These pieces aren't going to refinish themselves."

"No," Alex said, grinning and wanting to dance a little jig, much as she had on Logan's bed that first time they'd made love. "No, I guess they won't."

Much later, she realized that was the first time she'd referred to it that way. Lovemaking. She grinned then, too.

Chapter 16

Logan got out of his truck and headed toward the side door to the mudroom. It had been a long day. A long week. And not because anything had happened. Actually, with Thanksgiving being the next day, he'd expected quite the opposite. Something about families getting together under one roof usually guaranteed at least a few domestic situation calls, but he hadn't even had that to provide a merciful distraction.

It had rained the past three days. The remaining meetings with the subcontractors had been moved to after the holiday. He'd seen Owen twice in that time; both times he'd bent Logan's ear over the Eleanor situation. The holiday had bogged that process down a wee bit, too, but with a little finagling, he'd gotten Eleanor remanded to house arrest, so it wasn't as if she was sitting in a cell. *Thank God.* He hadn't trusted her with an ankle sensor, and frankly, didn't even want to picture that.

He'd worked it so that someone on each shift was keeping an eye on her house, and her, at all times. Thankfully, it had proven to be quiet duty. Eleanor hadn't made so much as a peep. Maybe she had finally learned her lesson, but Logan didn't take that on faith. Her court date was the Tuesday after the holiday, so he imagined that was when they'd see what was what with her state of mind. He had gently recommended that a check-up with her doctor might be a good idea. His ears were still blistered from that little conversation. He didn't hold much hope that the sentencing hearing was going to be peaceful.

He had learned one other thing from Owen's visits. Alex had postponed their tower climb until after Eleanor's court date. He'd been relieved to hear she was taking a bit more time. Between their supercharged clash and subsequent decision that she should room elsewhere, followed by her nightmare, moving out, and the whole thing at the hardware store and subsequent talk at the station it had not been the day to confront the single biggest professional obstacle she faced.

All that had a downside. Putting off going up inside the lighthouse, followed by three days of icy rain meant he hadn't seen, crossed paths with, or heard from Alex, which was why he toed open the door to the mudroom with a bit more of a shove than was necessary.

Rainy days, especially when they came in groups, always made the warped things more warped, but he was grateful for the excuse to shove at something. He knew Barb had been quite ready for him to leave that afternoon. In fact, she'd insisted on it.

He stepped into the mudroom, already taking off his hat and jacket, only to go completely still. The house was warm, which was welcome given the temperature had dropped after the rains had ended. But it was the rich scents of something amazingly wonderful mixing with the warm air that made him stop.

His first thought, considering there was no other car parked out front, was that one of his sisters had decided to surprise him for the holiday. He knew it wasn't Kerry. She was halfway around the world in Australia, of all places. Working a cattle station. She was not pregnant, engaged, or married while working a cattle station in Australia, so he was perfectly fine with that. He knew Fi was snowed under and snowed in, as New York had gotten blitzed by a lake-effect storm that had mercifully gone out to sea before hanging a left and hitting the Maine coast. Which left . . .

"Hannah?" Grinning, he stomped the dirt off his feet on the mat strode toward the kitchen in long strides, happy and privately relieved to have some one-on-one time with the sibling closest to him in age. "You should have let me know," he said as he stepped into the kitchen. "I'd have come and picked you up from the airport."

He stopped just inside the door when he realized he was talking to no one. The kitchen was empty. Of people, anyway. The stove had two pots on top, both covered, both simmering. He took a moment to lift the lids, sniffing in deep appreciation the rich scents of homemade spaghetti sauce in one, and a pan filled with the most amazing looking meatballs he'd ever seen in the other. Hannah wasn't really the domestic sort, but she'd been going through some rocky life stuff, so maybe cooking was a new form of therapy or something. He was all for it, if that was the case.

He managed to resist stealing a meatball and was heading out the door to find where his sister had wandered off to, when a handwritten note on the counter caught his eye. Frowning, he picked it up. In tidy handwriting, the note read

You mentioned the sunsets were spectacular from the top of the tower. I don't want to see my first one alone. I want to see it with you. Join me?

Alex

PS—Don't eat the meatballs. They're for tomorrow.

Logan read the note three times, then again for good measure. The moment he'd realized it was from Alex and not one of his sisters, and that she'd been the one cooking in his kitchen, back in his home, his heart had taken off like a sprinter running for gold. Not a single word or sighting in three days and she was back. Finally. It had felt like three eons.

He put the note down, then picked it up. He read it again, then carried it with him as he took the stairs three at a time to his bedroom. If he hadn't known she was already at the tower and been concerned about how she was doing, he'd have been like a girl on a first date, trying to figure out what to wear. He had no idea what Alex's intent was. She'd clearly come by to use his kitchen to make something for Delia's dinner tomorrow. Was it some kind of peace offering? Did she want to try friendship?

"Jesus, you're going to have a heart attack. Just get your ass out there already."

Five minutes later, in jeans, sweatshirt, boots, and his heavy tarp coat, and on legs shakier than he felt comfortable admitting, he was crossing the open ground on the north side of the house, heading toward the tower. She shouldn't have gone up alone, he thought; she should have waited. He'd told her not to go alone and she'd said she wouldn't. Hell, maybe she hadn't even gotten the door open yet.

The sun was headed toward the trees as he rounded the front of the tower, the wind making his ears sting and wish he'd thought to grab a wool cap. *Shit.* The door was open. He stepped inside, then immediately stopped. In his hurry to make sure she was okay, he hadn't thought about how he'd feel when he stepped back inside after such a long, long time. It surprised him how instantly familiar it felt, familiar in the way it would have if he'd just been inside last week, and not over a dozen years ago.

He'd spent a lot of time up in the tower as a kid. Funny how he'd forgotten that almost entirely. His memories were so focused on Jessica and how special the place had been to her. Hell, by the time they'd started dating the only thing he'd thought about was her . . . and sex. Sometimes together. Of course he hadn't cared about the tower.

He walked across the base floor, wrinkling his nose at the overwhelming scent of mold. The storm glass in the windows had actually held up, but the seals were all cracked, so water had gotten in. The damage to the interior walls and the floor wasn't minor.

He put his hand on the curved end of the rail, part of the iron steps attached to the interior walls, leading upward in a boxed spiral all the way to the Watch Room. He tugged at the rail. It groaned and wobbled, but nothing pulled away from the walls, which surprised him. He'd expected everything to be rusted through, especially with the amount of damp and salt that had been carried in.

He was tempted to call out for Alex. Instead he tested his weight on the first set of risers. A bit more groaning and wobble than he'd have liked, but he made it up the first set, then kept on, one set at a time, making sure they could hold his weight. He made it all the way to the Watch Room, and found himself smiling as a flood of memories came in the moment he stepped onto the landing. How many stories had his grandfather told him of the life of a light keeper and the generations of his own ancestors who had worked in that very room, preparing the lanterns every night? They were daring stories of rescues and wrecks, storms and squalls. More than he could count. His smile spread as he pictured Kerry giving Grandpa a heart attack, climbing like a monkey up the back side of the iron steps leading up to the lantern room and gallery.

It occurred to him that she would be enthralled by what Alex did for a living. Given Kerry's current location and occupation, he couldn't decide if it was a good thing or a bad thing that the two would likely never meet.

He crossed the room and started up the last set of iron steps to the lantern room to where the lanterns—the beacon itself—were housed. At the top, an iron walkway surrounded the storm-glass-enclosed lens. That's where he found her.

He didn't want to startle her, but she turned when he stepped out.

She smiled at him with such joy, his heart slid right out of his chest and straight to her feet, which was where it had pretty much been since she'd dazedly smiled and called him "Sex-god Voice" right before fainting in his arms.

"Hi."

"Hi yourself." He wasn't sure if her luminescent expression was due to his arrival, or due to her clearly having conquered her biggest fear. Selfishly, he hoped it was at least a little of both. He was so relieved to see her looking at peace with herself, that frankly, he'd have been happy to just watch her and not have her even know he was there.

But she did know.

She was leaning back against the storm glass housing, her hands tucked behind her back, the setting sun casting her face and the front of her body in a golden halo of soft, winter light.

"You're okay," he said, not making it a question.

She nodded. "Yeah. I am."

He saw the shimmer of tears spring to her eyes, but her smile was so radiant, he could only grin in response.

He stepped out onto the gallery and moved toward her until he could lean back next to her against the glass.

She turned her head and held his gaze for the longest moment, until the glassiness was gone and only the joy remained. Then she looked back out over the water. "It's as spectacular as you promised."

He finally looked away and did the same. Again, there was that deep, powerful tug inside him, and a sense of peace washed over him. "I shouldn't have waited so long."

She looked at him. "You're okay?"

"Yeah. I forgot how much time I spent up here as a kid.

My memories have been all tangled up with Jessie and I wish I hadn't forgotten all the stuff that came before." He took in as deep a breath as he could. "I really do miss this." *I miss you.*

They stood in silence as the sunlight moved farther away from the water and the sun itself started to dip farther behind the trees.

"My dad would have loved this place," she said. "All of it." Logan looked at her and felt what could only be described as pride. And respect. She'd taken on so much, had already handled so much, but instead of the tower being another burden to bear, she'd found a way to make it a blessing.

Her voice was throatier when she continued. "I feel closer to him. Up here. I think I always will. I thought it would be awful. Really awful. But it wasn't. It's not. It's . . . good here. Better than good. It's . . ." She shook her head.

A few moments later, her words barely reached him. "It's home."

Even knowing he shouldn't didn't stop him from sliding his hand over and taking hers.

She didn't go still or pull away. She didn't look at him. But after a moment, she slid her fingers through his.

He didn't know if it meant good-bye or something else. It didn't matter. What came next didn't matter. Not right then it didn't. What mattered was that she'd found a measure of peace, a haven from the worst of her grief. And that she'd wanted him there with her while she did.

"Yeah," he agreed, surprised to find his own voice a bit thick, his throat tight with emotion. He understood, but the home he was feeling was the slender fingers tucked between his. *She* was his home.

They didn't say anything else as the sun made its full descent and day became dusk. He could feel her shivering and held her hand more tightly, but didn't suggest they go in.

She'd know when she was finished doing what needed doing, this most important first time. A little chill, or even a
lot of chill, wasn't going to be the determining factor. As
long as she was holding on to him, he would be right there
with her.

"Thank you," she said at length. "For giving me the
tower. I mean, I know it's not mine—"

"Yeah, it is. It's the core of the McCrae family . . . but in
all the ways it needs to be, it will always be yours, too.
You're the one who's going to save it, after all."

She turned her head then, and he saw the tears track
down her cheeks, but the accompanying smile kept him
from reaching over to brush them away.

"Thank you for sharing this. With me," he told her.

"I wanted it to be yours again, too. I wasn't sure—"

"You were right. It is. Mine again, too." He smiled.
"Good instincts."

"I've been practicing." At his curious expression, she
added, "Trusting my instincts. Going with my gut."

He squeezed her hand. It was all he could do not to tug
her into his arms, shield her from the cold wind, and taste
her like he'd been aching to every minute of every day
since the last time they'd kissed.

"I used your kitchen," she said. "Hope you don't mind."

"It's fine. Smells amazing."

"F-for tomorrow," she said, her teeth chattering now.
"You g-going to D-Delia's?"

It was more dark than dusk, and he tugged on her hand.
"Come on. We can watch the rest from the other side of
the glass."

"K-kay."

They laughed at that and stepped back inside the lantern
room.

He closed the panel to the gallery and they stamped their
feet a few times and shook their hands, but it didn't do too

much to restore the blood flow to their extremities. "Not much warmer in here, really."

"I thought about bringing up a basket or something, but figured it wouldn't be much fun to have turkey and frostbite for dinner." She turned then and ran her hand over the lens that dominated the center of the room. "I was surprised it's a second-order Fresnel. Pretty powerful. I would have guessed fourth or even fifth."

"The other light across the bay was destroyed, so this became the main beacon. The Fresnel was installed about twenty-five years before the tower was decommissioned. I know my great-grandfather, who was the keeper at the time, had been making quite a ruckus about the U.S. not getting them installed fast enough."

"Well, it took almost forty years after they were invented to even start being installed. Stupid politics."

Both were shivering now and his teeth were starting to click, too. "Ready to go down?"

She shook her head even as she grinned and said, "Yes."

He let her go in front of him, waiting until she cleared each set of steps before he put his weight on them. She barely made them shimmy, whereas they made quite a protest with his added weight.

She paused and looked around the Watch Room, deep in shadows, more dark than light, but another round of shivers sent her across to the steps heading down to the base. He followed, same as before.

He caught up to her on the ground floor where she was looking up and around, and he could see the wheels already turning. "Missing your clipboard, are you?"

"You have no idea."

He chuckled and she shot him a smile. "You know, it's not as bad as I thought it would be in here. It's in much better shape than the cottage. But it's going to be monster to redo, well, everything."

"I know." *And I don't care. I hope it takes the rest of my life to fix it.* Hell, he'd have happily handed her the key to his entire kingdom, if he'd had one, just for the look of anticipation he saw on her face. He'd all but begged her to consider staying, when they'd been at the station earlier that week. Seeing her in her true element, he realized that had been more selfish than he'd imagined. He'd wanted to believe she could find a substitute in Blueberry for what her work made her feel, but looking at her, he couldn't imagine there was such a thing.

He wondered if he'd been too hasty in deciding he couldn't leave Blueberry. It wouldn't be the same after she'd gone. It would feel like nothing measured up, anymore. Good, but not as good as when she'd been there. Happy, but not as happy as when he'd shared it with her. God, who was he kidding? It was going to be awful.

Watching her studying, examining, her brain whirring and so fully in tune and invigorated, even as she looked as if she was going to shiver right out of her boots, he thought it might be slightly less awful if he could at least picture her like this. And know that wherever she was, this was how she'd be feeling, what she'd be experiencing. That couldn't be all bad.

"You look like someone stole your puppy."

He jerked his gaze to hers. "What? Oh. No, just . . . thinking."

"I've been doing a lot of that, too." She turned to the door. "But I don't want to talk about it here. I'm freezing. Come on, I have something else I want to show you, anyway."

She surprised him by grabbing his hand and tugging him out the door. Both had to put their shoulders into getting it closed again; then laughing, they ran like a pair of lunatics across the grass, freezing their asses off. She guided him to the side door on the north wing of the house. "In here." She tugged at the door, but he simply picked her up by bracing his hands on her arms and moving her bodily to the side, then gave a mighty tug until it popped open.

"Neanderthal."

He shot her a grin. "Good Neanderthal or bad Neanderthal?"

"Why do I think you'd take either as a compliment?"

"Because you know me?"

She shot him the kind of smile he hadn't seen from her since—since a time he'd be better off not thinking about if he wanted to make it through whatever else she had planned.

She led him down the long window room, as it had always been called, until they reached the glassed-in veranda that stretched across the center back of the house.

"I have to warn you, it's not going to be warm in there, either."

"Oh ye of little faith." She tugged the connecting door open and stepped inside, then turned and said, "Voilà!"

Knowing he was likely gaping, he stepped in behind her, almost forgetting to pull the door shut behind him as he took in the complete transformation of the veranda space.

The windows had been scrubbed until they glistened as much as they could, given the salt scrub finish on the outside. The panels below the windows had also been scrubbed, as had the cement floor and the rear wall. Even the eaves of the overhanging roof were cleared of cobwebs and brushed free of debris. An old, heavy Aubusson carpet had been dragged in to cover most of the floor, and he thought he saw another rug or two under that one. On top of all of that was a more traditional red and black plaid blanket. Piles of throw pillows ranging from small to overstuffed were piled around the corners. Candles of all shapes and sizes had been placed all around the room in colorful flickering groupings and two small space heaters hummed quietly from opposite corners.

In the center of the old plaid blanket sat a stunning walnut picnic basket. Actually, that particular kind, oversized, with compartments built inside, were called picnic hampers, he recalled. At least that's what Jessie's mom had called them. As far as he knew, the McCraes had never had one. He'd have remembered one as beautifully detailed and lovingly restored as this one. "When did you do all this?"

"Rainy days are not my friends," she said with a wry smile.

"I can see that."

"I hope you don't mind that I trespassed a little."

He just shook his head and looked around again.

"I didn't get too crazy as I'm not sure what all is going to have to happen to this room when we fully renovate, but for now I thought it would be a nice way to look out over the harbor during the winter months, view the sunsets, watch the lights came on along the harbor. And I thought we could start with that meal it was too cold to have up in the tower."

"I—yes. It's a wonderful idea." He'd already used up most of his control just keeping his hands off her and his mouth shut long enough to stop him from blurting out . . . well . . . a whole lot of things, so there wasn't much willpower left. He put what there was toward not getting his hopes up. About anything.

She stepped onto the blanket and sank down with her legs folded in front of her. She shrugged out of her coat and pulled off her hat. She raked her fingers through the curls, which did little to help the hat hair or static. Her quick eye roll and *what can I do?* shrug made him smile. And want her all the more.

Curling his fingers inward against the need to weave them through those flyaway curls and take her mouth like a man dying of thirst only she could quench, he sat down while his body would still let him. He should have chosen looser jeans. Not that it really mattered, since staring at her by candlelight for any length of time, while sprawled on that blanket with all those pillows so handily nearby was likely going to kill him, anyway.

"Oh, before I forget. I had a kind of epiphany today." She smiled brightly as she tugged the hamper closer.

His eyebrows climbed at her sudden animation, but he was grinning at the same time. *I love you, Alexandra MacFarland. I may never get to tell you, but God, I love you.* "I thought I saw smoke from the lightning strike."

"Just wait. You're going to thank me, so be nice."

"I'm always nice."

She nudged him with her toe and he nudged her back.

Grinning, he said, "So, what was the big lightbulb moment about?"

She talked while she opened up the hamper and set out the food. "I've been thinking about Eleanor."

He was no longer listening. Because out came a platter of fried chicken, a small basket of homemade biscuits, cheesy pasta in some kind of warming tray, and a chocolate cake that might have brought a tear to his eye. Topping it off, from the bottom of the basket, a little cooler produced a six-pack of cold beer.

"Marry me," he said, staring at the feast before him.

She laughed. "Glad you approve." She tossed a roll of napkins at him. "Here, you've got some drool on your chin."

He snagged them, but was still watching in awe as she unwrapped and set everything out. His stomach growled like a starved convict's.

"So, about Eleanor."

"Anything you want."

She laughed again. "You're making it way too easy, you know."

"I see no purpose in making it hard for arbitrary reasons." And dear God, he was still just as hard, even distracted as he was by the amazing smorgasbord she was setting out, even as he'd been when the only thing in the room he'd wanted to nibble on had been her. The last thing he really wanted to talk about at the moment was Eleanor Darby.

But fearing Alex might pack the food up if he didn't play along, he snagged a biscuit and said, "So, what about Eleanor?"

"I know her hearing thing is next week and I was thinking. You said something back when the city hall thing happened. About animal control relocating her raccoon."

"It wasn't her raccoon."

She nudged him again. "That's not what I'm getting at. Since you have an animal control service, do you also have some sort of animal shelter? I know Eleanor doesn't do well with people, and my guess is that includes cohabitating with four-legged critters. But she liked being a caretaker for the raccoon, as long as he stayed outside. And I was thinking, maybe her community service could be to volunteer at the animal shelter. If it's not a good fit, it could always be changed to something else. But by volunteering she'd be contributing to the town to pay for her transgressions, and, who knows, maybe it will be the thing that—"

"Keeps her from straying to a full-time life of crime?"

"Maybe. Hopefully. What do you think?"

He finished off a piece of chicken and thought he really wanted to taste her next. "I think for someone who hasn't lived here very long, you have pretty good instincts about the people who have."

"So, is that a yes?"

"That's an 'I'll make a recommendation to the judge.' But, yeah, I think he'll go for it."

"Excellent. Thank you!" She handed him an open beer, then lifted hers in a toast. "To Eleanor finding a path away from a life of crime."

"And out of my police station." They tapped cans, and took their sips.

He took a bite of pasta and groaned. "You know," he said, after finishing another bite. "When you get done restoring all the lighthouses in the world, you should think about feeding people for a living. It would be a true service to mankind. In fact, I'll even offer to personally help you establish the menu."

"Big of you,"

"I'm like that."

Her eyes took on a mischievous light, as if she was going to make a suggestive comment, but she looked back at her plate instead, eyes still twinkling, and picked up another biscuit.

He slid the hamper over and looked at it more closely. "This is beautiful. Is it Delia's?"

"Actually, it's mine."

He looked up, very surprised. "Really? Family heirloom?"

"Maybe someday. I hope so, anyway."

He frowned. "I'm—not following."

Her sunny confidence wavered and she suddenly found the biscuit she was picking apart to be the most interesting thing in the room.

"Alex?"

She worked at it another moment, then took what looked like a steadying breath and said, "Remember when I said back in the tower that I'd been doing a lot of thinking. About gut instincts?"

"Yes." He stomped hard and fast on the surge of hope that filled him, like a man stomping out a fire before it burned him alive.

"You asked me to think about what I wanted. That day, in your office, when—"

"I remember what day. And what I asked of you." He remembered every last word of that day. And how he wished he'd just given in and kissed her the way he'd wanted to.

Even if it was the last time, at least he'd have gotten a last time.

"I said I would. And I have been. I-I didn't go in the tower that day—which you know."

"Yes. It thought that was a good idea. It had been a big morning and before that . . . well, there had been a lot before that, too."

"You came to me that night, didn't you? When I had the nightmare again?"

He just nodded. They were moving into territory where no amount of self-control or fire stomping was going to protect him. Hope stubbornly reared its optimistic, rose-colored-glasses-adorned head. Despite knowing he was just setting himself up for a crushing blow, he couldn't quash it.

"I really hadn't thought past coming here and figuring out whether I could even continue doing what I've always done. But I've thought a lot about it, about what I want from my future. My professional future. And I've thought a lot about the life I want to go with it. You made me think. Hard. So did Eula. And Delia. About friendships and play-grounds and what it would take to fulfill my needs and give me the drive and focus I need to do something that feels worthwhile, that's as gratifying to me as this work is. I honestly couldn't imagine anything that could ever compete with a lighthouse."

Logan dipped his chin, knowing the truth of it. Hadn't he just witnessed how strong that affinity was? Much as he wanted it to be otherwise, it was not the time to pretend things were anything but what they were. "When you were out there, just now . . . you looked . . . ebullient."

"I was. I am. I can't wait to work on your tower."

"Your tower."

She flushed a little. It always charmed him when something caused that vulnerable side in her to come out.

My heart, he thought. *Right at your feet.*

"It is hard to think there wouldn't be others. After this one."

The vise grip on his heart returned with an even harder squeeze. *Here we go.*

"But it was harder to think that I'd have to leave Blueberry to see to them. I just . . . want both. But coming home for short stays between months- or even years-long projects isn't what I want, either. It was all I knew growing up in Thunder Bay, but it's already different here. I never really missed the bay because everything that was important to me went with me when I left." She looked at him. "I will miss the Cove."

He was surprised his heart hadn't turned to dust, the vise grip was so tight around it. "Alex, just—for the love of God, tell me before you kill me."

She looked honestly surprised by his outburst. "I am. I mean, it's—"

"Did you find the missing piece to the puzzle?"

She nudged the hamper toward him. "You tell me."

He looked at the beautifully restored walnut piece, then at her, then back at the basket, eyes widening. "You did this?"

"Every last freaking awesome inch of it. Yes, I did."

His gaze flew to hers. She looked so damn proud. And happy.

"That's . . . incredible. But how? Where did you even—?" Then it dawned on him. There was only one person. "Eula? You've been working for—"

"With. No one works for Eula. But . . . yes. That's where I went when I left the station. I just . . . wanted to find out. I wanted to do something, anything, to take a step forward. Like I told you in your office, I felt like I'd been on kind of a roll in the forward-step-taking department that day. She'd offered another path from my crossroads. And she was right. I had to know what they all were before I could decide which one to take. Other than going to Delia's to sleep, I've been at Eula's pretty much every minute since."

"Rain is not your friend," he added. "Well, at least you're productive. You know, some folks just read a book."

She shrugged, but looked inordinately pleased by his reaction.

It made him feel good that what he thought mattered to her.

"Eula just up and gave it to me when I finished it. She said it was a testimony, my testimony, and said she wanted me to have it."

"I can't believe you did this in three days. If you've never done this before, you're an amazingly fast learner." He looked at the hamper again, picking it up, studying the work. "When was this made originally?"

"Eighteen-sixty-two, according to Eula. She knows the provenance of all her pieces. Some of the stories are amazing. This one was a mess. I don't even know why I started with something so hard."

"Because it was the thing that needed you the most." *Like me.*

She stared at him, and he saw her throat work.

"Maybe." She looked at the hamper. "Probably."

"Did your background help at all? I mean, I know they're completely different realms, but did any of the language or terminology or restoration theory cross over?"

"Surprising amounts of it, yes. You're right, it's mostly apples and oranges in the broad spectrum, but when you break it down, it's really a lot of the same kinds of steps, just applying a different technology to how you go about them. I swear, Logan, if you could see some of the magic that woman works on the really damaged stuff . . . well, even you would start to believe in faeries and elves."

He looked up at Alex, and she could see the question on the tip of his tongue. But she beat him to it, laughing as she did. "No, as far as I can tell, they're not. I still don't know how that back room works, and frankly, I don't want to know. It will . . . spoil it somehow. She's teaching me. And I want to learn. Once I saw what I could do with something like this, I wanted to do it again. It really is like she said. Just sitting in that room, I felt there was half a lifetime of lighthouses right in front of me."

Her eyes were sparkling and she looked . . . ebullient.

Logan set the hamper aside. Then he very carefully moved their plates and empty drinks out of the way. "Come here."

"Logan, let me get the rest out. I need you to understand—"

"I get a turn. Okay?" He lifted his hand to her.

She held his gaze, then took his hand as she scooted across the blanket until she was in front of him, squealing when he pulled her into his lap.

It felt so damn good to have her in his arms again. He wasn't sure how he'd ever let her go. He looked down into all that stormy blue and said, "I'm all done pretending that I can even try not to want this, to want you. The more we're apart, the more I hate it. So, this is me telling you what conclusions I've come to in the past three days. And to hell with what comes next and to hell with protecting ourselves. We both know that life hands out awful, horrifying, painful crap, and we have to deal with it.

"Fergus made a comment that life is handing us the best of what can be, and how he didn't understand why we weren't going to take it just because we've seen the hard stuff. It's like we're doubly punishing ourselves and being idiots to boot, because we do have a choice this time. If we were smart, then we'd see that living through the hard stuff should make us appreciate the good, not run from it. Otherwise, what's the damn point? So . . . I might have you in my life for a month, a year, or, if I'm very, very lucky, every day until I draw my last breath. But I want you in it, Alex. Whether it's here, or in Timbuktu."

"There aren't any lighthouses in Timbuktu," she said, trying for a teasing tone.

He saw her heart in her eyes and his was beating too fast for him to do more than tug at one of her curls.

He was the one who was all big talk. Laying his heart at her feet was terrifying. Willing to put everything he was, everything he wanted out there for her to accept . . . didn't mean she had to, or that she'd see it his way. It was the risk he had to take. Having her in Blueberry Cove and not having her with him was worse than not having her in his life at all.

"Good," he said when he could finally speak past the big knot in his throat. "That's one less place I have to figure out how to live in."

"Logan—"

As he had once before, he cupped her face, rubbed his thumb over her bottom lip, and felt her tremble. Or maybe it was him. "Let me finish," he said. *Begged.* "You've been making all these strides figuring out things, maybe because you wanted to, maybe because I asked you to. But I know you did it because I said I couldn't see myself in your world. How could I? I don't know how I'd fit in because I haven't done what you're doing—finding the right puzzle piece by trying a few out. So . . . I'm just saying I'm willing to go. I'll work the puzzle, find the new playground, whatever the hell you want to call it. I just don't want to keep on doing anything, anywhere without you. I want you, Alexandra MacFarland. You're my playground."

Her eyes shimmered, even as the deep blue in them grew steadily darker. And he saw then what he most wanted to see. Beyond the desire, beyond the want. He saw . . . hope. The relief that came with that discovery was so massive, it took his breath away.

"I'm really glad to hear you say that because . . . Logan, I don't know if this new puzzle piece with Eula will fit. Long term. It fits now. I have time while I work on the cottage and the tower to keep at it, learn more, find out how deep the affinity might run. I know I don't want to walk away from Blueberry. I don't want to walk away from you. But it's even more than that.

"I also don't want to leave the people I'm just now finding. I'm feeling . . . connected. And I'm realizing why Delia likes her safety net. I like it, too. It used to go with me; my dad was my net. But now it's just me . . . and I don't much like it out on the tightrope all alone. In fact, now that I've found friends, a place that isn't home yet, but sure feels like it could be, and . . . you . . . being alone is going to be, well . . . awful."

"I hate you being gone from this house," he said, hearing the raw emotion in his voice, but no longer caring. "This used to be my security net. Now it's just . . . yeah. Awful."

She reached up and touched his cheek. "I hate being gone. I just . . . can't promise that Blueberry, even though I love it here, that staying in one place all the time will be a perfect fit for me, either. So . . . if in the end, I need to wander . . . are you really sure you'd be willing—"

He covered her hand, knowing his heart was right there in his eyes. And because he was the luckiest bastard in the universe, he was pretty damn sure hers was as well. "Alex, you have me. Okay? No rules. No boundaries. It's you and me. That's it, and that's everything. The rest we figure out as we go."

Eyes shining, she nodded. "Okay," she whispered, emotion in her voice, too. Then, as if testing this new step, a smile spread across her face and she said it louder. "Okay."

And then together, laughing, they shouted, *"Okay!"*

"Can I finally kiss you now?" she asked, framing his face in her palms. "This is pretty much killing me. Has been killing me. Every moment since we stopped, it's been killing me. Seeing you, hearing you, not having you, not even being able to just reach out and—"

He rolled her to her back in the middle of the blanket before she could finish. "That first night, you kissed me like I was the last man on earth." He brushed her wild, crazy hat hair away from her flushed cheeks and looked into the eyes of the woman he knew, without a single doubt, he was madly, deeply, head over heels in love with. "Now, because you are the last woman on earth, for me, I'd like to return that favor."

Proving she was never going to play just by his rules, that she'd always match him with a few of her own, she reached up and nipped his lip, making him groan and his body jerk in response. Grinning, she wriggled at his response. "I even get to be awake this time," she teased. "Yay, me."

He was grinning as he kissed her. Finally. *Finally.* He took his time, sinking in slowly, reveling in every gasp, every moan—his and hers—enjoying her taste, taking in her scent, and basically wallowing in being back where he thought he'd never be again. He kissed her intently, softly, passionately, teasingly until she was squirming, gasping, and bucking against him. Then he eased his mouth next to her ear and began undressing her, taking care to touch, to tease, to torment every part of her with his fingertips as he told her exactly how he planned to frolic in his very own, very private playground.

"Logan," she said, then moaned, making an almost keening sound as he followed the trail his fingertips had taken with his mouth, his tongue. Like the first night he'd had her in his arms, she clutched at him and cried out, but for entirely different reasons. "Don't let me go."

He brought her mouth to his as he moved over her, nudged her thighs apart. "It's okay," he promised her. "You're here now. I've got you." And he always would.

Epilogue

She was ripping up linoleum in the kitchen when he came downstairs the next morning.

"What does it say that after a night when you woke me up not once, but twice, and then I woke you up a third time, you're down here at the crack of dawn, working? It's enough to give a guy a complex."

She stopped and sat back on her heels, wiping the cracked putty flecks from her cheeks with the back of her hand. She was wearing one of his white work T-shirts and nothing else. Well, if you didn't count the knit cap on her head.

"And may I say that's very fetching headgear we're sporting this morning."

She reached up, touched her head, and closed her eyes. "Yeah. Well. I came down with the intent of making coffee for us. Then I caught my toe—again—on that stupid spot that's curled up and I just kind of snapped and reached down and yanked it up. Then I yanked some more, and I got into it and I guess I kind of forgot about the coffee."

"So, I guess I shouldn't ask about the hat? There wasn't some kind of horrible putty knife incident, was there?"

"My hair was getting in my eyes. It was on the table." She shrugged. Bending down, she grabbed the edge she'd been tugging and yanked some more.

For his part, he calmly stepped over the mess, bent down

and slipped an arm around her waist, and scooped her straight off the floor and back against his chest.

"Hey! Unfair gender advantage!" she called, as he shifted her over his shoulder. "Bad, Neanderthal, bad."

"That, too." He crossed the living room and climbed the stairs.

"Logan, I'm not even walking normally this morning. I don't think I can—"

"We're taking a shower."

"Oh?" Her voice dropped from shrill to sultry. "We?"

"Well, I can't have you walking funny when we get to Delia's. People will talk."

"True," she said, as he carried her straight to the bathroom. "And we can't have that."

"We're probably going to have a lot of things. Including that. But let's see if we can not embarrass the neighbors over Thanksgiving dinner."

"Yeah. We'll hold out until at least tomorrow."

He stepped in the shower and slid her off his shoulder until her feet touched the tiled floor.

"Hey," she said. "You're naked."

"That you just now noticed could stunt my ability to perform."

She snickered. "Yeah, right."

Grinning, he tugged her cap off and tossed it toward the bathroom door, then turned on the shower.

"Hey! I still have a shirt on."

He ran his hands down the front so the white T-shirt molded to her breasts. "Oh, yeah, you do."

"You're such a guy."

He bent down so he could suck on one of her nipples darkly outlined though the wet cotton. "Lucky you."

She grabbed his shoulders and held on as he worked his way down, gasping as he made it past the hem. "Oh, yeah I am," she breathed.

"We might be late for Delia's," he murmured.

"You know," she said between gasps, "I still have a room there. With a foldout couch."

"Maybe we should keep it. It's close to the station."

"You should take more lunch breaks anyway."

He worked his way back up and she had to clutch his shoulders just to stay upright. Her legs were officially jelly.

She felt him brush against her thighs. "You've managed to overcome your performance anxiety, I see. And feel. Dear . . . God. Would you hurry?"

"I thought you were worried about walking funny," he said, bracing his palms on her hips.

She reached down and took matters into her own hands. "So, you can carry me into Delia's. You seem to like hoisting me up." She wrapped her hands around him, smiling when he jerked and twitched at her touch. She liked that he wasn't the only one with the power. She stroked him and nipped his chin. "Only not over the shoulder. Be romantic."

"I can be romantic."

In a blink, he had her hiked up against the shower wall, urging her legs around his waist. Then he kissed her, deep, slow, and hard as he pushed up and inside her, inch by devastating inch, until she took him completely.

"Oh," she gasped against his throat as he started to move. "Yeah, you can."

They were very late to Delia's. He did carry her in, and it was very romantic. Everybody cheered.

"Look," she told Delia, blushing even as she grinned. "I made a new friend."

"I can see that. Fast learner. I like that about you." She gave Logan a onceover, then looked at Alex's flushed face. "Might have to rethink what I said about getting one of my own."

"Really." Alex wiggled her eyebrows. "We'll talk." She smiled. "That's what friends do, right?" Logan set her on her feet, then pulled her to his side. Alex slid her arm around his waist and leaned into him. "I've got time. I'm not going anywhere."

How to Restore Antique Brass Doorknobs

Want to give your home an instant boost? Bring the golden glow back to your antique doorknobs and add a little luster to your life!

Brass is made from a combination of two metals: copper and zinc. The quality of the brass has to do with the percentage of zinc in that combination. Forged or cast, brass is often used in home décor items because of its beautiful golden luster. However, it's an unstable metal that oxidizes easily and that chemical reaction creates a tarnished surface. Due to constant handling, brass doorknobs tarnish quickly and are in particular need of more regular maintenance.

There are many different approaches to cleaning tarnished brass, and while there are natural methods (did you know you could use household items like onions and Worcestershire sauce?) those methods take more time and the results are less dependable. (Not to mention who wants doorknobs that smell like onions and steak sauce?) Just keep in mind that when doing any restoration project, make sure you use proper ventilation, protection for hands (and eyes, mouth, and nose, if needed), and keep the cleaning solvents away from your kids and pets. Always read all the safety instructions on any product before using.

Supplies:
Latex gloves
Denatured alcohol or paint stripper

Ammonia
Vinegar
Salt
Commercial brass cleaner
0000 (very fine grade) steel wool
Soft T-shirt material or other soft cloths

1. First, you need to make sure you're dealing with true brass, and not just a knob that has been brass plated. An easy way to find out is by using a strong magnet. A magnet will attach to metal, like steel or zinc, that would be underneath brass plating. Magnets will not, however, stick to true brass alloys.
2. Remove any lacquer that might have been used to seal the doorknob in an effort to protect the brass from oxidizing. If there is a protective finish you can remove this with denatured alcohol or paint stripper. You can even try your nail polish remover, if the coating is relatively thin. Use proper ventilation and protect your hands. (See further information on safety precautions by reading the label of the particular product you use.)
3. Cleaning tarnished brass is a process of removing layers of grime and corrosion. This doesn't happen in one simple step. Several different processes must be used to fully remove its dulling effect. With the finest steel wool, #0000 grade, use a mixture of vinegar and salt to gently scour the doorknob, removing the surface layer of tarnish, grime, or corrosion. If the steel wool is too corrosive, or if the brass is highly detailed, an old soft T-shirt can be used instead.
4. To get through the next layer, soak the doorknob in ammonia to soften the grime and corrosion. Use caution as ammonia is caustic and can degrade the brass itself, creating pockmarks if left on too long. To neutralize the effects of the ammonia, spray with

diluted vinegar (mixed with water) to stop the process. Then repeat Step 3 as needed.

5. Finally, apply a thin layer of commercial brass cleaner or polish. Be aware that over-the-counter cleaners come in acidic and caustic formulas. Acidic is preferable as it reacts only with the tarnish. Caustic formulas are like the ammonia above, in that they can react directly with the brass itself. You may have to experiment a little to find the one that works best for you.

6. Now it's time to restore that lustrous glow! Buff your newly cleaned brass with a soft cloth to remove all polish, then repeat again with a clean cloth until the brass shines and all the tarnish is removed.

Come back to Blueberry Cove next May and visit Brodie Monaghan in HALF MOON HARBOR.

The morning of Brodie Monaghan's one-year anniversary as a resident in Blueberry Cove, Maine, began with a hard-on and a surprise visitor. Unfortunately for him, those events occurred in exactly that order.

Living right on the wharf in Half Moon Harbor, he loved waking to the sounds of the gulls calling back and forth as the tide slowly began to ebb. The sun making its way slowly and gloriously over the horizon and the low, reverberating thrum of the lobster boats chugging out of Blue's, heading toward Pelican Bay, was the best alarm clock known to man.

Brodie stretched fully, not minding as the sheet and quilt slid to the cypress floorboards in a tangle. Restless night. Again. He let the chilly May morning air ripple over his heated, bare skin, but it did little to calm down his body's morning state of affairs. He rubbed a hand over his face, felt the scratch of his morning beard, knew it was a match to the shaggy condition of his hair, then glanced down through barely open eyes. "Aye, yes, I know. I've been neglectin' ye, I have."

The part of his anatomy to which he'd directed the comment twitched as if in response, making Brodie grin, even as he sank his head back into his goose-down pillow and let his eyes drift shut. He was considering taking matters into his own hand—a poor substitute, but he was a man who be-

lieved in taking gratification where and when he could—
when a loud clatter on the docks below brought the rest of
his body upright, as well. Grunting, he rolled out of bed,
which was located in the converted loft of his boathouse.
Well, one of his boathouses. All of which were located on
his docks. His privately owned docks.

Probably that ruddy pelican had gotten his claws caught
up in the frayed, old, line ropes still piled out on the back
piers. He'd meant to get those hauled out before they'd
frozen into miniature ice piles last winter. He made a mental note to give Owen a call down at the hardware store and
see who might be available to help with that.

Before he could cross the narrow space to peek through
the porthole window, there was another thud, followed by
some very inventive swearing.

His grin returned. As an Irishman, he respected anyone
who was as passionate in their cussing as he was, but the
grin was more because he was fairly certain the colorful
curser in question was a woman.

Respect for the fair sex more than modesty on his part
had him grabbing and pulling on the pair of plaid pajama
bottoms he'd dropped beside the bed before climbing between the sheets the night before. "Down, boy-o," he said
to his still invigorated manhood, which also apparently ap-
proved of passionate, swearing women. "I promise I'll end
the drought and soon enough. But for now, behave. We've
company."

He climbed down the circular iron stairs to the open area
below. He'd had the space converted into kitchen and living room. The corner area where the picture windows in
the east and south walls came together was dedicated to his
drafting table and work desk.

Normally, he grinned every time he looked over the
newly finished space, sending silent thanks to Alex MacFar-

land for her fine craftsmanship and dedicated work ethic, but for once, his thoughts were mercifully on another woman. Perhaps he'd get lucky and this one wouldn't already be spoken for.

He flipped up the oversized latch and slid open the large plank doors original to the boathouse and stepped out onto the docks. Immediately, he wished he'd also grabbed a sweatshirt. And his Wellies. Late spring mornings were still pretty brisk Down East . . . as was the steady breeze coming off the water. Folding his arms and rubbing his hands over his chest, he trotted down the pier and around to the docks on the far side where the noise had come from.

"I should have left you in the car," he heard as he neared the back corner of the boathouse.

Definitely a woman. One with a decent bark, too. His morning mood was growing cheerier by the moment.

"Pants are ruined, heel busted. And I'm pretty sure I'll need some help getting these splinters out. Ouch! Damn, that one's deep. Seriously, how does someone your size cause so much trouble?"

Brodie slowed his pace. Ah, so she had wee ones. Or one of them, at least. Those usually came with a father of some sort. Present company excepted, anyway. *Didn't that just figure?*

"I have one moment of weakness—*one*—and this is what happens. I get you."

Just like that, Brodie's smile faded as did his respect. No child should be talked to that way, made to feel unwanted— as if they'd had a choice in the matter—even in the heat of the moment. Especially in the heat of the moment.

He rounded the back corner intent on . . . well, he wasn't sure, exactly, but no one was going to shout down a tiny tyke on his docks, or anywhere else in his presence. "Excuse me," he said, taking the short ladder up to the higher pier in a single hop. "This is private property and you'll be wanting to watch your tone with the wee one if you don't wish to make a direct exit, seaside."

She hadn't heard him. "Aw, come on now, there's no need for—cut it out with the look, okay? You're killing me here. Oh, no. *No!* I didn't mean—don't you even think about—augh!"

Brodie took one look at the woman sprawled all over his dock, tangled up in a pile of ropes—and the small, scruffy mutt presently planted on her chest. Tail a'wagging like mad, it was giving lots of wet, slobbery doggie kisses to its owner, instantly restoring his goodwill. "You tell her, laddie," he said with a chuckle. "That's a good boy."

At the sound of Brodie's voice, the wee bit of scruff looked up, spied him, and set off down the dock in a dead dash toward him, barking the whole way.

"Whomper! No! Stop! Down! Something! Hell, what's the right command? He's friendly!" she called out as the dog increased his speed. "But be careful, because he can jump really—"

At that exact moment, Whomper launched himself from the dock, and in an amazing display of vertical prowess that would make any of those lads in the NBA quite envious, he landed squarely against Brodie's chest.

"—high," she finished limply.

Brodie instinctively caught and clutched the dog, staggering back a step, but managing to remain upright. Simultaneously, he realized two things. One, he still wasn't wearing a shirt, and two, the dog's claws were remarkably sharp. He got a whiff of Whomper and realized a third thing. The tiny rascal had apparently found a dead fish he liked . . . and had become quite cozy with it.

In danger only of being asphyxiated by the smell of wet canine mixed with fish guts, and possibly licked to death, Brodie immediately held the thing away from his body.

"Whomper, lad." He shook his head and grimaced at the stench. "You sure know how to make an entrance, boy-o."

"I'm so sorry," the woman shouted. "He's kind of . . . exuberant."

"She's being kind to ye, laddie, now that ye've gone and made a scene."

His pronouncement was met by bright dark eyes, a lolling tongue, and a still wagging stub of a tail. Part terrier, part harbor doxy, most likely, his white scruffy fur marked with the occasional splash of black and brown, Master Whomper still managed to be quite the charmer. One pointed ear and one with a rakish tilt at the tip didn't hurt matters any, either. Brodie felt a certain kinship to the mutt. "Aye, 'tis a charmer you are, born and bred. Gets you out of a lot of scrapes, does it?" When the dog yipped in response, he grinned and gave the little fellow a fast wink. "Yes, I know. Comes in handy, that." The dog wriggled with renewed adoration.

Still holding him at arm's length, short hind legs dangling, Brodie strode down the dock toward the pup's entangled owner, who, he realized, was still cussing under her breath as she tried—and failed—to extricate her feet and heels from the heavy ropes.

"Might take both our charms combined to get you out of this one," he murmured to the dog. "That and a hot shower." He shuddered. Their commingled fishiness was impossible not to breathe in. "Good Lord, but we reek."

"I'm really sorry," the woman said, teeth gritting as she worked to get the strap on her shoes free from the frayed edges of the rope. "He's very well behaved . . . when he wants to be." She glanced up at the dog and gave him an arch look. "Like when luring unsuspecting women into taking him home."

Brodie grinned at the wriggling dog. "Well, mate, I'm finding you more interesting by the moment."

She eyed dog and man. "Perhaps he'd be happier with a fellow hound to room with, then."

Brodie barked a laugh at that. "I can see why you picked her from the crowd," he told the dog. "Women who know their own minds and aren't afraid to speak them are infinitely more interesting." He bent down and set the pup on the docks. "Now, be a good lad and don't run off whilst I free your mistress here. You've a bit of making up to do, I'd say, but we'll get ourselves cleaned up first, aye?"

Whomper planted his butt on the dock, tail going in a furious spin, panting happily. He looked up at Brodie like he'd caused the sun to rise all by himself.

Laughing, Brodie glanced from dog to owner. "You had no chance," he told her. "You realize that." He crouched down and swiftly pulled the knotted rope fibers free from the buckles on her heels.

She sighed. "I never thought of myself as a sucker for strays, but I guess there's always that exception."

She glanced up just then, and with the angle of his head blocking the bright beams of the rising sun, looked directly into his eyes for the first time.

Suddenly, he was the one all tangled up. And not quite sure why.

There was nothing extraordinary about her eyes. They were hazel, in fact, not quite distinctly green or blue, and possibly leaning a bit toward brown. She was pretty enough in that her features were all lined up just right. Her hair was a shiny sable brown and long enough to spread across a man's pillow, but as it was presently pulled back tightly against her head in a way that took it out of the equation entirely, there wasn't really anything that would turn a man's head in a crowd.

And yet, in that singular moment, he couldn't quite look away.

"Thank you," she said as her shoes were finally freed.

Was that a hint of breathlessness in her tone, or had he imagined it? "I should have worn more sensible shoes, I guess. I didn't think I'd be encountering any particularly tricky terrain."

He said nothing to that and their gazes continued to hold tight. Then she completely and quite surprisingly dazzled him by flashing a full-on smile. "I guess I was wrong about that. In more ways than one."

His smile spread more slowly, but ended just as broadly as her own.

"I'm Grace Maddox, by the way. Aren't you cold?"

"I passed cold several minutes ago. I would have said I was numb . . . only that smile of yours is like a blast straight from the sun, so that can't be the case now, can it?" He eased up from his crouched position, offering his hand to pull her up next to him. Her fingers were slender, but her grip was strong, and there were calluses on her palms. He'd barely registered the surprise of that before she slipped her hand from his and began brushing at her long black wool coat and slacks.

He took a step back, telling himself it was to save her from having to smell the fish and dog on him, then realized she'd been equally tainted. Yet a bit of distance seemed wise, at least until his equilibrium returned.

"I should let you get back to . . . wherever it is you came from," she was saying, "and get warmed up. Thank you for the rescue. I'm sorry to have disturbed your sleep."

"It's not often I'm awoken by a damsel in distress, but I can't say I minded it. Your smile was payment enough. Glad I could be of service."

Grace's gaze shifted from him to the still perfectly seated dog and that wry arch returned to her brow. "Yes, I can definitely see why the two of you bonded."

Brodie chuckled at that, then folded his arms and tucked his hands under them as his awareness of the morning chill returned with a vengeance. His actions had the unintentional result of pulling her gaze to his chest and arms, and on down over the rest of him where it appeared she got a bit hung up. He grinned, liking that she wasn't as impervious to him as she pretended to be. "What brings you down to my docks?"

Her gaze jerked up to his and the most becoming shade of pink colored her cheeks. "Your—?" She looked momentarily confused; then her expression cleared. "Oh, do you live on one of the boats in the harbor here?"

"At one point, I did, indeed. Now I reside in my boathouse. Converted boathouse," he amended, not sure why it mattered that she know that.

The confusion returned with an added frown. "*Your* boathouse? Which would be . . . ?"

"All of them, actually, but I live in that one." He nodded to the building at the far end of the lower pier. Her frown deepened and his grin faded a bit. "What is it, exactly, that brings you to my docks so early this fine spring morning?"

"Who are you?" she countered.

"Brodie Monaghan, madam." He sketched a quick, formal bow, despite being half naked, then grinned once more when Whomper barked in approval. "Current owner of Monaghan's Shipbuilders." He nodded to the weather-beaten company name painted on the side of the largest, centuries-old boathouse, which had been built by his ancestor's own hands. After decades of disuse and utter lack of maintenance, the proud company logo was barely distinguishable. Something he aimed to change, in due time. "And you, Grace Maddox . . . who are you?"

She nodded toward the largest of his four boathouses nestled at the opposite end of the cluster of buildings. "Owner of that boathouse." She pulled a sheaf of paperwork out of her leather satchel. "As of this morning."